Days of Blood & Starlight

ASTRAE
THISALENE
THE EMPIRE OF SERAPHIM
HALCYON SEA
CAPE ARMASIN
ADELPHAS MOUNTAINS
KIRIN CAVES
BAY OF BEASTS
BULLFINCH
LORAMENDI
FORMER FREE
FORMER FREE HOLDINGS
ERLING RIVER
THE SOUTHERN CONTINENT
ARANZU PLAINS
THE COAST RANGE
MARAZEL HILLS
KIR RIVER
THE SECRET COAST
THE HINTERMOST

N
S
HOLDINGS
SPIRIT VEIL
SAB DESERT
ARCH CARNIVAL
ERETZ

Days of Blood & Starlight

Laini Taylor

Little, Brown and Company
New York Boston

Little, Brown and Company

Hachette Book Group
1290 Avenue of the Americas, New York, NY 10104
Visit our website at lb-teens.com

Little, Brown and Company is a division of Hachette Book Group, Inc.
The Little, Brown name and logo are trademarks of Hachette Book Group, Inc.

First Paperback Edition: February 2014
First published in hardcover in November 2012 by Little, Brown and Company

Library of Congress Cataloging-in-Publication Data

Taylor, Laini.
Days of blood & starlight / Laini Taylor.—1st ed.
p. cm.
Sequel to: Daughter of smoke and bone.
Summary: "The otherworldly Karou struggles to come to terms with who and what she is, and how far she'll go to avenge her people"—Provided by publisher.
ISBN 978-0-316-13397-5 (hc) / ISBN 978-0-316-13398-2 (pb) / ISBN 978-0-316-22410-9 (int'l)
[1. Supernatural—Fiction. 2. Chimera (Greek mythology)—Fiction. 3. Mythology, Greek—Fiction. 4. Angels—Fiction. 5. Demonology—Fiction. 6. Prague (Czech Republic)—Fiction. 7. Czech Republic—Fiction.] I. Title. II. Title: Days of blood and starlight.
PZ7.T214826Day 2012
[Fic]—dc23 2012028752

Book design by Alison Impey

10 9 8 7 6 5 4 3

RRD-C

Printed in the United States of America

For Jim,
extremely

Once upon a time,
an angel and a devil held a wishbone between them.

And its snap split the world in two.

1

The Girl on the Bridge

Prague, early May. The sky weighed gray over fairy-tale rooftops, and all the world was watching. Satellites had even been tasked to surveil the Charles Bridge, in case the... visitors... returned. Strange things had happened in this city before, but not this strange. At least, not since video existed to prove it. Or to *milk* it.

"Please tell me you have to pee."

"What? *No*. No, I do not. Don't even ask."

"Oh, come on. I'd do it myself if I could, but I can't. I'm a girl."

"I know. Life is so unfair. I'm still not going to pee on Karou's ex-boyfriend for you."

"What? I wasn't even going to ask you to." In her most reasonable tone, Zuzana explained, "I just want you to pee in a balloon so I can drop it on him."

"Oh." Mik pretended to consider this for approximately one and a half seconds. "*No*."

Zuzana exhaled heavily through her mouth. "Fine. But you know he deserves it."

The target was standing ten feet in front of them with a full international news crew, giving an interview. It was not his first interview. It was not even his tenth. Zuzana had lost count. What made this one especially irksome was that he was conducting it on the front steps of Karou's apartment building, which had already gotten quite enough attention from various police and security agencies without the address being splashed on the news for all and sundry.

Kaz was busily making a name for himself as the ex-boyfriend of "the Girl on the Bridge," as Karou was being called in the wake of the extraordinary melee that had fixed the eyes of the world on Prague.

"Angels," breathed the reporter, who was young and pretty in the usual catalog-model-meets-assassin way of TV reporters. "Did you have any idea?"

Kaz laughed. Predicting it, Zuzana fake-laughed right along with him. "What, you mean that there really are angels, or that my girlfriend is on their bad side?"

"*Ex*-girlfriend," hissed Zuzana.

"Both, I guess," laughed the reporter.

"No, neither," admitted Kaz. "But there were always mysteries with Karou."

"Like what?"

"Well, she was so secretive you wouldn't believe it. I mean, I don't even know her nationality, or her last name, if she even has one."

"And that didn't bother you?"

"Nah, it was cool. A beautiful, mysterious girl? She kept a knife in her boot, and she could speak all these languages, and she was always drawing monsters in her—"

Zuzana shouted, "Tell about how she threw you through the window!"

Kaz tried to ignore her, but the reporter had heard. "Is it true? Did she hurt you?"

"Well, it wasn't my favorite thing that's ever happened to me." Cue charming laughter. "But I wasn't hurt. It was my fault, I guess. I scared her. I didn't mean to, but she'd been in some kind of fight, and she was jumpy. She was bloody all over, and barefoot in the snow."

"How awful! Did she tell you what happened?"

Again Zuzana shouted. "No! Because she was too busy throwing him through the window!"

"It was a door, actually," said Kaz, shooting Zuzana a look. He pointed at the glass door behind him. "That door."

"This one, right here?" The reporter was delighted. She reached out and touched it like it meant something—like the replacement glass of a door once shattered by the flung body of a bad actor was some kind of important symbol to the world.

"Please?" Zuzana asked Mik. "He's standing right under the balcony." She had the keys to Karou's flat, which had come in handy for spiriting her friend's sketchbooks from the premises before investigators could get their hands on them. Karou had wanted her to live here, but right now, thanks to Kaz, it was too much of a circus. "Look." Zuzana pointed up. "It's a straight drop onto his head. And you did drink all that tea—"

"No."

The reporter leaned in close to Kaz. Conspiratorial. "So. Where is she now?"

"Seriously?" Zuzana muttered. "As if he knows. Like he didn't tell the last twenty-five reporters because he was saving this excellent secret knowledge just for her?"

On the steps, Kaz shrugged. "We all saw it. She flew away." He shook his head like he couldn't believe it, and looked right into the camera. He was so much better-looking than he deserved to be. Kaz made Zuzana wish that beauty were something that could be revoked for bad behavior. "She *flew away*," he repeated, wide-eyed with fake wonder. He was performing these interviews like a play: the same show again and again, with only minor ad-libs depending on the questions. It was getting really old.

"And you have no idea where she might have gone?"

"No. She was always taking off, disappearing for days. She never said where she went, but she was always exhausted when she came back."

"Do you think she'll come back this time?"

"I hope so." Another soulful gaze into the camera lens. "I miss her, you know?"

Zuzana groaned like she was in pain. "Ohhh, make him shut uuup."

But Kaz didn't shut up. Turning back to the reporter, he said, "The only good thing is that I can use it in my work. The longing, the wondering. It brings out a richer performance." In other words: *Enough about Karou, let's talk about me.*

The reporter went with it. "So, you're an actor," she cooed, and Zuzana couldn't take it any longer.

"I'm going up," she told Mik. "You can hoard your bladder tea. I'll make do."

"Zuze, what are you..." Mik started, but she was already striding off. He followed.

And when, three minutes later, a pink balloon plunged from above to land squarely on Kazimir's head, he owed Mik a debt of gratitude, because it was not "bladder tea" that burst all over him. It was perfume, several bottles' worth, mixed with baking soda to turn it into a nice clinging paste. It matted his hair and stung his eyes, and the look on his face was priceless. Zuzana knew this because, though the interview wasn't live, the network chose to air it.

Over and over.

It was a victory, but it was hollow, because when she tried Karou's phone—for about the 86,400th time—it went straight to voice mail, and Zuzana knew that it was dead. Her best friend had vanished, possibly to another world, and even repeat viewings of a gasping Kaz crowned in perfume-paste and shreds of pink balloon couldn't make up for that.

Pee totally would have, though.

2

Ash and Angels

The sky above Uzbekistan, that night.

The portal was a gash in the air. The wind bled through it in both directions, hissing like breath through teeth, and where the edges shifted, one world's sky revealed another's. Akiva watched the interplay of stars along the cut, preparing himself to cross through. From beyond, the Eretz stars glimmered visible-invisible, visible-invisible, and he did the same. There would be guards on the other side, and he didn't know whether to reveal himself.

What awaited him back in his own world?

If his brother and sister had exposed him for a traitor, the guards would seize him on sight—or try to. Akiva didn't want to believe that Hazael and Liraz could have given him up, but their last looks were sharp in his memory: Liraz's fury at his betrayal, Hazael's quiet revulsion.

He couldn't risk being taken. He was haunted by another last look, sharper and more recent than theirs.

Karou.

Two days ago she had left him behind in Morocco with one backward glance so terrible that he'd almost wished she'd killed him instead. Her grief hadn't even been the worst of it. It was her *hope*, her defiant, misplaced hope that what he'd told her could not be true, when he knew with an absolute purity of hopelessness that it was.

The chimaera were destroyed. Her family was dead.

Because of him.

Akiva's wretchedness was a gnawing thing. It was taking him in bites and he felt every one—every moment the tearing of teeth, the chewing gut misery, the impossible waking-nightmare truth of what he had done. At this moment Karou could be standing ankle deep in the ashes of her people, alone in the black ruin of Loramendi—or worse, she could be with that thing, Razgut, who had led her back to Eretz—and what would happen to her?

He should have followed them. Karou didn't understand. The world she was returning to was not the one from her memories. She would find no help or solace there—only ash and angels. Seraph patrols were thick in the former free holdings, and the only chimaera were in chains, driven north before the lashes of slavers. She would be seen—who could miss her, with her lapis hair and gliding, wingless flight? She would be killed or captured.

Akiva had to find her before someone else did.

Razgut had claimed he knew a portal, and given what he was—one of the Fallen—he probably did. Akiva had tried tracking the pair, without success, and had had no option, ultimately, but to turn and wing his way toward the portal he himself had rediscovered: the one before him now. In the time he had wasted flying over oceans and mountains, anything might have happened.

He settled on invisibility. The tithe was easy. Magic wasn't free; its cost was *pain*, which Akiva's old injury supplied him in abundance. It was nothing to take it and trade it for the measure of magic he needed to erase himself from the air.

Then he went home.

The shift in the landscape was subtle. The mountains here looked much like the mountains there, though in the human world the lights of Samarkand had glimmered in the distance. Here there was no city, but only a watchtower on a peak, a pair of seraph guards pacing back and forth behind the parapet, and in the sky the true telltale of Eretz: two moons, one bright and the other a phantom moon, barely there.

Nitid, the bright sister, was the chimaera's goddess of nearly everything—except assassins and secret lovers, that is. Those fell to Ellai.

Ellai. Akiva tensed at the sight of her. *I know you, angel*, she might have whispered, for hadn't he lived a month in her temple, drunk from her sacred spring, and even bled into it when the White Wolf almost killed him?

The goddess of assassins has tasted my blood, he thought, and he wondered if she liked it, and wanted more.

Help me to see Karou safe, and you can have every drop.

He flew south and west, fear pulling him like a hook, faster as the sun rose and fear became panic that he would arrive too late. Too late and... what? Find her dead? He kept reliving the moment of Madrigal's execution: the *thud* of her head falling and the clatter of her horns stopping it from rolling off the scaffold. And it wasn't Madrigal anymore but Karou in his mind's eye, the same soul in a different body and no horns now to keep her head from rolling, just the improbable blue silk of her hair. And though her eyes were black now instead of brown, they would go dull in the same way, stare again the stare of the dead, and she would be gone. Again. Again and *forever*, because there was no Brimstone now to resurrect her. From now on, death meant death.

If he didn't get there. If he didn't find her.

And finally it was before him: the waste that had been Loramendi, the fortress city of the chimaera. Toppled towers, crushed battlements, charred bones, all of it a shifting field of ash. Even the iron bars that had once overarched it were rent aside as if by the hands of gods.

Akiva felt like he was choking on his own heart. He flew above the ruins, scanning for a flash of blue in the vastness of gray and black that was his own monstrous victory, but there was nothing.

Karou wasn't there.

He searched all day and the next, Loramendi and beyond, wondering furiously where she could have gone and trying not to let the question shift to what might have happened to her. But the possibilities grew darker as the hours passed, and his fears warped in nightmare ways that drew inspiration from every terrible thing he had ever seen and done. Images assaulted him. Again and again he pressed his palms to his eyes to blot them out. Not Karou. She had to be alive.

Akiva simply couldn't face the thought of finding her any other way.

3

Miss Radio Silence

From: Zuzana <rabidfairy@shakestinyfist.net>

Subject: Miss Radio Silence

To: Karou <bluekarou@hitherandthithergirl.com>

Well, Miss Radio Silence, I guess you're gone and have not been getting my VERY IMPORTANT MISSIVES.

Gone to ANOTHER WORLD. I always knew you were a freaky chick, but I never saw this one coming. Where are you, and doing what? You don't know how this is killing me. What's it like? Who are you with? (Akiva? Pretty please?) And, most important, do they have chocolate there? I'm guessing they don't have wireless, or that it's not an easy jaunt to come back and visit, which I *hope* is the case because if I find out you're all gallivanting-girl and still haven't come to see me, I might get drastic. I might try that one thing, you know, that thing people do when their eyes get all wet and stupid—what's it called? *Crying?*

Or NOT. I might PUNCH you instead and trust that you won't punch me back because of my endearing smallness. It would be like punching a *child.*

(Or a badger.)

Anyway. All is well here. I perfume-bombed Kaz and it got on TV. I am publishing your sketchbooks under my own name and have sublet your flat to pirates. Pirates with *BO.* I've joined an angel cult and enjoy daily prayer circle and also JOGGING to get in shape for my apocalypse outfit, which of course I carry with me at all times JUST IN CASE.

Let's see, what else? *strums lip*

For obvious reasons, crowds are worse than ever. My misanthropy knows no bounds. Hate rises off me like cartoon heat waves. The puppet show is good money but I'm getting bored, not to mention going through ballet shoes like there's no tomorrow—which, hey, if the angel cults are right, there *isn't.*

(Yay!)

Mik is great. I've been a little upset (*ahem*), and you know what he did to cheer me up? Well, I'd told him that story about when I was little and I spent all my carnival tickets trying to win the cakewalk because I really, *really* wanted to eat a whole cake all by myself—but I didn't win and found out later I could actually have *bought* a cake and still had tickets left over for rides and it was the worst day of my life? Well, he made me my own cakewalk! With numbers on the floor and music and SIX ENTIRE CAKES, and after I won them ALL we took them to the park and fed each other with these extra-long forks for like five hours. It was the best day of my life.

Until the one when you come back.

I love you, and I hope you are safe and happy and that wherever you are, someone (Akiva?) is making you cakewalks, too, or whatever it is that fiery angel boys do for their girls.

kiss/punch
Zuze

4

No More Secrets

"Well. This comes as a bit of a surprise."

That was Hazael. Liraz was at his side. Akiva had been waiting for them. It was very late, and he was in the training theater behind the barracks at Cape Armasin, the former chimaera garrison to which their regiment had been posted at the end of the war. He was performing a ritual kata, but he lowered his swords now and faced them, and waited to see what they would do.

He hadn't been challenged on his return. The guards had saluted him with their usual wide-eyed reverence—he was Beast's Bane to them, the Prince of Bastards, hero, and that hadn't changed—so it would seem that Hazael and Liraz had not reported him to their commander, or else the knowledge of it had simply not yet worked its way out to the ranks. He might have been more cautious than to just show himself with no idea what reception awaited him, but he was in a haze.

After what he had found in the Kirin caves.

"Should my feelings be hurt that he didn't come and find us?" Liraz asked Hazael. She was leaning against the wall with her arms crossed.

"Feelings?" Hazael squinted at her. "*You?*"

"I have *some* feelings," she said. "Just not stupid ones, like remorse." She cut her eyes at Akiva. "Or love."

Love.

The things that were broken in Akiva clenched and ground.

Too late. He had been too late.

"Are you saying you don't love me?" Hazael asked Liraz. "Because *I* love *you*. I think." He paused in contemplation. "Oh. No. Never mind. That's fear."

"I don't have that one, either," said Liraz.

Akiva didn't know if that was true; he doubted it, but maybe Liraz felt fear less than most, and hid it better. Even as a child she had been ferocious, the first to step into the sparring ring no matter who the opponent. He had known her and Hazael as long as he had known himself. Born in the same month in the emperor's harem, the three of them had been given over together to the Misbegotten—Joram's bastard legion, bred of his nightly trysts—and raised to be weapons of the realm. And loyal weapons they had been, the three of them fighting side by side through countless battles, until Akiva's life was changed and theirs were not.

And now it had changed again.

What had happened, and *when*? Only a few days had passed since Morocco and that backward glance. It wasn't possible. What had *happened*?

Akiva was dazed; he felt wrapped in skins of air. Voices

seemed to not quite reach him—he could hear them, but as from a distance, and he had the queer sensation of not being entirely present. With the kata he had been trying to center himself, to achieve *sirithar*, the state of calm in which the godstars work through the swordsman, but it was the wrong exercise. He *was* calm. Unnaturally so.

Hazael and Liraz were looking at him strangely. They exchanged a glance.

He made himself speak. "I would have sent word that I was back," he said, "but I knew that you would already know."

"I did know." Hazael was vaguely apologetic. He knew everything that went on. With his easy manner and lazy smile, he gave off an air of nonambition that made him unthreatening. People talked to him; he was a natural spy, affable and egoless, with a deep and entirely unrecognized cunning.

Liraz was cunning, too, though the opposite of unthreatening. An icy beauty with a withering stare, she wore her fair hair scraped back in harsh braids, a dozen tight rows that had always looked painful to her brothers; Hazael liked to tease her that she could use them as a tithe. Her fingers, tapping restlessly on her upper arms, were so lined with tattooed kill marks that they read at a distance as pure black.

When, on a lark one night and perhaps a little drunk, some of their regiment had voted on whom they would least like to have for an enemy, the unanimous victor had been Liraz.

Now here they were, Akiva's closest companions, his family. What was that look they shared? From his strange state of remove, it might have been some other soldier's fate that hung in the balance. What were they going to do?

He had lied to them, kept secrets for years, vanished without explanation, and then, on the bridge in Prague, he had chosen against them. He would never forget the horror of that moment, standing between them and Karou and having to choose—no matter that it *wasn't* a choice, only the illusion of one. He still didn't see how they could forgive him.

Say something, he urged himself. *But what?* Why had he even come back here? He didn't know what else to do. These were his people, these two, even after everything. He said, "I don't know what to say. How to make you understand—"

Liraz cut him off. "I will *never* understand what you did." Her voice was as cold as a stab, and in it Akiva heard or imagined what she did not say, but had before.

Beast-lover.

It struck a nerve. "No, you couldn't, could you?" He may once have felt shame for loving Madrigal. Now it was only the shame that shamed him. Loving her was the only pure thing he had done in his life. "Because you don't feel love?" he asked. "The untouchable Liraz. That's not even life. It's just being what *he* wants us to be. Windup soldiers."

Her face was incredulous, vivid with fury. "You want to teach me how to feel, Lord Bastard? Thank you, but no. I've seen how well it went for you."

Akiva felt the anger go out of him; it had been a brief vibration of life in the shell that was all that was left of him. It was true what she said. Look what love had done for him. His shoulders dropped, his swords scraped the ground. And when his sister grabbed a poleax from the practice rack and hissed "*Nithilam*," he could barely muster surprise.

Hazael drew his great sword and gave Akiva a look that was, as his voice had been, vaguely apologetic.

Then they attacked him.

Nithilam was the opposite of *sirithar*. It was the mayhem when all is lost. It was the godless thick-of-battle frenzy to kill instead of die. It was formless, crude, and brutal, and it was how Akiva's brother and sister came at him now.

His swords leapt to block, and wherever he had been, dazed and adrift, he was here now, just like that, and there was nothing muffled about the shriek of steel on steel. He had sparred with Hazael and Liraz a thousand times, but this was different. From first contact he felt the weight of their strikes—full force and no mistake. Surely it wasn't a true assault. Or was it?

Hazael wielded his own great sword two-handed, so while his blows lacked the speed and agility of Akiva's, they carried awesome power.

Liraz, whose sword remained sheathed at her hip, could only have chosen the poleax for the thuggish pleasure of its heft, and though she was slender, and grunted getting it moving, the result was a deadly blur of six-foot wooden haft edged in double ax blades with a spear tip half as long as Akiva's arm.

Right away he had to go airborne to clear it, couch his feet against a bartizan, and shoot back to gain some space, but Hazael was there to meet him, and Akiva blocked a hack that jarred his entire skeleton and shunted him back to the ground. He landed in a crouch and was greeted by poleax. Dove aside as it slammed down and gouged a wedge out of the hardpan where he had been. Had to spin to deflect Hazael's sword and got it right this time, twisting as he parried so the force of the blow slipped down his own blade and was lost—energy fed to the air.

So it went.

And went.

Time was upended in the whirlwind of *nithilam* and Akiva became an instinct-creature living inside the dice of blades.

Again and again the blows came, and he blocked and dodged but didn't strike; there was no time or space for it. His brother and sister batted him between them, there was always a weapon coming, and when he *did* see a space—when a split-second gap in the onslaught was as good as a door swinging open to Hazael's throat or Liraz's hamstring—he let it pass.

Whatever they did, he would never hurt them.

Hazael roared in his throat and brought down a blow as heavy as a bull centaur's that caught Akiva's right sword and sent it spinning from his grip. The force of it ripped a red bolt of pain from his old shoulder injury, and he leapt back, not quickly enough to dodge as Liraz came in low with her poleax and swiped him off his feet. He landed on his back, wings sprawling open. His second sword skidded after the first and Liraz was over him, weapon raised to deal the deathblow.

She paused. A half second, which seemed an eon coming out of the chaos of *nithilam*, it was enough time for Akiva to think that she was really going to do it, and then that she wasn't. And then...she heaved the poleax. It took all the air in her lungs and it was coming and there was no stopping it—the haft was too long; she couldn't halt its fall if she wanted.

Akiva closed his eyes.

Heard it, felt it: the skirr of air, the shuddering impact. The force of it, but...not the bite. The instant passed and he opened his eyes. The ax blade was embedded in the hardpan next to his cheek and Liraz was already walking away.

He lay there, looking up at the stars and breathing, and as the air passed in and out of him, it settled on him with weight that he was alive.

It wasn't some fractional surprise, or momentary gratitude for being spared an ax in the face. Well, there was that, too, but this was bigger, heavier. It was the understanding—and burden—that unlike those many dead because of him, he had *life*, and life wasn't a default state—*I am not dead, hence I must be alive*—but a medium. For action, for effort. As long as he had life, who deserved it so little, he would use it, wield it, and do whatever he could in its name, even if it was not, was never, enough.

And even though Karou would never know.

Hazael appeared over him. Sweat beaded his brow. His face was flushed, but his expression remained mild. "Comfortable down there, are you?"

"I could sleep," Akiva said, and felt the truth of it.

"You may recall, you have a bunk for that."

"Do I?" He paused. "Still?"

"Once a bastard, always a bastard," replied Hazael, which was a way of saying there was no way out of the Misbegotten. The emperor bred them for a purpose; they served until they died. Be that as it may, it didn't mean his brother and sister had to forgive him. Akiva glanced at Liraz. Hazael followed his gaze. He said, "Windup soldier? Really?" He shook his head, and, in his way of delivering insults without rancor, added, "Idiot."

"I didn't mean it."

"I know." So simple. *He knew.* Never theatrics with Hazael. "If I thought you had, I wouldn't be standing here." The haft of the poleax was angled across Akiva's body. Hazael grasped it, wrenched it free of the ground, and set it upright.

Akiva sat up. "Listen. On the bridge..." he began, but didn't know what to say. How, exactly, do you apologize for betrayal?

Hazael didn't make him grope for words. In his easy, lazy voice, he said, "On the bridge you protected a girl." He shrugged. "Do you want to know something? It's a relief to finally understand what happened to you." He was talking about eighteen years ago, when Akiva had disappeared for a month and resurfaced changed. "We used to talk about it." He gestured to Liraz. She was sorting the weapons in the rack, either not paying attention to them or pretending not to. "We used to wonder, but we stopped a long time ago. This was just who you were now, and I can't say I liked you better, but you're my brother. Right, Lir?"

Their sister didn't reply, but when Hazael tossed her the poleax, she caught it neatly.

Hazael held out his hand to Akiva.

Is that all? Akiva wondered. He was stiff and battered, and when his brother pulled him to his feet, another pain ripped from his shoulder, but it still felt too easy.

"You should have told us about her," Hazael said. "Years ago."

"I wanted to."

"I know."

Akiva shook his head; he almost could have smiled, if it weren't for everything else. "You know all, do you?"

"I know *you.*" Hazael wasn't smiling, either. "And I know something has happened again. This time, though, you'll tell us."

"No more secrets." This came from Liraz, who still stood at a distance, grave and fierce.

"We didn't expect you back," said Hazael. "The last time we saw you, you were . . . committed."

If he was vague, Liraz was blunt. "Where's the girl?" she asked.

Akiva hadn't said it out loud yet. Telling them would make it real, and the word caught in his throat, but he forced it out. "Dead," he said. "She's dead."

5

A Strange Moon Word

From: Zuzana <rabidfairy@shakestinyfist.net>

Subject: Hellooooo

To: Karou <bluekarou@hitherandthithergirl.com>

HELLO. Hello hello hello hello hello hello.

Hello?

Damn, now I've gone and done it. I've made *hello* go all abstract and weird. It looks like an alien rune now, something an astronaut would find engraved on a moon rock and go, *A strange moon word! I must bring this back to Earth as a gift for my deaf son!* And which would then—of course—hatch flying space piranhas and wipe out humanity in less than three days, SOMEHOW sparing the astronaut just so he could be in the final shot, weeping on his knees in the ruins of civilization and crying out to the heavens, *It was just hellooooooooo!*

Oh. Huh. It's totally back to normal now. No more alien doom. Astronaut, I just kept you from destroying Earth.

YOU'RE WELCOME.

Lesson: Do not bring presents back from strange places. (Forget that. *Do.*)

Also: Write back to signify your continuing aliveness or I will give you the hurts.

Zuze

6

The Vessel

There was one place besides Loramendi, Akiva told Hazael and Liraz, that he had thought Karou might go. He hadn't really expected to find her there; he had convinced himself by then that she had fled back through the portal to her life—art and friends and cafes with coffin tables—and left this devastated world behind. Well, he had almost convinced himself, but something pulled him north.

"I think I would always find you," he had told her just days ago, minutes before they snapped the wishbone. "No matter how you were hidden."

But he hadn't meant...

Not like this.

In the Adelphas Mountains, the ice-rimed peaks that had for centuries served as bastion between the Empire and the free holdings, lay the Kirin caves.

It was there that the child Madrigal had lived, and there

that she had returned one long-ago afternoon in shafts of diamond light to find that her tribe had been slaughtered and stolen by angels while she was out at play. The sheaf of elemental skins she'd gripped in her small fist had fallen at the threshold and been swept inside by the wind. They would have been turned by time from silk to paper, translucent to blue, and then finally to dust, but other elemental skins littered the floors when Akiva entered. No flash and flitter of the creatures themselves, though, or of any other living thing.

He had been to the caves once before, and although it had been years and his recollections were dominated by grief, they seemed to him unchanged. A network of sculpted rooms and paths extending deep into the rock, all smooth and curving, they were half nature, half art, with clever channels carved throughout that acted as wind flutes, filling even the deepest chambers with ethereal music. Lonely relics of the Kirin remained: woven rugs, cloaks on hooks, chairs still lying where they'd scattered in the chaos of the tribe's last moments.

On a table, in plain sight, he found the vessel.

It was lantern-like, of dark hammered silver, and he knew what it was. He'd seen enough of them in the war: chimaera soldiers carried them on long, curved staffs. Madrigal had been holding one when he first set eyes on her on the battlefield at Bullfinch, though he hadn't understood then what it was, or what she was doing with it.

Or that it was the enemy's great secret and the key to their undoing.

It was a thurible—a vessel for the capture of souls of the dead, to preserve them for resurrection—and it didn't look to have been on the table for long. There was dust under it but none *on* it. Someone had placed it there recently; *who*, Akiva couldn't guess, nor *why*.

Its existence was a mystery in every aspect but one.

Affixed to it with a twist of silver wire was a small square of paper on which was written a word. It was a chimaera word, and under the circumstances the cruelest taunt Akiva could fathom, because it meant *hope*, and it was the end of his, since it was also a name.

It was *Karou*.

7

Please No

From: Zuzana <rabidfairy@shakestinyfist.net>

Subject: Please no

To: Karou <bluekarou@hitherandthithergirl.com>

Oh Jesus. You're dead, aren't you?

8

The End of Aftermath

And this was Akiva's new hell: to have everything change and nothing change.

Here he was, back in Eretz, not dead and not imprisoned, still a soldier of the Misbegotten and hero of the Chimaera War: the celebrated Beast's Bane. It was absurd that he should find himself back in his old life as if he were the same creature he had been before a blue-haired girl brushed past him in a narrow street in another world.

He wasn't. He didn't know what creature he was now. The vengeance that had sustained him all these years was gone, and in its place was an ash pit as vast as Loramendi: grief and shame, that gnawing wretchedness, and, at the edges, an unfixed sense of... imperative. Of purpose.

But what purpose?

He had never thought ahead to these times. "Peace," it was being feted in the Empire, but Akiva could only think of it as *aftermath.* In his mind, the end had always been the fall of Loramendi and revenge on the monsters whose savage cheers had played accompaniment to Madrigal's death. What would come next, he had barely thought of. He supposed he had assumed he would be dead, like so many other soldiers, but now he could see that it would be too easy to die.

Live in the world you've made, he thought to himself, rising each morning. *You don't deserve to rest.*

Aftermath was ugly. Every day he was forced to bear witness to it: the slave caravans on the move, the burned hulls of temples, squat and defiled, the crushed hamlets and wayside inns, always columns of smoke rising in the distance. Akiva had set this in motion, but if his own vengeance was long spent, the emperor's wasn't. The free holdings were crushed—an accomplishment made easier by the pitiful fact that untold thousands of chimaera had fled to Loramendi for safety, only to burn alive in its fall—and the Empire's expansion was under way.

The populous north of the chimaera lands were but the cusp of a great wild continent, and though the main strength of Joram's armies had come home, patrols continued on, moving like the shadow of death deeper south and deeper, razing villages, burning fields, making slaves, making corpses. It might have been the emperor's work, but Akiva had made it possible, and he watched with bleak eyes, wondering how much Karou had seen before she died, and how acute had been her hate by the end.

If she were alive, he thought, he would never be able to look her in the eye.

If she were alive.

Her soul remained, but because of Akiva, the resurrectionist was dead. In one of his darker moments, the irony started him laughing and he couldn't stop, and the sounds that came from him, before finally tapering into sobs, were so far from mirth they might have been the forced inversion of laughter—like a soul pulled inside out to reveal its rawest meat.

He was in the Kirin caves when that happened, no one to hear him. He went back to retrieve the thurible, which he had hidden there. It was a day's journey, and he sat with the vessel and tried to believe it was Karou, but, laying his hand on the chill silver, he felt nothing, and such a depth of nothing overwhelmed him that he allowed himself the hope that it was not her soul within—it couldn't be. He would feel it if it were; he would know. So he made the journey back through the portal to the human world, all the way to Prague, where he peered in her window as he had once before, and beheld... two sleeping figures entwined.

His hope was like an intake of icy air—it *hurt*—and just as sharp and sudden was his jealousy. In an instant he was hot and cold with it, his hands clenching into fists so tight they burned. A flare of adrenaline coursed through him and left him shaking, and it wasn't her. It wasn't her, and for the fleeting flash of an instant, he felt *relief*. Followed by crushing disappointment and self-loathing for what his reaction had been.

He waited for Karou's friends to wake. That was who it was: the musician and the small girl whose eyes would give Liraz's a run for ferocity. He watched them throughout the day, hoping at every turn that Karou would show up, but she never did. She wasn't here, and there was a long moment when her friend stood stock-still, scanning the crowds on the bridge, the roofline, even the sky—such a searching look that it told Akiva she wasn't accounted for, either.

There were no whispers or edges of rumor in Eretz that hinted at her; there was nothing but the thurible with its singular, terrible explanation.

For a month Akiva let his life carry him along. He did his duty, patrolling the northwestern corner of the former free holdings with its wild coastlines and low, sprawling mountains. Fortresses studded the cliffs and peaks. Most, like this one, were dug into vertical seams in the rock to protect them from aerial assault, but in the end it hadn't mattered. Cape Armasin had seen one of the fiercest battles of the war—staggering loss of life on both sides—but it had fallen. Slaves now labored at rebuilding the garrison's walls, whip-wielding masters never far off, and Akiva would find himself watching them, every muscle in his body as tight as wound wires.

He had done this.

Sometimes it was all he could do to stop the screaming in his head from finding its way out, to mask his despair in the presence of kindred and comrades. Other times he managed to distract himself: with sparring, his secret occupation of magic, and with simple companionship and striving to earn the forgiveness of Hazael and Liraz.

And he might have gone on in that way for some time had not the end of... aftermath... come to the Empire.

It happened overnight, and it drew from the emperor such howling wrath, such bloodcurdling unholy fury as to turn storms back to sea and blast the buds of the sycorax trees so they shed their mothwing blossoms unopened in the gardens of Astrae.

In the great wild heart of the land that day by day fell prey to the halting onslaught of slave caravans and carnage, someone started killing angels.

And whoever it was, they were very, very good at it.

9

Teeth

"Hey, Zuze?"

"Hmm?" Zuzana was on the floor with a mirror set up on a chair before her, painting pink dots onto her cheeks, and it was a moment before she could look up. When she did, she saw Mik watching her with that small concern-crease he got between his eyebrows sometimes. Adorable wrinkle. "What's up?" she asked.

He looked back at the television in front of him. They were at the flat he shared with two other musicians; there was no TV at Karou's place, where Zuzana mostly lived now—the media circus having finally died down a little—and where they usually spent their nights. Mik was eating a bowl of cereal and catching up on the news while Zuzana got ready for the day's performance.

Though it was making them a bundle of money, Zuzana was getting restless with the whole thing. The problem with puppet shows is that you have to keep doing them over and over, which requires a temperament she didn't have. She got bored too easily. Not of Mik, though.

"What is it about you?" she had asked him recently. "I almost never like people, even in tiny doses. But I never get tired of being with you."

"It's my superpower," he had said. "Extreme be-with-able-ness."

Now he looked back from the TV screen, his concern-crease deepening. "Karou used to collect teeth, right?"

"Um, yeah," Zuzana said, distracted. She rooted around for her false eyelashes. "For Brimstone."

"What kind of teeth?"

"All kinds. Why?"

"Huh."

Huh? Mik turned back to the TV, and Zuzana was suddenly very alert. "*Why?*" she asked again, rising from the floor.

Pointing the remote to click up the volume, Mik said, "You need to see this."

10

Hive

"They knew we were coming."

Eight seraphim stood in an empty village. Evidence of sudden departure was everywhere: doors standing open, chimney smoke, a sack lying where it had tumbled off the back of some wagon and spilled out grain. The angel Bethena found herself turning again to the cradle that lay by the stile. It was carved and polished, so smooth, and she could see finger-divots worn into its sides from generations of rocking. *And singing,* she thought, as if she could see that, too, and she felt, just for an instant, the agonized pause of the beast mother who had admitted to herself, in that precise spot, that it was too heavy to take as they fled their home.

"Of course they knew," said another soldier. "We're coming for them all." He pronounced it like justice, like the edges of his words might catch the sunlight and glint.

Bethena cast him a glance, weary, weary. How could he

muster vehemence for this? War was one thing, but *this*... These chimaera were simple creatures who grew food and ate it, rocked their children in polished cradles, and probably never spilled a single drop of blood. They were nothing like the revenant soldiers the angels had fought all their lives—all their *history*—the bruising, brutal monsters that could cut them in half with a blow, send them reeling with the force of their inked devils' eyes, tear out their throats with their teeth. This was different. The war had never penetrated here; the Warlord had kept it locked at the land's edges. Half the time, these scattered farm hamlets didn't even have militias, and when they did, their resistance was pathetic.

The chimaera were broken—Loramendi marked the end. The Warlord was dead, and the resurrectionist, too. The revenants were no more.

"What if we just let them get away?" Bethena said, looking out over the sweet green land, its hazy hills as soft as brushstrokes. Several of her comrades laughed as if she'd made a joke. She let them think she had, though her effort at smiling was not a success. Her face felt wooden, her blood sluggish in her veins. Of course they couldn't let them go. It was the emperor's edict that the land be cleared of beasts. *Hives*, he called their villages. *Infestations*.

A poor sort of hive, she thought. Village after farm and the conquerors had not once been stung. It was easy, this work. So terribly easy.

"Then let's get it over with," she said. Wooden face, wooden heart. "They can't have gone far."

The villagers were easy to trace, their livestock having

dropped fresh dung along the south road. Of course they would be fleeing for the Hintermost, but they hadn't gotten far. Not three miles down, the path cut under the arch of an aqueduct. It was a triple-tiered structure, monumental and partially collapsed, so that fallen stones obscured the underpassage. From the sky, the road beyond looked clear, twisting away down a narrow valley that was like a part in green hair, the forest dense on either side. The beasts' trail—dung and dust and footprints—did not continue.

"They're hiding under the aqueduct," said Hallam, he of the vehemence, drawing his sword.

"Wait." Bethena felt the word form on her lips, and it was spoken. Her fellow soldiers looked to her. They were eight. The slave caravan moved at the lumbering overland pace of their quarry and was a day behind them. Eight seraph soldiers were more than enough to stamp out a village like this. She shook her head. "Nothing," she said, and motioned them down.

It feels like a trap. That had been her thought, but it was a flashback to the war, and the war was over.

The seraphim came down on both sides of the underpassage, trapping the beasts in the middle. Against the possibility of archers—there was no greater equalizer than arrows—they kept close to the stone, out of range. The day was bright, the shadows deepest black. The chimaera's eyes, thought Bethena, would be accustomed to the dark; light would dazzle them. *Get it over with*, she thought, and gave her signal. She leapt in, fiery wings blinding, sword low and ready. She expected livestock, cowering villagers, the sound that had become familiar: the moan of cornered animals.

She saw livestock, cowering villagers. The fire of her wings painted them ghastly. Their eyes shone mercury-bright, like things that live for night.

They weren't moaning.

A laugh; it sounded like a match strike: dry, dark. All wrong. And when the angel Bethena saw what *else* was waiting under the aqueduct, she knew that she'd been wrong. The war was not over.

Though for her and her comrades, abruptly, it was.

11

The Unfathomable Why

A *phantom*, the news anchor said.

At first, the evidence of trespass had been too scant to be taken seriously, and of course there was the matter of it being impossible. No one could penetrate the high-tech security of the world's elite museums and leave no trace. There was only the prickle of unease along the curators' spines, the chilling and unassailable sense that *someone had been there.*

But nothing was stolen. Nothing was ever missing.

That they could tell.

It was the Field Museum in Chicago that captured proof of the intruder. First, just a wisp on their surveillance footage: a tantalizing bleed of shadow at the edge of sight, and then for an instant—one gliding misstep that brought her clearly into frame—a girl.

The phantom was a girl.

Her face was turned away. There was a hint of high cheekbone;

her neck was long, her hair hidden in a cap. One step and she was gone again, but it was enough. She was real. She had been there—in the African wing, to be precise—and so they went over it inch by inch, and they discovered that something *was* missing.

And it wasn't just the Field Museum. Now that they knew what to look for, other natural history museums checked their own exhibits, and many discovered similar losses, previously undetected. The girl had been careful. None of the thefts were easily visible; you had to know where to look.

She'd hit at least a dozen museums across three continents. Impossible or not, she hadn't left so much as a fingerprint, or tripped a single alarm. As to what she had stolen... the *how* was quickly drowned out by the unfathomable *why*.

To what possible end?

From Chicago to New York, London to Beijing, from the museums' wildlife dioramas, from the frozen, snarling mouths of lions and wild dogs, the jaws of Komodo dragon specimens and ball pythons and stuffed Arctic wolves, the girl, the phantom... she was stealing *teeth*.

12

I Feel Happy

From: Karou <bluekarou@hitherandthithergirl.com>

Subject: Not dead yet

To: Zuzana <rabidfairy@shakestinyfist.net>

Not dead yet. ("Don't want to go on the cart!")
Where am I and doing what?
You might well ask.
Freaky chick, you say?
You can't imagine.
I am priestess of a sandcastle
in a land of dust and starlight.
Try not to worry.
I miss you more than I could ever say.

Love to Mik.

(P.S. "I feel happy. . . . I feel happy. . . .")

13

Asymmetry

Light through lashes.

Karou is only pretending to be asleep. Akiva's fingertips trace her eyelids, slip softly over the curve of her cheek. She can feel his gaze on her like a glow. Being looked at by Akiva is like standing in the sun.

"I know you're awake," he murmurs, close to her ear. "Do you think I can't tell?"

She keeps her eyes closed but smiles, giving herself away. "Shush, I'm having a dream."

"It's not a dream. It's all real."

"How would you know? You're not even in it." She feels playful, heavy with happiness. With *rightness.*

"I'm in all of them," he says. "It's where I live now."

She stops smiling. For a moment she can't remember who she is, or *when.* Is she Karou? Madrigal?

“Open your eyes,” Akiva whispers. His fingertips return to her eyelids. “I want to show you something.”

All at once she remembers, and she knows what he wants her to see. “No!” She tries to turn away, but he’s got her. He’s prying her eyes open. His fingers press and gouge, but his voice loses none of its softness.

“Look,” he coaxes. Pressing, gouging. *“Look.”*

And she does.

* * *

Karou gasped. It was one of those dreams that invade the space between seconds, proving sleep has its own physics—where time shrinks and swells, lifetimes unspool in a blink, and cities burn to ash in a mere flutter of lashes. Sitting upright, awake—or so she’d thought—she gave a start and dropped the tiger molar she was holding. Her hands flew to her eyes. She could still feel the pressure of Akiva’s fingers on them.

A dream, just a dream. Damn it. How had it gotten in? Lurking vulture dreams, circling, just waiting for her to nod off. She lowered her hands, trying to calm the fierce rush of her heartbeat. There was nothing left to be afraid of. She had already seen the very worst.

The fear was easy to banish. The anger was something else. To have that surge of perfect rightness overcome her, after everything…It was a filthy lie. There was nothing *right* about Akiva. That feeling had slipped in from another life, when she had been Madrigal of the Kirin, who loved an angel and died for it. But she wasn't Madrigal anymore, or chimaera. She was Karou. Human.

Sort of.

And she had no time for dreams.

On the table before her, dull in the light of a pair of candles, lay a necklace. It consisted of alternating human and stag teeth, carnelian beads, eight-sided iron filings, long tubes of bat bone, and, making it sag with asymmetry, a lone tiger molar—its mate having skittered under the table when she dropped it.

Asymmetry, when it came to revenant necklaces, was not a good thing. Each element—tooth, bead, and bone—was critical to the resulting body, and the smallest flaw could be crippling.

Karou scraped back her chair and dropped to her knees to grope in the darkness under her worktable. In the cracks of the cold dirt floor her fingers encountered mouse droppings, snipped ends of twine, and something moist she hoped was just a grape rolled off to rot—*Let it remain a mystery*, she thought, leaving it be—but no tooth.

Where are you, tooth?

It wasn't like she had a spare. She'd gotten this one in Prague a few days earlier, half of a matched set. *Sorry about the missing leg, Amzallag*, she imagined herself saying. *I lost a tooth.*

It started her laughing, a slappy, exhausted sound. She could just imagine how that would go over. Well, Amzallag probably wouldn't complain. The humorless chimaera soldier had been resurrected in so many bodies that she thought he'd just take it in stride—no pun intended—and learn to do without the leg. Not all of the soldiers were stoic about her learning curve, however. Last week when she had made the griffon Minas's wings too small to carry his weight, he had not been forbearing.

"Brimstone would never make such a ridiculous mistake," he'd seethed.

Well, Karou had wanted to retort, with all the gravity and maturity she could muster. *Duh*.

This wasn't an exact science to begin with, and wing-to-weight ratios—well. If Karou had known what she would be when she grew up, she might have taken different classes in school. She was an artist, not an engineer.

I am a resurrectionist.

The thought rose up, flat and strange as always.

She crawled farther under the table. The tooth couldn't have just vanished. Then, through a crack in the stone, a breeze fluted over her knuckles. There was an opening. The tooth must have fallen through the floor.

She sat back. An icy stillness filled her. She knew what she would have to do now. She would have to go downstairs and ask the occupant of the chamber beneath if she could search for it. A deep reluctance pinned her to the floor. *Anything but that.*

Anything but *him*.

Was he there now? She thought so; she sometimes imagined she could feel his presence radiating up through the floor. He was probably asleep—it *was* the middle of the night.

Nothing would make her go to him in the middle of the night. The necklace could just wait until morning.

At least that was the plan.

Then, at her door: a knock. She knew at once who it was.

He had no compunction about coming to *her* in the night. It was a soft knock, and the softness disturbed her most of all—it felt intimate, secret. She wanted no secrets with him.

"Karou?" His voice was gentle. Her whole body tensed. She knew better than anyone what a ruse that gentleness was. She wouldn't answer. The door was barred. Let him think she was asleep.

"I have your tooth," he called. "It just landed on my head."

Well, hell. She couldn't very well pretend to be asleep if she had just dropped a tooth on his head. And she didn't want him to think she was hiding from him, either. Damn it, why did he still affect her this way? Severe and straight-backed, her braid swinging in a blue arc behind her, Karou went to the door, drew back the ancient crossbar—which was primarily a defense against *him*—and opened it. She held out her hand for the tooth. All he had to do was drop it on her palm and walk away, but she knew—of course she knew—it would not be that simple.

With the White Wolf, it never was.

14

This Desolation of Angels

The White Wolf.

The Warlord's firstborn, hero of the united tribes and general of the chimaera forces. What remained of them.

Thiago.

He stood in the corridor, elegant and cool in one of his creaseless white tunics, his silken white hair gathered loosely back and tied with a twist of leather. The white hair belied his youth—the youth of his body, at least. His soul was hundreds of years old and had endured endless war and deaths beyond counting, many of them his own. But his body was in its prime, powerful and beautiful to the full extent of Brimstone's artistry.

It was high-human in aspect and had been made to his own specifications: human at a glance but beast in the details. A carnal human smile revealed sharp cuspids, his strong hands were tipped in black claws, and his legs transitioned at mid-thigh from human to wolf. He was very handsome—somehow both rugged and refined, with an undertone of the wild that Karou felt as a lashing danger whenever he was near.

And no wonder, considering their history.

He had scars now that he hadn't when she knew him before, when she was Madrigal. A healed slash cleaved one of his eyebrows and spidered up into his hairline; another interrupted the edge of his jaw and jagged down his neck, drawing the eye along his trapezius to the smooth form of his shoulders, straight and full and strong.

He had not come unscathed through the last brutal battles of the war, but he had come through alive and, if possible, even more beautiful for the scars that made him seem more *real.* In Karou's doorway now, he was all too real, and too near, too elegant, too *there.* Always, the White Wolf had been larger than life.

"Can't sleep?" he asked. The tooth was cupped in his palm; he didn't offer it up.

"Sleep," said Karou. "How cute. Do people still do that?"

"They do," he said. "If they *can.*" There was pity in his look—pity!—as he added softly, "I have them, too, you know."

Karou had no idea what he was talking about, but she bristled at his softness.

"Nightmares," he said.

Oh. Those. "I don't have nightmares," she lied.

Thiago was not deceived. "You need to care for yourself, Karou. Or"—he glanced past her into her room—"let others care for you."

She tried to fill her doorway so that no slice of space might be construed as an invitation to enter. "That's okay," she said. "I'm good."

He moved forward anyway, so that she had to either back away or tolerate his nearness. She stood her ground. He was clean-shaven and smelled faintly, pleasingly, of musk. How he managed to be always pristine in this palace made of dirt, Karou did not know.

Scratch that. She *did* know. There was no chimaera who would not stoop gladly to see to the White Wolf's needs. She even suspected his attendant, Ten, of brushing his hair for him. He scarcely had to speak his will; it was anticipated, it was already done.

Right now his will was to enter her room. Anyone else would have subsided at his first hint of approach. Karou did not, though her heartbeat hammered a small-animal panic to be so near him.

Thiago didn't press. He paused and studied her. Karou knew how she looked: pale and grim and waning thin. Her collarbones were oversharp, her braid was a mess, and her black eyes were glossed with weariness. Thiago was gazing into them.

"*Good?*" he repeated, skeptical. "Even here?" He brushed her biceps with his fingers and she shrugged away, wishing she were wearing sleeves. She didn't like anyone to see her bruises, and him least of all; it made her feel vulnerable.

"I'm fine," she said.

"You would ask for help, wouldn't you, if you needed it? At the very least, you should have an assistant."

"I don't need an—"

"There's no weakness in asking for help." He paused, then added, "Even Brimstone had help."

He might as well have reached into her chest and seized her heart.

Brimstone. Yes, he'd had help, including, ostensibly, *herself.* And yet, where had she been while he was tortured, butchered, burned? What was she doing as his angel murderers stood guard over his scorched remains and ensured his evanescence?

Issa, Yasri, Twiga, every soul in Loramendi. Where was she when their souls drifted off like cut kites and ceased to be?

"They're dead, Karou. It's too late. They're all dead."

Those were the words that had destroyed Karou's happiness one month ago in Marrakesh. Just minutes before, she and Akiva had held her wishbone between them and snapped it, and her life as Madrigal—all the memories that Brimstone had taken away for safekeeping—had come rushing back. She could feel the heat of the block she'd laid her head on as the executioner raised his blade, and she could hear Akiva's scream—a thing ripped from his soul—as if its echo had been trapped in the wishbone, too.

Eighteen years ago, she had died. Brimstone had resurrected her in secret, and she had lived this human life with no knowledge of the one that came before it. But in Marrakesh it had all come back to her, and she had...*awakened*—joined her life already in progress—to find herself with the fractured wishbone in her hand and Akiva miraculously before her.

That was the most astonishing thing—that they had found each other, even across worlds and lifetimes. For a pure and shining moment, Karou had known joy.

Which Akiva had ended with those words, spoken in deepest shame, most wretched sorrow.

"They're all dead."

She hadn't believed it. Her mind simply would not approach the possibility.

Following the maimed angel Razgut from the skies of Earth into those of Eretz, she had clung to the hope that it would not be—*could not be*—as Akiva had said. But then she had found the city, and...there *was* no city. She still couldn't wrap her mind around the devastation. She had *lived* there once. A million chimaera had lived there. And now? Razgut, foul thing, had *laughed* at the sight; that was the last she remembered of him. From that moment, she'd been in a daze, and couldn't remember how they'd parted, or where.

All she'd known in the moment was the ruin of Loramendi. Over that blackened landscape hung something Karou had never felt before: an emptiness so profound that the very atmosphere felt *thin*, it felt *scraped*, like an animal hide stretched on a rack and hacked at and hacked at until it was clean.

What she was feeling was the utter absence of souls.

"It's too late."

How long she had wandered in the ruins, she could not afterward have said. She was in shock. Memories were at work in her. Her life as Madrigal was twining itself into her self as Karou, and it was fraught with death, with loss, and at the core of her stunned grief was the knowledge that she had enabled it. She had loved the enemy and saved him. She had set him free.

And he had done *this*.

Bitter, bitter, this desolation of angels.

When a voice splintered the silence, she had spun around, her crescent-moon blades leaping in her hands with the will to make angels bleed. If it had been Akiva there in the ruins, she could not have spared his life again. But it was not him, or any other seraph.

It was Thiago.

"You," he had said, with something like wonder. "Is it really you?"

Karou couldn't even speak. The White Wolf looked her over from head to toe, and she shrank away. Her memories burned. Revulsion roiled like snakes in the pit of her belly, and from within the deadness of her shock she was lit with fury—at the universe, for this newest cruelty. At him, for being the one left alive.

Of all possible souls to survive the slaughter: her own murderer.

15

Fractured

She should have known that night, long ago in another life, another flesh, that she was followed, but joy had dulled her caution.

She was Madrigal of the Kirin. She was in love. She was in the grip of a huge, bold dream. For a month of secret nights, she had flown in darkness to the temple of Ellai, where Akiva waited, restless with new love and on fire as she was to remake their world. She always savored the moment of arrival—her first glimpse of his upturned face as she slipped down through the canopy of the requiem trees, and how he would see her and light up with a joy to answer her own. It was the image she would keep with her in the days that followed—Akiva's lifted face, so perfect and golden, bright with such amazement and delight. He reached up to draw her down. His hands skimmed up her legs as she descended, took her hips and gathered her right out of the air so that their lips met before her hooves ever touched ground.

She laughed against his mouth, her wings still open behind her like great dark fans, and he sank down, reclining on the moss right there with her astride him. They were giddy and hungry, and made love in the middle of the grove in plain sight of the bright-eyed evangelines whose night symphony was their music.

In plain sight of those who had followed Madrigal from the city.

Later, it made her sick to realize that they had watched. They had waited and watched, not content with the treason of mere kissing, but needing a more outrageous raft of crimes—to see it all, and to hear what they would talk of afterward.

And what had they been rewarded with?

The lovers moved languidly into the small temple, where they sipped from the sacred spring and ate bread and fruit that Madrigal had brought. They worked at magic. Akiva was teaching Madrigal his invisibility glamour. She could manage it for a moment, but it required a heavier pain tithe than she could sustain on her own to hold it in place. In the temple, she flickered in and out: there, not there.

"What shall I do," she mused, "for pain?"

"Nothing. No pain for you. Only pleasure." He nuzzled her, and she pushed him off, smiling.

"Pleasure won't help me stay invisible long enough for it to count."

They couldn't hide forever, and would need to be able to come and go in both their lands, among chimaera and seraphim, unseen as needed. They were working out whom to recruit to their cause; they were poised to begin. It would be a critical moment, giving themselves away to their first few chosen fellows, and they talked them over in turn.

They also discussed whom to *kill.*

"The Wolf," Akiva said. "As long as he is alive, there is no hope for peace."

Madrigal sat silent. *Thiago, die?* She knew Akiva was right. Thiago would never accept less than the total demise of the enemy, and certainly she had no personal love lost for him, but to kill him? She toyed with the wishbone hanging around her neck, conflicted. He was the soul of the army and a unifying hero of her people. The chimaera would follow him anywhere. "That's a problem," she told Akiva.

"You know it as well as I do. Joram, too," said Akiva.

If possible, the emperor was even more bloody-minded than Thiago was. He also happened to be Akiva's father. "Do you... do you think you can do it?" asked Madrigal.

"Kill him? What am I for but killing?" His tone was bitter. "I am the monster he created."

"You're not a monster," she said, drawing him to her, stroking his brow, which was always hot as fever, and kissing the ink lines on his knuckles as if she could forgive him the lives they represented. They let talk of killing fall away and wished in silence that they could have the world they wanted without having to kill for it.

Or, as it turned out instead, *die* for it.

Outside, Thiago decided that he had heard enough, and he set fire to the temple.

Even before they smelled smoke or saw the lick of fire, Madrigal and Akiva were jolted by the screams of the evangelines. They'd never even known that the creatures *could* scream. They leapt apart, spun instinctively for weapons that weren't there. They'd left them on the moss outside, along with their shed clothes.

"So careless" was the first thing Thiago said when they were drawn up short, rushing from the burning temple to find a company of soldiers waiting. The White Wolf, front and center, had Madrigal's crescent-moon knives, one in each hand. He let them swing back and forth, hooked from his fingertips. Behind him, one of his wolf retinue held Akiva's swords. He chinged the blades together in a taunt.

One beat followed the sound, a single beat of stillness, and then chaos leapt in.

Akiva raised his arms, summoning magic. What he intended to do, Madrigal never knew, because Thiago was ready for him, and four revenant soldiers had already thrown up their palms, hamsas outfaced to the angel. A fury of sickness hit him. He staggered, dropped to his knees, and they were on him with the butts of their swords, their heavy gloved fists and booted feet, and one whipping reptilian tail wrapped in chains.

Madrigal tried to run to him but was caught by Thiago's fist slamming into her belly so hard it lifted her off her feet. For a weightless, airless moment she didn't know up from down, and then she hit the ground. Bones jarred. Blood rose up her throat, filled her mouth and nose.

Choking, gasping, sick. Pain. Pain and blood. She coughed for breath. Naked, she curled around the pain. Overhead:

smoke, trees catching fire, and then Thiago. He stared down at her, his lip curled in a snarl.

"Foul thing," he growled in a tone of deepest revulsion. "Traitor." And then, the vilest thing of all: *"Angel-lover."*

She saw murder in his eyes and thought she would die right there on the moss. In some deep place, Thiago was fractured. He was sometimes called the Berserker for his savage killing sprees in battle; his trademark was tearing out throats with his teeth. It was a very dangerous thing to make him angry, and Madrigal flinched from a blow that never came.

Thiago turned away.

Maybe he wanted her to have to watch. And maybe it was just base instinct—an alpha urge to destroy a challenger. To destroy Akiva.

There was so much blood.

The memory was lurid, mixed with choking smoke and the shrieks of serpent-birds roasting alive, and though it wasn't Karou's proper memory but Madrigal's, it was still her own, arising from her deeper self. It was all her, and she remembered everything: Akiva on the ground, his blood running into the sacred stream, and Thiago, wild-eyed but eerily composed and utterly silent, laying into the angel's body with blow after blow, his own face, his white hair shining with fine bloodspray.

He would have killed Akiva then, but one of his more level-headed followers stepped in and pulled him off, and so it hadn't ended there. Madrigal had heard the awful, echoing screams of her lover for days afterward as he was tortured in the prison of Loramendi, where she awaited her own execution.

That was the Thiago whom Karou saw—killer, torturer,

savage—when he appeared before her a lifetime later in the ruins of Loramendi.

But . . . it all looked different now, didn't it? How, after all, in the light of what had come to pass, could she argue that he had been wrong?

Akiva should have died that day, and so should she. It *had* been treason, their love, their plans, and worst of all: her fool mercy, to save the angel's life not once but twice, so that he might live to become what he was now. The Prince of Bastards, they called him, among other names. Thiago had made certain she heard them all—Lord of the Misbegotten, Beast's Bane, the Angel of Annihilation—and behind each name lurked the accusation: *Because of you, because of you.*

If it weren't for her, the chimaera would still live. Loramendi would still stand. Brimstone would be stringing teeth, and Issa, sweet Issa, would be fretting over his health and winding serpents around human necks in the antechamber of the shop. The children of the city would still run riot on the Serpentine in all their many shapes, and they would grow up to be soldiers, as she had, and be cycled through body after body as the war went on. And on.

Forever.

Looking back now, Karou could scarcely believe her own naiveté, that she had believed the world could be some other way, and that she could be the one to make it so.

16

The Inheritors

In her doorway, Karou thrust out her hand and said, "Thiago, just give me the tooth."

He stepped closer, so that his chest butted at her fingertips and she had to pull them back. Her pulse stuttered. He was so near; she really wanted to move away, but to do so would give him space to enter, and she must not do that. Since joining with him, she had tried hard never to be alone with him. His nearness made her feel small, so weak by contrast, and so... human.

With a magician's flourish, he opened his hand, revealing the molar as if he were daring her to take it. What would he do if she did—grab her hand?

She hesitated, wary.

"Is it for Amzallag?" Thiago asked.

She nodded. He had asked her for a body for Amzallag, and that's what he was getting. *Aren't I the compliant little helper*, she thought.

"Good. I've brought him." He raised his other hand, which held a thurible.

Karou's belly flipped. So it was already done. She didn't know why this part of the process unsettled her so much; she supposed it was the image of two creatures going off into the scree and only one coming back. She hadn't seen the pit, and she hoped she never would, but some days she could smell it: a fug of decay that gave reality to what was usually remote. Thuribles were clean and simple; the new bodies she made were as pristine as Thiago's clothes. It was the other bodies that bothered her—the discarded ones.

But in that way, as in pretty much every way, she was alone. Thiago was unfazed. He swung Amzallag's thurible as if he had not just murdered a comrade and pushed his body into a pit of rotting corpses. The comrade had been willing, after all; anything for the cause, and the old bodies just didn't serve the new purpose, so Karou was replacing them, one by one.

The Wolf fixed her with his pale stare, so intense it made her want to back up a step. "It has begun, Karou. What we've been working for."

She nodded. A chill ran through her. Rebellion. *Revenge.* "Has there been news?" she asked.

"No. But it's early yet."

Several days ago Thiago had dispatched five patrols of six soldiers each. What exactly their missions were, Karou didn't know. She had asked, but she hadn't exactly argued when Thiago told her, "Don't worry about that, Karou. Save your strength for resurrection."

Wasn't that what Brimstone had done? He had left the war to the Warlord, and she was leaving the rebellion to the Wolf.

"I admit I've been pacing." Thiago tossed the tooth up and caught it. "I was glad to have a reason to come up. Won't you let me help you, Karou?"

"I don't need help."

"It will help *me*, to have something to do." With that, he moved forward so that she had to step aside or risk something like an embrace, and then he was past her. He was in her chamber, and it seemed to grow smaller around him.

It was a beautiful room, or had been once. The high ceiling glinted with mosaics, and faded silk panels lined the walls. A pair of windows with carved shutters stood open to the night, their ledges three feet deep, revealing the fortress thickness of the walls. It wasn't very big; there were other rooms that would be more suitable to Karou's work, but she had claimed this one because of the crossbar at the door and the feeling of safety it gave her—though a fat lot of good that did her now that Thiago was on the wrong side of it.

Stupid, she thought. Hanging back at the open door, she told him, "I'd rather work alone."

He approached her worktable. Setting the tiger molar down with a *click*, he looked at her. "But you are not alone. We are in this together." His intensity—his seeming sincerity—was piercing. "We are the inheritors, Karou. What my father and Brimstone were to our people, you and I are to those who remain."

And what a heavy inheritance it was: no less than the fate of the chimaera races and all their hopes for survival.

The chimaera were barely clinging to the world. Thiago's band of soldiers was all that remained of the chimaera army, and only through Karou's collaboration did they have any hope of mounting a real opposition.

When she'd joined them they were hardly more than sixty: a handful of wounded survivors of the defense of Cape Armasin, who had escaped through the mine tunnels, along with others they had met as they moved across the ravaged land. They were mostly soldiers, with a few useful civilians such as the smith Aegir and a pair of farmwives to see to the cooking. And though sixty was a paltry number for a rebel force, they did have more hope than that.

They had thuribles. They had souls.

Karou's best guess: Several hundred slain soldiers waited in stasis in the silver vessels, and it was up to her to bring them back to the fight.

"We are in this together," Thiago had said. She looked at him hard and waited for the usual revulsion to rise, but it didn't. Perhaps she was just too tired.

Or... perhaps Fate laid out your life for you like a dress on a bed, and you could either wear it or go naked.

Across the room, he had found her case of tools. It was a pretty thing, embossed leather the color of saffron, and looked like it might be a cosmetics case.

It was not.

He spilled its contents onto the table. There were some everyday objects—straight pins, a small blade, a hammer, pliers, of course—but mostly there were vises. They weren't flashy: just plain brass screw clamps like the ones Brimstone had used.

It was amazing the pain you could cause with such simple objects, if you knew what you were doing. Karou had had them handmade to order by a smith in the medina of Marrakesh who hadn't asked questions but had guessed their purpose and smirked at her with a knowingness that had made her feel dirty. As if she enjoyed this.

"I'll tithe," said the Wolf, and Karou felt, in the void of her curiously absent revulsion, relief rush in.

"Really?"

"Of course. I would have before, if you had ever let me come in. Do you think I like knowing that you're locked in here alone, suffering?"

Yes, she thought, but at the same moment she experienced a twinge of doubt for all her suspicion, and all the nights of barred doors. Thiago would give his pain to her magic so that she didn't have to. How could she say no to that? Already he was stripping off his impeccable white shirt. "Come." He smiled, and she saw in him a fatigue to mirror her own. "Let's do it and be done."

Karou gave in. She pushed the door closed with her foot and went to him.

17

The Pain Tithe

There is intimacy in pain. Anyone who has comforted a sufferer knows it—the helpless tenderness, the embrace and murmur and slow rocking together as two become one against the enemy, pain.

Karou did not comfort Thiago. She didn't touch him more than she had to as the pain invaded his body. But she was alone with him in the candlelight, and he was half-clad and subdued, his handsome face grave with endurance, and while she certainly felt what she expected—a grim pleasure to give back some small measure of the anguish he had once caused her—it wasn't *all* she felt.

There was gratitude, too. A new body lay on the floor behind them, freshly conjured from teeth and pain, and for a change, the pain had not been her own. "Thanks," she said grudgingly.

"My pleasure," replied Thiago.

"I hope not. That would be sick."

He gave a tired laugh. "The pleasure is not in the pain. It's in sparing *you* the pain."

"How noble." Karou was removing the vises and his arm was heavy in her hand, his muscle so dense that she'd had trouble fitting the clamps, and was having trouble again, wrenching them off. She cringed as she torqued his triceps out of shape, leaving an angry welt. He winced, and an apology slipped automatically from her lips. "Sorry," she said, and wanted to bite it back. *He had you beheaded*, she reminded herself. "Actually, I'm not. You had that coming."

"I suppose I did," he agreed, rubbing his arm. With a hint of a smile, he added, "Now we're even."

A small bark of a laugh, almost but not entirely without mirth, burst from Karou. "You wish."

"I do, Karou. Karou."

The laugh died quickly; Thiago said her name too much. It was like he was claiming it. She started to draw away, her hands full of vises, but his voice stopped her. "I've had this thought that if I could tithe for you, I could... atone... for what I did to you."

Karou stared at him. The Wolf, *atone*?

He looked down. "I know. There's no atoning for it."

I can think of a way, thought Karou. "I'm... I'm surprised that you think you have anything to atone for."

"Well." He spoke softly. "Not for everything. You gave me no choice, Karou, you know that, but I might have done things differently, and *I* know that. The evanescence... it was beyond the pale." He looked at her, beseeching. "I wasn't myself, Karou. I was in love with you. And to see you with... him, like that. You drove me a little mad."

Karou flushed and felt laid bare all over again. At least, she thought, struggling to maintain her composure, this human flesh had never been exposed to him the way her natural body had. Still, the way he was looking at her, she gathered that he'd forgotten nothing of that night in the requiem grove.

She fumbled with the vises, returning them to their case.

"There's something I've wanted to tell you, but I didn't think you were ready to hear it." A drop in his voice alarmed her. He sounded . . . confessional.

"I really should finish—" she tried to say, but he cut her off.

"It's about Brimstone."

The mention of Brimstone gripped Karou as it always did: like hands at her throat; a throttling, breathless assault of grief.

"He and I had our differences," Thiago admitted. "That's no secret. But when I found out that he had saved you, that your soul wasn't lost . . . Perhaps you think I was furious that he had defied me, but nothing could be further from the truth. And now . . . Believe me when I say that every day I wake filled with gratitude for his mercy." He paused. "Every time I look at you, I bless him."

Look who's become a fan of mercy, Karou thought. "Yes, well. It was good luck for you that a spare resurrectionist happened along."

"I won't lie. When I saw you in the ruins, I almost fell to my knees. But *luck* is too small a word for it, Karou. It was *salvation*. I had been praying to Nitid for hope, and when I opened my eyes and saw you there—*you*—like a beautiful hallucination, I thought she had answered me, and delivered to me the only person Brimstone ever trained."

Karou wouldn't have said Brimstone had *trained* her; that made it sound like he had intended for her to succeed him, and she knew that he would have carried his burden alone to the end of time sooner than pass it to her. *Brimstone, Brimstone.* Most of the time she accepted that he was gone—she *knew* he was—but there were moments when a certainty besieged her out of nowhere: that his soul was in stasis, hidden, waiting for her to find it.

Those moments were shining points of hope, brief and followed by crushing guilt, when she would admit to herself just how badly she wanted to hand Brimstone back this burden. *Selfish.*

In her deepest heart, she was glad he was free of it, finally at rest. Let someone else bear this weight. It was *her* turn—and who deserved it more than she did? The ugliness and misery, the wind-borne stench of the pit, the isolation and fatigue, the *pain.* And if Brimstone hadn't exactly trained her, he had taught her enough to manage, if only just. She was getting better, faster—*thinner, wearier*—and with no help from gods or moons or anything else, thank you very much. She told Thiago, with a rough edge to her voice, "Nitid had nothing to do with it."

"Maybe not. It doesn't matter. I'm just trying to say thank you." There was a tremulous pathos in his ice-blue eyes. Keenly the intimacy of the moment struck Karou—their aloneness in the flickering light, his bare skin—and her revulsion came flooding back, nasty as bile.

"You're welcome," she said. She pulled his shirt off the chair back and threw it at him. "Get dressed, would you?"

She turned away again, trying to mask her disquiet. The only sound was the ring of the thurible's chain as she took it from the table and suspended it from a hook over Amzallag's new body.

It lay before her, huge and inert. Monstrous. She couldn't believe that Brimstone would be proud of her now, but, as Thiago had persuaded her, these were monstrous times, and the rebels needed to maximize the impact of their small force.

It at least bore a resemblance to Amzallag's accustomed bodies, being stag and tiger with the torso of a man, but it was much bigger—the iron filings were for size and heft, and fittingly were scavenged from the cage of Loramendi. It was a hulking thing; no armor would fit it. Every muscle was bunched and pronounced, and the flesh had a grayish cast: The excess of iron did that. Its head was tiger, the fangs as long as kitchen knives. And then there were the wings.

Ah, the wings.

The wings were the reason that living soldiers needed new bodies at all. It was Karou's own fault. It had been her idea to come... here. She glanced at the window and the singular moon that was framed in it. Was she crazy? Stupid? Maybe. It had just been too much, keeping always on the move in Eretz, hiding in ruins and mine tunnels and scanning the sky for seraph patrols. She'd have lost her mind and her nerve keeping on like that, and the chances were that if they'd stayed they'd have been discovered by now, but still, she had to admit she hadn't thought out all the ramifications of the move.

The pit, chiefly.

The soldiers needed to be able to come and go through the

portal *in the sky*. They needed wings. For the journey here, those who could fly had carried those who could not—multiple trips back and forth, and those too large to be lifted had been slain and gleaned and carried that way. That was a day Karou would never forget, and now that they were here, the wingless were relegated to guard duty until she was able to remake them, at which time they could join the incursions into Eretz.

It was that simple. *Simple, ha.* Karou shuddered just to look at the fearsome thing on her floor and know that Amzallag's previous body—the last one of many that Brimstone had made for him—had been thrown away like an old suit of clothes, so that Amzallag could become *this*. For a moment, she could only see it as its prey would see it, the horror and the hopelessness of escape, those wings, which, unfolded, would quite blot out the sky. Her hands grew clammy. *What am I doing?*

What am I making?

And... *What have I brought into the human world?*

It was like surfacing from a dream to glimpse cold reality for just an instant before sleep dragged her back down. Karou's horror subsided. She was arming soldiers, that's what she was doing. If she didn't, who would make the seraphim pay for what they'd done?

As for bringing them into the human world, this place was remote and forgotten; the chance of encountering people was slim to none. And if a small voice in her head liked to whisper, *That's not good enough, Karou*, she was getting used to tuning it out.

She took a deep breath. All that remained now was to guide Amzallag's soul into his new skin, and that was a simple matter for incense. She reached for a cone and turned back to Thiago. He had put his shirt back on, she was glad to see. He looked very tired, his eyes heavy-lidded, but he mustered a smile.

"All ready?" he asked her.

She nodded and lit the incense.

"Good girl."

She bristled at the words and the caressing tone in which he spoke them. *Am I?* she wondered as she sank to her knees to raise the dead.

18

Arisen

Coming up on the silent village, the slave caravan thought nothing of a sky winged by blood daubs. The anomaly would have been an *absence* of blood daubs; in this work, carrion birds were a given. Usually, however, the carrion was of the beast variety.

Not so now.

The dead were strung up on the aqueduct: eight seraphim with their wings fanned wide. From a distance, they seemed to be smiling. Up close, it was an ugliness to shock even a slaver. Their *faces*...

"What did this?" someone choked out, though the answer was writ plain before them. In sweeping letters, in blood, a message was painted on a keystone of the aqueduct.

From the ashes, it read, *we are arisen*.

They panicked and dispatched messengers for Astrae. Being ill-defended, they didn't delay to cut down their soldiers but hurried on, driving their chimaera chattel with whips. A marked change had come over the captives at the sight of the dead—a brightness, a keen and shifting eagerness. The blood scrawl was not the only message; the smiles were a message, too.

The corners of the dead angels' mouths had been carefully slit, widened into rictus grins. The slavers knew exactly what it meant and so did the slaves, and all eyes grew sharp—some with fear; others, anticipation.

Night came and the caravan made camp, posted guards. The dark was pocked by small sounds: a scurry, a snap. The guards' hands were hot on their hilts; their blood jumped, eyes darted.

And then the slaves began to sing.

This had not happened on any previous night. The slavers were accustomed to whimpers from the huddle of captives, not song, and they didn't like it. The beasts' voices were raw as wounds, forceful and primal and unafraid. When the seraphim tried to silence them, a tail lashed forth from the huddle and knocked a guard off his feet.

And then, between one leap of the campfire's flame and the next, they came. Nightmares. Saviors. They came from *above*, and the slavers' first confused thought was that reinforcements had arrived, but these were no seraphim. Wings and screaming, spike horns, antlers, lashing tails and hunched ursine shoulders. Bristles, claws.

Swords and teeth.

No angel survived.

Freed slaves melted away into the landscape, dragging the

swords and axes—and yes, the whips—of their captors. They would be less easily subdued in the future.

All fell still. Here, too, a message was scribed in the blood of slaughter—the same words as would be found at many such scenes in the days to come.

We are arisen, it read. *It is your turn to die.*

19

Paradise

Once upon a time, an angel and a devil fell in love and dared to imagine a new way of living—one without massacres and torn throats and bonfires of the fallen, without revenants or bastard armies or children ripped from their mothers' arms to take their turn in the killing and dying.

Once, the lovers lay entwined in the moon's secret temple and dreamed of a world that was like a jewel box without a jewel—a paradise waiting for them to find it and fill it with their happiness.

* * *

This was not that world.

20

A Country of Ghosts

Akiva, Hazael, and Liraz walked among the dead angels. They didn't speak, only looked, and their silence was brittle with anger. These corpses, they were *torn*, as mice by cats. Akiva couldn't tell if he had known them—the blood daubs had done their work—but on several of the faces there remained enough flesh to make out the mutilation. The obscene smiles had not been seen for generations, but all seraphim and chimaera knew them from graven memory. This was the Warlord's signature.

It was what he had done to his seraph masters when he rose up from slavery a thousand years ago and changed the world. It was a powerful and unmistakable symbol of rebellion.

"Harmony with the beasts," said Liraz under her breath, and Akiva tensed. His words, thrown back at him, and what could he say in response? That these same soldiers had left a string of burned villages in their wake and were no one's idea of innocent? It would sound as though he thought they deserved this.

He didn't, but he couldn't feel outrage, either, only sinking sadness. These soldiers had done what they had done, and been done unto in return. This was how it went.

In the cycle of slaughter, reprisal begat reprisal, forever. Now was not the time to philosophize, though, not with blood daubs circling overhead, skawing at them to be gone and leave them to their feasts. He kept his thoughts to himself.

The sun was rising. It touched the stalks of jess with a fairy glimmer, and the tassels fanned like wings in the breeze. Green-gold, gold-green, not yet ripe and never now to ripen. Soldiers were touching fire to the field's edge, and the flames would spread fast in this tinder heat. Before the sun was fully up, the jess would be crackling, and so would the slain. Fire take the dead. There were no funerals for soldiers.

A shout from above. "You there! What are you doing?"

Akiva tilted back his head. The rays of the early sun lit his amber eyes, and the seraph in the air saw who he was and blanched. "Forgive me, sir. I... I wasn't informed that you were here."

Akiva launched into the air to meet him, his brother and sister coming up behind him. "We've come with the reinforcements from Cape Armasin," he said.

The largest garrison in the former free holdings, Cape Armasin had sent soldiers to bolster the small southern contingent in response to these attacks.

The young patrol leader, whose name was Noam, looked slightly dazed to find himself face-to-face with Beast's Bane. "It's good to have you, sir," he said.

For the second time: *sir.* Liraz made a noise in her throat.

Akiva was no sir. Though fame afforded him a certain esteem, he was Misbegotten, and his rank was as it had ever been, and would ever be: low. "What have you learned?" he asked.

The soldier was wide-eyed. "The fight was under the aqueduct, sir." It stood just behind them, a massive, ancient span, trees enough sprouting from the cracks in its stones to make it a kind of aerial forest. It would have been built by seraphim, Akiva knew, in the early days of the Empire's first expansion, many centuries gone by, when the angels had come to this wild land of primitive, hostile beast tribes and civilized it. Subdued it.

Subdued. What a gentle word for the slave-making and spirit-crushing that had brought the chimaera under the Empire's fist. The Warlord had destroyed that fist, but it was back, and now Akiva was a part of it.

"An ambush," Noam added. "They were killed in the underpassage, and strung up there." He indicated the red message painted on the aqueduct's soaring upper story.

Arisen. Arisen.

Akiva stared at the words. *Who?*

Liraz spoke. "Could the villagers have done this?"

Noam glanced at the dead. "It's a Caprine village," he stated simply, which Akiva understood to mean that the placid sheep-aspect beasts could never have committed such an act, let alone wrestled the corpses up the aqueduct.

"Are there enemy dead?" he asked.

"No, sir. Only our own, and no blood on their weapons."

So they hadn't managed a single stroke in self-defense? And these had been seasoned soldiers who had survived the war itself.

"And down there, sir." Noam indicated the line of the road wending south through the hills. "The slave caravan was hit, too."

Akiva looked. The scene was pastoral: a softness of valleys, hills shading one behind the next like the shadows of shadows, all of it as tranquil as birdsong. And there, lingering just above the horizon, was Ellai. A ghost moon all but vanished by the dawn. *I saw what happened here*, she might have taunted. *And I laughed.*

"The slaves?" he asked Noam.

"Gone, sir. Into the woods. The slavers were . . . fed chain."

"Fed *chain*?" repeated Hazael.

Noam nodded. "The slaves' shackles."

Akiva watched his brother and sister for a reaction, but they gave away nothing. *What would you do*, he wished he could ask them, *if someone put our people in chains?*

Slaves were held to be a necessary evil in the affairs of empire, but Akiva did not share that belief, and didn't mourn the loss of slavers. Soldiers, though, were another matter, and here were eight more. The death toll was sharp and rising. There had been five attacks in all. In one furious night, at Duncrake, Spirit Veil, the Whispers, the Iximi Moors, and here, in the Marazel Hills, seraph "cleansing" patrols had been taken by surprise, killed, mutilated, and left as gruesome messages for the Empire.

It was worse than war, he thought, to bleed out your life while your faraway folk danced hallelujah and raised their cups to the peace.

Peace, indeed.

Akiva looked down. The flames were halfway across the field by now, the first soldiers already swallowed up. Squalls swam in the rising heat, dropping down almost lazily to pick off the smoke-stunned grassjacks that fled in clouds ahead of the blaze.

"Sir?" asked Noam. "Can you tell what did this?"

Revenants, Akiva thought at once. He had seen enough dead-strewn battlefields to know that only the biggest, most monstrous and unnatural chimaera could have caused such rending of flesh. But the revenants were gone. "Probably some survivors of the war," he said.

"There's talk," said Noam, hesitating. "That the old monsters aren't really dead."

The Warlord and Brimstone, he meant. "Believe me." Akiva was besieged by memories of their last moments. "They're dead and more than dead."

And what would this wide-eyed young soldier say if he knew how fervently the hero Beast's Bane wished they weren't?

"But the message. *We are arisen.* What else could it mean but resurrection?"

"It's a rallying cry. That's all." The Warlord and Brimstone had gone beyond all retrieval. He had watched them die.

But... he had watched Madrigal die, too.

A sliver of doubt slid under his certainty. Was it possible? Akiva's pulse gave a short, sharp spike. He thought of the thurible he had found, its small message scrawled in a bold hand: *Karou.* If there was another resurrectionist, maybe the word was not such a terrible taunt as he had believed.

No. He couldn't let himself hope. "There was only ever Brimstone," he said, more harshly than he'd intended.

Liraz was watching him, her eyes drawn ever so slightly narrow. Did she know what he was thinking? She knew about the thurible, of course. "No more secrets," she had said, and there weren't. Did a brief flare of hope count as a secret? If it did, it was one he felt justified in keeping.

Noam nodded, accepting his word. With a light tone, as if he were repeating foolishness he himself did not believe, he said, "Others are saying it's the ghosts." His eyes, though, betrayed a real fear, and Akiva couldn't blame him. Brimstone's last words chilled him, too.

He remembered how Joram's voice had reverberated through the agora of Loramendi in the silence after all resistance was crushed. The Warlord and Brimstone had been on their knees; they had been kept alive to witness the deaths of everyone else.

Everyone else.

"*You* doomed them," Joram had hissed in the Warlord's ear. "You were never going to win. You are *animals*. Did you really think you could rule the world?"

"That was not our dream," the Warlord had said with quiet dignity.

"Dream? Spare me your beast dreams. Do you know what my dream has been?" asked Joram, as if there were any who didn't know he sought to dominate all Eretz.

The Warlord's stag antlers were broken, ragged. He had been beaten, and it seemed to cost him great effort to hold up his head. At his side, Brimstone wasn't managing even that. He was hunched forward, his weight on one splayed hand, the other arm wrapped across his middle where he bled from a gash, and his great shoulders heaved as he tried to draw breath.

He wasn't long for life, but still he managed to raise his head and answer.

That *voice*. It was the only time Akiva ever heard it, and the sound of it—the *feel* of it—would never leave him. Deep as the beat of a stormhunter's wings, it had seemed to lodge in the base of his skull and live there.

"Dead souls dream only of death," the resurrectionist told the emperor. "Small dreams for small men. It is *life* that expands to fill worlds. Life is your master, or death is. Look at you. You are a lord of ashes, a lord of char. You are filthy with your victory. Enjoy it, Joram, for you will never know another. You are lord of a country of ghosts, and that is all that you will ever be."

It sounded like a curse, Akiva had thought, and it had pitched Joram into a fervor. "It shall be a country of ghosts, I promise you that. A country of corpses. No beast shall crawl but that it drags a weight of shackles and is so scored by the lash that it can hardly raise its head!"

Anger was the emperor's resting state. Seraphim were beings of fire, but it was said that Joram burned hot, like the core of a star. It gave him enormous appetites—such an inferno to feed—and when it snapped into rage it was terrible, beyond all reach of reason or control.

He killed Brimstone on the spot. One slash; surely he meant to sever his head, but Brimstone's neck was thick and he failed, and as Brimstone collapsed in a torrent of blood, Joram wrenched up his sword and raised it for another try. With a bellow of rage, the Warlord, ancient creature, lowered that rack of broken antlers and launched himself at the emperor. It took two soldiers leaping in to put him down, but not before he speared Joram on one jagged prong and felled him, not killing him, not even seriously wounding him, but stealing his dignity on his day of triumph.

And ever since, Joram had been delivering on the promise he had made: a country of ghosts, indeed.

"If ghosts could pick up killing where the living left off," Akiva told Noam, "we'd have wiped each other out long ago."

Again Noam nodded, accepting his words as wisdom. "Sir?" he asked. "Are there new orders?"

Liraz finally couldn't take it anymore. "You don't have to call him sir," she said. "You know what we are." Misbegotten. Bastards. Nothing.

"I . . ." Noam stammered. "But he's—"

"Never mind," said Akiva. "No. No new orders. What are the standing orders?" They had just arrived; he didn't know. "Are we to track the rebels?"

But Noam shook his head. "There's nothing to track. They just vanished. We're . . . we're to answer them."

"Answer them?"

"The messages, the smiles. The emperor . . ." He swallowed audibly; he was being careful, weighing his words for Akiva's benefit, but they lacked conviction. "The emperor can send a message, too."

Akiva was silent, taking this in. At Cape Armasin he had been lucky: in the north, there had been no one left to kill. Here it was another story. Fleeing villagers, freed slaves, chimaera trying to make their way to the Hintermost, where they believed they might find sanctuary, a way through the mountains to a new life. And now he was supposed to hunt them down? Make a message out of them?

Beast's Bane. He should be good at it.

A mixture of desperation, fatigue, and helplessness overcame Akiva. He wanted no part of Joram's message.

Corpse smoke gusted up from the field, and the angels beat their wings and backed away from it to come to rest atop the aqueduct. Noam noticed gore and broken feathers where the soldiers had been strung up, and emotion broke through his martial stolidness. "What is it all *for?*" he asked wildly—of the sky, of no one. "I can't remember. I . . . I don't think I ever knew." He fixed abruptly on Akiva. "Sir," he implored, Liraz's scold forgotten. "When will it end?"

It won't, thought Akiva. He looked into the eyes of this young soldier and knew that soon enough, whatever was in him that made him ask *why* would be dead, of necessity—another soul ripped out to make way for a monster. Armies need monsters, as the old hunchback had told him in Morocco, to do their terrible work. Who knew that better than Akiva? He looked at Hazael, Liraz. Was it too late for them? For himself?

Desperate and tired, helpless and besieged by the meat scent of burning comrades, he did something he had not done in a very long time, not since Madrigal was ripped naked from his arms at the temple of Ellai.

He imagined two futures for Eretz: One as Joram would have it, the other as it might be.

A different sort of life.

21

Scared Enough

Sveva woke with the thunderclap jolt and sick, scrambling lurch to consciousness of one who has fallen asleep on watch. Every particle of her body and mind slammed from dream to dread in the space of a twig's snap and she was awake, looking, listening.

Blinking. It was dawn. Through the fringe of the trees, the sky was soft and pale. How long had she slept? And the twig snap—had she heard it or dreamt it?

She sat very still listening. All was quiet. After a few minutes, she relaxed. They were safe. Sarazal still slept; she didn't need to know Sveva had fallen asleep; she scolded her enough as it was. With a sigh, Sveva uncurled her forelegs from beneath her. They were slim as a fawn's, the fur still lightly speckled; she was the smaller of the two girls, the younger. She was the one used to getting away with things, not doing her share.

But that was before.

When they got back home, she would be perfect. No more dreaming days, or hiding from their mother's call. Their mother. How worried she must be now, and the whole tribe; did they know it had been slavers who got them? They'd just gone out to run, the two of them, needing the wind in their hair after a day at their looms. It was Sveva, the fastest, who had kept them going, too far, too far. She'd given her sister no choice but to chase her. She couldn't leave her—older sisters didn't do things like that. This was Sveva's fault.

Did the tribe think they were dead? It made her sick to imagine their grief. *We're okay*, she thought; she thought it hard, willing the message to fly across the land and reach her mother's mind. Mothers could sense things, couldn't they?

We're okay, Mama. We're free. We were freed!

She couldn't wait to tell how it had been, the revenants come from the skies like vengeance made flesh. And what flesh! So huge, so terrible. Well, one of them had not been terrible: a tall one with long, spike horns had taken a knife off a dead angel and put it in her hand; he had been handsome.

Oh, who had ever had such a story to tell? She would tell it fast, before Sarazal could butt in. She was better at stories anyway; she remembered the good details, like how all the slaves had stood together singing. They were from all different tribes, but every one of them knew the words of the Warlord's ballad. The sound of their mingled voices, Sveva thought, had been like the sound of the world itself: earth and air, leaf and stream, and tooth and claw, too. And snarl, and scream. Some of the other slaves had frightened her almost as much as the slavers, but they'd all gone their separate ways once their shackles were off. Most had fanned south, carrying whips and swords, going to warn anyone they could find. Sveva herself clutched her knife—it was in her fist now, too big for her small hand to grip properly—but they were headed north and west.

Home. We're coming come.

Once Sarazal was better, anyway.

Sveva was chewing her cheek, worrying about her sister's leg—she could smell the wound, even through the herb fragrance of her poultice—when she heard another snap. Her skin flashed cold and she stared into the thickness of the forest where night still clung in the shadows of the dense damsel trees.

It was probably just a skote, she told herself, or a tree creeper. Right?

Her heart was pounding; she wished Sarazal would wake. Older sisters could be tiresome when you just wanted to dither away a day, but they were a comfort when you found yourself fugitive in a strange forest, prey to sounds and shadows and in need of someone to tell you it would be all right.

Silently, Sveva gathered herself upright, her deer legs extended before her, her sylph-slender human torso rising slowly. The Dama were the smallest of the centaurid tribes, slight, lithe deer centaurs known for their speed. Ah, their speed; they were the fastest of all the chimaera, and since Sveva was the fastest of the Dama, she liked to boast that she was the fastest creature in all the world. Sarazal said not necessarily, but true or not, Sveva loved to run, and longed to. They could have been halfway home by now, to the spiking ezerin forests and high moss plains of Aranzu where the Dama ranged, unfixed and wild.

They *would* have been halfway by now, if not for Sarazal's leg.

Sarazal still hadn't stirred. She lay curled in the fur-soft bracken, eyes closed, face relaxed and tranquil, and as much as Sveva wished she would wake, she couldn't bring herself to rouse her. For days, Sarazal had had a hard time sleeping with the pain. All because of the shackle. Now that their ordeal was over, it was this that Sveva fixed her hatred on. It was interesting the way a small hate could grow inside a big hate and take it over. When she thought of the slavers now—dead though they were, she would hate them forever—it was Sarazal's shackle more than anything else that made her chest and face feel tight with swallowed fury.

With chimaera being so many different shapes and sizes, the slavers carried all manner of shackles and used whatever fit—all sizes of iron bands and steel chains, on legs, waists, necks. Never arms, though. It was Rath, another slave—a fearsome Dashnag boy whose long white fangs made Sveva shrink up like a wilting flower—who had told them why.

"An arm you could cut off and get away," he'd said. "An arm you could do without."

Oh.

"*I* couldn't," Sveva had replied with some superiority. *Savages*, she remembered thinking, as if perhaps it was a lack of finer feelings that made Dashnag so casual about their limbs.

"That's because you don't know what's waiting for you."

"And you do?" she'd snapped. She shouldn't have. Rath could have eaten her face with a bite, but she couldn't help it. Was he trying to scare her? As if she wasn't scared enough.

Maybe, she thought, she *hadn't* been scared enough. She was now, though. The sweet stink of infection was coming off her sister, and she knew that when she reached out to touch her, she would be hot with fever. The herbs weren't working.

Sveva had found them—feversbane even. At least, she was almost sure it was feversbane. Half-sure at least. But she could see the wound, Sarazal's leg lying delicate on its bracken pillow, and it didn't look any better. She traced her own painful chafe marks with her fingertips and felt the guilty weight of luck she didn't deserve.

The slavers had bound Sveva around her small waist with an iron manacle probably meant for some giant bull centaur's legs, but when they'd gotten to Sarazal—she was last; it was only luck, bad luck—they'd found nothing to fit her, and made do with a scrap of iron tightened just above her left fore fetlock. The metal had cut, the cut had swollen, and then the makeshift shackle had done its real damage, slicing further into the swelling, biting deeper with every step. Sarazal's limping had gotten so bad that the slavers would have had to leave her behind if the revenants hadn't come. Rath said they would have sooner but that Dama were valuable, and Sveva didn't need him to tell her that if they did leave Sarazal, or any of them, it wouldn't be alive.

But the revenants *had* come—from where, the moons only knew, on wings such as she had never seen, more terrifying than anything out of a nightmare—and just in time. Sarazal could barely walk now, and they hadn't gotten far, with Sveva too small to be much help supporting her.

She sighed. No more sounds from the shadows, that was

good, but the shadows were fading away. It was day. It was time to wake Sarazal. Reluctantly, Sveva touched her shoulder. Her skin *was* hot, and when she fluttered her eyes open they weren't right—they had that shine and blear of sickness. Sveva's guilt churned in her stomach like a live thing. She wanted to pull her sister's head into her lap, comb out her tangled cinnamon-stick hair with her fingers, and sing to her, not the Warlord's ballad but something sweet, with no one dying in it. But all she did was murmur, "It's morning, Sara, time to get up."

A whimper. "I can't."

"You can." Sveva tried to sound cheerful, but a desperate panic was building in her. Sarazal was really sick. What if she... *No.* Sveva slammed the thought shut. That couldn't happen. "Of course you can. Mama will be watching for us."

But Sarazal only whimpered again and tried to nestle deeper into the bracken, and Sveva didn't know what to do. Her sister was always the one bossing and planning and coaxing. Maybe she should let her sleep a little longer, she thought, let the feversbane work.

If it *was* feversbane. What if it wasn't? What if it was doing more harm than good?

That's what Sveva was worrying over when the voice came from behind her. No snapping twigs gave warning—it was just there, almost in her ear, stabbing icy jolts of fright all through her. "You have to go."

Sveva whirled around, brandishing her too-big knife, and there was Rath. The Dashnag boy with his long white fangs, he was half in the shadow and half out, and for all that he was still a boy, he was just so big. Sveva's gasp was long and unsteady, a reeling drag of terror. Rath gave her a long look, and Sveva could read no expression on his beast face. He had a tiger's head and cat eyes that caught the light and silvered. He was a hunter, a stalker, an eater of flesh. She could outrun him easily, she knew that... except that she couldn't, because if she were running, it would mean she had left Sarazal behind.

"What are you doing here?" she cried. "Were you following us?"

Rath's voice came from low in his throat. "I was looking for the revenants," he said. "But they're gone, and I wouldn't count on them saving you twice."

Was that a threat? "You leave us alone," she said, putting herself in front of Sarazal.

Rath made an impatient sound. "Not from me," he said. "If you were watching the sky, you'd know."

"What?" Sveva's heart drummed. "What do you mean?"

"Angels are coming. Soldiers, not slavers. If you want to live, it's time to go."

Angels. Sveva's hatred kindled. "We're hidden here," she said. The leaf cover of the damsel canopy would be unbroken green from above, leagues and leagues of it. Two Dama girls were like two acorns. "They'll never see us."

"They don't need to see you to kill you," said Rath. "Look for yourself." He indicated an opening in the brush that Sveva knew gave way to a little rise and a ridge, with a view out onto the sweep of the hills. She glanced at Sarazal, who was sleeping again, her lips moving and eyelids fluttering with unhappy dreams. Rath made another impatient sound, and Sveva went. She moved sideways, her cloven hooves dancing and anxious, and when she was past him she burst into speed and leapt up the rise.

She saw smoke.

Across the valley, between themselves and their way home, some half-dozen plumes of ink-black smoke rose from the forest at intervals. Licks of vivid fire were discernible below, and above, shimmering in the air like heat mirages: seraphim.

They were going to burn them out. Burn this land. Burn the world.

Stunned, she came back to Rath. "Did you see?" he asked.

"*Yes*," she spat, angry. Angry with *him*, as if it were his fault. Anger was better than the panic that pulsed just beneath it. She stooped to gather her sister to her feet, but Sarazal resisted.

"No," she said, her voice small as a child's. "I can't, I can't."

Sveva had never seen her sister like this. She tried to draw her upright. "Come on," she said. "Sarazal. You *can*. You have to."

But Sarazal shook her head. "Svee, please." Her face crumpled; her eyes squeezed tight. "*It hurts*." It was the first time she had admitted the pain, and her voice was a whisper from a deep place, long and pleading. "Go," she said. "You know I can't. I won't blame you. No one will. Svee, Svee, maybe you *are* the fastest in the world." She tried to smile. Svee was Sveva's baby name; it cut her to the heart to hear it. "So run!" Sarazal cried.

And Sveva shook her. "I'll lie down and die with you, do you hear me? Is that what you want? Mama will be so mad at you!" Her voice sounded shrill, cruel. She just had to get her sister moving. "And don't even try to say you would leave me. I know you wouldn't, and I won't, either!"

And Sarazal did try to rise, but she cried out as soon as she put weight on her swollen leg, and sank back down. "I can't," she whispered. Her fevered eyes were wide with terror.

Then Rath sprang. Sveva had half forgotten him. She didn't see the start of the leap, only its finish, when he came down on the bracken before them, impossibly light for his bulk, and grabbed Sarazal up, one big arm hooked under her sleek deer belly, her human torso pulled tight to his shoulder. Sarazal gasped, going rigid with pain and fear, and Rath said nothing. Another leap and he was moving again, away from the oncoming fire and the shimmer of angels without even a backward glance at Sveva.

After one numb pulse of surprise, she followed him.

22

The Tooth Phantom

"But why *teeth?*" Mik asked Zuzana. "I don't get it."

Zuzana, marching up the sidewalk ahead of him, stopped dead and whirled to face him. He was pulling her giant marionette on its wheeled cart and had to lurch to a halt to avoid running her over. She stood there tiny and imperious, a pout and a scowl vying for dominance of her expression. She said, "I don't know why. That's not the point. The point is that she was *here*. In Prague."

She left the rest unsaid, the pout winning out so that for a moment she looked unguardedly wounded. Karou—the "Tooth Phantom," as they were calling her, little guessing that she and "the Girl on the Bridge" were one and the same—had apparently, at some point in her string of crimes, hit the National Museum. The local news had featured a curator shining a penlight into the jaws of a slightly moth-eaten Siberian tiger.

"As you see, she didn't take the fangs—only the molars," the man had said, defensive. "That's why we didn't notice. We have no reason to look inside specimens' mouths."

Clearly, the Phantom was Karou. Even if the glimpse of footage wasn't enough to positively identify her, Zuzana had a resource that the various police forces of the world did not: her friend's sketchbooks. They were piled in a corner of Mik's room, all ninety of them. From the time Karou was old enough to hold a pencil, she had been drawing this story of monsters and mystical doorways and *teeth.* Always teeth.

Mik's question was a good one: *Why?* Well, Zuzana had no idea. Right now, however, that was not her primary concern.

"How could she be here and not come see us?" she demanded. One eyebrow was up, cool and furious, and her scowl muscled her pout into submission. In her platform boots and vintage tutu, with her face upturned and fierce, in doll makeup with pink-dot cheeks and fluttery foil lashes, she looked every inch the "rabid fairy" that Karou had dubbed her.

Mik reached out to cup her shoulders. "We don't know what's going on with her. Maybe she was in a hurry. Or she was being followed. I mean, it could be anything, right?"

"That's what pisses me off the most," Zuzana said. "That it could be anything, and I know nothing. I'm her best friend. Why won't she let me know what she's doing?"

"I don't know, Zuze," said Mik, his voice soft. "She said she feels happy. That's good, right?"

They were poised at the verge of the Charles Bridge on their way to stake out their spot for the day's performances. They'd gotten a late start this morning and the medieval bridge was fast filling with artists and musicians, not to mention more than a fair share of the world's apocalyptic weirdos. Anxiously, Mik watched an old-man jazz band trundle by carrying battered instrument cases.

Zuzana was oblivious. "Ugh! Don't get me started on that e-mail. I want to kill her a little bit. Was it a riddle? Monty Python references? Sandcastles? *What the hell?* And she didn't even mention Akiva. What does that mean?"

"It's not promising," Mik acknowledged.

"I know. I mean, are they together? She would mention him, right?"

"Well, yeah. Like you write her all about me, telling her all the funny things I say, and how every day I get more handsome and clever. And you use smileys—"

Zuzana snorted. "Of course. And I sign everything Mrs. Mikolas Vavra, with a heart dotting the *i*."

Mik said, "Huh. I like the sound of that."

She punched his shoulder. "Please. If you ever *did* ask me to marry you, don't even think I would identify myself as some addendum of *you*, like an old lady signing her rent check with perfect penmanship as Mrs. Husband Name—"

"But you'd say yes, is that what you're saying?" Mik's blue eyes twinkled.

"What?"

"That sounded like the only quibble is what you'd call yourself, not whether or not you'd say yes."

Zuzana blushed. "I didn't say that."

"So you *wouldn't* marry me?"

"Ridiculous question. I'm eighteen!"

"Oh, it's an age thing?" He frowned. "You don't mean wild

oats, do you? We're not going to have to take some stupid break so you can experience other—"

Zuzana put a hand over his mouth. "Gross. Don't even say it."

Mollified, Mik kissed her palm. "Good."

She spun on her heel and walked on. Mik gave the huge puppet a tug to get it rolling again, and followed. "So," he called to her back, "just out of curiosity, you know, purely conversation and all, at what age *will* you be entertaining offers of marriage?"

"You think it'll be so easy?" she called back over her shoulder. "No way. There will be *tasks*. Like in a fairy tale."

"That sounds dangerous."

"Very. So think twice."

"No need," he said. "You're worth it." And Zuzana's face warmed with pleasure.

They managed to find a wedge of unclaimed space on the Old Town end of the bridge, where they parked the marionette. It towered there in its black trench coat like some sinister bridge guardian, a dark counterpoint to the clutch of white-robed figures beyond. Angel-cult rabble. They were loitering, lighting their vigil candles and chanting—at least until the next police sweep, which would temporarily scatter them. How unflagging they were in their belief that the angels would return here to the scene of their most dramatic sighting.

You know nothing, Zuzana thought with scorn, but her superiority was wearing thin. So she had met one of the angels. So what? She was just as ignorant now as everyone else.

Karou, Karou. What could it mean that she had been here

and not even said hello? And that e-mail! Yes, it was absurd, mysterious to the point of *clubbing her on the head*, but . . . there was just something so *off* about it.

It struck Zuzana then: a lightning flash of memory.

I feel happy. . . . I feel happy. . . .

Karou did not feel happy. Zuzana was suddenly sick. She pulled out her phone to make sure she was right. The clip was easy to find online; it was a classic. "Don't want to go on the cart!" That was the clue. *Monty Python and the Holy Grail*: She and Karou had gone through a phase when they were fifteen, they must have watched it twenty times. And there it was, at the end of the "Bring out your dead" scene.

"I feel happy. . . . I feel happy. . . ."

Desperate singsong. It was what the old man said to convince them he was all right just before they clubbed him on the head and threw his body on the plague cart. Jesus. Leave it to Karou to communicate in *Holy Grail*. Was she trying to say that she was in danger? But what could Zuzana possibly do about it? Her heart was beating fast now.

"Mik," she called. He was tuning his violin. "Mik!"

Priestess of a sandcastle? In a land of dust and starlight?

Was that a clue, too?

Did Karou want to be found?

23

Priestess of a Sandcastle

The kasbah was a castle built of earth, one of the hundreds that studded these southern reaches of Morocco, where they had baked in the sun for centuries. Once, they had been home to warrior clans and all their retinue. They were primeval fortresses, proud and red and tall, with crenellations like the hooked teeth of vipers, and arcane Berber patterns etched on the high, smooth walls.

In many of the kasbahs, small clutches of warriors' descendants still eked out lives while time worked its ruin around them. But this place, when Karou found it, had been left to the storks and scorpions.

A few weeks ago, when she came back into this world to collect teeth, she had been, well, reluctant to return to Eretz. Not that she doubted for a second that she would; it was just that returning to that place was so hard. To that world in general with its waft of death, and the mine tunnel in particular. The echoes and the eerie, fluting cries of cherub bats, the dirt, the darkness, the pale tuber roots that pulsed like veins, no privacy, gruff "comrades," always eyes on her, and . . . no doors. That was the worst part, not being able to close a door and feel safe, ever, especially while she was working—because in magic she went to a place inside of herself and was entirely vulnerable. And forget about sleep. She'd had to find an alternative.

It was no small matter secreting a growing army of chimaera in the human world. They needed a place that was big, isolated, and within range of the Atlas portal Razgut had shown her, so that they could come and go between worlds. Electricity and running water would have been nice, too, but she hadn't expected to find a place that fit even the critical needs.

The kasbah did, perfectly.

It looked for all the world as Karou had described it in her one brief e-mail to Zuzana: like a sandcastle, a very big sandcastle. It was monumental: an entire town, really—lanes and plazas, neighborhoods, a caravansary, granary, and palace—all of it echoing empty. Its creators had dreamed on a legendary scale, and to stand in its flagstone court, mud walls and peaked roofs jutting overhead, was to feel shrunk to the size of a songbird.

It was gorgeous: embellished with scrollwork iron window grilles and carved wood, jewel mosaics and soaring Moorish arches, jade-green roof tiles, and the white plaster lacework of long-dead craftsmen.

And it was collapsing into ruin. In some quarters the roofs had fallen in entirely, and several towers were reduced to a single standing corner with the rest melted clean away. Staircases led nowhere; doors opened onto four-story plunges; towering arches loomed precarious, riven with cracks.

Above and behind it, slopes scraped north, where the teeth of the Atlas Mountains bit off the sky. Before and below, the earth rolled down a slope of scree and scrub toward the distant Sahara. It was a bleak vista, so still that it seemed the twitch of a scorpion's tail for miles around should draw the eye.

All this Karou could see from her room at the highest point in the palace. A wide, walled court lay below. Several chimaera stood in the arcaded gallery that faced the main gate, and they fell silent when she drifted down before them. She had gone out her window—the lanes were in terrible repair and walking was treacherous, on top of which: *Why walk when you can fly?*—and her silent flight, no stirring of wings, always unsettled them. They stared at her now with the colored eyes of raptors and oxen and lizards, and made no greeting as she passed.

The heat of the day was as powerful as a hand pressing on her head, but still she had put on a sleeved tunic to cover her bruised arms, and she'd slung her knife belt on over that. Her crescent-moon blades hung at her hips, a reassurance that she wished she didn't need. All the chimaera were armed at all times, so she didn't stand out; her "comrades" didn't need to know it was *them* that she feared.

Almost as soon as she entered the great hall, someone whispered, "*Traitor.*"

It came behind her back, a hiss too toneless to place. It pierced her, though she gave no outward sign, continuing on and hearing holes gape open in conversations. It might have come from Hvitha, who was serving himself food, or Lisseth or

Nisk, who were already at the table. But Karou's money was on Ten, for no better reason than that Ten, a wolf-aspect female and the lone surviving member of Thiago's retinue, was friendlier to her face than most. Which of course made her totally suspect.

I love my life, thought Karou.

If it had been Ten, though, the she-wolf was all innocence as she hailed Karou and offered her a plate. "I was just going to bring it up to you," she said.

Karou gave her a suspicious look that took in the plate, as well.

Ten didn't miss it. "You think I'd poison you? Well. Wouldn't I be sorry next time I died?" She laughed, a husky sound from her wolf jaws. "Thiago asked me to," she explained. "He's meeting with his captains or I'm sure he would have done it himself."

Karou took the plate of couscous and vegetables. That was another benefit of being here: In Eretz food had been hard to come by; they had subsisted mainly on boiled jess, which had the mouthfeel of modeling clay and not much more flavor. Here, a battered truck served Karou for occasional trips to buy bulk bags of grain, dates, and vegetables in the nearest towns, and behind the great hall a dynasty of stringy chickens now ruled over a small courtyard.

"Thanks," Karou said. Thiago had brought her dinner several nights now so that her work would not be interrupted, and she had to admit it was easier than coming down to the dubious reception of her comrades—on top of which, the Wolf had tithed. His arms were almost as bruised as her own now, covered in blotches and blooms from the palest yellow to the deepest purple, overlapping and ever-changing.

"An art form all its own," he had called them, and paid her the strangest—and *ickiest*—compliment of her life: "You make beautiful bruises."

This evening, however, he had not come, and it was when she realized that she was waiting for him—*waiting for the Wolf*—that Karou had slammed to her feet and gone straight out the window.

She let Ten guide her to the table. The hall wasn't crowded at this hour. A quick scan and she gauged that half the soldiers here were her own handiwork. It was easy to tell: wings, sheer size. There was Amzallag: hers; Oora: not. Nisk and Lisseth, both hers; Hvitha and Bast: not. Not yet, anyway. But there was a reason the hissed *traitor* had come behind Karou's back: they all knew that in the days, weeks, possibly even *hours* to come, their souls would pass through her hands. One of them might even be walking to the pit with Thiago tonight; who knew? What they *did* know was that they were going to die; they were used to it.

They were not used to trusting a traitor with their resurrection.

"Nectar?" said Ten. A joke. She gestured to the big drum that held river water, and scooped Karou up a cup. After they were settled in their places, she said, "I saw Razor earlier."

"Oh?" Karou was instantly wary. Razor was a Heth bone priest she had brought back that morning from the stash of thuribles. It had been a tricky resurrection, one of Thiago's special requests.

Ten nodded. "He was perplexed by his head."

"He'll get used to it."

"But a lion's head, Karou? On a Heth?"

As if Karou didn't know what kind of heads Heth had. They were fairly horrific, actually, with great compound eyes and scissoring ant mandibles that resembled crab claws. How had Brimstone handled that? Karou had no insect teeth in her supply, and she had never known him to have any, either. "Thiago wanted him. Lion was the best I could do on short notice." *And better than he deserves*, she thought. Razor was a stranger to her, but she had sensed a dark character while she worked. Every soul made a unique impression on her mind, and his was... *sticky*. Why Thiago had made him a priority she didn't know, and hadn't asked, as she hadn't asked about the others. She did her work and the Wolf did his.

"Well," allowed Ten, "I suppose he *is* much prettier now."

"Right?" said Karou. "I'm expecting his thank-you any day."

"Yes, well, don't sheathe your claws," said Ten. It was a chimaera expression, roughly equivalent to *don't hold your breath*, though more menacing, with the implied necessity of self-defense. *Good advice*, thought Karou.

Her mouth was full when Ten said, casually, "Thiago suggested that I help you."

The couscous felt like Play-Doh on Karou's tongue. She couldn't answer, and struggled to swallow.

"Well," said Ten. "It's an enormous undertaking for one person, isn't it?"

Karou finally swallowed her Play-Doh. *Brimstone was one person*, she thought, but she didn't say it. She knew she didn't fare well in that comparison. Besides, Brimstone had not been alone, had he?

"I would be your assistant," Ten went on. "Like the Naja woman, what was her name?" At this blithe mention of Issa, Karou stiffened. Ten didn't notice, and didn't wait for a response. "I could take care of the menial things to leave you free for the part only you can do."

"No," said Karou, sharp as a bite. *You're not Issa.* "Tell Thiago thank you, but—"

"Oh. I believe he meant for you to accept."

Well, of course Thiago meant for her to accept; he meant for everyone to accept his will and enact it at once. And she *did* need help. But Ten? Karou couldn't stand the thought of the she-wolf always at her elbow, watching her.

There was something savage about Ten, about most of the company, in fact, that Karou was having a hard time reconciling with her memories of her chimaera kindred—had they always been like this and she just couldn't see it? There had been, for instance, the matter of the sweet arza tree, not long after she'd joined with them. Nothing sweet about it anymore, the tree was burned like everything else around Loramendi, huge and skeletal as a great bone hand clawing up from the earth. There had been charred orbs swaying in its boughs, and Karou hadn't understood what they were until she'd heard some soldiers talking of using "the arza fruit" for archery practice.

She hadn't even thought—*stupid, stupid*—before saying, "Oh, that's fruit? It's big."

The way they'd looked at her. She couldn't recall it without a scald of shame. It was Ten who had said, "They're *heads*."

Karou had blanched. "You're shooting at *heads?*" All she could think was: *But they're* ours. *They must have been chimaera,* and Ten had asked, "What else would we do with them?"

A beat passed in incredulity before Karou said, "We could *bury* them."

To which Ten had replied, with vicious zeal, "I'd rather avenge them."

It was a fearsome thing to say, and Karou had gotten a chill—and a small spark of admiration, she had to admit—but it kept coming back to her later, and her admiration didn't last. Why not both? Bury the dead *and* avenge them. It was barbaric to leave corpses lying about, and she knew this wasn't simply her human feeling.

She experienced a queer collision of reactions these days. Karou's were foremost, and most immediate, but Madrigal's were hers, too: her two selves, coming together with a strange kind of vibration. It wasn't disharmony, exactly. Karou *was* Madrigal, but her reactions were informed by her human life and all the luxuries of peace, and things that might have been commonplace to Madrigal could still jar her at first. Burnt heads strung from a sweet arza tree? If Madrigal hadn't seen exactly that, she had witnessed enough horror that it had no power to shock her.

But in Madrigal's lifetime the chimaera had buried their dead, if they could. It wasn't always possible; countless times they'd gleaned souls and left the bodies on the battlefield, but that was of necessity. This was...brutish. To take target practice at the dead? It wasn't only Karou's human self that shrank from that. What had the past eighteen years been like that the chimaera had given up such a basic hallmark of civilization as *burial*?

Now, leaning forward, Ten told Karou, "Thiago needs more soldiers, and faster. It is critical."

"It would slow things down more to try to teach you what to do."

"Surely there's something."

Surely there was. Plenty of things. She could make and mold the incense, clean the teeth, tithe. But something in Karou clenched at the thought. *Not Ten.* For years Ten had been attached to the White Wolf—his personal guard, one of a pack that moved always in his shadow, in battle and out of it.

She had been in the requiem grove.

"A smith would be more helpful," said Karou. "To band the teeth in silver for stringing."

"Aegir is busy. *Forging weapons.*" Ten's tone suggested that banding teeth was beneath the smith's dignity.

"And what am I forging, *jewelry*?" Karou matched her tone. She met Ten's eyes, which were golden-brown like a true wolf's, unlike Thiago's pale blue, a color never seen on the animal. *He should be called the White Siberian Husky,* Karou thought pettishly.

"Aegir can't be spared." Ten's voice was getting tight.

"I'm surprised Thiago can spare *you*." *Who will brush his hair for him?*

"He considers this very important."

Ten's words were hard and clipped now, and it began to dawn on Karou that she might not win this, and also that her arguments against Ten's help weren't sound. She could see

Thiago's point; she was no Brimstone, that was sure. The Wolf was trying to mount a rebellion, and there were still a score of flightless soldiers awaiting their walk to the pit, not to mention the landslide of thuribles in her room that had barely begun to diminish.

And the patrols had not yet returned from the first wave of the rebellion.

If anything had happened to them . . . Just the thought made Karou want to sag down and weep. Of those thirty soldiers, half were newly wrought—hard-earned flesh-and-blood bodies, her arms still blooming with bruises to show for them.

Of the rest, one was Ziri, the only chimaera in the company who, Karou was reasonably sure, had not cheered at her execution.

Ziri.

As Thiago said, it was early yet. Karou sighed and rubbed her temples, which Ten took as assent, her jaws doing their wolf version of a smile.

"Good," she said. "We'll start after dinner."

What? No. Karou was trying to decide whether to retrieve the threads of the argument when, peripherally, she saw a large figure enter the room and stop hard. She knew that shape, even at the edge of sight. She should; she'd just made it.

It was Razor.

24

Angel-Lover

All talk in the hall ceased. Heads swung to look at Razor, poised on the threshold and staring straight at Karou.

Her gut twisted. This was the worst part, always. There were the ones like Amzallag who walked to the pit and woke knowing where they were, with whom, and all that had happened in Eretz. And then there were the souls from the thuribles: the soldiers who had died at Cape Armasin and didn't even know that Loramendi had fallen, let alone that they were in another world.

Without exception they blinked at Karou dully, not recognizing her. How could they? A blue-haired girl without wings or horns? She was a stranger.

And, of course, she never heard what was said later, when they were told the truth. She liked to imagine someone speaking on her behalf—*She's one of us; she's the resurrectionist; she brought you back, she brought us here, and look: food!*—but thought it was more likely something along the lines of: *We have no choice; we need her.* Or even, in her darker moments: *Much as we'd all love to, we can't kill her.* Yet.

Though, by the look of things, no one had given Razor that message.

"*You,*" he snarled.

He leapt.

Fast—faster than Ten, who stumbled—Karou was on her feet and clear of the table. Razor landed on it just where she'd been sitting. It gave way under his weight with a powerful *crack*, its two ends shooting up in the air as it collapsed in a V beneath him. The water drum tipped, spilled, hit the ground with the warp clamor of a gong, and bodies were in motion, everyone a blur but the Heth, who was poised, focused. Vicious.

"*Angel-lover,*" he spat, and shame lit Karou like a flare.

It was a term of utter degradation; in all Karou's human languages, there was no insult so loaded with disgust and contempt, no single word that cast such a pall of filth. It was that bad even when it was figurative, a slur.

Never, before her, had it been literal.

A flick of his tail, and Razor spilled forward. That was what the motion looked like. His body was reptilian—Komodo dragon and cobra—and even big as he was, he moved like the wind over grass.

Karou had done that. She had given him that grace, that speed. *Note to self,* she thought, and leapt clear. She was graceful, too, and fast. She danced backward. Her crescent-moon blades were in her hands. She hadn't been conscious of drawing them. In front of her, the lion face that had been so beautiful in its resting state on her floor was made grotesque by Razor's hatred. He opened his jaws, and the voice that came out was scraping, bitter, an anguished roar.

"Do you know what I have lost because of you?"

She did not know, and didn't want to. *Because of you, because of you.* She wanted to cover her ears, but her hands were occupied holding blades. "I'm sorry," she said, and her voice sounded so slight after his, and unconvincing even to her own ears.

Ten was there, saying something low and urgent to him; whatever it was, it had no effect. Razor lunged past her. And past Bast, who made no move to intervene. Granted, she was half his size, but Amzallag could easily have stopped him, and he seemed uncertain, looking back and forth between the two. Karou danced away again. The others just stood there, and in her breast a spark of anger leapt and caught. *Ungrateful assholes*, she thought, which struck an unexpected nerve of humor. She and Zuzana used to call everything assholes—kids, pigeons, fragile old ladies who scowled at Karou's hair—and it had never stopped being funny. Assholes, crannies, *orifii.* Now, in the path of this lion-dragon, sticky-souled thing, Karou felt her face crimped by the unlikeliest of expressions: a smile.

It was as sharp as her crescent-moon blades. And with-Razor's next move, she held her ground and held her knives. Gritting her teeth, she dragged one curved edge hard across the other in a shriek of steel that got his attention for an instant—a pausc just long enough for Karou to consider *What now? Will I have to kill him?* Can I?

Yes.

And then: a flash of white and it was over. Thiago was

between them, his back to Karou as he ordered Razor to stand down, and she didn't have to kill anyone. The Heth obeyed, his restless tail upending chairs at every pace.

Lisseth and Nisk intercepted him and Karou stood there, poised between breaths, blades in her hands and blood thrumming up and down her arms, and for an instant she felt like Madrigal again—not the traitor but the soldier.

Just for an instant.

"Take her back to her room."

That was Thiago to Ten, as if Karou were an escaped mental patient or something. Her smile vanished. "I'm not done eating," she said.

"It looks like you are." He glanced ruefully at the broken table and spilled food. "I'll bring something up to you. You shouldn't have to endure this." His voice was kind, cloyingly so, and when he drew close to ask softly, "Are you all right?" Karou kind of wanted to scratch his face off.

"I'm *fine*. What do you think I am?"

"I think that you are our most valuable asset. And I think that you need to let me protect you." He reached for her arm; she jerked it away, and he raised his hands in a gesture of surrender.

"I can protect myself," she said, trying to recapture the brief vibration of power that had possessed her. *I am Madrigal*, she told herself, but faced with the White Wolf, all she could think was that Madrigal had been a victim, and she couldn't hold on to the sensation of power. "Whatever you might think," she said, "I'm not helpless." But she sounded like she was trying to convince herself as much as him, and without even thinking about it, she wrapped her arms around her middle in a childish gesture of self-protection. She unwrapped them instantly, but that just made her look fidgety.

Thiago's voice was soft. "I never said you were helpless. But Karou, if anything happened to you we'd be finished. I need you safe. It's that simple."

Safe. Not from the enemy but from her own kind—into whom she poured all her care, her health, her pain, day after night after day. Karou gave a hard laugh.

"They need time," Thiago said. "That's all. They'll come to trust you. As I do."

"*Do* you trust me?" she asked.

"Of course I do, Karou. Karou." He looked sad. "I thought we were moving past all of that. There's no room for petty grudges in these times. We need all of our focus, all of our energy, on the cause."

Karou might have argued that her execution wasn't exactly a petty grudge, but she didn't, because she knew he was right. They did need all their energy on the cause, and she hated that he had had to remind her of it like she was some schoolgirl acting up, and even more, she hated the shaky feeling that was hitting her now that her adrenaline rush was drying up. As much as she resented being packed off to her room at Thiago's command, it was her room that she wanted, its solitude and safety, so she put her crescent-moon blades back in their sheaths and, trying to act like it was her own idea, she turned and went. She held her head high, but she knew, every step of the way, that she wasn't fooling anyone.

25

Enemy Queue Forms Here

Ten escorted Karou to her room, and she must have taken Karou's quiet for complaisance, because she chatted away, offering unwelcome critique on recent resurrections, and was caught completely off guard at the top of the stairs when Karou shut the door in her face and slammed down the crossbar.

A moment of stunned silence, and then the thumping began. "Karou! I'm supposed to help you. Let me in. *Karou.*"

"I love you, crossbar," whispered Karou, and petted it.

Ten's voice rose steadily, scolding, huffing. Unbuckling her knife belt, Karou ignored her. On her table lay a half-strung necklace, but she didn't want to pick it up, and she didn't want company—or babysitting. She wanted a pencil and a page, and to render the exact look on Razor's face as he came at her, the V of the broken table and the blur of figures at the periphery who'd done nothing to help her. Drawing had always been how she processed things. Once they were on paper they were *hers*, and she could decide what power they would hold over her.

She took up her sketchbook and smoothed it open. In the margin she saw the ragged remnants of a torn-out page and recalled, as vividly as if she were looking at it, the sketch of Akiva that had been there. He'd been asleep in her flat. She had destroyed that sketch, of course. She had destroyed them all.

If only she could do the same with her memories.

Angel-lover.

Even the thought of the word brought on shame. How could she have done it: loved Akiva—or rather, thought she had? Because now, whatever there had been between them wore that pall of filth—*angel-lover*—and looked nothing like love. Lust, maybe. Youth, rebellion, self-destructiveness, perversity. She'd barely known him; how could she have thought it was love? But whatever it had been . . . could it ever be forgiven?

How many chimaera would Karou have to resurrect before they accepted her?

All of them. That was how many. Every last one who had died because of her. Hundreds of thousands. More.

Which was, of course, impossible. Those souls had evanesced, including the ones dearest to her. They were lost. Was that it, then? No possibility of redemption?

This was her life, and it was her nightmare, too, and sometimes the only way she could bear it was by telling herself it would end. If it *was* a nightmare, she would wake up and Brimstone would be alive; everyone would be alive. And if it wasn't a nightmare? Well then, it would end in one of the very many ways that lives end. Sooner or later.

She drew, and captured Razor's snarl with awful vitality.

You really want to know what I'm up to, Zuzana? Here it is. I'm trapped in a sandcastle with dead monsters, forced to resurrect them one after the next, all while trying to avoid getting eaten.

It sounded like a pitch for a Japanese game show, and Karou couldn't help laughing again, though only for a second, because Ten heard from the other side of the door and let out a soft snarl. *Great.* The she-wolf probably thought she was laughing at *her*.

Enemy queue forms here, wrote Karou below her sketch.

Oh, Zuze.

She cast an eye over her tooth trays and damned them for being so full. She'd been too efficient on her collecting trip; it would be some time before she could plead the necessity of going out again. The faster she worked, though, the faster the time would come, and when it did, she would do more than e-mail Zuzana. She would find her. She would slouch down for tea and goulash with her and Mik at Poison Kitchen and tell them everything, then bask in their outrage on her behalf.

They would agree with her that ungrateful Heth bone priests did not deserve regal lion heads but perhaps hamster next time, or maybe Pekingese.

Or better yet, she imagined Zuzana saying in her sharp way, *to hell with them all.*

I'm not doing it for them, Karou would reply. It was a practiced thought, one she clung to. *It's for Brimstone. And for all the chimaera the angels haven't yet managed to murder.* She had only to remember Loramendi to feel the desperation of her duty. There was no one else to do this work but her.

From somewhere outside came the sentry's call, a single short high whistle. Karou jumped up and was at the window in a stride. A patrol was returning, the first of the five. Unblinking, she leaned out her window and scanned the sky. There: from the direction of the mountains where the portal hung high and unseen in the thin air. They were still too distant to make out silhouettes and know which team it was, but, squinting, she could see that they were six. That was a reason to be glad; one team at least was intact.

Nearer, nearer, and then she saw him: tall and straight, his horns like a pair of pikes. Ziri. A knot loosened in her chest that she hadn't known was there. Ziri was okay. She could make out the others now, and soon enough they were circling over the kasbah and dropping into the court, half on wings of her creation, no two the same in size or form but all alike in menace: armed to kill, leathers black with blood and ash. She was glad to see Balieros, too, but her relief was really for Ziri.

Ziri was Kirin; he was kin.

When Karou looked at him, her Madrigal memories grew bright, and she remembered the men of her tribe as she hadn't seen them in so long. She had been only seven years old when she was orphaned by angels. She was away from home that day, a free child in a wild world, and had returned to the aftermath of the slave raid and the end of life as she knew it. Death and silence, blood and absence, and, deep in the caves, huddled together: a handful of elders who had managed to save the very smallest of the babies.

Ziri had been one of those babies, tiny and new as a kit with its eyes still shut. Karou had some small memories of him in Loramendi later: he used to follow her around blushing—her foster sister, Chiro, teased her that he had a crush on her. "Your little Kirin shadow," she had called him.

"It's not a crush," Madrigal had argued. "It's kinship. It's longing for what he never had."

She'd felt deeply for him, an orphan like her but with no memories of their home or their people to hold on to. There had been some elder Kirin left, and a few other orphans his age, but Madrigal was the only Kirin in her prime whom he had ever seen.

Funny, now the tables were turned, and it was her looking to him and seeing what *she* had lost. He was grown now, and tall even before the antelope horns that added several more feet. His legs were human tapering to antelope, as her own had once been, and, coupled with his vast bat wings, gave him the same buoyant gait all the Kirin had possessed—a lightness as if the earth underfoot were incidental and he might at any instant go airborne and rise leagues above it all.

Only there was no lightness in him now. His tread was heavy and his face grim, and as the patrol assembled in formation to await their general, he was the only one to give a glance up at Karou's window. She half raised her hand to him, her bruised arm screaming at the simple gesture, which...he did not return. He lowered his head again as if she weren't even there.

Stung, Karou let her hand fall.

Where were they coming from? What had they seen? What had they done?

Go down and find out, came a whisper in the back of her

mind, but she didn't heed it. Whatever went on in the ashfall landscape and blood-crusted world of war where her creations went forth to do violence, it wasn't her concern. She conjured the bodies; that was all.

What more could she possibly do?

26

Grievous Harm

The Wolf was in the window right below Karou's. As soon as Ziri lifted his eyes to look for her, he saw white and dropped his head again. It was barely enough time to register the look of half hope on her face as she raised her hand to him, tentative. Lonely.

And then he shunned her.

The Wolf had told him he must have no contact with her. He had told them all, but Ziri thought those pale eyes had lingered on him when he said it, and that he was the one Thiago watched most closely. Because he was Kirin? Did he think that fact alone would bond them, or did he remember Ziri as a child? At the Warlord's ball?

At the execution.

He had tried to save her. It would be funny if it wasn't so pathetic—how he had crouched in the crawl space under the tourney stands, getting up his courage, gripping his edgeless training swords as though they might deliver her. The stands had been erected in the agora so the folk could better watch her die; it was a spectacle. Madrigal, so still and straight, so beautiful, had made the stamping masses seem like animals, and he, a skinny boy of twelve, had thought he could storm the scaffold and . . . what? Cut her pinion, her manacles? The city itself was a cage; she would have had nowhere to go.

It hadn't mattered. He'd been laid out by the hilt of a soldier's sword before his feet ever touched the platform. Madrigal never even saw his fool heroics. Her eyes had never left her lover.

That was another lifetime. Ziri hadn't understood her treason then, or where it could lead. Where it *had* led. But he wasn't a lovestruck little boy anymore, and Karou was nothing to him.

So why were his eyes drawn to her window? To *her*, on the rare occasions she came down?

Was it pity? A glance was all it took to see how alone she was. In the first days, in Eretz, she had been pale, trembling, mute—clearly in shock. It had been harder then, not to go to her or speak even a word. She must have seen it—how something in him leapt to answer her grief, her loneliness, and now she sought him out with that look of half-hope whenever she saw him, as if he might be a friend.

And he turned away from her. Thiago had been clear: The rebels needed her but couldn't make the mistake of trusting her. She was treacherous and must be managed carefully—by him.

And here he was now, come down to greet the patrol.

"Well met," said Thiago, striding out like the lord of the manor. Lord of the *ruins*, rather, but if this mud castle was a comedown for the great White Wolf, he claimed it as he had ever claimed anything—or everything: as his to do with as he wished until he seized the next and better thing. He would have the throne in Astrae before he was through, he claimed, and seraphim for slaves, and as ludicrous a claim as it seemed in light of their circumstances, Ziri would never underestimate the Wolf.

Thiago was a soldier's soldier. His troops worshipped him, and would do anything for him. He ate, drank, and breathed battle, never more at home than in a campaign tent strewn with maps, hashing strategy with his captains or, better yet, hurling himself at angels with his teeth bared and bloody.

"Reckless," the Warlord had fumed once, furious when his son had been killed and come back in a new body. "A general need not die at the front!" But Thiago had never been one to hang back in safety and send others forth to die. He *led*, and Ziri knew firsthand how his fearlessness spread like wildfire in the fray. It was what made him great.

Now, though, with the chimaera hanging on to the frayed end of their existence, it seemed his father's words had gotten through. When the patrols had gone out to Eretz, he'd stayed behind—with clear reluctance and even bad grace that put Ziri in mind of guardsmen who drew duty during the festival times. It was a heavy thing, to *miss out*. He had paced, wolf-restless, hungry, *envious*, and he came alive now at his soldiers' return.

He clasped them by the arm one by one before coming to a halt before Balieros.

"I hope," he said, with a grim smile to indicate he doubted it not, "that you have done grievous harm."

Grievous harm.

The evidence of it painted them, splash and spatter. Blood: dried to a dull dark brown, black where it gathered in the creases of gauntlets and boot heels and hooves. Every edge and angle of Ziri's crescent-moon blades was grimed with it; he couldn't wait to clean them. Mutilating the dead. Perhaps it was a proud thing, these cut smiles that had been the Warlord's message long ago. Ziri only knew that he felt foul, and wanted to go to the river and bathe. Even his *horns* were crusted with blood where they had impaled an angel who flew at him while he was grappling with another. The patrol had done grievous harm indeed.

It had also protected Caprine farmfolk from an enemy sweep, freed a caravan of slaves, armed them, and sent them wide to spread word of what was coming. But Thiago didn't ask about that. To hear him, he might have forgotten there were folk in the world who weren't soldiers—enemy or own—or any cause left but killing.

"Tell me," he said, avid. "I want to know the looks on their faces. I want to hear how they screamed."

27

Great Wild Heart

Some time around midday, the Dashnag boy, Rath, still carrying Sarazal, led Sveva down a steep wooded slope into a ravine. It was narrow enough that the forest canopy was unbroken overhead, and Sveva thought that the pale damsel boughs arching upward to meet in the middle looked like the arms of maidens joined in dance. Sunlight reached through them, sometimes in bright spears and sometimes dappled lacework, green and gold and ever shifting. Small winged things drifted and hummed from the depths to the heights of this little ravine that was their entire world, and, down below, a creek could be heard, spry as music.

All this will burn, thought Sveva, leaping a drift of vines and shying sideways down the slope behind Rath.

The fires were still behind them, and with the wind from the south carrying the smoke away, they couldn't even smell it, but they had come several times to hillocks and glimpsed the sky roiling black behind them.

How could the angels do it? Was it so important to catch or kill a few chimaera that they would destroy the whole land? Why did they even want it, just to ravage it?

Why can't they just leave us alone? she wanted to scream, but she didn't. She knew it was a childish thought, that the wars and hates of the world were too big for her to understand, and that she was no more important in the scheme of things than these moths and adderflies drifting in their shafts of light.

I am important, though, she insisted to herself. And so was Sarazal, and so were the moths and the adderflies, and the slinking skotes, and the star tenzing blooms so small and perfect, and even the tiny biting skinwights, who, after all, were just trying to live.

And Rath was important, too, even if his breath smelled like a lifetime of blood meals and bitten bones.

He was helping them. When he had grabbed up Sarazal, Sveva hadn't really believed he meant to drag her away and make a meal of her, but it was hard not to be afraid when her heartbeat skittered sideways at the mere sight of him. Dashnag ate flesh. It was what they were, same as skinwights were skinwights, but that didn't mean she had to like them. Or him.

"We don't eat Dama," he'd said without looking at her, after she'd caught up to him—which was easy, she was so much faster than he was, and he was encumbered by carrying Sarazal. "Or any other higher beasts. As I'm sure you know."

Sveva knew that this was supposedly the case, but it was a hard thing to take on faith. "Not even if you're really hungry?" she had asked, skeptical and in some strange way wanting to believe the worst of him.

"I *am* really hungry, and you're still alive," he'd replied. That was all. He kept going, and Sveva had a hard time staying afraid, because Sarazal was asleep with her head on his shoulder and he stayed upright, holding her, when it would have been easier for him to leave her and throw himself forward into the long, loping run the Dashnag used to take down prey. He hadn't, though.

He'd led them here, and now that they were well down in the ravine, Sveva could hear and smell what he had heard and smelled several miles back with his sharp predator's senses: Caprine.

Caprine? This was why he had cut east, to catch the trail of these slow, bobbing herdfolk, who, to judge from the smell, still had all their livestock with them?

Rath stopped at the bottom of the slope, and when Sveva drew even with him, he said, "From the village, I think, the one by the aqueduct. You remember."

As if she could forget the place where the seraph soldiers were strung up with their red Warlord smiles. She would never forget it as long as she lived, the horror mingled with the hope of salvation. The village had been empty; she had supposed its occupants must be dead, and was glad now to know they weren't, but she didn't know why Rath was following them.

"Caprine are slow," she said.

"So they'll need help," Rath replied, and Sveva felt a flush of shame. She'd been thinking only of their own escape.

"They might have a healer, too," Rath added, looking down at Sarazal, who rested against his chest, her eyes still closed, wounded leg curled gingerly in the crook of his arm. It was such an incongruous sight, the predator cradling the prey, that Sveva could only blink and feel that she'd hit the stony bottom of her own shallow depths.

Did she know anything at all?

* * *

This land was immense. It seemed to Akiva as though he could rise higher and higher into the air and it would keep unrolling in every direction, endless and green, forever. He knew that wasn't the case. In the east the earth rose and stepped up a long, low crust of hills to become high desert for days, days into weeks of red clay and barbed plants, where venomous beetles as large as shields burrowed down and lay in wait for months, years, for prey to pass within reach. Some nomads were rumored to live around the sky islands, such as the jackal-headed Sab, but seraph patrols that went that way either reported no signs of life or vanished into the depths and never returned to report at all.

To the west lay the Coast Range, and beyond that the Secret Coast, home to tidal villages and folk who could live in the water or out of it, and who slipped away fish-fast at the sight of the enemy, retreating to deepwater refuges until the danger had passed.

And to the south: the formidable Hintermost, the highest mountains in Eretz as well as the broadest by triple the scope of any other mountain range in the world. They made an epic wall of gray ramparts and natural crenels, gorges riddled through with rivers that cut into the heart of the rock and out again, and slopes glinting with waterfalls by the thousands. There were said to be passes—mazy ravines and tunnels—leading to green lands on the far side, impassable but with the guidance of the frog-fleshed native tribes who dwelt mostly in darkness. And in the highest reaches, ice formations looked like crystal cities from a distance, but proved desolate wind mazes up close, unnavigable but by the stormhunters who nested there, sitting their huge eggs and riding gales that would dash anything else to death in half a wingbeat.

Such were the natural boundaries of this southern continent that the seraphim had long ago sought to tame, and the green earth that lay below Akiva now was its great wild heart, too huge to hold, even if every soldier in the Empire's array of armies was sent to try. They could—and would—burn villages and fields, but more chimaera here were nomads than farmers, fleet and elusive, and the seraphim couldn't burn it all, even if they were to try, which—contrary to these billows of black smoke—they were not.

The fires were only to corral the fugitives south and east, to where the forests thinned and creeks filtered down to join the great Kir River, and they might be able to flush them out. And if they succeeded?

Akiva hoped they wouldn't. In truth he did more than hope: He put all his skills as a tracker to work at *un*tracking. Wherever he gauged chimaera might be—where a crease in the canopy hinted at a creek, for example—he made efforts to lead the team a different way, and because he was Beast's Bane, no one questioned him. Except maybe Hazael, and then only with his eyes.

Liraz wasn't with them; their team was a dozen strong, and she'd been assigned to another. Akiva couldn't help wondering, over the course of the day, with what zeal his sister was pursuing her orders.

"So what do you really think?" Hazael asked him out of the blue. It was getting on into evening, and they had yet turned up no fleeing slaves or villagers.

"About what?"

"About who's behind these attacks."

What *did* he think? He didn't know. All day Akiva had been at war with hope—trying not to *let* himself hope, partly because it was so wrong a feeling to take away from a site of massacre, and partly out of simple fear that it might prove fruitless. Was there another resurrectionist? Was there not?

"Not ghosts, anyway," he gave as a safe answer.

"No, probably not ghosts," Hazael agreed. "It is curious, though. No blood on our soldiers' blades, no tracks leading away save the fleeing folk, and five attacks in one night—so how many attackers in all? They have to be strong to do what they did, and probably winged, to come and vanish without tracks, and I'd guess they had hamsas, else our soldiers must have gotten in some strikes. This was just an opening act." It was a studied assessment; Akiva had thought of all these things himself. Hazael gave him a long look. "What are we dealing with here, Akiva?"

He finally had to say it. "Revenants. It has to be."

"Another resurrectionist?"

Akiva hesitated. "Maybe." Did Hazael understand what it meant to him if there *was* another resurrectionist? Could he guess his hope—that Karou might live again? And what sympathy could he have for his hopes? Suppose his forgiveness hinged on Karou being dead, as if Akiva's madness might be in the past, something to be gotten over so they could keep on as usual.

There could be no more "as usual" for Akiva. What *could* there be?

"There!" called the patrol leader, jarring him out of his thoughts. Kala was a lieutenant of the Second Legion, the largest by far of the Empire's forces, sometimes called the common army. She was pointing down into a gully where the fringe of trees didn't quite come together, and where, as Akiva watched, one flicker of movement begat another, and another, and then a rush of bodies. Herd movement. The Caprine. His gut seized, and his first impulse was anger: *What fools, in all this great wild land, to let themselves be seen.*

It was too late to divert attention from them; there was nothing he could do but follow as Kala led the team down toward the trees. She was alert for ambush, and motioned Akiva and Hazael to sweep wide to the gully's far side, which they did, staring hard into the broken space between treetops, hoping for a clear view, which they did not get—only glimpses of fleece and ambling motion.

Akiva held his swords bitterly. His training was very clear. Take up a weapon and you become an instrument with as pure a purpose as the weapon itself: to find arteries and open them, limbs and sever them; to take what is alive and deliver it unto death. There was no other reason to hold a weapon, no other reason to *be* one.

He didn't want to be that weapon anymore. Oh, he could desert, he could vanish right now. He didn't have to be party to this. But it wasn't enough that *he* cease to kill chimaera. He had dreamed so much bigger than that once.

The trees were a whisper of green as he and Hazael descended with the others, and the voice that filled his head was one he had heard only once. *It is life that expands to fill worlds. Life is your master or death is.* When Brimstone had spoken those words, they'd meant nothing to Akiva. Now he understood. But how could a soldier change masters?

How, with swords clenched in both hands, could one hope to keep blood from spilling?

28

The Worst Kind of Silence

So many different kinds of silence, Sveva thought, pressing her face into Rath's shoulder and trying not to breathe. This was the worst kind. This was make-a-sound-and-die silence, which, though she had never experienced it before, she understood instinctively grew more fraught the more souls you shared it with. One might trust oneself to be quiet, but thirty-odd strangers?

With *babies*?

They were huddled under a lip of earth carved out by the creek in fuller seasons; the water passed before them, flicking at their hooves—and Rath's huge clawed paws—and its burble might at least cover some small sounds—whimpers or sniffs. Of which, Sveva noted, she heard none and nothing. With her eyes closed, she might have been alone, but for the heat of Rath on one side and Nur on the other. The Caprine mother held her baby tucked against her, and Sveva kept expecting Lell to cry, but she didn't. This silence, she thought, was remarkable: a perfect, shimmering thing, and fragile. Like glass, if it shattered, it would never come back together again.

If Lell cried, or if someone's hoof lost purchase and skidded on the bank, or if any sound rose over the innocent burble of the creek, they would all die.

And if the innermost frightened-child part of her wanted to blame Rath for them being here at all, she couldn't. Oh, not for lacking of trying. It was good to have someone to blame, but the problem with Sveva and blame was that if she kept tracing it back, there was only *her*, racing down the valley ahead of Sarazal, wind in her hair and not heeding her sister's call to turn back. This wasn't Rath's fault, and what's more, she and her sister would probably be dead already if not for him. And the Caprine, well, they would be dying *right now*. Right this very moment.

What an odd and terrible thing to know.

If Rath hadn't scented the Caprine and followed them, caught up to them, and joined them, then this fraught silence would not exist at all; this same air would be pierced with bleating screams, and Lell *would* be crying, sweet small bundle, and all the others, too, instead of the aries.

* * *

"Aries!" said Hazael, laughing—laughing with relief, it seemed to Akiva—and he saw that in the gully were only aries: shaggy, curling-horned livestock, and no Caprine sheepfolk, no chimaera at all.

"You and you." Kala pointed out two soldiers. "Kill them.

The rest of you..." She turned in a half circle, surveying her team; she hung in the air, wings sweeping wide enough to brush the leaning trees at the gully's edges and shed sparks. "Find their owners."

* * *

Sveva heard the screams of the aries and pressed her face harder into Rath's shoulder. Rath had persuaded the sheepfolk to drive off their flock and double back along the creek bed, climb out of that ravine and into another—this one—and take shelter. They were too many, all together, and the aries were too loud, too unruly to trust with their lives; they'd be seen, he'd said, and he'd been right.

Now the aries were dying.

Sveva clutched her sister's hand; it was limp. The screams of the aries were terrible, even at a distance, but they didn't last long, and when they finally trailed away she imagined she could feel the angels wheeling in the sky overhead. Angels, hunting. Hunting *them*. She clutched the hilt of her own stolen knife and it made her feel her smallness all the more, made as it was for an angel's big brute fist.

Maybe she would stab one with it. What would *that* feel like? Oh, her hate was hot; she almost hoped she got the chance. She'd always hated angels, of course, but in a faraway, vague kind of way. They'd been monsters from bedtime tales. She'd never even seen one before she was captured. For centuries this land had been safe—the Warlord's armies had kept it so. What ill luck, then, to live in the time of failed safety! Now, suddenly, seraphim were real: leering tormentors, beautiful in a way that made beauty *hideous*.

And then there was Rath, dreadful in a way that made dreadful . . . well, if not beautiful, then regal, at least. Proud. How curious, to take comfort in the bulk of a flesh-eater at her side, but she did. Again, Sveva felt herself scraping at her own shallows; since she was taken slave, her world had fallen open. She had beheld seraphim and revenants; she had seen death and smelled it, and today, just today, she had learned more of folk than in all her fourteen years together. First Rath, then the Caprine: sheepfolk she had called herdbeasts, and would have left to fend for themselves. Nur had made a poultice for Sarazal and given her some spice in water, hoping to break her fever. They had shared their food, and Lell, who smelled of grass, had taken to Sveva and ridden astride her back for a time, her little arms wrapped around Sveva's waist where just days ago a great black shackle had been.

Sveva's eyes were closed. Her face was against Rath's shoulder, and her hip hard against Nur's, and the silence held them together. It was the worst kind of silence, but a good kind of closeness. These weren't her folk, but . . . they *were*, and maybe that meant that anyone could be anyone's, which was a sort of nice thing to think, with the world falling apart. Sveva wondered if she would ever get home to her mother and father so she could tell them that.

She tried to pray, but she had only ever prayed at night, and it seemed to her that the moons made poor protectors when angels chose to hunt by day.

In the end, it wasn't Lell who gave them away, but Sarazal.

She jolted awake, her limp hand suddenly clenching and pulling free of Sveva's. The fever had come down; Nur's spice and poultice had worked, and Sarazal's big dark eyes, when they fluttered open, were much clearer than when Sveva had looked at them last. Only... they fluttered open to see Rath's fearsome face mere inches from her own.

And Sarazal opened her mouth, and screamed.

29

The Devils Will Still Be There in the Morning

"Listen to this one," said Zuzana. "She-devil sighting in southern Italy—"

"Blue hair?" asked Mik. It came out muffled. He had a pillow over his face and had been trying to sleep.

"Pink, actually. I guess the legions of Satan are exploring their color options." She was sitting up in bed, reading off her laptop. "So, she scaled the side of this cathedral and *hissed*, at which point the witness was able to ascertain, at a distance of some hundred feet, that her tongue was forked."

"Good eyes."

"Yeah." She puffed out her cheeks and backpaged to her Google search screen. "What a bunch of morons."

Mik peered out from beneath the pillow. "It's bright out there," he said. "Come into my lair."

"*Lair.* That's some fancy lair you've got, mister."

"It's exactly the right size for my head."

"Uh-huh," Zuzana said vaguely. "Here's one from yesterday, um, Bakersfield, California. Blue hair, cool coat, floating. Hurray! We've found Karou! What she's doing in Bakersfield, California, stalking schoolchildren is unclear." She gave a derisive snort and returned to the Google screen.

The world, it would seem, was overrun with blue-haired devils. The same message boards that reported angels among us were keeping abreast of the devil situation, too, and in a quirk of coincidence—*ahem*—ever since the widely televised showdown on the Charles Bridge, devils tended to have blue hair, black trench coats, and tattoos of eyes on the palms of their hands.

Karou was the face of the Apocalypse, which Zuzana happened to think was a pretty kick-ass brand of infamy. She had even made the cover of *Time* magazine with the headline "Is This What a Demon Looks Like?" There was this gorgeous picture someone had taken that day as she faced the angels, her hair wild, hamsas outthrust before her, a look on her face of fierce concentration with a hint of... wild delight. Zuzana remembered the wild delight. It had been a little freaky. *Time* had tried to interview her for the piece, and strangely enough had failed to print her expletive-riddled response. Kaz, of course, had not disappointed them.

"Come sleep," Mik tried again. "The devils will still be there in the morning."

"In a minute," Zuzana said, but it wasn't a minute. An hour later she had made a cup of tea and moved to the armchair beside the bed. The message boards weren't getting her anywhere; that was where the crazies went to play. She narrowed her search. She'd already traced the IP address of Karou's single e-mail to Morocco, which wasn't a surprise. The last she'd heard from her friend she'd been in Morocco. This wasn't Marrakesh, though, but a city called Ouarzazate—pronounced War-za-zat—in a region of palm oases, camels, and kasbahs at the fringes of the Sahara desert.

Dust and starlight? Why, yes. One would imagine.

Priestess of a sandcastle? Kasbahs did look extraordinarily like sandcastles. Too bad there were, like, fifty million of them scattered over hundreds of miles. Still, Zuzana was excited. This had to be right. She got that dorky song "Rock the Casbah" stuck in her head and hummed it as she drank tea and paged through dozens of sites that mostly came up as trek outfitters or "authentic nomad experience" kasbah hotels, all of them with these sparkling swimming pools that didn't look terribly nomad-y to her.

And then she came across a travel blog a French guy had written about his trek in the Atlas Mountains. It was only a couple of days old and mostly it was just landscape pictures and camel shadows and dusty children selling jewelry at the roadside, but then there was this one shot that caused Zuzana to set her teacup aside and sit up. She zoomed in and leaned close. It was the night sky with a perfect half pie of a moon, and—obscure enough that she wouldn't have noticed them if she weren't looking—shapes. Six of them, with wings, they were visible mostly for the way they blotted out the stars. Hard to determine scale in a sky photo, it was the subtitle that got her.

Don't tell the angel chasers, but they have some seriously big night birds down here.

30

A Poor Judge of Monsters

Karou went to the river to bathe—feeling almost absurdly indulgent about shampooing her hair, and more so about the wastrel fifteen minutes she took to let it dry fanned out on a hot rock—and when she got back to the fortress, the crossbar was missing from her door.

"Where is it?" she demanded of Ten.

"How would I know? I was with you."

Yes, she had been, never mind that Karou hadn't wanted her. It wasn't *safe* for her to go off alone, Thiago had said, even to the shallows of the river that spilled out of the mountains and passed just downhill of the kasbah, *in plain sight of the sentry tower*—with some large rocks that she valued for the hiding of nudity from keen eyes. The chimaera were as intrigued by her humanity as Issa and Yasri had always been, but were less kind about it.

"What a queer plain thing you are," Ten had observed today,

with an up-and-down look that took in Karou's tailless, clawless, hoofless, and otherwise *less* self.

"Thanks," Karou had said, sinking into the river. "I try."

She'd had a fleeting impulse to let the current carry her away under the water, just downstream a ways where she could be free of the she-wolf's presence for, oh, a half hour? Ten had been quite the fixture over the past several days: her assistant and chaperone, overseer and shadow.

"What will you do when I have to go back out for teeth?" Karou had asked Thiago that morning. "Send her with me?"

"Ten? No. Not Ten," he'd replied, in such a way that Karou had instantly taken his meaning.

"What, *you*? *You're* going to come with me?"

"I admit, I'm curious to see this world. There must be more to it than this desert. You can show me."

He was serious. Karou's stomach had seized. She'd been joking about Ten, but *him*? "You couldn't. You're not human—you'd be seen. And you can't fly." *And you're* vile, *and I don't want you.*

"We'll think of something."

Will we, Karou had thought, imagining Thiago in Poison Kitchen with his wolf feet kicked up on a coffin, spooning goulash into his cruel, sensual mouth. She wondered if Zuzana would swoon over his beauty as she had Akiva's, and immediately thought: *No. Zuze would see right through him.*

But there was a flaw in that. Zuzana hadn't seen through Akiva, had she? And neither had she. Apparently Karou was a poor judge of monsters, which was most unfortunate considering her current situation.

"Who took it?" she demanded. Her heartbeat was out of whack, coming in little staccato bursts.

"What are you carrying on about? It's only a piece of wood."

"It's only my *safety*."

This was to be the cost of clean hair? How was she supposed to sleep when anyone could waltz right in? She slept poorly enough as it was. It struck her then, a swift little thought like the jab of a needle, that she had slept just fine with Akiva only a few feet away, that night in her flat in Prague. What was wrong with her sensors that she had felt safe with *him*? "This was *your* idea, wasn't it? Because I locked you out the other day?" Even the wall brackets had been pried away, so she couldn't just find another beam and slot it in place. "Do you want someone to kill me in my sleep?'

"Calm down, Karou," said Ten. "No one wants to kill—"

"Oh, really. No one *wants* to, or no one *will*?"

Did she expect Ten to sugarcoat it? "Fine. No one *will*," said the she-wolf. "You are under the White Wolf's protection. That's better than any piece of wood. Now, come. Let's get back to work. There's Emylion to finish, and Hvitha goes to the pit tonight."

And that was that? She was just supposed to sidle meekly into her room and get back to work on the Wolf's resurrection wish list? Like hell. Karou turned back toward the stairs, but Ten stood in her way, so she crossed the room to where the window stood open. If Thiago wanted her watched, she thought, he'd do better to assign a shadow who could *fly*.

Ten realized what she was about to do and said, "Karou..." just as she stepped into the air and, after floating there just long enough to throw a defiant glare Ten's way, let herself fall. *Fast.* A great whoosh of air, and she pulled up short at the last second to land in a crouch four stories down.

Ow. Pulled up a little *too* short. The soles of her feet smarted, but it had surely looked dramatic. Ten's head was out the window, and Karou fought the impulse to flip her off—the British V version, which was so much cooler than the American single-finger—but it was ridiculous either way. *Don't be such a human*, she told herself, and went looking for the Wolf.

He was probably in the guardhouse, the half-razed structure where he held court with his captains, drawing maps in the dirt and then scuffing them away, pacing, ranting, planning. Karou started in that direction and passed Hvitha, who gave her a sharp nod and didn't slow his steps. *I guess I'll see you later*, thought Karou with a twist of pity. Hvitha hadn't exactly been kind to her, but he hadn't been unkind, either—he hadn't been anything—and it couldn't be very nice walking around knowing he was scheduled to have his throat slit in a few hours. Such a waste, it seemed, of Brimstone's craftsmanship.

Not my call.

Karou passed clothes draped over a wall to dry in the sun, and it came to her that this place was beginning to feel downright inhabited—thanks to herself. Nine more soldiers in the past few days—her pace was improving with Ten's help, but holy hell, her arms were a mess—and life seemed everywhere amplified. She could hear Aegir's hammer and see smoke rising from the forge, smell the almost-but-not-quite-nothing smell of boiling couscous, and also the not-nearly-nothing-*enough* waft of rankness from the buttress that had become the default piss wall of soldiers who couldn't bother to walk out of the kasbah—or, hello, *fly*.

You're welcome for the wings, now use them to pee farther away please thank you!

An argument, a hoot of laughter, and from the court: the *ching* of newly wrought blades heaved in newly wrought hands as her most recent revenants got the feel of their bodies, wings and all. She paused under an arch to watch and caught sight of Ziri at once. He was with Ixander, her greatest monstrosity to date, and was positively dwarfed by him.

Ixander had always been big—he was Akko, one of the larger tribes and a mainstay of the army—but now he stood grizzly height, maybe ten feet, thickset and tusked to Thiago's specifications. His wings were almost as big as a stormhunter's, and the muscle required to anchor them made his hunched bear back enormous. The body was inelegant, and Karou was sorry about it. Her brief contact with his soul had surprised her with its . . . meadowiness.

The impression of souls was synesthetic: sound or color, flashes of image or feeling, and Ixander's had been meadowy. Dappled light and newbloom and quiet—the opposite of the colossal beast body that he seemed now, with Ziri's help, to be mastering.

Ziri cast himself to the sky, graceful and silent, and beckoned Ixander to follow, which he did with neither grace nor silence. His wingbeats gave the air a sonic thrashing and kicked up flurries of dust that reached Karou even across the court. In the air, the pair began to drill fighting stances, and Karou found her focus not on Ixander but on Ziri, as she forgot her outrage and her errand and was sucked back across years by the sight of a Kirin in flight.

Every time, it was like falling backward into Madrigal. She never felt more chimaera than in the first instant of catching sight of Ziri—and never more human than in the next, when it caught up to her what she was now. It wasn't disappointing. She was who she was. It was just the slightest bit disorienting, a brief vibration between two selves that would always be separate, like two yolks in one shell.

"You could be Kirin again, you know," Ten had told her at the river.

"What?" Karou, rinsing her hair, had thought she must have misheard.

"You could be chimaera. It might be easier for the others to accept you." Again she'd given Karou that up-and-down look and chuffed at her unfortunate humanness. "I could help you."

"Help me?" She had to be joking. "What, you mean *kill* me? Thank you sooo much!"

But Ten was not joking. "Oh, no. Thiago would do that, of course. But I would resurrect you. You'd just need to show me how."

Oh, is that all? "Tell you what," Karou had said with a big mock-cheerful smile. "Let's do *you* instead. I have *all kinds* of ideas for your next body." Ten hadn't particularly liked that, but Karou did not care much what Ten liked. She was still annoyed. Was this something Ten and Thiago had discussed? Maybe it would be easier to blend in if she looked like a chimaera, but it didn't make sense to even think about it now. Karou needed to be human to get the rebels' food for them, as well as cloth for clothes, and material for Aegir's forge, not to mention teeth. But would they expect it of her, eventually?

Well, they could expect all they wanted. She looked at the hamsas on her palms; they almost seemed like a signature. Brimstone had made her this body, and she was keeping it.

Laughter called her back to the moment. Ziri and Ixander were sparring, and Ixander had lost his balance and begun to spiral groundward. Trying to right himself, he thrust back on awkward wingbeats to crash into the crumbled parapet that edged the court, where he set off a cascade of dirt and ended up hanging by one hand from the wall. *Laughing.* And Ziri was laughing, and others, and the sound was so alien, so light. It made Karou realize she was spying, because they never laughed when she was around and would surely stop if they saw her. She drew back, not wanting that to happen.

Ziri darted forward in the air and smacked Ixander's hand with the flat of his blade, making him lose his grip on the parapet and drop to the ground with a roar. He landed with concussive force and tried to swat at Ziri, who was taunting him from above, still laughing as he darted just near enough to whack Ixander on the helmet before pulling clear. Some of the others gathered around taunting—in unmistakable good humor—and when Ixander leapt airborne in pursuit, they cheered.

All five patrols had returned from Eretz, not a single casualty, barely even a wound. Thiago had been in a fine mood, and the atmosphere in the kasbah was one of glory, though *what* glory, or what their mission had been, Karou still didn't know. One of the farmwives who cooked the food had made Thiago a new gonfalon to replace the one that had burned with

Loramendi; it was more modest, made of canvas, not silk, but it bore a white wolf and the words *Victory and vengeance* that were his motto. And now, apparently, all of theirs.

Privately, Karou preferred the Warlord's heraldry: antlers sprouting leaves to signify new growth, but she was far from immune to the desire for vengeance—it was huge and ugly in her: a primal drumbeat, a baring of teeth—and she had to admit Thiago's motto made a better rallying cry for a rebellion.

The banner hung from the gallery at the head of the court, seeming to declare the Wolf's eminence. *Where's mine?* Karou thought, with an inward surge of hilarity. Why not? *We're in this together*, Thiago had told her. So what would he do if she made her own gonfalon to string up beside his? And what would be on it? A string of teeth? A pair of pliers? No. A vise, and her motto could be *Ouch*.

She smiled to herself. It was funny, she thought, but her smile turned wistful because she had nobody to tell. In the court, the soldiers were still laughing, and she was in the shadows and no part of it.

Ixander was moving with much more ease now, and it took her a moment to understand why—it was because he wasn't trying so hard. He was moving as bodies are meant to move, without thought. She experienced a surge of pride, seeing the bear heft of him snap to a smooth glide. Ziri's taunting had provoked him to forget his self-consciousness—which Karou guessed was Ziri's plan—and Ziri paid the price for it now as Ixander caught him around the neck and fake-throttled him before tossing him right out of the air. Ziri hit the ground at a reeling run and skidded to a halt on his cloven hooves practically nose-to-nose with Balieros, the big bull centaur who was his patrol leader.

Balieros shook his head, his shoulders shaking with laughter, and, putting an arm around Ziri's shoulder, walked back with him to watch Ixander fly.

Karou got a lump in her throat. How easy they all were with each other, and quick to laugh. Once she had been part of their soldiers' closeness, sharing barracks and battle camps, meals and songs. She had saved lives and gleaned souls; she had been one of them.

But she'd made her choices, and now she had to live with them.

When the laughter abruptly ceased, Karou gave a start, thinking the soldiers had seen her spying, but they weren't looking in her direction. A beat later, Thiago strode into view. Karou recalled that she had been going to demand her crossbar back, but now her outrage-courage left her. It wasn't just him, though the Wolf certainly had an effect on her courage. It was whom he was with.

The Shadows That Live.

They were beautiful in their way, and sinuous in their stride. Tangris and Bashees were identical: sphinxlike panther creatures of dusky black, fine-boned and softly furred, with the heads of women and wings of dark owl feathers that were perfectly silent in flight. They weren't large, or terrible, but Thiago treated them with a deference he showed no other soldiers, and it was no wonder. No one else could do what they did. Karou's hands turned clammy. Was he sending them on a mission?

He was.

This time she couldn't wonder dumbly what nature of mission, or pretend not to understand. The Shadows That Live were legend, and they were . . . special . . . and so their mission must be special, too.

They lifted away and flew, leaving silence behind them. No one called good-bye or wished them luck. They didn't need luck. Somewhere in Eretz, some angels needed it badly, but they wouldn't get it. Whoever they were, they were as good as dead already.

31

Tally

Akiva could have done without fire that night at camp. He'd had enough fire for one day: the sky was still curdled with smoke from the blazes they'd set to herd fugitive chimaera out of the safety of the forest. When he looked up, he couldn't see a single star. But fire was a camp fixture and focal point. Soldiers were gathered around it to clean their blades and eat and drink, and though he had no appetite, he did have a thirst. He was on his third flagon of water, sunk in thoughts as murky as the sky, when a voice caught his attention.

"What are you doing?"

It was a sharp demand, and it came from Liraz. Akiva looked up. His sister was on the far side of the fire, lit lurid by its glow.

"What does it look like?" This from a Second Legion soldier Akiva didn't know. He was sitting with two others, and when Akiva saw what it was they held—what they were about to do—his fists clenched.

Tattoo tools, such as they were. A knife and ink stick were all it took to record kills on flesh.

"It looks like you're about to add to your tally," said Liraz, "but that can't be, can it, because no self-respecting soldier would ink today onto their hands."

Today. Today. What had Liraz's patrol done today? Akiva didn't know. Her look, when he and Hazael had found her after their own bleak day, had seemed to dare him to ask her, but he didn't want to know. Injuries had been sustained by some in her group—whiplashes, some bite wounds. None serious, but telling enough. Akiva hadn't offered up what he had done, either, hours earlier in that gully to the south and east. He and Hazael hadn't even talked about it, had barely exchanged a glance to acknowledge that it had happened at all.

The point was that the tally was for battle kills, for soldiers slain. Not fleeing folk.

"They were armed," the soldier said with a shrug.

"Oh, is that all it takes in the common army?" asked Liraz. "Give a slave a knife and it becomes a worthy opponent?" She gestured to his hands, to all the black marks already ticked onto his fingers. "How many of those fought back? Any of them?"

The soldier rose suddenly to his feet. He was a foot taller than Liraz, though if he imagined that gave him an advantage, he would learn his mistake. Akiva rose, too—not because he thought his sister was going to need his help, but more out of surprise at the nature of her anger.

"I earned my marks," said the soldier, looming over her.

Liraz didn't back down. Through clenched teeth, and with acid contempt, she said, "Not today you didn't."

"And who are *you* to decide?"

Her lips drew up over her clamped teeth in a vicious smile. "Ask around."

Maybe it was the smile, or something he saw in her eyes, but the soldier wavered in his looming swagger. "Is that supposed to scare me?"

"Well, it gave *me* chills." Hazael had appeared. "I'd be happy to tell you stories, if you really want to know. I've known her all my life."

"Lucky you," said one of the others, which kicked off some stupid laughter.

"Oh, I know." Hazael was earnest. "It's good to have someone around to save your life. How many times has it been, Lir? Four?" he asked her.

She didn't reply. Akiva stepped up beside them. "Making friends, Lir?"

"Everywhere I go."

Akiva nodded to the other soldiers. "You know she's right," he said. "You shame yourself taking pride in today's work."

"Just following orders," said the soldier, who had grown uneasy in Akiva's presence.

"And were you ordered to enjoy it?"

"Come on," said one of the others, pulling at his friend's elbow, and as they retreated, mutterings of "Misbegotten" could be heard in low tones.

Liraz called to their backs, "If I see fresh ink on any of you tomorrow, I'm taking fingers."

The looming one let out an incredulous laugh and looked back.

"Try me," she said.

"*Don't* try her," said Hazael. "Please? I think she'd enjoy having a finger collection a little too much."

Once they were gone, Liraz sat down. She gave Akiva a sideward glance. "I don't need Beast's Bane settling my arguments."

Hazael was offended. "What about me? I'm pretty sure it was *me* they were afraid of."

"Yes, because nothing instills fear quite like bragging how many times your sister has saved your life."

"Well, I left out how many times I've saved your life," he said. "I believe we're currently even?"

"I wasn't settling anything," Akiva broke in. "Just agreeing with you." He hesitated. "Liraz, what happened today?"

"What do you think?" was her only reply. What he thought was that they had come across some of the other escaped slaves from the caravan, and, as the soldier had said, followed their orders. By the way Liraz was staring into the fire, he judged that she had taken no pleasure in it, but he wouldn't have expected her to. She might glory in a well-fought battle, but never in a slaughter. The question was, how committed was she to following orders? And... might she surprise him, as Hazael had?

Akiva looked at his brother now and found Hazael looking back. The gaze held, over their sister's head, and it amounted to their first acknowledgment of what they had done that day in the gully.

Or, more to the point, what they had *not* done.

When Akiva had heard the scream—brief, bitten off, but unmistakable—Hazael had been nearer to its source than he. Only by a few wingspans, but still it was Hazael who responded first, suddenly folding his wings and plunging down to land in the rocky creek bed, crouched in a ready stance in case he needed to burst skyward again. A half a heartbeat and Akiva was beside him, and saw what he saw, huddled in a concavity in the ravine: a quivering mass of terrified sheepfolk.

The Caprine were one of the mildest of the chimaera tribes, so ill-suited to fighting that they were exempt from the army. The fact was that many chimaera tribes made poor soldiers: they were too small, or configured ill for holding weapons, or they were aquatic, or they were timid, or they were large but lumbering and slow. There were as many reasons as there were tribes, and it was why Brimstone had had to do what he had done for so long: too many of his people were simply not made for fighting at all, and certainly not for fighting seraphim.

The main might of the chimaera army had always been drawn from some dozen of the fiercer tribes, and it was with surprise that Akiva recognized one such in the center of this huddle. A Dashnag, among Caprine. A small one, not yet grown, but even a small Dashnag is a brutish thing, though this one was holding a slender deer centaur girl in his thick arms—her hand was clamped over her own mouth; it was she who had screamed, and her limpid deer eyes were impossibly huge in her sweet small face. Another deer girl was shrunk in fright against the boy's side, and though Akiva couldn't know precisely what had brought these folk together in this moment, the tableau was simple, and it painted in miniature what the angels had done to Eretz: Through terror, they had united it against them.

All this in an instant, and the Dashnag boy was setting the centaur girl aside, gently, and there was fear in his eyes, but he would defend these folk. Akiva's swords were in his hands, but he didn't want them.

This isn't who we have to be, he thought. "Haz—" he started to say.

His brother turned to him. He looked puzzled, a squint drawing at his eyes. "That's strange," he said, cutting Akiva off. "I could have sworn I heard something down here."

It took Akiva a beat to understand, and then a rush of relief—and reprieve, and gratitude—flooded through him. "Me, too," he said, cautious, hoping he was reading his brother right. The Dashnag boy was watching them intently, every muscle poised to spring. All the Caprine and the two Dama girls were staring unblinking. A baby started to murmur—a baby—and its mother clutched it tighter. "Must have been a bird," Akiva ventured.

"A bird," Hazael agreed. And…he turned away from the fugitives. He took a few splashing steps in the creek, casual, even a little comical, and bent to pick one of the blooms that grew on reedy stalks at the water's edge, tucking it into a notch in his mail. It was still there.

He took it out now, and presented it to Liraz. Akiva tensed, wondering if he was going to tell her that they had spared a whole village worth of chimaera today, and even a Dashnag who, though a boy, would certainly grow into a soldier. What would she think of that? But Hazael only said, "I brought you a present."

Liraz took the flower, looked at it, and then at Hazael, expressionless. And then she ate it. She chewed the flower and swallowed it.

"Hmm," said Hazael. "Not the usual response."

"Oh, do you give flowers often?"

"Yes," he said. He probably did. Hazael had a way of enjoying life in spite of the many restrictions they lived under, being soldiers, and worse, being Misbegotten. "I hope it wasn't poisonous," he said lightly.

Liraz just shrugged. "There are worse ways to die."

32

Death Ruled Them All

"There you are," said Ten, exasperated, catching up to Karou in her spying place.

"Here I am," agreed Karou, eyeing the she-wolf. "Where are they going?"

"Who?"

"The sphinxes. Where did he send them? To do what?"

"I don't know, Karou. To Eretz, to do what they do. Can we get back to work?"

Karou turned back to the court. The soldiers had gathered around Thiago in a knot, all watching the sky where the Shadows That Live had vanished. *Go*, she willed herself. *Go ask.* But she just couldn't find it in herself to stroll over and feel all those eyes settle on her in that flat way they had, or to put forth her voice and breach their silent, watchful intensity.

So when Ten put a hand on her arm and said, "Come. Emylion, then Hvitha. We have an army to build," Karou was almost relieved. *Coward.*

She let herself be led.

* * *

After two days of Nur's ministrations, Sarazal could put weight on her leg again, though Rath mostly still carried her—now in a sling that they'd fashioned for his back—and Sveva felt the burden of her sister's life lift from her own shoulders. Sarazal would be fine, and they'd find their tribe again, just . . . not right away. It was a hard thing, going in the wrong direction, but it was far too great a risk to go north. Too many seraphim lay between them and home.

We're okay, Mama. We're alive. Sveva kept sending her thoughts out over the land, imagining them to be squalls bearing notes that her mother could just unroll and read. She almost convinced herself of it; it was too hard to admit the truth: that their people must believe them lost. *Angels spared us,* she thought to her mother, still reeling from the miracle of it. Her life felt new: lost and found, both lighter and heavier at the same time.

If you meet an angel with eyes like fire, and another with a bog lily tucked in his armor, she thought to her mother, *don't kill them.*

The herd moved south toward the mountains, with their rumors of safe haven. They met others along the way and urged them to get moving. A pair of Hartkind joined them, but they were careful not to let their convoy grow. It wasn't safe to travel in large groups. Well, nothing was safe, but you did what you could. Unless they had dense tree cover, they moved only by night, when seraphim were easy to spot, their fiery wings painting light onto the darkness.

Lell rode on Sveva's back, and it seemed the most natural thing in the world now to hoist her up there whenever they got moving, and fall into step behind Rath, where she could keep a good eye on Sarazal.

"I can't wait to run again," said her sister under her breath one morning as they plodded up a hillside at Caprine pace.

"I know," Sveva said. And then, at the top of the hill, they got their first glimpse of the Hintermost: hazed by distance and impossibly huge, their snowy peaks merging with the clouds like some white country of the air. "But it's good to be alive."

* * *

The seraph patrols were having poor hunting. The land was too big and wild, its inhabitants scarce and getting scarcer.

"Someone is warning them," said Kala one morning, when they had come upon another abandoned village. Villages were rare; more common were simple farms where small clans lived off the land, but these, too, they'd been finding deserted. In the evenings, around the fire, soldiers still cleaned their swords, but it was more of habit than necessity. The country seemed to empty ahead of them; they'd scarcely drawn blood in days. Whispers about ghosts persisted. Some blamed the slaves, though they all knew it would have been a remarkable feat—of both courage and logistics—for those few freed creatures to warn this whole vast land of the coming scourge.

The only logical conclusion, though there was no evidence to support it, was that it was the rebels.

"Why won't they show themselves?" stormed a soldier of the Second Legion. "Cowards!"

Akiva wondered the same thing. Where *were* the rebels? He happened to know that it wasn't rebels warning the folk.

It was him.

At night, while the camp slept, he cloaked himself in glamour and slipped from his tent. Wherever the next day's sweep was to lead them, he went ahead, and when he found a village or farm or nomad's camp, he let himself be seen, frightening off the folk and hoping they would have the good sense to stay gone.

It was something. It wasn't enough, and his exhaustion was not sustainable, but he didn't know what else to do. What can a soldier do when mercy is treason, and he is alone in it? It might have bought some of these southern folk time to reach the Hintermost, though. It should have.

But it didn't.

Because overnight, on dark, silent wings, while Akiva was struggling to save the enemy one family at a time, the rebels were sending the Empire such a message that Joram's response must blow away any hope he had of allaying the killing.

"Life is your master, or death is," Brimstone had said, but in these days of blood, there was no luxury of choice.

Death ruled them all.

Once upon a time, the sky knew
the weight of angel armies on the move,

and the wind blew infernal
with the fire of their wings.

33

The Shadows That Live

At the seraph garrison at Thisalene—not on some far shore or lonely sweep of beast-ranged wilderness, but hooked to the cliffs of the curved Mirea Coast in the heart of the Empire itself—a sentry watched from his tower as the sun rose over the sea and his comrades failed to stir. Not a rustle from the hundred soldiers trained to rise at first light, no sound at all. The barracks lay quiet in the dawn, and the silence was surreal and deeply wrong. Quiet was for night. There should have been clamor, cooksmoke, the early, desultory chime of blades on the practice ground.

He knew he should have been relieved of duty by now, but he couldn't make himself leave his post. Terror held him where he was. Nothing moved but the sea, the sun. It was as if all living things in the world had frozen except for him. When the first blood daub circled, he finally unfroze, leapt from his tower, and flew down to discover bunk after bunk of sleeping comrades who would never wake.

A hundred throats opened neat as letters. A hundred red smiles, and on the wall, also in red, a new message:

THE ANGELS MUST DIE.

It was an echo of the emperor's own infamous words, so long thundered from the heights of the Tower of Conquest and drummed from infancy into every seraph's consciousness, citizen or soldier: *The beasts must die.*

He should have deserted, that soldier. He must have known he would hang for his failure; it was unpardonable, even if it was true what he reported, stricken and babbling, when he reached the city, just north along the coast. Thisalene was the Empire's main slave port, a mere half day's journey overland from the capital—an hour at most on wing—and was heavily armed and fortified. Soldiers from his own regiment rotated in to patrol the seawalls, and he feared to find them dead, too, and gasped out, "Thank the godstars! You must triple the watches. They're alive. They're back and we are all killed!"

The commander was sent for, and by the time he arrived, the soldier's shock had worn off. The first thing he said was, "I never fell asleep, sir, I swear it."

"Who says you did? What happened, soldier? You're covered in blood."

"You have to believe me. I would never sleep at my post. They're alive. I would have seen any natural thing—"

"Speak sense. Who's killed? Who's alive?"

"*We* are killed. Sir. I never closed my eyes! It was the Shadows That Live. It had to be. They're back."

34

Celebration

Karou was good at a lot of things, but driving wasn't one of them. She wasn't actually old enough for a license, which struck her now as funny. She didn't know about Morocco, but in Europe you had to be eighteen, which she wouldn't be for another month—that is, unless you counted her two lives together. *Should've asked for credit for that*, she thought as she bounced and skidded off-road in the old blue truck she used for getting supplies to the kasbah.

A big bump kicked the truck up onto two tires, where it hung in suspension for a long moment before slamming back down with an impact that bounced Karou at least a foot off the driver's seat. *Oof.* "Sorry!" she sang over her shoulder, sweetly, insincerely. Ten was in the back, hidden from view.

Karou aimed for another bump.

"If I didn't want to be here, you know, I'd have left already," she'd said to Thiago before setting out, she-wolf in tow, against her protestations. "I don't need a prison guard."

"She's not a guard," he'd replied. "Karou. Karou." The intensity of his eyes was as unnerving as ever. "I just can't stand to watch you go off alone. Humor me? If something were to happen to you, I'd be lost." Not *we* would be lost. *I* would.

Ick.

It could be worse, of course. Thiago could have come himself, and there had been a tense moment when she'd feared he might. But with the Shadows That Live due back from their mission, he'd chosen to wait at the kasbah.

"Get something for a celebration," he'd told her. "If you can."

The hairs on the back of her neck stood up at that. "What are we celebrating?"

In answer, Thiago only pointed up at his gonfalon and smiled. *Victory and vengeance.*

Right.

So, Karou wondered, what does one bring to a celebration of victory and vengeance? Booze? Hard to find in Morocco, and it was just as well. Booze was the last thing she needed to be giving the soldiers.

Well, okay, maybe not the *last* thing.

When she reached Agdz, with its long, dusty main street that looked more Wild West than Arabian Nights, she avoided the shop on the north end, the one she remembered had rifles in the window. She didn't want to risk Ten seeing them from her hiding place and asking what they were.

Wouldn't *that* make a nice treat for the celebration? No doubt about it.

Looming large in Karou's mind, always, was the issue of guns. At the thought of them, her hand went to her stomach, where three small, shiny scars remembered the bullets that had torn through her once, in the hold of a ship in St. Petersburg where all around her girls and women had bled from toothless mouths and cried, and run.

Karou hated guns, but she knew what they could mean for the rebellion. A dozen times she'd considered telling Thiago about human killing technology, and a dozen times she'd stopped herself. She had a lot of reasons, starting with her personal feelings and the people she would have to deal with to procure arms—weren't things bad enough without adding arms dealers to the mix? But she could have dealt with that if it weren't for the bigger reason, the thing she always came back to.

Brimstone had never brought guns into Eretz.

She could only guess why not, but her guess was simple: because it would start an arms race, and accelerate the pace of killing beyond reckoning, and that was the last thing he would have wanted. He had told her—*Madrigal*-her—in the last moments before her execution, that for all these centuries he had only been holding back a tide, trying to keep his people alive until some other way could be found, some truer way. A path to life, and peace.

Life and peace. Victory and vengeance.

And never the twain shall meet.

In town, Karou bought apricots, onions, courgettes by the crateful. She wore a cotton hijab over her blue hair, and jeans with a long-sleeved jellaba to blend in. They wouldn't mistake her for Moroccan, but with her black eyes and perfect Arabic, they wouldn't take her for a Westerner, either. She took care not to let her hamsas be seen, and bought cloth and leather, tea and honey. Almonds and olives and dried dates. Feed for the chickens and discs of flat bread. Red slabs of marbled meat—not a lot; that wouldn't keep. Couscous, tons of it—sacks so big she could barely heave them but still had to wave away help on account of having a wolf-headed monster stowed away in the back of her truck. *Thanks, Ten.*

She told an inquisitive woman that she worked for a tour provider. "Hungry tourists" was the response. Indeed. It occurred to Karou that she had literally bought enough food for a small army, and she couldn't even laugh about it.

She kept thinking of the sphinxes, and what they must be doing.

Which pretty much killed her will to come up with some celebration for the soldiers. She tossed Ten a bottle of water and closed up the back of the truck. But on the way out of town she spotted a shop that made her reconsider. Drums. Berber tribal drums. Sometimes on campaign there had been drumming in camp. Singing, too. There had been no singing at the kasbah, but she thought of Ziri and Ixander clowning in the court, the laughter that she'd had no part in, and she bought ten drums, and drove the long way back as day slid into dark.

She was overseeing the unloading when the Shadows That Live returned.

* * *

"I thought the Shadows That Live were the Shadows *That Died*," said Liraz.

Word had come from Thisalene, and Akiva was reeling. The horror, the body count, the bold stroke. The *fool* stroke. To attack so near Astrae was to pierce the perceived sanctity of the Empire itself. Did these rebels even know what they had begun?

Hazael sighed, blowing out a long, weary breath. "Is it just me, or have you noticed that chimaera prefer not to be dead?"

"Well then," said Liraz. "We have that in common at least."

"We have more in common than that," said Akiva.

Liraz turned her eyes on him. "You more than most," she said, and he thought she meant something biting about "harmony" with the beasts, but she dropped her voice and said, "Slipping about invisible, for example?" and Akiva went cold.

Did she know what he had been doing these past nights, or did she just mean his glamour in general? Her gaze lingered, and there seemed a keen specificity to it, but when she continued, it was only to say, "If *Father* knew you could do that..." and trail away with a whistle. "He could have his own personal Shadow That Lives."

Akiva looked around. He didn't like to talk about it in camp—his magic, his secrets. Even calling the emperor "Father" was punishable, first because use of his honorific was law, and second because the Misbegotten had no claim to paternity. They were weapons, and weapons had no fathers, or mothers, either, and if a sword could claim a maker, it was the blacksmith, not the vein of ore whence came its metal. Of course, that didn't stop Joram boasting how many "weapons" came from his own "vein of ore." The stewards kept lists. There had been more than three thousand bastard soldiers born in the harem.

Of which barely three hundred remained, and too many of those were deaths recent.

Akiva saw that there was no one within earshot. "You could do it, too," he reminded Liraz. He had taught his brother and sister the glamour so they could pass in the human world, helping him to burn the black handprints onto Brimstone's doors. They managed it, though not with ease, and not for long.

She made a sound of disgust. "I think not. I prefer my victims to know who killed them."

"So they can dream of your lovely face for all their eternal slumber," said Hazael.

"It's a blessing to die at the hand of someone beautiful," answered Liraz.

"So, not at Jael's hand, then," remarked Hazael.

Jael. Akiva glanced at the sky. The name was a sharp reminder.

"No. Godstars." Liraz shuddered. "There is no blessing that will help *his* victims. Do you know, there are two reasons I am glad I am Misbegotten, and both of them are Jael."

"What reasons?" Akiva couldn't imagine why anyone, especially his sister, would be glad to be the emperor's bastard.

The Misbegotten were the most effective and least rewarded of all of the Empire's forces. They could never command, lest they strive above their station, but were only fodder for the ranks, given out on loan to regiments of the Second Legion to do the dirty work. They had no pensions, being expected to serve until their deaths, and were not permitted to marry, to bear or father children, to own land, or even to live elsewhere than their barracks. It was a sort of slavery, really. They weren't even given burial but only cremation in common urns, and since their names were borrowed more than owned, it was deemed meaningless to engrave them on a stone or placard. The only record of life a Misbegotten left behind was his or her name stricken from the stewards' list so that it could be given over to some new mewling babe soon enough to be ripped from its mother's arms.

Live obscure, kill who you're told, and die unsung. That could have been the Misbegotten's creed, but it wasn't. It was *Blood is strength.*

"Being Misbegotten," said Liraz, counting the first reason on her finger, "I will never serve under Jael."

"A good reason," Akiva agreed. Jael was the emperor's younger brother, and the commander of the Dominion, the Empire's elite legion and a source of endless bitterness to the bastards. Any Misbegotten would best any Dominion soldier in sparring or—if it ever came to it—combat, yet the Dominion were held supreme in every way. They were richly attired and provisioned from the coffers of the Empire's first families—who filled their ranks with second and third sons and daughters—and they had been richly rewarded at war's end, too, gifted with castles and lands in the carve-up of the free holdings.

An elder bastard half sister named Melliel had dared to ask Joram if the Misbegotten would be given their due, and their father's answer had been, in his sly way making even the refusal a boast of his virility, "There aren't castles enough in Eretz for all the bastards I've sired."

Still, for all the benefits the Dominion enjoyed, they served at Jael's pleasure, and Jael's pleasure was, by all accounts, a gruesome thing.

"Go on," said Hazael. "What else?"

Liraz counted off another finger. "Second, being Misbegotten, I will never *lie* under Jael."

Akiva could only stare at her, aghast. It was the first time he had ever heard his sister make reference to her own sexuality, even in such an oblique way. She wore her ferocity like armor, and it was purely asexual armor. Liraz was untouchable and untouched. The image of her... beneath Jael... was one to reject immediately, abhorrently.

Hazael looked aghast, too. "I should hope not," he said, sounding weak with disgust.

Liraz rolled her eyes. "Look at the pair of you. You know our uncle's reputation. I'm only saying I'm safe, because I'm blood, and thank the godstars for that if nothing else."

"Damn the godstars," said Hazael, indignant. "You're safe because you would gut him with your bare hands if he ever tried to touch you. I'd say that *I* would do it, but I know that by the time anyone else got there *our uncle* would already be pulled inside out, and less ugly for it, too."

"Yes, I suppose." Liraz sounded weary, looked it. "And what of all the other girls? Do you think they don't want to pull him inside out, too? And what then? The gibbet? It comes down to life, doesn't it, and whether it's worth keeping on with, whatever happens. So... *is* it?" She looked to Akiva. Was she asking him?

"Is what?"

"*Is* life worth keeping on with, whatever happens?"

Was she talking about living broken, living with loss? Did she count his loss a real one, and did she really want to know, or was there a barb in this somewhere? Sometimes Akiva felt like he didn't know his sister at all. "Yes," he said, wary, thinking of the thurible, and Karou. "As long as you're alive, there's always a chance things will get better."

"Or worse," said Liraz.

"Yes," he conceded. "Usually worse."

Hazael cut in. "My sister, Sunshine, and my brother, Light. You two should rally the ranks. You'll have us all killing ourselves by morning."

Morning. They all knew what would happen in the morning.

Liraz rose to her feet. "I'm going to sleep while I can, and you two should, too. Once they get here, I think there will be very little rest for anyone."

She walked off. Hazael followed. "Coming?" he asked Akiva.

"In a minute."

Or not. Akiva looked to the sky. It was still dark for as far as he could see, but he imagined he felt a change in the air: a pull from the draft of many, many wings. It was illusion, or prophecy, or just dread.

He had a long way to go tonight, territory to cover, chimaera to save. No rest for him. The Dominion were coming.

35

Roles to Play

The sphinxes stretched out delicate cat feet to land, small tufts of dust eddying around them. The rest of the chimaera host were emerging from doors and windows to gather in the court and hear their report, and there was Thiago, striding from the guardhouse. Karou's mind was sharp with wondering. What had they done? Not just the sphinxes, but all the patrols. It was with a sense of unreality that she found her feet carrying her toward all the others.

"Karou," Ten called after her, but she kept walking.

Thiago caught sight of her and paused, watching her approach. The soldiers followed his gaze, the sphinxes, too. All regarded her with identical nonexpressions, but Thiago smiled. "Karou," he said. "Did everything go all right in town?"

"Oh. Fine." Her hands were clammy. "You don't have to stop. I was just going to listen."

The Wolf cocked his head slightly, looking perplexed. "Listen?"

"To the report." Karou felt herself shrinking, faltering. "I just want to know what we're doing."

She didn't know what she expected Thiago to say, but not this: "Is there someone in particular that you're worried about?"

Karou's face went hot. Insidious implication. "No," she said, affronted. She was also rattled, realizing that anything she said now would come across as concern for seraphim. For Akiva.

"Well then, *don't* worry." Another smile from the Wolf. "You have enough to think about. You've lost the whole day today, and I need to have another team ready by tomorrow. Do you think you can do that?"

"Of course," Ten answered for her, and she took Karou by the arm as she had the day before. "We're just going."

"Good," said Thiago. "Thank you." And he waited for them to be gone before resuming speaking.

Karou felt pinched awake from some stupor. It wasn't that Thiago didn't want her bothered with details, it was that he flat-out didn't want her to know what he was doing. As Ten drew her away, she locked eyes—briefly—with Ziri. He looked so guarded. Thiago's remark . . . Did they all think she still loved Akiva? And they didn't even know about Marrakesh and Prague, or that she'd met him again so recently. Met him and . . . *No.* Nothing. She'd left him behind. That was what mattered. This time, she had made the right choice.

When they were out of the court, Karou pulled her arm from Ten's grip, wincing as it dragged at her bruises. "What the hell?"

she said. "I think I have a right to know what my pain is paying for."

"Don't be a child. We all have our roles to play."

"Oh. And yours is what, babysitter? I'm sorry, I mean *traitor*-sitter?"

Ten's eyes flashed with defiance. "If Thiago asks it, yes."

"And you'll do whatever he asks."

For a second Ten only stared at her as if she were dim-witted. "Of course" was her answer. "And so will you. *Especially* you. For the good of our people, and the memory of all we've lost, and the very great debt you owe."

Karou's shame response was instant, but it was followed this time by a surge of anger. They would never let her forget what she had done. She was here willingly, when she, unlike they, had a choice in the matter. She had a whole other life, and right now she really just wanted to fly back to it, back to Prague and her friends and art and tea and worrying about nothing more dire than butterflies in her belly—*Papilio stomachus*, she recalled with an ache. How quaint and small that life seemed now, like something you could fit inside a snow globe.

She wouldn't go. Ten was right: She did owe a debt. But she was sick to death of the cowering thing she'd become. She thought Brimstone would scarcely recognize this compliant little shame-creature; she had certainly never followed his orders so meekly.

When they had climbed the stairs back to her room, she picked up the necklace she had begun earlier, while Ten, impatient, spilled her case out on the table. Brass clamps clattered in all directions. Karou picked one up but didn't put it on. She was in no state to conjure a body now.

What wasn't she allowed to know?

"Do you want me to tithe?" Ten asked. Karou looked up at her. The she-wolf didn't offer up her pain very often, and Karou surprised herself by saying, "No. Thanks." It was only when she heard her own reply that she realized she was going to do something.

What am I going to do?

Oh.

She toyed with the vise, twisting the screw tighter, looser. Did she even remember how? It was a long time ago.

What shall I do for pain?

Nothing. No pain for you. Only pleasure.

Still fidgeting with the vise, she said to Ten, "I don't suppose you know the story of Bluebeard."

"*Blue*beard?" Ten eyed Karou's hair. "A relative of yours?"

Karou shot her a wry smile. "I have no relatives, remember?"

"No one does anymore," Ten said simply, and Karou realized it was true. Everyone here had lost...everyone. They were a people with nothing more to lose.

"Well," she said, calmly fitting the vise over the web of flesh and muscle that connected her thumb and palm. It was a tender spot. "Bluebeard was this lord, and when he brought his new bride home to his castle, he gave her the keys to every door and told her she could go anywhere she wanted except this one little door down in the cellar. And there she must *never* go." She tightened the screw, and her pain began to open like a flower.

"And I suppose that was the first place she went," said Ten. "The minute his back was turned."

Ten had just turned to reach for the teapot. At Karou's words, she spun back around, and cursed.

Karou knew by her reaction that it had worked; she had remembered Akiva's invisibility manipulation after all. Funny, the pain had seemed like a big deal back then. Not anymore. It throbbed to the tune of her heartbeat and felt nearly as natural.

It didn't occur to Ten that Karou might not have moved from her seat. She just thought she was out the window again, and so when she unfroze, she lunged toward it, and Karou slipped out the door. Ironically, the absence of the bar made it easier for her to get away. Holding the glamour in place, she whipped down the stairs and out to the court to hear whatever she could before Ten bolted down with the news of her vanishing.

It wasn't much.

It wasn't her shadow that gave her away. The glamour didn't conceal shadows, so she kept to the shade and she didn't make a sound. She was certain of that. She wasn't even touching the ground. Still, she had been in the court only a couple of minutes, just long enough to learn the sickening nature of the "message" that the rebels had been sending to the seraphim, and...the emperor's response—dear god, the sky dark and bright with Dominion, a merciless display of might, hopeless, *hopeless*—before Thiago cut off midsentence, pivoted on the pads of his wolf feet, and, lifting his head just slightly, nostrils flaring delicately, scented the air.

And looked at her.

She froze. She was already still, and she was yards away, but she stopped breathing and watched those colorless eyes with dread. They couldn't quite fix on her, but they narrowed. Again he sniffed. He couldn't see her, she knew that, and neither could the rest of the company, who followed his gaze. Still—*stupid, stupid*—they knew she was near the same way Thiago did.

They were creatures. They could *smell* her.

36

Feel Like Smiling

She took the vise off at the river, let go of the magic, and watched herself flush visible again. Her hand was blue where the clamp had bitten. A bruise. Had anything ever been more insignificant than a bruise?

Would Thiago guess about the glamour? That had been stupid of her. If he suspected she could do that, he and his spy would never take their eyes off her again. Not to mention, if he suspected she could do that, he would want to know *how*. He would want all his soldiers to know how, and shouldn't Karou want that, too, if it could help them?

Help them kill more angels in their sleep?

That was what Tangris and Bashees did. No one knew exactly how; they had a way of pulling the shadows around themselves to stalk unseen among the enemy, but glamour alone couldn't account for the mass killings conducted in perfect silence. Who slept so deeply that they wouldn't wake to gasp as their throat was cut? Yet these victims slept on as throat by throat they died and all breath was subtracted from the room until only the killers' remained.

Karou didn't know why it bothered her so much. It was painless. And how many chimaera had those soldiers killed, and surely with less kindness.

Kindness? What an appalling thought.

Karou sat arguing with herself, wishing more desperately than ever for someone to talk to. There were conflicts in herself she just couldn't settle. This brutality that she was a part of, she had been half pretending it was all a bad dream in an effort to get through her days, because she just couldn't come to terms with it.

With war.

Her life as Karou had in no way prepared her for this. War was something from the news, and she didn't even watch the news, it was too terrible. And if she'd thought that Madrigal could help her, as if her deeper self might enable her to accept this ugly reality, she was mistaken there, too. Why had Madrigal done what she'd done, conspiring with Akiva for peace? Because she'd had no stomach for war even when it was her life. She had always been a dreamer.

And what was happening in Eretz... The rebels had made it worse, so much worse. They had knocked down a hornet's nest. The cut smiles, the cut *throats*, the blood scrawl. What had Thiago been thinking, taunting the Empire like that? And the emperor's answer was swift and enormous. For the chimaera it would be cataclysmic. The full might of the Dominion, sent to crush civilians?

What had Thiago thought would happen? What had *she* thought?

She hadn't thought; she hadn't wanted to know, and now look.

I feel happy. . . . I feel happy. . . .

Karou took off her shoes and put her feet in the cool water. Back at the kasbah they would be searching for her, and they should find her easily enough. She waited in plain sight, and at length she heard wings, and then a shadow fell over her. It was horned, and for an instant it aligned with her own shadow so the horns seemed hers.

Ziri.

Ziri had been the one on his patrol to do the cutting. His curved blades—just like her own—were suited to it; he had only to hook the corners of a corpse's mouth and with a flick of his wrist it was done: smile rendered. *And this is what has become of my little Kirin shadow.* She turned to look up at him. The sun was behind him; she had to shade her eyes. Now that he'd found her, he didn't seem to know what to do. She saw his gaze trail down her arms—bruises and tattoos intermingling—before returning to her face. "Are you . . . all right?" he asked, hesitant.

These were the first words he had spoken to her. If they had come earlier she would have been so glad. From her first frightened days with the rebels, she had hoped he might be a friend, an ally; she'd thought she recognized something in him—compassion? The sweetness of his younger self? Even now, she could see that boy in him, those round brown eyes, his gravity and bashfulness. But he had stayed away from her all these weeks, and now when he finally chose to speak to her, it didn't matter at all.

"You seem..." He faltered, discomfited. "You don't seem well."

"No?" Karou could have laughed. "Imagine that." She stood, brushed off her jeans, and picked up her shoes. She looked up at Ziri. He had grown so tall, she had to tilt her head back. On one of his horns there was a hack mark, several ridges shaved away, and you had only to look to see that the horn had saved his head from a killing blow. He was lucky. She'd heard the other chimaera say so. Lucky Ziri.

"Don't worry about me," Karou told him. "Next time I feel like smiling, I guess I know who to ask."

He flinched like he'd been slapped, and she stepped around him, went up the dusty riverbank and toward the kasbah. She didn't fly, but walked. She was in no hurry to get back.

* * *

The emperor's brother looked *cut in half.* A scar ran from the top of his head right down the center of his face, hooking under his chin and stopping—unfortunately—just shy of his throat. And it was no thin tracery either, but a puckered, livid keloid that overcame what remained of his nose and split his lips aside to reveal broken teeth. No one knew how he'd gotten it. He claimed it was a battle scar, but whispers contradicted him—though so many and so varied that it was impossible to guess which, if any, might be true. Even Hazael, with his way of finding things out, had no idea.

Whatever its cause, the scar's result was to make it almost unendurable to hear Jael eat, which he was doing now with sounds very like the gluckings of a dog licking its tenders.

Akiva kept his face impassive, as ever, though truly it felt like a feat. No one could tempt a lip curl quite like the Captain of the Dominion.

"Think of it as a hunting party," Jael said casually when he had downed half a cold smoked songbird with a gulp of ale, not bothering to wipe at the dribble that spilled from his ruined mouth. "A very large hunting party. Do you hunt?" he inquired of Akiva.

"No."

"Of course not. Soldiers have no luxury for sport. Until the enemy becomes the quarry. I think you'll enjoy it."

Not likely, thought Akiva.

The full weight of the Dominion hung poised to fall on the fleeing folk of the southern continent, several thousand troops now staging to cut off their escape to the Hintermost and then move steadily northward, killing every living thing in their path.

"I said it was too soon to withdraw our main strength," said Jael. "But my brother didn't believe the south was a threat."

"It wasn't," said Ormerod, the Second Legion commander who had, until now, been overseeing this sweep and who was, Akiva thought, unhappy at being displaced. They were at table in his pavilion—not Akiva's usual place. Far from it. Bastards did not sit at high table or dine with their superiors. He was here, to his surprise and *not* delight, at the request of Jael.

"The Prince of Bastards," the captain had cried, catching

sight of him on his arrival. Akiva had had to work with him in the past, and even when their passions had aligned—the destruction of Loramendi, for example—he'd despised him, and had sensed the feeling was mutual. And yet: "What an honor," Jael had said that morning. "I hadn't thought to look for you here. You must join us for breakfast. I'm sure you have thoughts on our situation."

Oh, Akiva did, but not such as he could share at this table.

"The south wasn't a threat before and it isn't now," Ormerod continued, and Akiva admired his forthrightness.

He could go so far as to agree with that. "Whoever is striking at seraphim, it isn't these common folk."

"Yes, well. The rebels are hiding somewhere, aren't they?" Jael sighed. "*Rebels*. My brother is put out. He just wants to plan his new war. Is that so much to ask? And here comes the old one, back from the dead." He laughed at his own witticism, but Akiva wasn't laughing.

New war? So soon? He wouldn't ask. Curiosity was weakness, and both Joram and Jael enjoyed drawing it out and letting it fester unrewarded.

Ormerod apparently hadn't learned that lesson. "What new war?"

Jael kept his eyes on Akiva, and his look was direct, amused, and personal. "It's a surprise," he said, smiling—if you could call it a smile, the way his mouth skewed wide, pulling his scarred lips white.

There is a smile a chimaera could improve upon, thought Akiva. But if Jael was trying to taunt him, he would have to do better than this. There was no surprise. Who else could Joram's next target be but the renegade seraphim whose freedom and mystique had riled him for years?

The Stelians.

To Akiva, his mother's people were more phantoms than these rebels arisen from nowhere. He gave Jael no satisfaction. At the moment, his concern was the battle at hand, and these southern lands where seraph fire had yet to touch death to every green and growing thing, every flesh and breathing thing. And now? Despair moved through him, restless, refusing to settle. He thought of the folk he had spared and warned. They would be cut off, trapped, captured, killed. What could he do? Several thousand Dominion. There was nothing *to* do.

"To Joram it may be a bother, but to me it's a boon, this rebellion," Jael was saying. "We must have something to do. I believe that an idle soldier is an affront to nature. Don't you agree, Princc?"

Prince. "I don't imagine nature spares us a thought except to weep when she sees us coming."

Jael smiled. "Quite right. The land burns, the beasts die, and the moons weep in the heavens to see it."

"Be careful," warned Akiva, finding a thin smile of his own. "The moon's tears are what created chimaera in the first place."

Jael gave him a cool and considering look. "Beast's Bane, spouting beast myths. Do you *talk* to the monsters before you kill them?"

"One should know one's enemy."

"Yes. One should." Again, that look: direct, amused, and personal. What did it mean? Akiva was nothing to Jael but one of his brother's legion of bastards.

But when at last the meal came to an end, he had to wonder what more there was to it.

Jael pushed back his chair and stood. "Thank you for your hospitality, Commander," he said to Ormerod. "We fly in an hour." He turned to Akiva. "Nephew. Always charming to see you." He turned to go, stopped, turned back. "You know, I probably shouldn't admit it now that you're a hero, but I argued for killing you. Back then. No hard feelings, I hope."

Back when? Akiva regarded Jael evenly. When had his life been up for discussion?

Ormerod shifted uneasily and sputtered a few words, but neither Akiva nor Jael paid him any mind.

"The pollution of your blood, you know," said Jael, as if it ought to be obvious. So. His mother, again. Akiva rewarded the quip with no more interest than he had shown earlier for the taunt about the new war. Of his mother he had only snatches of memory and the emperor's cryptic taunt: *Terrible what happened to her.* What was Jael's interest? "My brother had faith his blood would prove the stronger—*blood is strength* and all that—and now he says he was right. You were a test, and you passed, gloriously, and I suppose there's no argument to be made against you now. Pity. One does so hate to be wrong about these things."

With that, Jael of the Dominion, second-most powerful seraph in the Empire, turned to go, pausing just long enough to toss a command back at Ormerod—"Have a woman sent to my tent, would you?"—and kept walking.

Ormerod blanched. His mouth opened but no sound came out. It was Akiva who rose to his feet. Liraz's words came back to him, and "all the other girls" she'd spoken of. It occurred to him only now that his sister had given voice to a fear. Not directly; she wouldn't, but now he felt the fear for her, and for "all the other girls," too. And not only fear. Fury. "We have no women here," he said. "Only soldiers."

Jael stopped. Sighed. "Well, one can hardly be choosy in a battle camp. One of them will have to do."

* * *

A world away, the White Wolf readied his troops. He gathered them in the court at darkfall and sent them off in teams, every last one with wings. Nine teams of six, plus the sphinxes, ever their own team. Fifty-six chimaera. It had seemed like so many in the tithing, so many bruises, but Karou, watching from her window, pictured them against a sky full of Dominion and knew that they were nothing. She remembered the shine of the sun on armor, the flaming breadth of seraph wings, and the terrible sight of the enemy arrayed in force, and she felt numb. What did they hope for, going off like this? It was suicide.

They lifted, as squadrons, and flew.

Ziri did not look to her window.

37

Suicide

It was not suicide.

The squadrons did not turn south when they passed through the portal. The fifty-six didn't fly for the Hintermost to the aid of the creatures who peered up through the forest canopy to see why the sun faltered and what it was that the sky was delivering to them. Truly, what could fifty-six have done against so many? Suicide wasn't in Thiago's nature. It would have been a pointless exercise, a waste of soldiers.

The rebels didn't witness the running and falling of desperate chimaera, the running and falling and pushing up again and clutching at babies and hoisting of elderly by elbows. They didn't see the anguish of their kindred. They didn't see them die by the scattered hundreds, chased from burning forests and cut down in sight of safety. And they didn't die defending them, because they weren't there.

They were in the Empire, causing anguish of their own.

“Our advantage now is twofold,” Thiago had said. “One, they don’t know where we are, they still don’t know who or *what* we are. We are ghosts. Second, we are now *winged* ghosts. Thanks to our new resurrectionist, we have freer movement than we have ever had before, and we can cover much greater distance. They won’t be looking for us to strike at them on their own terrain.” He had let a silence settle before adding, with the perverse gentleness that was his way, “The angels have homes, too. The angels have women and children.”

And now they would have fewer of them.

* * *

Only one team leader defied his order: Balieros. The stalwart bull centaur would not turn his back on his people. Once the teams separated to make for their assigned territories, he put it to his soldiers to choose, and they followed him proudly. Bear Ixander; griffon Minas; Viya and Azay, both Hartkind as the Warlord had been; and Ziri. They flew south, their wings churning clouds and pushing the long leagues behind them. As swiftly as they crossed the land they had once defended, it was an epic swath of country, and they were a day in flight before they saw the bastions of the Hintermost in the distance.

A mere six soldiers into a maelstrom of enemy wings—it *was* suicide, and could end in only one way.

They knew it, they flew toward it, hearts on fire and blood pounding, in their doom infinitely more alive than their comrades who went the other way with every expectation of survival.

* * *

"So," said Hazael, coming quietly to Akiva's side as they awaited the order to fly. They followed Ormerod today, their patrols combined to follow the Dominion, who had already gone. "What do we do now, brother? Do you suppose there will be many birds out today?"

Birds?

Akiva turned to him. They had never spoken of the chimaera in the gully. "Must have been a bird," they had agreed at the time, pretending not to see the huddled folk right in front of them.

"Not nearly enough, I think," said Akiva.

"No, I suppose not." Hazael put his hand on Akiva's shoulder and let it weigh there for a moment. "Maybe some, though." He turned away; Liraz was coming. He intercepted her, leaving Akiva to his thoughts.

Maybe some. His spirits lifted, just a little.

When the fly order came, he left his despair in camp and took instead only his sense of purpose. He didn't deceive himself that it would be a day of heroics. It would be a day of death and terror, like so many other days, too many other days, and one—or was it two?—renegade seraphim couldn't hope to save many lives.

Maybe some, though.

38

The Inevitable

Rattle of thuribles, clatter of teeth.

Karou's fingers were restless at her trays. Sift, string. Teeth, teeth. Human, bull. Jade chips, iron. Iguana teeth—little saw-blade nasties—bat bones. Sift, string. When she came to the antelope teeth, she sat back and stared at them.

"Who are those for?"

Karou startled, and clasped her fist around them. She'd forgotten Ten for a moment. Watching. The she-wolf was always *watching.*

"No one," she said, and set them aside.

Ten shrugged, and returned to the task of mixing incense.

In London, at the Natural History Museum, Karou had hesitated beside the beautiful bull oryx for minutes, her hands tracing up its long, ridged horns, remembering what it was like to bear that weight on her own head.

"You could be Kirin again," Ten had said, but the thought

had never even occurred to Karou. The antelope teeth weren't for her. They were for Ziri, and she hadn't even wanted to take them. Superstitiously, it had seemed to her that the preparation *invited* his death—like digging a grave before someone died. Yes, death was expected, death was routine, but . . . not for Ziri.

Lucky Ziri.

Remarkably, he was still in his natural flesh. Through speed, skill—*luck*, he would be the first to say—he had never yet been killed. And, as foolish, as hypocritical as it was to care about his "purity," Karou did. He was the last of her tribe, the last true flesh of her kind. There was something sacred in that, and when he had flown out on that first assault, a small, cold dread had crystallized in her and grown, only subsiding when she saw him return.

And now she was waiting again—just to see him, and know that the Kirin were not yet gone from the world—but this wasn't like before. This time, she didn't see how he could possibly come back. Her parting words to him—her *only* words to him—had been so cruel, as if he were to blame for any of it. Would she ever get the chance to unsay them?

Sift, string. Teeth, teeth.

The hours passed and her dread grew. The sun rose, dragging all the hours behind it, and never had a day in this place seemed so sluggish, so hot, so unending. Karou felt aged by the time it finally subsided to twilight. Again and again she found the antelope teeth in her palm.

In the end, that night in London, she had taken her pliers to the oryx's mouth. It wasn't an invitation to Ziri's death, she had persuaded herself, but a way of preparing herself for its inevitability. All chimaera soldiers died. Maybe now his time had come. She tried to imagine him coming back in a thurible, his true flesh—the last Kirin body in all of Eretz—abandoned somewhere, broken or burned—and found that she could handle it.

So long as it kept her from considering the other possibility: that he might not come back at all.

39

Task Number One

On an unpaved road in southern Morocco, a car crunched to a stop, disgorging two passengers and their backpacks before pulling away with a backdraft of dust and Berber shouts for luck. Zuzana and Mik shielded their faces, coughing. The drone of the engine grew faint, and as the air cleared and they could look around, they found themselves at the edge of a vast emptiness.

Zuzana tilted back her head. "Holy. Mik. What are the creepy lights?"

Mik looked up. "Where?"

She gestured to the sky—the entire sky—and he shuttled his gaze back and forth twice before settling on her and asking, "You mean... *the stars*?"

"No way. I've seen stars. They're, like, these faraway specks in space. Those are *right there*."

What by the light of day was an austere land the unrelieved

color of dust became, in the dark, a midnight tapestry ludicrous with stars. Mik laughed, and Zuzana laughed, too, and they cursed and marveled, their necks craned all the way back. "You could pick those bastards like *fruit*," Zuzana said, reaching up and waggling her fingers at them.

They soon fell silent and stood looking out over the rough and rugged crust that was this land. It was like something out of a documentary—and not the feel-good kind. His voice bright, Mik said, "We're not going to die out there, are we?"

"No." Zuzana was firm. "That only happens in movies."

"Right. In real life, fool city folk never die in the desert and turn into bleached skeletons—"

"To be crushed under the hooves of camels," added Zuzana.

"I don't think camels *have* hooves," said Mik, sounding less than certain.

"Well, whatever they have, I would kiss a camel right about now. We probably should have gotten some camels."

"You're right," he agreed. "Let's go back."

Zuzana snorted. "Really, intrepid desert explorer. We've been here less than five minutes."

"Right, and where is *here*, exactly? How do you know this is the right spot? It all looks the same."

She held up a map. Overscribbled in red ink and fluttering with Post-its, it was not an object to inspire confidence. "*Here*-here. Don't you trust me?"

He hesitated. "Of course I do. I know how much work you've put into this, but... it's not exactly our area of expertise."

"Please. I'm an expert *now*," she said. She would have aced any quiz on southern Morocco after the research she'd done, and thought she should qualify as an honorary nomad for her efforts. "I know this is where she is. I'm sure of it. Come on, I even learned how to use a compass. We have water. We have food. We have a phone—" She looked at her phone. "Which doesn't get a signal. Well. We have water. We have food. And we told people where we're going. Sort of. What's the risk?"

"You mean, besides . . . the monsters?"

"Oh, *monsters*." Zuzana was dismissive. "You've seen Karou's sketchbooks. They're *nice* monsters."

"Nice monsters," Mik repeated, staring out at the stark starlit wilds.

Zuzana wrapped her arms around his waist. "We've come all this way," she cajoled. "It can be one of your tasks."

He perked up at that. "You mean the fairy-tale tasks?"

She nodded.

"Well, okay then. In that case, we'd better get moving." He hoisted his backpack on and held hers up as she slipped her arms through the straps.

They stepped off the road, and all lay before them.

"Maybe I should have asked before," said Mik. "But how many tasks are there?"

"There are always three. Now come on. It should be about twelve miles." She grimaced. "Uphill."

"Twelve miles? My love, have you *ever* walked twelve miles?"

"Sure," said Zuzana. "Cumulatively."

Mik laughed and shook his head. "Good thing you left your platforms behind."

"As *if*. They're in your pack."

"My—?" Mik heaved his shoulders up and down, jouncing

his pack and the attached violin case with it. "I *thought* it felt heavier."

Zuzana looked innocent. On her feet were her approximation of sensible shoes. They *were* sneakers, but their foam soles were thicker than was strictly necessary, not to mention zebra-striped. She gave Mik's hand a tug and plunged into the desert. They were both alive with the thrill of adventure, but it was Zuzana who practically gave off a hum, so tightly wound was her excitement. She was going to see her friend again.

Not to mention a giant sandcastle.

Full of monsters.

40

Wrong

Another night crawled above the kasbah, the stars never so slow in their arc as when lives were in question.

Karou distracted herself with work, a new urgency in the building of bodies. She tried not to think as if she were starting from scratch, but it was hard, with such grim odds.

It could be days before they knew anything. It was an epic long way to the Hintermost, with all the free holdings and the vast southern continent between here and there. Without wings, it would have been several weeks' overland trudging, but overland trudging was a thing of the past, and thank goodness for that. Karou remembered, when she was Madrigal, chafing at the unbearable pace of her battalions. But with wings, depending on what happened, the patrols could be back in days.

Or never.

The possibility that no one would come back at all was very real, and the strain of knowing that, and waiting, waiting to know something by *never actually knowing*, it was as old as war itself and it was the worst kind of dragged-out, miserable, gradual understanding she could think of.

So she was startled to hear the sentry's call just after dawn—too soon—and she was out the window in a stride, a string of teeth still clasped in her hands. She leapt up the parapet on tiptoe and kept going, up and into the sky. It was barely thirty-six hours and there were shapes on the horizon, a full patrol. It seemed like a miracle.

Another minute and they were near enough that she could make out Amzallag's bulk. It was Amzallag's team.

No Ziri then.

Yet. She ignored her disappointment, glad at least to see Amzallag, and just marveled that a team—any team, if not the one she was most hoping for—had returned intact from such a fight, and so quickly! She settled to perch on the green palace roof tiles and watch them land. Thiago came out to meet them as he always did, clasping arms and not seeming out-of-the-usual pleased or surprised. She couldn't hear what they said, but she could see that the soldiers' sleeves were stiff with blood.

Another patrol returned, and another.

The sun climbed, the squadrons came home to roost one by one, and the miracle of it began to feel suspect. How was it possible that they had lost no one? By midmorning every team was accounted for but Balieros's, and Karou could barely swallow around the lump in her throat.

"Where did they go?" she asked Ten back in her room, making a fidgeting effort at work.

"What do you mean? They went to the Hintermost," said

the she-wolf, but Karou knew it was a lie. Aside from the fact that they were back too soon, too *alive*, and the mood was wrong. It was *heavy*.

From her vantage point she saw the soldier Virko, who with his spiraling ram's horns reminded her a little of Brimstone, go behind the piss-rampart and fall to his knees to vomit. The sound of his retching rose and fell, traveling in waves across the court where the rest of the company, milling in a queerly quiet way, fell even quieter, and seemed to avoid looking at one another.

Amzallag sat under the arcade cleaning his sword, and when Karou looked down an hour later or even longer, he was still cleaning it, his movements jerky, angry.

The sight, though, that made Karou's mouth fill with the sweet saliva that precedes gagging, was Razor. Whatever the teams had been doing for the past day and a half—which was not by any calculation enough time to reach the Hintermost and return—had added a swagger to his whisper-smooth reptilian stride, and...he carried a sack. It was a brown cloth sack, heavy and full, and...stained with some fluid seepage, its color indeterminate, thanks to the brown of the sack. Fighting back the gag, Karou knew what the seepage was, and its color, and no matter how she had berated herself for her willful ignorance just a couple of days earlier, she did not want to know any more than that.

She found the antelope teeth again in her hand and put them down. She kept going to the window. Ten snapped at her for aimlessness, but she couldn't focus. This was wrong.

Wrong.

Wrong.

And then, finally, at the slow waning of the day's hottest hour, the sentry called again. *Ziri.* Karou was out the window and into the air. The sky was pure cobalt, cloudless and depthless, hiding nothing.

It was also empty. She turned to the sentry tower, confused. Oora was standing duty, and she wasn't even looking in the direction of the portal. The Wolf appeared beside her, and Oora pointed downhill, into the distance. Karou had to squint to see what they were looking at, and when she did, she breathed, "No. No no. *No.*"

Humans, two of them, slipping as they climbed the scree.

They were headed straight for the kasbah.

41

Mad Alchemy

This time, when angels came upon them, Sveva searched their eyes, and none were fire, and she swept their armor, and saw no lilies. Different angels. Bad luck.

To come so close to safety…

She'd really thought they'd made it. The mountains were so big, they'd kept seeming nearer than they were, and within reach. And then at the top of a slope that just had to be the last one—the last hill before the land *must* feather into those great granite folds that were like the world's own walls—another valley would yawn open at their feet. Another expanse to cross, another rise to climb. It was like a trick.

But this one, this really was the last. Sveva could see the very place where a row of huge bulged stones met a meadow.

"They look like toes on a big fat foot," she'd just said, not two minutes ago, smiling with the others. And she'd spun Lell, and the babe had laughed. "The mountain's toes," she'd sung. "We've reached the mountain's toes!" And she was prancing, hugging the little Caprine to her chest, still singing her happy nonsense—"I wonder if it's stinky in between the mountain's toes"—when Sarazal cried, "Svee!"

And she looked, and they were there. Angels. The wrong angels.

Still, Sveva tensed in a place between hate and hope that hadn't even existed a few days earlier. They had met mercy once; why not twice? Mercy, she had discovered, made mad alchemy: a drop of it could dilute a lake of hate. Because of what had happened in the gully, seraphim were more than slavers and faceless winged killers to her.

And yet, when these seraphim came pressing down, swords already red and no mercy in their eyes, she had no trouble screaming, "Kill them!"

Rath sprang.

The angels hadn't seen him. They were almost smirking, this pair in shining armor. They saw a flock of Caprine, a couple of Dama, some grizzled old Hartkind—easy kills all. And the Dashnag? He'd been last up the rise; they didn't see him until he was on them, already inside the reach of their swords and dragging them down to the ground, grappling, tearing.

They were screaming.

Sveva didn't want to watch, but she made herself, which is how she saw one of them free an arm and raise his sword, slamming it onto Rath's back. She shoved Lell at Sarazal and darted in with her slaver's knife and stuck it. She stuck it right in the gap the angel's armor left bare. She stabbed him in the armpit, deep, and he dropped his sword.

And died.

So that's what it feels like, she thought as her boldness gave way to trembling. *It feels awful.* Her knife was slippery and her gorge was rising. Sarazal grabbed her shoulder. "Svee, come on!" Urgent. And then they were swimming in shadows, all of them. Shadows wheeling, weaving. More angels overhead. Sveva threw back her head.

A lot more angels.

Rath roared. Sveva looked at her sister, at Lell, at Nur with her arms outstretched, trying to reach her child, at all the other Caprine and the old Hartkind couple, and she held on to her knife and pointed to the stone toes in the distance. "Run!" she screamed. They did.

She stood with Rath.

Look at me, she thought with weird, cold pride. Everything was sharp and sure. Stabbing was awful, and she'd never have believed she would stand when she could run. She loved to run. But standing felt good, too. She looked at Rath. He looked at her. She thought he might urge her to go, but he didn't. Maybe he just knew it wouldn't matter, that there was no safety, but maybe . . . maybe he liked not being alone. He was, after all, just a boy.

Sveva smiled at him, and there they stood, so near the end of their journey they could feel the mist of waterfalls from on high, but they were in the shadows of angels now, and not likely to ever come out again.

Unless of course there was another miracle.

When the figures crested the tree line, Sveva almost couldn't believe it. If she hadn't seen them before, she would have been as afraid of them as she was of the angels. They were much scarier than angels.

They were revenants. Chimaera.

Saviors. It was so much like the night at the slave caravan, but it was day now and she could see them clearly. She recognized some of them: there was the griffon who had unlocked her shackle, and the bull centaur who had untwisted the metal scrap that bound Sarazal. Sveva searched for the other—the handsome horned one who had put this knife in her hand—but him she didn't see.

The rebels were five against thrice that number, but they tore through the seraphim like a calamity.

After the first clash, and the first thuds of fallen bodies—enemies all—Rath did turn to Sveva and urge her to go. His eyes were alight. "I knew they'd come back," he said fervently. "I knew they wouldn't abandon us. Sveva, go. Catch the others. Take care of them, and tell them I said good-bye." He put a big clawed hand on her shoulder. "Good luck."

"But what about you?"

"I told you before, I was looking for the rebels." He was happy; she saw that this was what he had wanted all along. "I'm going to join them," he said.

And he did. When Sveva fled, Rath stayed and fought with the rebels.

And died with them, right there at the toes of the mountains.

And was dragged with them into a big pile.

And burned.

42

Lucky Ziri

"Come on," said Hazael. "There's nothing more we can do."

More? That would imply they had done something. They had found no opportunity. Too many Dominion, too much open ground. Akiva shook his head and said nothing. Maybe his night flight had spurred folk from their resting places, maybe chased them near enough that some had made the ravines and tunnels ahead of the angels. He would never know. All he would know was this before him.

The sky was spring blue and mountain-clean. Pristine. The smoke was still contained to thin columns, here and there. From this high rock perch the world became a lace of treetop and meadow, and the runoff rivers in the sun were like veins of pure light curving through the contours of hills. Mountains and sky, tree and stream, and the spark of wings as Dominion squadrons moved from site to site, setting their fires. This place was damp, ferny: mist veils and waterfalls. It wouldn't burn easily.

In such a place, with such a vista, it was almost impossible to accept what had happened here today. The blood daubs gave it away, though.

There were so many. The carrion birds could scent blood in the air from miles away. Judging from their numbers—and from the jerking eagerness of their usually languid spirals—there was plenty of it in the air today.

"And there are our birds," Akiva said, defeated.

Hazael took his meaning. "I'm sure some got to safety," he said. It was a moment before Akiva realized he'd said it with Liraz right there. She was looking at them. He waited for her to say something, but she just turned away, looked up into the peaks.

"They say you can't fly over them," she said. "The wind is too strong. Only stormhunters can survive it."

"I wonder what's on the other side," said Hazael.

"Maybe it's a mirror of this side, and seraphim there have chased their chimaera into tunnels, too, and they meet in the middle, in the dark, and find out there's no safe place in all the world, and no happy ending."

"Or," said Hazael, overbright, "maybe there are no seraphim on that side, and there's the happy ending. No *us*."

She turned from the peaks, abrupt. Her tone, which had been curiously remote, turned hard. "You don't want to be *us* anymore, do you?" Her gaze shuttled back and forth between them. "You think I can't see it?"

Hazael pursed his lips, glanced at Akiva. "*I* still want to be us," he said.

"So do I," said Akiva. "Always." He thought back to the sky of the other world, when he had stopped the pair of them in their pursuit of Karou and made himself tell them—finally—the truth. That he had loved a chimaera, and dreamed of a different life. He'd gambled then that his sister was more than the emperor's weapon, and if she had shunned the idea of harmony, at least she hadn't turned on him. Did he think he was the only one who was sick of death? Look at Hazael. How many others? "But a better us," he said.

"A better us?" Liraz asked. "Look at us, Akiva." She held up her hands to show her ink. "We can't pretend. We wear what we've done."

"Only the killing. There are no marks for mercy."

"Even if there were, I would bear none," she said. Akiva met her eyes, and he saw a kind of torment in her.

"You have only to begin, Lir. Mercy breeds mercy as slaughter breeds slaughter. We can't expect the world to be better than we make it."

"No," she said, faint, and for a moment he thought she was going to say more, go deeper, demand his secrets. Confess hers? But when she turned away, it was only to say, "Let's get out of here. They're burning bodies, and I don't want to smell the char."

* * *

Ziri watched the blaze. He was upslope on a ridge, in the safety of the trees.

Safety. The word felt absurd. There was no safety. The angels might as well light the whole world on fire and be done with it. The things he had seen burn in these last months. Farms, entire rivers slick with oil. Children running, fleet and screaming—*aflame*—until they could run and scream no more. And now, friends.

His grip on his knife hilts was so fierce it felt as if his fingers would gouge through the leather to the steel beneath, and through that, too. *Safety*, he thought again. It was worse than absurd, it was profane. It had also been his mandate on this mission: to be *safe*.

Balieros had ordered him to *hide*.

In every engagement there was to be someone kept back, designated safety against such an eventuality as this, to glean the souls of the others should they be slain. It was an honor, a deep trust—to hold his comrades' perpetuity in his hands—and it was torture.

Lucky Ziri, he thought with bitterness. He knew why Balieros had chosen him. It was such a rare thing for a soldier to be in his natural body; the commander had wanted to give him a chance to keep it. As if he cared about that. Being the one left alive was worse. He'd had to watch the slaughter and do nothing. Even that Dashnag boy had fought—and well—but not Ziri, though his mind and body had screamed to fly into the fray.

The one breach he had permitted himself was to cut down a seraph who pursued the little Dama girl, the deer centaur, pretty as a doll. She was the same girl he'd helped free from the slavers up in the Marazel Hills, and she was holding the knife he'd given her. To think that they had come so far and nearly died right here. He saw the group of them, Dama and Caprine, vanish into a crease in the rocks, and that was good. It had been something solid to hold on to as he watched his comrades die. To know that it was not for nothing.

The five of them had taken fivefold the lives they gave, and the Dashnag boy added to the count. Ziri had watched the seraphim gape and gesture over the corpses—Ixander, especially, whom it took three of them to drag when it finally came to it. They pulled the bodies into a pile, and then, unholy butchers, they hacked off *their hands* before setting them alight, hacked them off and kept them—*why?* As trophies?—then lit the whole clearing and watched the blaze devour the mutilated remains. Ziri smelled them now—mingled with the sweet char of grass was the odor of scorched fur, horns, and, horribly, the cookfire scent of meat—and he imagined his comrades' souls hovering over the clearing, maintaining a tenuous connection with their burnt bodies for as long as they could.

He couldn't wait much longer. Burning hastened evanescence, and it had been hours already. Soon it would be too late. If Ziri hoped to save his comrades, he had to do it *now.*

The angels had lingered from morning into afternoon, but finally they were going, lifting skyward in all their abominable grace, and flying away.

He moved steadily down the slope, keeping to the thickest cover, and by the time he came to the edge of the clearing the enemy was gone from the horizon. He surveyed the clearing. The seraph fire was an infernal thing, and burned so hot that the bodies had been eaten to nothing. A wind was rising, stirring the mound of ashes, carrying it into Ziri's eyes and worse: sundering what little the souls had left to cling to. He lit four cones of incense in his thurible and held it steady. Five soldiers and one volunteer. He hoped he had them all, the boy, too.

He'd done all he could. He closed the thurible with a twist and slipped the gleaning staff back through its loop across his back. He scanned the sky. It was empty, but he knew he had to wait until dark to fly—more hiding, more waiting. The Dominion were everywhere, still spreading the emperor's message with their terrible efficiency, and, as he had seen… enjoying themselves.

At first, in the rebels' opening strike, Ziri had hated cutting the Warlord's smiles on the dead, but right now, all he could think was that the angels' black joy must be answered.

And what if the act of answering sparked a black joy of its own? What would Karou think of that? *No.* Ziri pushed down the thought. He had taken no joy in it, but he couldn't blame Karou for her scorn. It had surprised him, at the river, how deeply it cut—how she looked at him, how she walked away. He'd covered his shame with anger in the moment—who was *she* to scorn *him*?—but he couldn't fool himself anymore. When Balieros had pulled the patrol aside to ask if they were with him—if they wished to slaughter enemy civilians or aid their own—Ziri's first thought had been of Karou, of erasing her scorn and replacing it with something else. Respect? Approval? *Pride?*

Maybe he was still that lovestruck little boy, after all.

Ziri shook his head. He turned back toward the cover of the trees. And saw them standing there watching him: three angels with their arms crossed.

43

An Amusing Story

"*You,*" said Ziri.

It was often said among chimaera that all seraphim look alike, with such sameness of parts as make them up, but any chimaera would know this angel on sight. The scar that split his face was unique.

Ziri whistled. "Wait until my friends hear that I killed the Captain of the Dominion. They won't believe it."

Jael laughed. It was a wet sound. He stepped forward, and his soldiers fanned out to encircle Ziri. Three angels didn't upset him overmuch, even if one of them was the emperor's brother. Three was easy. He heard a sound behind him and glanced back to see another...six...emerge from the far wood. *Ah.* And when he turned back, another three behind Jael. A dozen.

So death, then.

Probably.

"Do you know," Ziri said to Jael, "every last chimaera soldier claims to have given you that scar. It's a game we play when we're bored, who can come up with the best story. Would you like to hear mine?"

"Every last chimaera soldier?" said Jael. "And how many is that these days, four? Five?"

"Yes, well. One chimaera *is* worth"—he made a show of counting them and a show of smiling—"*at least* a dozen seraphim. So that should be taken into account." He had drawn his blades at the first sight of them. They gave him a wide berth now, but he knew that they would close in and try to take him. He welcomed it. All the anguish of the past hours was alive in his hands—a hot thrum where he clasped his hilts. "The story goes like this," he said. "We were having dinner together, you and I. As we do from time to time. It was grimgrouse. Overspiced. You killed the cook for that. *Temper.*" He added, as an instructive aside, "You know, in a story, it's the details like that that make it seem real. Anyway, you got a bone stuck in your mustache. Did I mention you had a mustache?"

Jael did not have a mustache. Around him, Ziri sensed the Dominion tightening. Jael stood at a safe remove, his face showing calculated forbearance. "Did I," he said.

"A sad, wispy specimen, but never mind. I went to cut the bone out, using *your* sword, and that was my mistake right there. It's much bigger than I'm used to." He held up his crescent moons to illustrate his point. "And, well, I missed. Spectacularly, really, though I always say: I wish I'd missed in the other direction." He mimicked slashing a throat. "Nothing personal."

"Of course not." Jael ran a fingertip down the long, jagged line of his scar. "Do you want to know how I really got it?"

"No, thank you. I'm this close to believing my own version." A flicker of movement. Behind Ziri, a soldier; he spun, his knives glinting, the sunlight bright and beckoning along their well-honed curves. The steel wanted blood and so did he. The soldier pulled back.

"You can lower your weapons," said Jael. "We aren't going to kill you."

"I know," Ziri replied. "I'm going to kill you."

They thought this was funny. Several laughed. But not for very long.

Ziri was a blur. He took the laughers first, and two angels were dead where they stood, throats gaping open before the others could even draw their weapons.

If any of them had ever fought a Kirin, they wouldn't have felt such comfort in their numbers as to stand so near him with their swords sheathed. Well, their swords came out fast now. The two bodies slumped to the ground, and another two angels were bleeding before ever steel rang on steel. Then it was a melee. *Nithilam*, as the seraphim called it. Chaos.

Ziri was outnumbered, but he turned it to his advantage. He moved so fast in the spinning kata of moon blades that the seraphim scarcely knew where to look for him. They followed; he spun. They got in the way of one another's strikes. Ziri's part was easier: everything was enemy. Everything was target. His crescent-moon blades seemed to multiply in the air; this was what they were made for, not slicing smiles but taking on multiple opponents, blocking, slashing, piercing. Two more angels fell: gut wound, cut tendons.

"Keep him alive!" roared Jael, and Ziri was aware, even in the spiral and glint of flesh and steel, that this was not good news.

He lunged at them, gripping his hilts hard so blood wouldn't flow beneath his fingers and make his grip slippery. He flew at them, took the fight airborne, and cut and killed, but he never held out any real hope of escape. These were seraph soldiers; he was fast, but they were far from slow, and they were many. Not for the first time in his life, he wished for hamsas. The marks might have weakened them, given him a chance. By the time they disarmed him their host was halved, but he himself bled only from shallow wounds—which he attributed as much to their discipline as to his own agility. They wanted him alive, and so he was.

He was on his knees before them, and no one was laughing now. Jael came toward him. He had lost his smugness; his face was rigid, the scar livid white against the red of his fury. Ziri saw the kick coming and curled to absorb the blow, but it still caught his stomach hard and drove the breath from him.

He turned the gasp into a laugh. "What was that for?" he asked, straightening back up. "If I've done something to give offense—"

Jael kicked him again. And again. Ziri ran out of laughter. Only when he was choking up blood did Jael come close enough to rip the gleaning staff off of his back. His eyes were hard with triumph, and Ziri felt the first burn of fear.

"I have an amusing story, too, only mine is true. I met your

Warlord and Brimstone recently, and I burned them like I burned your comrades and that is how I know that they are dead and gone, and that *this*"—he held up the thurible—"can only be for someone else. So... who?"

Ziri's blood had become strangely loud in his head. It was dawning on him what this was about, that the seraphim had laid a trap in the clearing and waited to see if anyone came gleaning. The rebels had been ghosts, as the Wolf had said; now they were real. He had tipped their hand. "I'm sorry." Ziri feigned confusion. "Who what now?"

Jael looked down. He stirred the ashes with the tip of his sword. "You will tell me who the resurrectionist is," he said. "Sooner would be better. For you, I mean. Myself, truly I don't mind if it takes... a bit of work."

Well, that didn't sound like fun at all. Ziri had no experience of torture, and when he thought of it, there was one face that came to mind.

Akiva's.

Ziri would never forget the day. The agora, all of Loramendi turned out to watch, and Madrigal's lover forced to watch, too. The seraph had been on his knees as Ziri was now, weak from beatings and hamsas and undone by grief. Had he given up anything to the Wolf? Ziri didn't think so, and strangely enough, the thought gave him strength. If the angel could withstand torture, he could, too. To protect Karou, and with her, the chimaera's hope, he thought he could endure anything.

"Who is it?" asked the captain again.

"Come closer," replied Ziri with a bloody grin. "I'll whisper it in your ear."

"Oh, good." Jael sounded pleased. "I was afraid you were going to make it easy." He gestured to his soldiers, and two stepped in to seize Ziri's arms. "Hold him," he said. He stabbed the gleaning staff into the black earth and began to roll up his sleeves. "I'm feeling inspired."

44

Some Luxuries

"I said no humans would be hurt." Karou's voice, already hoarse from arguing, sounded like a growl to her. "That was the first thing. No humans hurt. Period." She was pacing in the court. Chimaera were gathered in the gallery and on the ground, some basking in the sun and others withdrawn in shade.

As if he were teaching her a hard life truth, Thiago said, "In war, Karou, some luxuries must be put aside."

"Luxuries? You mean not killing innocent people?" He didn't say anything. That *was* what he meant. Karou's stomach twisted in a knot. "Oh god, no. Absolutely *no*. Whoever they are, they're nothing to do with your—" She stopped. Corrected herself. "*Our* war."

"But if they endanger our position here, they are everything to do with it. You had to know the risk, Karou."

Had she known? Because of course he was right that it would only take a hiker telling tales to bring a media storm down on the kasbah. And then what? She didn't like to think of it. The military, surely. Once upon a time, a tale of monsters in the desert might have been dismissed as backpackers smoking too much hashish, but times had changed. So, what now?

"They might keep going," she said, but that was feeble and they both knew it. It was a hundred degrees out and there was no other destination for many miles. Besides which, even at a distance it was obvious the hikers weren't doing so well.

They were dragging uphill, pausing every minute or so to bend over with hands on knees, slug water from canteens, and then . . . the small one doubled over and heaved. They were too far for the accompanying sound to carry, but it was obvious that they were at risk of heat exhaustion, if not already suffering from it. The pair leaned together for a long time before they got moving again. Karou paced. The hikers needed help, but this was oh so very much not the place that they would find it. If they only knew what they were headed toward. But even if they did know, they were clearly in no state to turn back.

Thiago was calm, always so maddeningly calm—until he *wasn't*, anyway—because the hikers posed no urgent danger. He was content to let them approach. And then what?

The pit?

Again Karou's stomach seized. She could smell it today. Maybe because it had fresh fodder—Bast had finally taken her walk with the Wolf. Karou had already conjured her new body; it lay on her floor even now—and maybe because the breeze was one of those mild but insistent wafts from just the right direction. It might have been saying, *Here, smell this. Here, smell this*, over and over.

Karou stopped pacing and stood before the Wolf. She put her shoulders back and tried not to shake, tried to sound like someone to be reckoned with as she said, "I'm going to go down there and help them, and I'll take them around the back gate into the granary." It was cool in the granary, and isolated. The truck was there. "I'll give them some water, they will see no one, and then I'll drive them to a road." She paused. She heard herself, and knew she wasn't conveying the forcefulness she wanted. "You won't have to do anything," she said, but her voice cracked and her head filled with cursing. What a perfect time to sound like an adolescent boy. "I'll take care of it."

"Very well," Thiago said. His expression was so arranged. Karou imagined she could see the strings holding it in place, this benign Thiago-mask, and it made her furious. It was like beating her fists against a wall talking to him. "Go on, then," he urged.

And she went, trying to have some dignity and not stomp like a powerless child. She went out the gate, and the breeze was stronger here: rot rot, wrong wrong. Bodies putrefying in a pit, and if she didn't help them, the hikers would end up there, too, and any other humans who had the misfortune to wander too near this godforsaken place. What had she done, leading the rebels into this world?

But then she thought of Eretz, and what the rebels' prospects would have been if she hadn't—and the prospects for all chimaera—and she didn't know what was right anymore. She'd wanted to believe that they could be trusted to have some humanity. They were soldiers, not brute killers, and not wild animals, either, whose appetites functioned beyond the reach of reason. She knew Amzallag wouldn't harm anyone without justification, and neither would Balieros, or Ziri, or most of the others. But she had only to think of Razor—and his sack—to know that all bets were off.

She had to remind herself to keep her feet on the ground as she left the kasbah; it was her first impulse now to fly, so unaccustomed had she become to human society, and it wasn't easy walking on the shifting scree.

She realized that her hair was uncovered. What if the hikers recognized her? They really could be a danger. But what was she supposed to do?

It didn't take long for them to spot her. Coming down the slope from the fortress, she would be the only moving thing in sight. They were still too far off for her to see clearly, but she heard the cry that came at her, and she stopped walking like she'd hit a barrier. It came rolling over the rocks and scrub, full-throated but dissolving at the edges into weakness.

The voice.

It just wasn't possible. But the cry was "Karou!" and the voice was Zuzana's, and Karou had certainly learned that "possible" and "impossible" were rough categories at best. *Oh god, no*, she thought, staring at the figures and seeing what she had never expected to see: Zuzana and Mik, *here*.

Not them, not here.

How? How?

Did it matter? They were here, and they were in danger—of heatstroke, of chimaera—and Karou's heart pounded and swelled within her—with panic, with . . . *gladness* . . . and more panic, and more gladness, and a surge of anger—what were they *thinking*?—then tenderness, astonishment, and her eyes were wet when her feet left the earth and she flew down the slope and caught them and crushed them in a hug that threatened to finish what the heat had begun.

It was really them. She drew back to look at them. Zuzana had sagged down with exhausted relief. Tear tracks stood out against the red of her cheeks, and she was laugh-crying, crushing Karou's hands with a vise-tight grip—a squeeze right on the bruised web of her hand that made her gasp.

"Jesus, Karou," Zuzana rasped, her voice spent in crying out. "The freaking desert? It couldn't have been Paris or something?"

And Karou was laugh-crying, too, but Mik wasn't laughing or crying. He had a careful hand at Zuzana's back, and his face was tense with concern. "We could have died," he said, and the girls fell silent. "I should never have agreed to this."

After a beat, Karou agreed. "No, you shouldn't." She took in the desert panorama with new eyes, imagining coming across it on foot. "What on earth were you thinking?"

"What?" Mik stared at her, looked to Zuzana then back to Karou. "Didn't you want us to come?"

Karou was taken aback. "Of course not. I would *never*... God. How did you even find me?"

"*How?*" Mik was helpless with frustration. "Zuze figured out your riddle, that's how."

Riddle? "What riddle?"

"The riddle," Zuzana said. "Priestess of a sandcastle, in a land of dust and starlight."

Karou blinked at her. She remembered writing that e-mail; she had just brought the chimaera through the portal to the kasbah, and had been in Ouarzazate scrounging supplies for Aegir. "*That's* how you found me? Oh, Zuze. I'm so sorry. I didn't mean for you to come here. I never thought..."

"Oh, you've got to be kidding me." Mik raised his hands to his head and turned his back. "We've come to the godforsaken navel of nowhere and you don't even want us here."

Zuzana looked crestfallen. Karou felt horrible. "It's not that I don't want you!" She dragged her friend into another crushing hug. "I *do*. So much. So much. It's just...I would never have brought you into...this." She gestured to the kasbah.

"What *is* this?" Zuzana asked. "Karou, what are you *doing* out here?"

Karou opened her mouth and closed it again, twice, like a fish. Finally, she said, "It's a long story."

"Then it can wait," Mik said firmly. Karou had never seen anger on his face before, but he was flushed with it now, his eyes narrow with accusation. "Can we please get her out of the sun?"

"Of course." Karou took a deep breath. "Come on."

She shouldered one of their packs and dragged the other. Mik helped Zuzana up the slope, and Karou didn't take them the long way around to the granary, but the more direct route to the main gate, where they froze on the threshold and stared.

Again, Karou saw with new eyes, imagining how these creatures must look to humans.

Thiago stood looking bemused, Ten just behind him. Thiago himself you could almost mistake for human, but Ten was another story with her wolf head and humped shoulders. As for the rest of the court, it was a horror show: soldiers gathered in the gallery and on the ground, even on the rooftops, strangely still but for the lash of a tail here and there, the flick of a wing. Their monstrous size, their many and varied eyes, unblinking. Razor, too near for comfort, flicked out his serpent tongue, and Karou found herself in a ready stance, light on her toes, in case he should leap.

Mik spoke in a hoarse stage whisper. "Let's just get this out of the way so I can relax. Karou, your friends aren't going to eat us, are they?"

No, Karou thought. *They are not.* She whispered back, "I don't *think* so. But try not to look delicious, okay?"

She was rewarded with a snort from Zuzana. "That poses a problem, seeing as how we are *totally delicious*." A half beat later, anxiously: "Wait. They don't understand Czech, right?"

"Right," said Karou. The whole time, she was looking at Thiago and he was looking at her. The stench of the pit was in the air, and it was then that the nightmare surreality of the life she had been living was sucked away as by a vortex, just gone, and everything was real. This was *her life*, not a grim dream she would wake from, and not purgatory but her actual life in the actual world—*worlds*—and now her friends were in it, and it was their life, too.

It made a difference.

"These humans are my guests," she said, and she felt the words come from some iron place within her that hadn't existed an hour ago. She didn't speak loudly, but there was such a change in her voice. Coming from that iron place, it was heavy and true; it wasn't persuasive, or desperate, or antagonistic. It just was. She approached the Wolf, nearer than she liked to be to him. She forced herself to breach his physical space, the way he did hers, tilted back her head, and said, "Their lives are not a luxury. These are my friends, and I trust them."

"Of course," he said, smiling, the perfect gentleman. "That changes everything." He nodded to Mik and Zuzana and even welcomed them, but his smile, it was just wrong. Like he'd learned it from a book.

45

Dead

"Who was *that*?" Zuzana whispered as Karou led her and Mik out of the big courtyard where the monsters were gathered. "The other white meat?"

Karou's laugh sounded like a choke. "Oh god," she said when she could breathe again. "And now that's what I'm going to think every time I see him. Watch your step."

They were on a rubble-strewn path, Mik holding Zuzana's elbow, and they had to pick their way over a collapsed wall. Zuzana peered around. From a distance, the kasbah had looked regal in a crazy sandcastle way, but inside it was pretty desolate. Not to mention—she stepped over a timber bristling with giant rusty nails and skirted the edges of a gaping hole—*dangerous.* And it *smelled* bad, too, like piss and worse. What *was* that smell? Why was Karou living here? And the creatures back there... They weren't entirely unlike the drawings in her sketchbooks, but they weren't *like* them, either. They were much bigger and freakier than anything Zuzana had imagined.

As for the white guy, he looked almost human; he was supernaturally hot—holy, those eyes, those shoulders, he'd be right at home on the cover of a romance novel—but there was something so icy about him that she'd gotten a shiver in spite of practically melting to death in this desert hell.

"That was Thiago," Karou said. "He's... in charge."

Zuzana had gotten that much from his lord-of-the-manor air. "In charge of what, exactly?" she asked. Something occurred to her and she stopped walking. "Wait. Where's Brimstone?"

Karou stopped, too, and her stricken expression was all the answer Zuzana needed. "Oh no," she said. "Not—?" *Dead?*

Karou nodded.

Dead. That word was not supposed to be part of this adventure. Horrified, Zuzana asked, "And... Issa? Yasri?"

Again Karou's expression was her answer.

"Oh, Karou, I'm so sorry," Zuzana said, and when she looked to Karou now, she really looked, not with the pure relief that had gripped her on first sight, but *seeing* her. She was too thin, *sharp*, her lips were chapped, her hair in a slapdash braid, her shirt—some Moroccan-style loose cotton shift—was wrinkled as if she lived in it, and her eyes had that bruised sleepless look. And not just sleepless; she looked... *depleted.*

Another shiver went down Zuzana's spine. What had she walked into, brought Mik into? She'd gotten so caught up in the mystery and the challenge; of course she'd known something was going on with Karou. Her cryptic e-mail had made that clear, but she hadn't really considered it might involve the word *dead* and this stench in the air that she was sure now was *rot.*

She swallowed hard. She had a fat headache, her feet were killing her, she really, *really* wanted a shower, and she had a sad presentiment that ice cream was out of the question, but there was someone she hadn't asked after yet. She hesitated, afraid of seeing another bleak answer written on her friend's face. "What about Akiva?"

An answer appeared on Karou's face all right, but it wasn't the one Zuzana had expected. The bleakness transformed to severity. Karou's jaw clenched, her eyes narrowed. "What about him?" she asked, hard.

Zuzana blinked. *What?* "Um. Is he . . . alive?"

"Last I heard," Karou said, and turned away. "Come on."

Zuzana and Mik looked at each other wide-eyed and followed in her wake. Karou's tense posture was a warning to keep silent, but Zuzana chose to ignore it. Frankly, it pissed her off. She'd come all this way; she'd solved a riddle that wasn't even a riddle; she'd found Karou *in the middle of the Sahara desert*—okay, they weren't really in the Sahara desert but close enough, and if she ever told this story she was absolutely going to say she had hiked into the middle of the Sahara desert in zebra-striped sneakers. Whatever. She really didn't think she deserved to be stonewalled. "What happened?" she asked her friend's back.

Karou glanced over her shoulder. "Let it go, Zuze. I'll tell you everything else, but I don't want to talk about him."

How bitterly she said it. "Karou." Zuzana reached for Karou's arm; when her friend winced from her touch, she drew back her hand. "What?" Zuzana asked. "Are you hurt?"

Karou stopped walking. She let go of the packs she was dragging and hugged her arms to herself, looking so lost. So beautiful and so lost. How was it fair that she looked so beautiful with such an obvious lack of effort? "I'm fine," she said, trying for a smile. "It's you two Lawrence of Arabias I'm worried about. Would you just shush and let me get you inside?" Karou looked to Mik for support, and of course he agreed with her.

"Come on, Zuze, we can catch up on everything later."

Zuzana sighed. "Fine. Bullies. But I might die of curiosity."

"Not if I can help it," said Karou, and Zuzuna gave Mik's hand an involuntary squeeze, because it didn't sound like she was joking.

* * *

Karou was still trying to push the thought of Akiva from her mind when they reached the palace. Just the mention of his name was enough to make her feel turned to stone. Well. Stone was better than pulp, and she was never going to let anyone make her feel like that again.

She stepped aside to usher her friends through the door. As dusty and worn on the outside as the rest of the kasbah, inside, the palace was, well, it was dusty and worn, too, but it was also unexpectedly lavish. Once home to the sloe-eyed brides of tribal chiefs and all their chittering broods, it was a complex of many grand rooms. There were pilasters of etched alabaster, badly chipped, and lantern niches in the shape of keyholes. The walls were paneled with faded silk, the ceilings carved in

Arabic honeycombs, and a grand staircase swept upward, tiled in cracked lapis the color of Karou's hair.

Zuzana turned in a slow circle, taking it all in. "I can't believe you live here," she said. "No wonder you gave me your dinky flat."

"Are you kidding?" Karou had to laugh at the absurdity of the comparison. "I miss that flat so much." And that *life*. "Trade you."

"No, thanks," said Zuzana at once.

"Wise girl." Karou started up the stairs, pausing to offer Zuzana her arm. Between herself and Mik, who was not exactly peppy, they helped her up to the first landing, where a corridor led to Thiago's suite and the small antechamber where Ten slept. A twist, and there were more stairs. "I still can't believe you're here," Karou said as they climbed. "You have to tell me how you did it. After you get some rest, that is. You two can have my bed while you're here."

"Where will you sleep?" asked Mik.

"Oh, don't worry about that. I don't sleep much."

Zuzana's eyebrow rode high. "Really. Or eat, apparently. Or groom." At the sight of that eyebrow—insult notwithstanding—Karou was flooded with love. Zuzana, *here*. It boggled. She crushed her in another hug, which did not stop Zuzana from asking, "So what *do* you do, exactly?"

Karou released her. "I'll tell you everything else," she had said, and she'd meant it. She'd been desperate for someone to talk to, hadn't she, and now, like a wish granted, Zuzana and Mik were here. It felt like magic.

Karou took a deep breath, mindful of the state in which she

had left her room, and put her hand to the heavy cedar door. “You sure you want to know?”

Eyebrow.

“Okay then.” Karou pushed open the door. “Come in and I’ll tell you.” Innocently, as they moved past her, she added, “Oh, and don’t trip over the body on the floor.”

46

Un-Alive

Some months had passed since Karou had first tested truth-telling on Zuzana back in Prague. It had been so unfamiliar then, talking about her secret life, that she hadn't known how to begin. She'd just blurted it all out, angels and chimaera and all, and if Kishmish hadn't appeared at that very moment—on fire—she would probably have lost her friend forever.

Well, the things she had to tell now made that first round of confessions sound plain tame, but Mik and Zuzana were primed to believe. They had, after all, just walked into a kasbah full of monsters. Still, the idea of resurrection might take some getting used to.

"*Ohmygodwhyisthereadeadmonsteronyourfloor?*" was Zuzana's breathless question when she saw Bast's new body sprawled before her.

"Well. She's not *dead* exactly," Karou hedged.

Zuzana reached out a dust-caked sneaker and gave the inert flesh a nudge. "She's not *alive*."

"True. Um. Let's call her . . . *un-alive*."

And thus did Zuzana and Mik learn that *un-alive* could mean *dead*—and usually did—but it could also mean *new*. "I made it earlier," Karou told them, much as she might say she had knitted a hat, or baked a cake.

Zuzana was calm, effortfully so. She perched herself at the edge of Karou's bed and folded her hands in her lap. "Made it," she repeated.

"Yes."

"Explain, please."

Karou did explain, as succinctly as possible, gesturing to her tooth trays and neglecting to mention the small matter of the pain tithe. She also poured water into a basin so her friends could bathe their faces and feet—*in that order*, she specified with mock gravity—made mint tea, and set out dishes of almonds and dates. When they were done with the basin, she emptied it out the window without looking, hoping Thiago or Ten might be walking below, but no shout or growl answered the splash, and she closed her shutters against the heat.

She performed the resurrection right away, partly because it was easier to show what she did than tell, but also to clear the room of bodies so her friends could relax.

The awakening was the easy part. The magic was already done, so no tithe was required or rolling up of sleeves to reveal ugly bruised arms. Karou felt such shame for her bruises, and didn't want Zuzana to see them, but it wasn't called for at this stage. All she had to do was hang up the thurible Thiago had brought her, light a cone of incense, and place it on the body's brow. Zuzana and Mik watched the whole procedure without blinking, though there was really nothing to see. The scent of sulfur, the creak of chain, these were the only signs. Karou alone could sense the soul that emerged from the vessel, lingering for just a moment before funneling itself into its new body.

Bast had, until now, looked rather like an Egyptian cat goddess: the slender human form, high breasts, feline head with exaggerated ears; Karou had maintained the feline aspect as much as she could, but had, at Thiago's request, sacrificed much of the human. This new body was all sleek muscle, not as big as some, being made for agility. The arms and upper torso remained human for versatility with weapons—Bast was a good archer—but the haunches were leopard, for leaping and springing. And of course there were the all-important wings, sprawled open to take up much of the floor. Karou was glad this wasn't one of her more monstrous creations, first for the sake of Zuzana and Mik, and now, unexpectedly, Bast.

Bast's soul, she discovered, had a delicate beauty ill-suited to a soldier, and she wondered briefly what sort of life she might have had in a different world. Well, she thought as Bast opened her eyes, they would just never know.

Zuzana gave a small gasp. Mik just stared.

Bast lifted her head, eyes widening at the sight of new humans, but said nothing. She focused on her new self, testing her limbs with small gestures before rising unsteadily to find paws where hands and feet had been.

"All right?" Karou asked.

The soldier nodded and stretched her entire supple spine.

The gesture was unmistakably feline; she might almost have been a cat waking on a window ledge. "It's well done," she said, her voice like a purr in her newly made throat. "Thank you."

Something clenched in Karou's chest. None of them had ever thanked her before. "You're welcome," she said. "Do you need help down the stairs?"

Bast shook her head again. "I don't believe so." She stretched again. "As I said, it's well done." Again, that clenching in Karou's chest. A compliment. It was kind of ridiculous how grateful she felt for those few words. When the door settled closed behind Bast, she turned to her friends.

"Well," said Mik, leaning back on one elbow, eyes lazy with feigned cool. "That wasn't weird."

"No?" Karou dropped into her chair and rubbed her face. "My weird gauge must be off. I'd have guessed it was at least a little weird."

"Again," said Zuzana.

"What?" Karou dropped her hands and looked at her friend.

Zuzana's expression was vivid with amazement. "Again, again." She bounced up and down at the edge of the bed, childlike, clapped her hands and demanded, "When can I do it? You're going to teach me, right? Of course you are. That's why you brought me here."

"Teach you? I *didn't* bring you here—"

But Zuzana wasn't listening. "This is so much better than puppetry. Holy hell, Karou. You're making *living things*. You're freaking *Frankenstein*!"

Karou laughed and shook her head. "No, I'm not." She'd had ample time to consider and discard that comparison. "The whole point with Frankenstein is where the soul comes from." If a human created "life," there could be no soul, only a poor benighted monster with no place in the world—or heaven or hell, either, if you were concerned about that, which Karou was not. "I have the souls already." She pointed to the pile of thuribles. "I'm just making the bodies."

"Oh, is that all?" drawled Mik. "Ho hum."

But Zuzana was fixed on the dozens and dozens and *more* dozens of thuribles. Her eyes went round, her mouth, too. "All of those?" She was across the room in a flash, pulling one from the middle of the pile and setting off a minor landslide. "Let's make one. Please? Show me how you make the body." She was still bouncing; Karou feared she might ricochet. "I'll be your Igor. Please please please? Look." She went hunchback and dragged a leg. "What is your wish, Herr Doktor?" Snap, she was herself again. "Please? Whose soul is this? How can you tell? *Can* you tell?"

She had a million more questions and didn't give Karou time to answer any of them. Karou looked helplessly at Mik, who sat back and shrugged, as if to say, *this one's all yours.*

"Oh my god." Zuzana snapped motionless as an idea seized her. "Art exhibit. Can you imagine?" She set the scene with spokesmodel hands. "Balthus Gallery, a half-dozen chimaera bodies in, like, decorative sarcophagi, and at the opening everyone's all, *ooh, ahh, what's your medium, they're so lifelike*, and we just smile all Mona Lisa and swirl our wine around in our glasses? That would be the best thing ever. But no! Even better. We bring them to life! The smoke, the smell, those lantern things, and then these sculptures *lift their heads and get up.* Everyone would just think it was puppetry or something, what else could it be, and they'd be trying to figure out how we did it, and they'd be all posing for pictures with monsters and not even know it."

She kept going, and Karou laughed helplessly and tried to stop her. "That is never going to happen. You understand that, right? *Never.*"

Zuzana rolled her eyes. "Duh, killjoy, but wouldn't it be awesome?"

"It would be pretty awesome," Karou allowed. She hadn't really thought of her work as art, which struck her now as silly, especially in the wake of Bast's compliment. A memory rose from her Madrigal life, how when she was a child newly in Brimstone's service she had loved to come up with ideas for new chimaera, and had even drawn pictures to show him what she had in mind. She wondered if that was what had made Issa start her—*Karou*-her—with drawing. Sweet Issa, how she missed her.

"But you'll let me help you, right?" Zuzana was earnest. She handed Karou the thurible she had pulled from the pile. "Let's do this one first. Who is it?"

Karou took it and just held it. She didn't want to say that Thiago decided who got resurrected and when. "Zuze," she said instead, "you can't."

"I can't what?"

"You can't help me. You can't stay here."

"What? Why?" Zuzana began to come out of her spell of wild glee.

"Trust me, you don't *want* to stay here. I'm going to take you back as soon as you're rested enough to travel. I have a truck—"

"But we just got here." She looked so betrayed.

"I know." Karou sighed. "And it's so great to see you. I just want to keep you safe."

"Well, what about you? Are *you* safe?"

"Yeah, *I* am," she said, aware as she said it how *un*safe she felt pretty much all the time. "Me, they need."

"Uh-huh." Zuzana regarded her unhappily. "About that. Why *you*? Why are you here, with them? How is it *you* are doing *this*?"

That was a whole other neighborhood of the truth, and Karou felt as reluctant to broach the subject of her true nature as she was to reveal her bruises. Why all the shame? She took a deep breath.

"Because," she said, "I'm one of them."

"What kind?"

Karou blinked. It was Mik who had asked, and the question was so casual she thought she must have misheard. "What?"

"What kind of chimaera were you? You were resurrected, right? You have the tattoo eyes." He gestured to her palms.

Karou turned to Zuzana and found her looking every bit as unflabbergasted as Mik. "That's it?" she said. "I tell you I'm not human, and you're all tra-la-la?"

"Sorry," said Mik. "I think you neutralized our capacity for surprise. You should have started with that, and *then* told us you raise the dead."

"Anyway," added Zuzana. "It's kind of obvious."

"How is it obvious?" Karou demanded. She had believed she was human her whole life; she would not be persuaded that she had somehow been unconvincing at it.

"Just this aura of weird you have." Zuzana shrugged. "I don't know."

"Aura of weird," Karou repeated, flat.

"*Good*-weird," said Mik.

"So what kind?" Zuzana asked.

The question was so light, so offhand. Karou felt her palms go clammy. It was, after all, her *tribe* they were asking about, the family that had been ripped away from her so long ago. Flashes of the day besieged her, the long blood streaks on the floors where bodies had been dragged to the cave mouth and heaved over the drop. She breathed. They didn't get it. Of course they didn't. In their life it was not necessary to worry whether someone had been orphaned by slave raiders before you asked after their family.

Once upon a time she had had parents, a home, kin. Once upon a time, she had belonged somewhere, perfectly and without trying. "I was Kirin," she said softly. *I am Kirin*, she thought, though everything Kirin had been taken from her: her tribe and her home by angels, her true flesh by the White Wolf, and now, maybe...Ziri. "I'll show you," she heard herself say.

She reached for her sketchbook and pencil and held them a moment, tight, wondering if she could do this. She had tried to draw Madrigal before, but found her hand deflecting her pencil into some other effort. She was afraid—of getting it wrong, of getting it right, of what she would feel at the sight of her former self. Would she feel like it was her true form, and long for it? Or would it be strange, as if she had never even been that long-ago girl? Either way, she couldn't imagine it would make her happy.

Still, she thought it was time, and so she started to draw. A curved line. Another. Her horns took shape. Zuzana and Mik watched. Karou almost felt as if she were watching, too, rather than creating the image, and she was a little surprised by what emerged on the page. By *who* emerged.

"Um. You were a *guy*?" asked Zuzana.

Karou released her pent-up breath in a laugh. "No. Sorry. That's not me; that's Ziri. He's . . ." It felt too brutal to say he was the last living member of her tribe, so she said only, "He's Kirin, too."

"Oh, phew. I don't know why it would be freakier if you were a not-human *guy* in your previous body than a not-human *girl*, but it would."

Mik asked, "Where is he? Is he here?"

"His team is overdue back from a mission in Eretz."

Zuzana must have heard the anxiety in her voice. "What does that mean, *overdue*? Arc thcy okay?"

"Maybe. I hope. They might just be late."

Or they might be dead.

47

Assassins and Secret Lovers

Day passed to night, and Karou found herself faced with the undesirable task of explaining the toilet situation to Zuzana. That is, the *lack-of-toilet* situation.

To her surprise, Zuzana said only, "Well, that explains the smell."

It seemed Karou really *had* neutralized their capacity for surprise. She decided the best course would be to go to the river so they could bathe and take care of immediate needs with some privacy. "Privacy," in air quotes, as it were. Thiago met them on the way out, his courtly, overly solicitous manner stilted and old-fashioned as he insisted that Ten accompany them. "Just to be sure you're safe," he said.

Safe, thought Karou. *Right*. "Don't worry," she said. "I'm not going to make a break for it."

"Of course not," he said, and she knew that she couldn't if she tried. She wouldn't be able to escape the creatures she had made. Winged, powerful, and with keen animal senses, they'd be on them in no time. *Good going, me*, she thought as, with the she-wolf trailing, she led her friends out the gate and down the slope to the river. With the heat of the day gone, the cold water was less than inviting—plus, Ten's hunched presence on a rock was small inducement to shed clothes—so they didn't bathe properly, but only splashed themselves, scrubbed their faces and necks, and lay out on a rock to dry.

"Star bathing," said Karou.

"Seriously." Zuzana reached up as if to brush the stars with her fingertips. "I always thought pictures of night skies like this were faked or enhanced or something."

"Like those giant moon photos," added Mik.

Karou turned to them. "Did I tell you there are two moons in Eretz? And one of them really is that big."

"Two moons?"

"Yeah. The chimaera—*we*—worship them." She didn't, though, not anymore. Once upon a time she had believed there was a will at work in the cosmos, but if there had been, it had abandoned her at the temple of Ellai. "Nitid is the big one. She's the goddess of just about everything."

"And the other one?"

"Ellai," said Karou, remembering the temple, the *hish-hish* of the evangelines, the *shush* of the sacred stream. The blood. "She's the goddess of assassins and secret lovers."

"Cool," said Zuzana. "That's the one I'd worship."

"Oh, really. And which are you, an assassin or a secret lover?"

"Well," Zuzana said in a smarmy voice, "*my love is no secret*," and rolled on her side to kiss Mik. "Guess that makes me an assassin. How about you?" She turned back to Karou.

Karou's throat tightened. "*Not* an assassin," she said, and instantly regretted it.

A pause came between them, and it was so full of Akiva that Karou imagined she could smell him. *Stupid*, she scolded herself for opening the subject; it was like she *wanted* to talk about him. The pause grew, and for a moment she thought Zuzana was going to let it pass, for which she was grateful. She did not want to talk about Akiva. She didn't want to think about him. Hell, she wanted to unknow him, to go back in time to Bullfinch and turn another way on the battlefield as he bled out his life into the sand.

"I wish you'd tell me what happened," said Zuzana.

"I don't want to talk about it."

"Karou, you're *miserable*. What good is having friends if they can't help you?"

"Believe me, it's not something you can help me with."

"Try me."

Karou's whole body was rigid. "Yeah? Okay," she said, staring up into the stars. "Let's see. You know how, at the end of *Romeo and Juliet*, Juliet wakes up in the crypt and Romeo's already dead? He thought she was dead so he killed himself right next to her?"

"Yeah. That was awesome." A pause, followed by "Ow," suggested elbow punctuation on the part of Mik.

Karou ignored it. "Well, imagine if she woke up and he was still alive, but..." She swallowed, waiting out a tremor in her voice. "But he had killed her whole family. And burned her city. And killed and enslaved her people."

After a long pause, Zuzana said in a small voice, "Oh."

"Yeah," said Karou, and closed her eyes against the stars.

* * *

The sentry's call came as they were walking back up the slope. A throat-deep rumble that Karou recognized as Amzallag's, and at once she was rising into the air, squinting in the direction of the portal. At first she saw nothing. Was it more humans? No. Amzallag was pointing to the sky.

And then the stars shimmered. A figure was cutting across the night, visible first only as a canceling of stars. One figure, alone—*one*, only one?—and... its wingbeats were labored and uneven. It pitched, dropped, caught, pushed on, pain in every movement. And there were soldiers in the air going to meet him and help him—*him*, Karou saw that it was *him*. It was Ziri. Alive. She wanted to go, too, but there were her friends on the ground below, and anyway, she didn't imagine Ziri could want to see her, not after the last thing she had said to him, so she dropped back down and said, "Come on. Hurry."

Ten wanted to know what she'd seen, so she told her, and the she-wolf loped on ahead while Karou took her friends by the elbows and rushed them uphill, practically lifting them off the ground in her hurry.

"What?" Zuzana demanded. "Karou, what?"

"Just come," she said, and by the time they got there, Nisk and Emylion were lowering Ziri to the ground before Thiago.

His wings hung limp, and the Wolf knelt to support him, and Karou was there, a roaring in her ears as she searched for the source of the blood, the blood that was all over him. Where was it was coming from? Ziri was bent over, head down, arms pulled tight against his body, and . . . something was wrong with his hands. They were dark with blood and crooked stiff, like claws—oh god, what had happened to his hands?—and then he lifted his head, and his face . . .

Karou sucked a breath.

Behind her, she heard Zuzana cry out.

Ziri was as white as shock, and that was one thing Karou saw, but the rest was . . . it was confused, he was white but he was also gray, ash-gray—his chin, his mouth . . . his lips were black, clotted and crusted, and even that wasn't the worst thing. Karou's gaze skittered away and lost focus and she forced it back.

What had they done to him?

Of course. Of course they had done this. They had cut him as he had cut them, but he was still alive, wearing that terrible smile. He was . . . *carved.* Bleeding, white with shock and blood loss. His eyes searched for her and found her and focused with a snap—a whiptail snap when their eyes met—and her own jumped wider and he was telling her things with his look, but she couldn't understand, the words were missing, there was only the urgency.

Then he pitched forward and Thiago caught him, but not before one of his long horns hit the flagstone, snapping off the tip with a crack like a gunshot. Ten lunged forward and took his other arm, and he hung limp between the two as they lifted him and carried him away. Karou grabbed the piece of horn—she didn't know why—and went in quick short steps in their wake, gesturing for Zuzana and Mik to follow.

"Wait," she said, when Thiago and Ten came to the door of the keep where the soldiers slept. "Take him to my room. I think . . . I think I might be able to heal him."

Thiago gave a nod and changed direction. Ten followed his lead, and Karou, behind them, felt a sudden prickling at the back of her neck and turned. She scanned the path behind her. It was strewn with detritus; the wall beyond was high and the stars were bright, but there was nothing else.

She turned back and hurried up the path.

* * *

Akiva fell to his knees. He hadn't breathed since he saw her. He gasped now and his glamour failed, and if Karou had still been looking back she would have seen the shape of him cut in and out of the air, wings limned in fire and sparks like bursting embers. He was not twenty feet from her.

From *Karou.*

She was alive.

Soon, everything else would come rushing at him. Like the ground to a falling man, it would come rushing up and hit him all at once—the place, the company, her words; one implication would lead to another and shatter him—but around that intake of breath the world hung silent and bright, so bright, and Akiva knew only this one thing, and held on to it and wanted to live inside of it and stay there forever.

Karou was alive.

Once upon a time, a girl lived
in a sandcastle,

making monsters to send through a hole in the sky.

48

Fascinating Guest

"Captain, we've found . . . something. Sir."

Jael favored the scout with the baleful look his soldiers knew well. The Captain of the Dominion was not hot-tempered like his brother. His anger was a cool, intentional thing, but just as brutal—arguably more so, as he had full control when he committed his worst acts, and was more able to enjoy himself. "Am I to understand," he said softly, "that by 'something' you don't mean the rebel?"

"No, sir, not him." The scout stared past Jael's head at the silk wall of the pavilion. It was night and the breeze was up. The folds of the tent flapped in a light breeze, and the glow of lanterns painted its ripples crimson and fire, ever-shifting, mesmerizing. Jael knew; he'd been staring at it himself until his steward showed the scout in, but he didn't imagine the scout was mesmerized. He imagined he just didn't like to look at his captain's face.

"Well, what then?" he asked, impatient. It was the rebel he wanted—the Kirin who, unbelievably, had slipped through his fingers—and he could little imagine that anything else would hold his attention at the moment.

He was wrong.

"We're not sure what it is, sir," said the scout. He sounded bewildered. He looked repulsed. Jael was used to that look; he got it enough. They tried to hide it, but there was always a tell: a tic, a sliding away of the eyes, a subtle pursing of the lips. Sometimes it irritated him enough that he gave them something to take their mind off their revulsion. Like agony, for example. But if Jael were to punish everyone who was disgusted by his face, he would be kept very busy indeed. And anyway, this particular revulsion wasn't for him. When he realized that, his curiosity stirred.

"We found... *it*... hiding in the ruins of Arch Carnival. It had a fire."

"*It?*" prompted Jael. "A beast?"

"No, sir. It's like no beast I've seen. It says... It says it's a seraph."

Jael let out a spray of laughter. "And you can't *tell*? What manner of fools surround me that can't recognize our own kind?"

The scout looked acutely uncomfortable. "I'm sorry, sir. At first I thought it was impossible, but there's something about the thing. If what it says is true—"

"Bring it here," said Jael.

And they did.

He heard it before he saw it. It spoke the tongue of seraphim and it was moaning. "Brothers, cousins," it implored, "be gentle with this poor broken thing, take pity!"

Jael's steward held the flap of the tent open and beheld the creature first. The fellow was stoic from years in his service and all that that entailed, so when Jael saw him blanch, he took notice.

Two soldiers dragged the thing by its armpits. Its body was a bloated ball, its arms were reedy and ropey, and its face...

Jael did not blanch. The things that disgusted others were a fascination to him. He rose from his chair. Went closer and knelt before the thing to peer at it, and when *it* looked at *his* face, *it* recoiled. This was funny—that such a monster could feel disgust—but Jael did not laugh.

"Please!" it cried. "I have been punished enough. I have come home at last. The blue lovely made me fly again, but she was wicked, oh, false girl, she tasted of fairy tales, but let her have her ash city, let her mourn her dead monsters, she cheated me. The wish *ran out*. How many times must I fall? It has been a thousand years. I have been punished enough!"

Jael understood that he was looking at a legend. "Fallen," he said, amazed, and he took in the creature's fine eyes, sunk in the bloat of its purple face. He looked at its dangling, useless legs and the splinters of bone jutting from its shoulder blades where, in a long-distant past—a past out of stories whose books had been burned and lost—its wings had been ripped from its body.

"So you're real," said Jael, and he felt no small awe that the thing could be alive after all that it had endured.

"I am Razgut, good brother, have pity. The other angel, he

was cruel, oh, his fire eyes were bright, but he was a dead thing, he wouldn't help me."

Fire eyes. Suddenly, Jael found the creature's gibberish as fascinating as his history.

With a flash of unexpected strength from those reed-thin arms, Razgut jerked free of the soldier holding him and seized Jael's hand. "You who know what it is to be broken, brother, *you* will pity me."

Jael smiled. It was when Jael smiled that he felt most keenly what his face was: a mask of scar tissue, a horror. He didn't mind being a horror. He lived. The one who had cut him, well, she had lived long enough to rue her poor aim, and then long enough to rue having ever lived at all. Jael was ugly, and though his teeth were broken *he* was most avowedly not, and as for pity, it had never troubled him. Still, he let Razgut clutch at his hand. He waved the soldiers off when they tried to drag the creature back, and he ordered his steward to bring food.

"For our guest," he said.

Our fascinating guest.

49

A True Smile

All of Karou's careful hiding of her bruises was undone the moment she rolled up her sleeves and dumped her tool case out on her table. It was a small shock lost in larger shocks, though, and Zuzana said nothing. Karou didn't look at her; she didn't want to see her friend's reaction. She focused on Ziri.

Thiago and Ten put him on her bed—so much for Zuzana and Mik sleeping there tonight—and Ten went for boiled water to wash his wounds. Ziri had not regained consciousness, which was a mercy since Karou had nothing to give him for the pain. Why would she? She wasn't a healer.

But...she supposed she *was*; she could do what an ordinary healer could not—at least, in theory. The same magic used in conjuring flesh could also knit and heal it. It was even possible to repair a dead body and restore its soul to it, though this could only be done immediately after death before any decomposition began, and if the injuries were not too extensive. As soldiers tended not to die at the resurrectionist's door, the gleaning of souls was the practical alternative. Also, Brimstone had said that it was usually easier to conjure a new form than restore a broken one.

He had compared it to mending a slice in knitted wool: the wool skein had been one continuous fiber in the original creation and was now fraught with interruptions, each its own snafu of loose ends and lost stitches. The interruptions could be put right, but it took maniacal craft, and the whole was unlikely to emerge quite as it had been before.

Karou knelt to examine Ziri's injuries. As terrible as the smile looked, she felt sure she could manage. It had been sliced clean by a very sharp blade, and the muscles affected were on the large side, their configuration straightforward. There might be some scarring, but what of that?

Thiago leaned over her shoulder. "Is that... ash?" he asked.

Karou realized that it was. It was ash blackening Ziri's mouth and lips. The inside of his mouth was black, too. "It looks like he *ate* it," she said.

"Or was fed it," replied Thiago darkly.

Fed ash? By *who?* Karou reached for Ziri's hands, gently curling them open. When she saw what had been done to him, a soft sound of anguish escaped her lips. His hands were pierced through, as if he had been crucified. The left one was torn entirely from the center of his palm out through the webbing between his third and fourth finger, as if he had wrenched it free of whatever had pinned it. The imagined pain brought a trembling white noise to her ears. She laid the hands back gently on Ziri's chest.

"So. Can you heal them?" asked Thiago.

Karou heard skepticism in his voice, and didn't blame him for it. Hands were ridiculously complex. She'd had to draw and label them in anatomy classes in art school: all twenty-nine bones, seventeen muscles just in the palm, and... over a hundred ligaments. "I don't know," she admitted.

"If you can't, tell me now."

She went cold. "Why?" she asked, though she knew the answer.

"If he can't use his hands, this body is of no use to him—or to me."

"But it's his natural flesh."

Thiago shook his head, not unsympathetic. "I know. And as rare a thing as that is, do you think he'll thank you for salvaging it if he can't hold his blades?"

Is that all that matters? Karou wondered, and the bleak answer was: *yes.*

She felt the Wolf looking at her, but she kept her eyes on Ziri. Broken, brutalized Ziri. Lovely, long-limbed Ziri, graceful echo of a dead people. What manner of monstrous body would Thiago ask for to replace this perfect one? It wouldn't come to that. She would keep Ziri from the pit. She would. "I'll heal him."

Thiago began, "If it would be faster to make him a new—"

"I can do it," Karou snapped, and the Wolf sat back.

When she turned to face him, he was giving her a considering look. "All right, then. Try. But first I need to question him."

"What? Wake him?" Karou shook her head. "It's better this way—"

"Karou, what do you think happened to him? He's been

tortured, and I need to know by who, and if he gave anything away."

"Oh." She saw the sense in that, and as much as she hated to wake Ziri to his pain, she did, as gently as she could.

It was terrible to see his eyes flutter open and cloud with agony. They sought her face, then flickered to the Wolf and back to her. Again she saw in them the urgency that had been there when he first arrived, and felt sure there was something he wanted to tell her.

Thiago was his best self as he knelt at his soldier's side to question him. "Who did this?" he asked in a soothing tone, but it quickly became evident that Ziri couldn't speak, not with the severed muscles in his cheeks. The Wolf had to settle for yes and no questions, which Ziri answered with nods and head shakes that clearly caused him pain.

"Did you tell them anything?" asked Thiago, who had learned no more than that "they" were seraphim.

Ziri gave a head shake, immediate and resolute.

"Well done. And... the rest of the team?"

Ziri shook his head again. Tears gathered in his lashes, and Karou understood that he meant they were dead. She had already supposed so, but the news still hit her like a punch. Five soldiers, dead. Balieros. Ixander. She remembered the unexpected softness of Ixander's soul and how she'd wished to do better by him than that monstrous body.

"Were you able to glean their souls?" asked the Wolf, and Karou leaned forward, hoping.

Ziri hesitated. His eyes went to her. Despairing. Confused. He neither nodded nor shook his head. What did it mean?

Thiago asked him again, but Ziri's eyes fluttered shut, his lashes releasing tears to track down his ash-smudged face, and he moaned. He was lost in pain, and after a few more attempts, Thiago had to let it go with the reassurance that Ziri had not compromised their position. He stood. "Go ahead," he told Karou, "and luck to you."

She wished she could assert that luck had nothing to do with it, but the truth was she was praying for it herself. She was almost ready to ask Nitid for help. "Thank you," she said, and as he went out, she reached for some vises from her table.

Ziri made an inarticulate sound and she looked to him to find him shaking his head, agitated. She didn't understand at first, but then he hit himself on the chest with his mangled hands and she got it. He wanted her to use his pain.

"Oh, no. No. You'd have to stay conscious to tithe—"

He nodded, hit his chest again, and tried to speak. His face contorted and fresh blood pulsed from the slashes. "Stop," Karou cried, reaching out to restrain his hands. Their fingers curled together and he held hers tight in spite of the agony it must be causing him. He nodded again.

There were tears in Karou's eyes now. "Okay," she said, wiping them away. "Okay."

Ten returned with water and cloths, and Karou set about cleaning Ziri's wounds. She had some antiseptic, and as she dabbed it on she felt Ziri's pain amplify in the air around him, almost like currents of electricity. It was a terrible waste to let it all dissipate while she cleaned his wounds. She needed help. She turned to Ten, but one look at the she-wolf's heavy, ungentle hands and she looked away again. She couldn't entrust Ziri's wounds to her. She looked over her shoulder. Zuzana and Mik were still in the room, standing against the far wall. Zuzana was wide-eyed, pale, and watching her intently. Surely this was not what she had meant when she had petitioned to be Igor, resurrectionist's assistant, but she did have fine small hands and years of training at delicate work.

"Zuze, do you think you can help me? You don't have to if you're not comfortable—"

"What can I do?" She came at once to Karou's side.

Ten tried to assert herself, but Karou waved her off and explained to Zuzana what she needed, and though her friend paled further, she took the clean gauze and water basin and antiseptic and turned to Ziri. "Hi," she said. Aside to Karou: "How do you say *hi* in Chimaera?"

Karou told her, and she repeated it, and Ziri couldn't say it back, but he nodded.

"This is the one you drew," said Zuzana. "From your tribe."

"Yes."

"Okay. Well. Let's get started."

Karou nodded encouragement and watched for a moment to make sure Zuzana would be all right, and then, with a deep breath, she sank into the slash-and-burn landscape of Ziri's pain and began to gather it, and use it.

* * *

She didn't know how long she was within herself, in that strange place where she worked at Brimstone's magic. This wasn't the continuous, meditative, and fluid feel of a conjuring, but a faltering, puzzling piecing-together and picking at loose ends, trying to reconstruct what had once been whole. It seemed to take a very long time; she existed in a curious sense of suspension, like she was underwater and should have to surface to take a breath, but didn't, and when she finally did come up it was like rising from black water. She blinked, breathed. The sun had risen; the shutters were closed but light seeped in around the edges, and though the fortress walls kept out the worst of the heat, the coolness of night had gone; it felt like much of the day had gone with it.

"Karou." It was Zuzana's voice, hushed with reverence. "That was... amazing."

What was? Karou tried to focus her eyes. They were dry, as if she hadn't blinked in hours, which maybe she hadn't. She looked around. Ten was gone. Zuzana was still at her side; Mik was on her other side, his arm around her, and she realized with a slumping weariness that he was pretty much all that was holding her upright. Her exhaustion felt like gravity, inexorable. Her head had never been so heavy.

Finally she looked at Ziri, who had kept conscious for hours as well, feeding her his pain, and she found him looking back. He smiled at her. It was a smile full of exhaustion, sorrow, and other unreadable things, but it was a true smile, and not an ugly message carved in flesh.

She had done it.

She drank in the sight of his face. She had mended him, and almost without a trace of scarring. And his hands? That was the true test. She reached for them, held them and looked, and at first her breath caught because the scarring was ugly, knotted, and she thought she had failed, but then he flexed his fingers and the movements were fluid, and she breathed again. She breathed out a laugh and tried to rise. Dizziness broke over her.

The room fell sideways.

And that was all there was for a while.

50

Like Juliet

Zuzana perched on the edge of Karou's bed. Her friend lay asleep, eyes closed, the skin around them deep blue. Her breathing was steady and deep. At her side lay Ziri, also sleeping, and their breathing had fallen into rhythm. Zuzana had bathed her friend's face with cool water, and her hands and wrists, too, before laying them at her sides. "She needs rest," she said to Mik. "And I need food. Tell me you're not starving."

In response, Mik flipped open his pack and dug something out. "Here," he said.

Zuzana took it. It was—or had been—a bar of chocolate. "It melted on hell hike."

"And then *un*melted. In a new and exciting shape."

Zuzana inhaled deeply in the direction of the window, and fanned air at Mik. "Do you smell that? It's food. Excitingly shaped chocolate can be dessert. We can share it with the chimaera."

Mik's concern-crease appeared. "You don't really want to go down there without Karou."

"I do."

"And share your chocolate."

"Yes."

"Okay. Who are you, and what have you done with the real Zuzana?"

"What do you mean?" she asked, putting on a stiff affect and flat voice. "I am the human called Zuzana, and I am not trying to lure you out to the monsters. Trust me, meaty human—I mean Mik."

Mik laughed. "I'm only not freaked out by that because you haven't been out of my sight since we got here." He took her hand. "Don't go out of my sight, okay?"

She regarded him mildly. "What about the bathroom?"

"Ah. That." They had made a pact never to be one of those couples who use the bathroom in front of each other. "I must maintain my mystique," Mik had told her solemnly, holding her hand in both of his. Now he said, "Well, we should at least have a code word then, to determine whether the other one is an impostor. In case, you know, a monster steals my body in the five minutes I'm peeing."

"You think they can steal bodies? And more importantly, you can pee for five minutes, and yet you wouldn't even pee on Kaz for me?"

"I'll be apologizing for that forever, won't I? But seriously. Code word."

"Fine. How about... *impostor*?"

Mik was expressionless. "Our impostor code word should be *impostor?*"

"Well, it's easy to remember."

"The whole point is to be sly. If I suspect you're not really you, I need to find out without you knowing I know. Like in movies. I'll have my back to you, you know, facing the camera, and I casually say, uh, *haberdasher* in conversation—"

"*Haberdasher?* That's our code word?"

"Yes. And you fail to respond to it and my expression goes all bleak and horrible"—he demonstrated bleak and horrible—"because I've just found out your body has been taken over by hostile forces, but by the time I turn around I'm cool. I pretend to be fooled while I quietly plot my own escape."

"Escape?" She stuck out her lower lip. "You mean you wouldn't try to save me?"

"Are you kidding?" He pulled her against him. "I would stick my head down monster throats looking for you."

"Yes. And hope that they'd conveniently swallowed me without chewing. Like in fairy tales."

"Of course. And I cut them open and out you pop. Though they would be missing out on your amazing flavor if they didn't chew." He nibbled her neck and she squeaked and pushed him off. "Come on then, brave monster-throat-looker-downer, let's go get some dinner. I am almost positive it will not be *us* on the menu." She sniffed the air. "If only because they're already cooking it." When he started to renew his protest, she held up a hand. "What are you more afraid of: them, or me with low blood sugar?"

His stern caution-mouth twisted into a smile. "I'm not sure."

"Bring your violin," she said, and with a shrug, he did. Zuzana laid her hand on Karou's forehead before leaving, and then they were out the door, skipping down the stairs on the trail of food.

* * *

Karou's sleep was haunted and dangerously deep. She lost the thread of her days and nights, or her lives—human and chimaera—and wandered through tableaux of memory like they were rooms in a museum. She dreamed of Brimstone's shop and her childhood there, of Issa and Yasri and Twiga, scorpion-mice and winged toads and . . . Brimstone. And even in her sleep she felt as if her vises were clamping down on her heart.

She dreamed of the battlefield at Bullfinch, the fog, and her first sight of Akiva as he lay dying.

Of the temple of Ellai. Love and pleasure and *hope*, the hugeness of the dream that had filled her in those weeks—she had never in either of her lives been as happy as that—and the delicacy of the wishbone that she and Akiva had held between them, their knuckles resting together in the moment before the snap.

And finally, Karou dreamed herself in a crypt, waking like a revenant—or like Juliet—on a stone slab. All around were bodies burned beyond recognition, and in their midst stood Akiva. His hands were on fire and his eyes were pits. He stared across the piled dead at her and said, "Help me."

She came awake and upright in an instant, and day had again passed to night, and there was a warm presence at her side.

"Akiva," she gasped. It spilled from the dream, this name that carved a piece out of her when she even so much as *thought* it. Spoken aloud it was sharp and cruel, a spike, a *slap*—and not only to herself but Ziri, if he heard. Because it was not Akiva beside her. Of course it wasn't, and what ran through Karou's mind in that instant was bitterness, a double pang: one for when she thought it was him.

And one for when she realized it wasn't.

* * *

Akiva started at the sound of his name, the sound of Karou's voice, the sight of her upright, awake, and so near. He couldn't stop the surge of heat that answered her cry, a flare that must surely have rolled off his wings and touched her across the room. Touched her and . . . the one lying beside her, who didn't move or open his eyes even when she cried out.

Akiva held himself still, glamoured, and Karou didn't so much as look around; her eyes were on the Kirin, and Akiva couldn't guess what had made her call *his* name, but whatever it was, it seemed already forgotten. She stared down at the Kirin and Akiva closed his eyes. He quieted his breathing and reassured himself that she couldn't hear his heartbeat as he moved toward the window.

He wanted to stay. He never wanted to take his eyes off Karou again, but now that she had awakened—he'd just had to know that she *would*—he couldn't stomach spying on her like this. And he wasn't sure he could handle what might come next, when the Kirin woke.

He wouldn't wonder what there was between the two of them. He had no right to wonder.

She was alive, that was what mattered.

That, and…*she* was the resurrectionist. That realization carried a numbness that blotted out nearly everything else.

Nearly.

Seeing her sleeping at another man's side was too big to blot out. It was too like the sight of her friends through her window in Prague, and Akiva was shaken by the same absurd jealousy as he had been then, when for a moment he'd thought it was her. If he had any decency in him he would wish her happiness with one of her own kind, because whatever else was uncertain in these terrible days, one thing was sure: There was no hope that she could still love *him*.

Karou reached for the Kirin's hand and it was more than Akiva could bear. He hurled himself out the window and was gone.

51

The Better to Kill You With

Karou bent to examine Ziri's hands and see more closely the healing that she had worked on them. She felt the disturbance in the air behind her, but Ziri's fingers closed on hers in the moment she would have turned, and the sparks that gusted in the window skittered across the dirt floor and spent themselves unseen.

"You're awake," Karou said. Had he heard what name she called out?

"I'm glad we're alone," Ziri said, and her reaction was to pull her fingers free and shift away from him. *What did he mean?* But he looked stricken by her response and seemed to become aware all at once of the unexpected intimacy of the scene. "No, not..." He broke off, flushed, sat up and back, putting space between them on the bed. His blush made him look very young. He added with haste, "I mean, because I have to tell you what happened. Before he comes back."

He? *Who?* For a breathless instant Akiva's name came again to Karou's mind and she pushed it away in frustration. "Thiago?"

Ziri nodded. "I can't tell him what really happened, Karou. But I need to tell *you*. And I... I need your help."

Karou just looked at him. *What did he mean? What kind of help?* She felt slow, still wrapped in the haunting spell of her dreams, and there was something nagging at her that she couldn't seem to focus on.

Ziri rushed to fill the silence. "I know I don't deserve your help, not with the way I've treated you." He swallowed, peered down at his hands, and flexed his fingers. "I don't deserve *this*. I shouldn't have listened to him." Shame weighed heavily on his expression. He said, "I wanted to speak to you, and I should have. He ordered us not to, but it always felt wrong."

Karou processed this. "You mean... Thiago ordered you not to speak to me? All of you?"

Ziri nodded, tense and miserable.

"What reason did he give?"

With reluctance, he told her, "He said we couldn't trust you. But I do. Karou—"

"He said that?" She felt slapped. She felt stupid. "He told *me* he was working on you all, that you'd come to trust me as he did."

Ziri said nothing, but the message was clear. Thiago had been lying to her all along, and how could it even surprise her? "What else did he say?" she demanded.

Ziri looked helpless. "He reminded us, often, of your... treason." His voice was soft, his posture hunched. "That you sold our secret to the seraphim."

She blinked. "Sold—?" *What?* This did surprise her, the magnitude of this lie. "He said *that?*"

Ziri nodded and Karou reeled. Thiago had been telling the chimaera that she sold secrets to the seraphim? No wonder they hissed *traitor* at her. "I never sold anything," she said, and it occurred to her: She hadn't sold anything, and she hadn't *told* anything, either. She'd been so busy wallowing in her shame these past weeks that she hadn't even questioned whether it was justified. What exactly was her crime? Loving the enemy, that was a grave thing; setting him free, graver still, but they didn't *know* she had done that, and anyway… *she* had not told Akiva the chimaera's deepest secret.

Thiago had.

The White Wolf was blaming her for his own breach, keeping her isolated from the rest of the company, feeding steady lies in both directions. All to control her, and her magic, and it had been working neatly for him, hadn't it? She'd done everything he asked.

Not anymore. Her heart was beating fast. She looked at Ziri. "It's not true," she said, and it came out like a twisted whisper. "I didn't tell… the angel." She couldn't say his name again. "I never told him about resurrection. I swear it." She wanted him to believe her, for someone to know and believe that though she might be a traitor in some measure, she had not done *that*. And then it came to her that *Brimstone* might have thought she had.

She felt sick. If he *had*, he must have forgiven her for it, because he had given her life, safety, and even—though she hadn't realized it until she lost him—love. And it killed her to think he might have believed she had betrayed his secret, his magic, his pain. Even more, it killed her that she would never be able to tell him the truth. Whatever he had thought, he had died thinking it, and the finality of it brought his death home to her in a way that nothing really had so far.

"I believe you," Ziri said.

That was something, but not enough. Karou held her stomach, which, in spite of being empty to concavity—or maybe because of it—was rolling with nausea. Ziri reached out an uncertain hand and drew it back. "I'm sorry," he said, distressed.

She nodded, steadied herself. "Thank you for telling me."

"There's more—"

But then, shocking in its volume: a sound from outside. A shriek, a wail. Karou's heartbeat was midskip when it hit her what it was that had been nagging at her. It was *absence*. Zuzana's and Mik's. *Where were her friends?*

And who had just screamed?

* * *

Out in the court, Zuzana covered her ears and gritted her teeth.

Mik was more diplomatic. He nodded to the chimaera named Virko, who had just drawn an earsplitting *skreeek* from his violin. "That's right," he said. "That's, um, how it makes sound."

Virko was holding the instrument more or less correctly. Though it was dwarfed by the jut of his jaw, his big hands managed the bow all right. One thing Zuzana had noticed was that many of the chimaera had human hands—or human-*ish*—even though the rest of their body might be solidly beast. Judging from the array of swords and axes and daggers and bows and other implements of killing and dismemberment that they carried around, she gathered that manual dexterity was an imperative.

The better to kill you with, my dears.

For all that, though, weapons and claws and such, they weren't that scary. Oh, well, they were scary as hell to look at, but their *manners* weren't menacing. Maybe it was because Zuzana and Mik had crossed paths first with Bast, the one from Karou's floor, who had understood their pantomime of eating and brought them with her to the food, introducing them around with words Zuzana and Mik could not understand.

"Do you want these humans grilled or minced in a pie?" Mik had translated under his breath, but Zuzana could see that he was in awe more than he was scared. The chimaera had seemed more curious than anything else, really. Maybe a bit suspicious, and there were some who turned her blood cold for no better reason than the unblinkingness of their stares; she stayed away from those, but overall it had been fine. Dinner was bland but no worse than what they'd eaten at a tourist trap in Marrakesh on their way here, and they'd learned a few words of Chimaera: *dinner*, *delicious*, *tiny*, the last—she hoped *only* the last—in regard to herself. She was quite the object of fascination, and submitted to pats on the head with unusual good grace.

Now, in the court, it was Mik's violin that was the object of fascination. Virko produced a few more hellish shrieks and a sawing sound before another chimaera shoved him and growled something that must have meant *give it back*, because Virko handed it over and gestured to Mik to play, which he proceeded to do. Zuzana had learned to recognize his signature pieces, and this was the Mendelssohn that always raised the hairs on the back of her neck and made her feel happy and sad, salty and sweet at the same time. It was big and intricate, kind of... *cute* in some places, but epic in others, and wrenching, and Zuzana, standing back and watching, saw the change it worked on the creatures arrayed around her.

First: the startle, the surprise that the same instrument that had produced Virko's *skreeek* could do *this*. There was some exchange of glances, some murmurs, but that fell away quickly and there was only wonder and stillness, music and stars. Some soldiers hunkered down on haunches or settled on walls, but most stayed standing. From doorways and windows others peered and slowly emerged, including the unsoldierly stooped figures of the two kitchen women.

Even the Other White Meat looked transfigured, standing stock-still in all his weirdly repellant beauty, a look of deep and terrible longing on his face. Zuzana wondered if she could have been wrong about him, but dismissed the thought.

Anyone who would wear all white like that clearly had issues. Just looking at him made her wish she had a paintball gun, but hell, you couldn't pack for *every* eventuality.

* * *

Karou shook her head in wonder. Zuzana swaying lightly in the court while Mik played his violin for such an audience; back in Prague she could never have imagined this scene.

"How did they come to be here?" Ziri asked. He had risen, too, and stood behind her looking over her shoulder.

"They found me," Karou said, and the simplicity of it filled her with warmth. They had looked for her, and found her; she wasn't alone, after all. And the music... It rose and swelled, seeming to fill the world. She hadn't heard music in weeks, and felt like some gasping part of her was gulping it and coming back to life. She climbed onto the window ledge, ready to step off and drift down to join her friends in the court, but Ziri stopped her.

"Wait, please."

She looked back.

"I don't know when I'll have another chance to talk to you. Karou, I... I don't know what to do."

"What do you mean?"

"The souls." He was agitated. He turned and paced away from her, stooped to reach for something, and came back up with a thurible. "My team," he said.

"You saved them?" Karou stepped back into the room. "Oh, Ziri. That's wonderful. I thought—"

"I'll have to report to Thiago, and I don't know whether to tell him." He weighed the vessel on his palm.

Karou was confused. "Whether to tell him that you saved your team? Why wouldn't you?"

"Because we disobeyed his order."

Karou didn't know what to say to that. Disobeyed the Wolf? That just didn't happen. After a pause, she asked, "Why?"

Ziri was very grave, very careful. "Do you know what the order was?"

"The... the Hintermost. To defend against the Dominion." She said it, but she didn't believe it.

He shook his head. "It was a counterattack. On seraph civilians."

Karou's hand flew to her mouth. "What?" she asked, her voice paper-thin.

Ziri's jaw worked as he nodded. "It's a terror campaign, Karou." He looked ill. "It's all we can attempt, he says, being so few."

Terror, thought Karou. *Blood. Blood.* How many had died in Eretz on both sides over the last days?

"But we disobeyed him. We went to the Hintermost. It was..." His eyes were out of focus, haunted. "Maybe Thiago was right. There was nothing we could do. There were too many of them. I was safety, and I watched the team die."

"But you got their souls. You gleaned—"

"It was a trap. I walked right into it."

"But...you escaped." She was trying to understand. "You're here."

"Yes. That's what I don't understand." Before she could ask what he meant, he took a deep breath and reached into his bloodied, ash-stained tunic, taking something from an inner pocket. Karou saw a flash of vivid green, but that was all. Whatever it was, it was small and fit neatly into his hand. He said, "They had me, Karou. *Jael* had me. He was going to make me tell him." His eyes, large and brown and bruised with exhaustion, were wide with a strange intensity. "About *you*. And...I would have. I wanted to think I wouldn't break, but I would have." He choked out the words. "Eventually."

"Anyone would." Karou kept her voice even, but a panic was building in her. "Ziri, what happened?"

52

A Summoning of Birds

"Akiva." Liraz's voice, sharp. She'd pointed down and away, down the slope where rock furrows met green, to a small clearing hazed by the smoke of a dead fire, a blot of ash at its center. And angels. "Jael," she'd hissed, then looked to her brothers, grim, as they saw the rest for themselves.

Jael's soldiers had a chimaera surrounded.

From such a distance, all Akiva had known was that it was a Kirin, the first he had seen since Madrigal died, but as soon as the Kirin moved—cutting, killing, like dance—Akiva understood that here was no fleeing freed slave, but a soldier.

Jael had found a rebel. All Akiva's unspent mercy and thwarted purpose came down to this moment. And when the Dominion finally fought the Kirin to the ground, and when Jael stood over him, rolling up his sleeves, Akiva had known that all his hope came down to this moment, too. A resurrectionist. The thurible. Karou. Would Jael find the rebels, or would he?

How had Hazael put it? "Do you suppose there will be many birds out today?"

As it happened, there were. From his high slope perch, Akiva had scanned the deep distance: blood daubs and squalls circled in great numbers, disappointed by the fires that cheated them of flesh. Of course, Hazael hadn't meant literal birds.

But even Hazael didn't know what Akiva was capable of.

* * *

It began as a sound, Ziri told Karou. Gathering and building, a tremulous, encircling murmur growing to a roar. At first he had thought it was something of the angels' making, but it distracted them, too. His captors looked around, alarmed. They were holding him down, two to a side. He was on his back in the ash, his arms wrenched wide, hands…secured. Jael had him pinned, each hand speared through by a sword from a soldier he had killed.

Every kick jarred the blades, and the pain only began in his hands but didn't end there. It got in his head; it possessed him. It was everything, and in the small moments between kicks, when he could keep still and let it abate, the fear came back—the fear of what he would do and say to make it stop.

He had told them nothing yet, but they were far from through with him. Jael knelt over him with a helm full of ashes. "This was a friend of yours just a few hours ago," he said. "Open wide."

"No!"

They clawed his mouth open with their fingers. Ziri felt the hot steel of the helm against his lip, and tasted ash as it began to spill. He fought, he struggled, but in it fell and filled his throat and he was choking on his own dead, drowning in death. His struggling gasps sucked it into his lungs and he was burning from within, all ash and no air, and time spun interminable. Bright lights in pinpoints and the seraphim blurred: their leering faces, Jael's sucking hole of a mouth flecked with spittle from his exertions. The pain closed in, the burning and the gasping, the hot awful closing-in airless *dying*…

Dying.

And then water.

It choked him, too, but it cleared the ash and then he was coughing it all out and breathing water and ash but also *air*, and not dying.

"Is this helping your memory any?" Jael asked. "I can do this all day."

The physical misery was overwhelming. Ziri saw how it could take over, how pain could become puppet master and make you do things. Tell things.

No.

The helm came again. He tensed, fought. Clenched his teeth, and they couldn't pry his mouth open.

That was when they cut his smile.

The helm was again to his lips when…the sound. The angels stopped, the helm fell aside as they spun in confusion. They drew their weapons, and the hum grew to an overwhelming, all-encompassing drone and kept growing. It became more than sound. It became *shade*.

The sky took on a life of its own. Chaotic and every-colored. Shifting. *Loud.* Pressing in.

It was a phenomenon.

It was . . . a distraction.

"Birds," Ziri told Karou, shaking his head in wonder. "Blood daubs first and then others. Every kind. I don't know how many thousands. The sky filled with birds, Karou, *filled with birds*, and they were on us."

"They attacked?" Karou was leaning forward, her eyes wide.

Ziri shook his head. "They just came. Around us. Between us. Driving the angels back."

She cocked her head in that way she had, and it made Ziri want to reach out and lay his hand—his newly healed hand—full against the long, fair column of her neck—or, he thought, flushing as he recalled the feel of her body's warmth against his when they had lain side by side, to just draw her to him and tuck her against him and hold her. He looked away again, stared hard and unblinking at the wall.

His hand pulsed as if the small thing he held were still alive; it wasn't. It was his own blood thrumming in his veins . . . because *he* was alive. He didn't understand it, and he didn't know what to say next, so he held out his hand and opened it.

Karou saw the tiny feathered corpse. She just looked at it, blank, not making the connection, and Ziri doubted for the hundredth time that this blue-haired human girl was truly Madrigal. Surely she couldn't forget *this*.

And then her eyes flew wide and her gaze lifted to his, startled.

It was a hummingbird-moth. Its furred wings were soft gray and crushed; its body was brilliant viridian with a band of scarlet at the throat. When the birds had descended—birds of every kind, birds of the day and the night, shadowlarks, evangelines, bat-winged crows and blood daubs, songbirds, raptors, even stormhunters, their wings still flecked with snow—Ziri had seized the opportunity to escape. It had meant tearing one hand free. The swords that held him were driven too deep into the earth to shift, so he had set his teeth and...pulled. The blade had been blessedly sharp. His hand came away in a scream of agony, red pulsing filling Ziri's vision, chaos and adrenaline drowning out some of it, maybe, and somehow he had used that mangled hand to free the other.

The seraphim tried to grab him. He couldn't hold blades, so he lowered his head and used his horns, caught one soldier in the side, but his horns weren't sharp enough to pierce mail and the soldier only fell and Ziri had to drop a knee, crushing his throat. Another he swept off his feet with a long low kick, and he was looking for Jael, intent on doing what he had said he would and killing the Captain of the Dominion, but he couldn't find him. The gleaning staff still stood in the earth, so he grasped it in his mangled hands as the thickness of birds became a maelstrom and he could scarcely see his enemies through the fury of feathers. Or they him.

In the rushing of wings, he chose flight.

He didn't stop then to consider how or why this thing had happened, and certainly not *who*—it didn't occur to him that there *was* a who until he got well away, clear and unpursued, far, far, and fell against a tree to breathe. The hummingbird-moth was dead when he discovered it. It was entangled in his mail, a small victim of the chaos, and—it seemed to him at once—a sign.

Hesitating, he told Karou, "I can't say for certain that… *he*…did this—"

"*He?*" Karou was wary. "I don't know who you mean."

Ziri looked at her long and searching. In no single detail did she resemble Madrigal. The shape of her face was different; her eyes were black, not brown. Her mouth was less wide, her hair was blue, she had no horns, she was human. With the memory of Madrigal bright in his mind—and the night of the Warlord's birthday that had been the beginning of the end—Karou seemed unconnected to it all, and he could almost believe her denial. He asked himself, did she really need to know? It wasn't as if he *wanted* to talk about the angel. Her lover. Maybe it was enough that he had shown her the bird. Let her think what she wanted. As he had said, he didn't know for certain.

But…he believed there was only one possible explanation for his being alive, and he couldn't keep silent. "I never saw him," he said, and Karou didn't ask who he meant. She was silent, still wary, guarded. "Maybe I'm wrong," Ziri said, "but I don't know what else to think. I've never heard of a summoning of birds but that one night, at the Warlord's ball. The…the shawl."

Her eyes widened in surprise. "How did you know about that?"

Ziri's face grew hot. He looked down and admitted, "I was watching you."

Eighteen years ago at the Warlord's ball, Ziri had been a boy in a crowd, and he had watched Madrigal dance with a stranger and wished it were him, wished he were grown, wished, wished, uselessly wished. Of course he hadn't guessed that the stranger was a seraph, but he had seen what no one else there had: that he was the same man in different masks, and she danced with him again and again. There had been something melting and supple about her movements that hinted at adult mysteries—as opposed to the brittle way she held herself with Thiago—and when the drifting hummingbird-moths fanned down from the constellations of lantern light to settle on her bare shoulders, Ziri had seen that, too, and understood that it was magic, and that the stranger had done it. The man had lifted Madrigal up, cloaked in her living shawl, and brought her back down again, and even a boy could see that there was magic between them, and more than magic.

Ziri had been a watchful child, and had seen many things he was too young to understand. He'd had to watch Madrigal die, and he hadn't understood the fervor—the ecstasy—of the crowd. He hadn't understood why the only one who mourned her was the enemy, driven to his knees and bloody from torture. Ziri would never forget Akiva's screams—absolute despair, rage, helplessness. It remained the worst thing he had ever heard.

He had seen Thiago that day, too, a chill white presence on the palace balcony, motionless and unmoved.

Ziri had begun to hate someone on that day, and it wasn't Akiva.

"I don't know why, Karou," he said. "But I think the angel saved my life."

53

Heroes

"We should have killed him when we had the chance," Liraz said under her breath as she and Hazael walked in step through the Dominion camp.

"We *didn't* have the chance," Hazael reminded her. "There were too many damn birds in the way."

"Yes, well, I hoped he'd been suffocated or pecked to death or something," she replied.

She was talking about Jael, who they were headed to see. For reasons yet mysterious, their charming uncle had asked to see them. "Couldn't Akiva have *made* the birds kill him?"

Hazael shrugged. "Who knows what our brother can do. I don't think he quite knows himself. And I don't think he'd ever tried anything that big before. It cost him."

It had. The effort of the summoning had left Akiva gasping and shaking, his eyes tight shut so that Hazael and Liraz had not seen until it was done how blood vessels had burst and turned them red.

"For the life of one chimaera," said Liraz.

"For the life of one, yes, and the hope of more," said Hazael.

"The hope of *her*," said Liraz, not without bitterness. How could she not hate this phantom of a girl who was neither alive nor dead, human nor chimaera—what the hell *was* she, anyway? It was just so very far outside of everything, so deeply abnormal, and... Liraz knew that at the root of it was jealousy, and she hated that. Akiva was hers.

Oh, not in that way. He was her brother. But Hazael and Akiva were her people, her *only* people. They had hundreds of other brothers and sisters, but this was different. It had always been the three of them, and though she had come close to losing them in battle more than once, until recently she'd never had to worry about losing them in this way. Misbegotten didn't love and marry. It was forbidden. And... it would be worse, she thought, because it would be their choice. They wouldn't die, or be taken from her. They would go freely to make their life around another person and leave her behind.

She had said she didn't feel fear, but it was a lie; this was her fear: being left alone. Because of one thing she was certain, and it was that she could never love, not like that. Trust a stranger with her flesh? The closeness, the quiet. She couldn't imagine it. Breathing someone else's breath as they breathed yours, touching someone, opening for them? The vulnerability of it made her flush. It would mean submission, letting down her guard, and she wouldn't. Ever. Just the thought made her feel small and weak as a child—and Liraz did not like to feel small and weak. Her memories of childhood were not kind.

Only Hazael and Akiva had gotten her through it. She'd thought that she would do anything for them, but it had never occurred to her that "anything" might mean letting them go.

"I wonder if he's found them," she said now to Hazael. The rebels, she meant. She spoke low; they were nearing Jael's pavilion. "We should have gone with him."

"We have our part to play here," he said, and Liraz only nodded. She hadn't wanted to let Akiva go off alone again, but how could she stop him? The worst thing of all would be making him hate her. So they'd watched him struggle to glamour himself invisible—he had been so weary after the summoning—and follow the Kirin into the bird-torn sky, while she and Hazael had returned to the camp. To play their part, as they had before, and cover for him.

Never before, though, had they been summoned before the Captain of the Dominion to tell their lies and half-truths.

"Ready?" asked Hazael.

Liraz nodded and went first through the flap. The same flap Loriel had come through, was it just the day before? Liraz felt the brief contact of her brother's fingertips at the small of her back and carried the connection with her as she faced Jael.

Loriel said she was fine. She said it was nothing—just a man, and men wash off.

She was older than most of the female soldiers, more worldly. She had volunteered—to spare some virgin being thrown to Jael, she said—and though Liraz had not been in danger, being Jael's own blood, she thought it was an act of courage unlike any she had ever witnessed. Braver than taking the vanguard or doubling back for wounded comrades. Braver than facing a host of revenants. Liraz had done those other things, but she knew she could never have walked into this tent and out of it again, not like that.

"My lord," she said now, with the appropriate deep bow. Drawing even with her, Hazael did the same.

"Niece, nephew," he drawled. It was mockery, but Liraz was glad of it. *And don't forget it*, she thought. She lifted her head and looked at him.

And really did not like what she saw on his face. It was aimed at her, cutting Hazael out, and it was... interest. Unmistakable and unsettling. "What is your name?" he asked her.

"My sister is Liraz," Hazael spoke up. "And I am Hazael."

But Jael repeated only, "Liraz." He said it wetly, followed it with a heavy sigh. "Misbegotten. What a pity. You're a fresher fruit than some others who've come my way. But my brother does have a way of... inserting himself."

Hazael laughed. "I get it," he said, and succeeded this time in drawing Jael's eyes from her. "Inserting himself. That's funny."

Stop, Liraz willed him, but Jael only smiled. Hazael's laughter sounded genuine. He had a gift for laughter.

Now that Jael troubled to look at Hazael, he saw what everyone did when the pair of them stood side by side, and looked back and forth between brother and sister. "Twins?" he asked. "No? The same mother, at least."

But Hazael shook his head. "No, sir, only our father's blood shining through."

Liraz was stunned enough to turn her head and stare. To

name Joram "father," to Jael? She knew what he was doing, trying to keep the focus on himself. *Stop it*, she willed him again, but Jael didn't take offense. Maybe because of the foolish good humor of Hazael's manner, and maybe because his thoughts were elsewhere.

"Indeed," said the captain. "Though that's not the case with the Prince of Bastards, is it? I would say his Stelian taint rose to the top."

Taint? It was true that Akiva looked nothing like Joram; more than that, Liraz couldn't say. She didn't remember her own mother, let alone Akiva's. *What did Jael want?*

"I'm told that Akiva is not in camp. Is that right?"

"Yes, sir," they said in unison.

"And I'm told that if anyone knows where he is, it's you two."

"He's still out hunting, sir," said Hazael. "For the rebels."

Not even a lie, thought Liraz.

"Admirable. Our stalwart Beast's Bane never rests. But you came back without him?"

"I was hungry, sir," said Hazael, contrite.

"Well, I suppose we can't all be heroes."

His disdain snapped something in Liraz. "And did you catch any rebels?" she asked, with none of Hazael's comic contrition. "Sir."

His eyes swiveled back to her. A beat, and he answered firmly, "No."

Liar, she thought, recalling the sight of him brutalizing the Kirin. He'd enjoyed himself. Feeding him the ashes of his comrades? It made her sick. Funny, how easy it had been to root for the enemy when the enemy was up against Jael. Well, the form and nature of the enemy had surely helped. Had he been Heth or Akko or some snarling, beast-aspect revenant, it would have been harder to take his side, Jael or not. But the Kirin, it had been thrilling watching him fight—Liraz had even thought for a moment that he might prevail and escape. He was so quick. She hadn't seen a Kirin since she was a green soldier on her first forays and she had forgotten what they were like. So when Akiva had told them, in a quiet, choked voice, that Madrigal had been Kirin, too, the last of Liraz's revulsion had loosened and evaporated.

In spite of the rebel's creature elements, there had been a lean and elegant grace to him that was not animal. Not at all. She hadn't wanted him to die.

The same couldn't be said of Jael. No elegance, no grace. She would have been glad to see him choked with ash. How badly, she wondered, had he hurt that soldier? And how many others had he delighted in torturing in just that way? "No?" she heard herself say, goading him. "Maybe they really are ghosts."

Oh, fool. Jael's look of lazy interest sharpened and sparked. "They are animals," he replied simply, in an offhand manner as if he couldn't care less. He took another step toward her. "You know, you remind me of someone." He was studying her face, her body. "Not in particulars. She was dark, not fair, but you have the same... fire... that she had."

Had. Liraz forced her eyes to the floor. *Don't push him, don't test him, he is* Jael. *Do you really think bastard blood will constrain him if you anger him?*

"Can we relay a message to Akiva for you?" asked Hazael, trying again to draw their uncle's attention away. "He should be back in a day or two."

"No." Jael stepped back. "No message. I'm returning to Astrae. But no doubt we'll meet again."

* * *

"I can't believe you went downstairs without me," Karou said, exasperated.

"What?" Zuzana was impenitent. "I was starving and our hostess was passed out on the bed with a hot monster boy."

Hot monster boy? "God. That makes it sound..." Karou threw up her hands and shook her head. It was silly to be so retroactively anxious about something that hadn't happened, but when she thought of what Zuzana and Mik had walked right into, it made her cold. When she had finally gone down to the court she'd found Zuzana sitting between, of all possible chimaera, Tangris and Bashees, having much the same sort of pointing-and-charades "conversation" one has anywhere while traveling and meeting people who don't speak your language. Only... these weren't "people."

"You don't understand." Karou hadn't wanted to freak her friends out before, but they were obviously not freaked out *enough*. "Do you know what they're called? They're the Shadows That Live, Zuze. They're assassins."

"Like me," said Zuzana cheerfully.

Karou thought maybe she should hold her head so it didn't come apart. "No, *not* like you. Not pretend assassins. *Real* assassins. They slit angels' throats in their sleep."

"Yikes." Zuzana grimaced and grabbed her throat. "But the angels are the bad guys, right?"

Karou really didn't know how to respond to that. None of it was real to Zuzana. "They're just really creepy, okay?" she said, hearing how lame she sounded, then hesitated. How could she be sure of anything, in light of the fact that she'd been living in a theater of Thiago's lies? "*Aren't* they?"

Zuzana shrugged. "I don't know. They were cool."

Cool. The Shadows That Live were *cool.* "And I suppose Thiago is a peach, too."

"Eww," said Zuzana with a shudder. "*No.* Nonpeach. Wormy peach."

Well, at least they agreed about that.

"You should get some sleep," Karou said.

Mik was already stretched out on the bed, barely conscious, and Zuzana's energy looked to finally be winding down. "I know." She yawned. "I will. What about you?"

"I slept already," Karou said. *With Ziri.* How strange. And now they were allies with a shared secret. Thiago didn't suspect. They'd heard him coming and had time to pretend sleep before he walked in—in a less intimate arrangement than before, with Karou on the chair beside the bed. They had already decided that Ziri *would* tell the general about the gleaned souls, and that Karou would somehow manage the resurrections in private so that she could give Balicros and the others their cover story when they woke. If all went well, Thiago never needed to know that they had disobeyed orders. She wasn't sure what she'd do with the extra soul Ziri warned her she might find: the Dashnag boy who'd fought and died with them. Stasis, she guessed.

Of course, this was all only the beginning of the problem.

The large and looming issue was: What *now*? This terror campaign. Karou had believed—as far as she had peered out of her misery to really think about it—that the objective of the rebellion was the protection of chimaera. Thiago was protecting no one. Maybe it was true that he lacked the numbers to do any more than that, which he would say was her fault, but...had he given up on everything else?

"That can't have been enough rest," said Zuzana. "You can sleep here. I'll scooch over."

Karou shook her head. "Be comfortable. I wouldn't be able to sleep anyway." There was too much spinning in her mind. What to do? *What to do?* "I think I'm going to go for a walk while it's still cool. In the morning it's back to work." Zuzana's face brightened, and Karou said, "Yes, Igor. You can help. And thanks for earlier. You were awesome."

"*Me? You* were awesome. Holy. Karou. You're my hero."

"Yeah? Well, you're mine, so we're even."

Mik, contrary to appearances, was not quite asleep. He rallied to say, "I want to be someone's hero, too."

"Oh, you are," Zuzana assured him, throwing herself on top of him. She kissed him with a smack. "My fairy-tale hero, one task down and two to go." Karou didn't know what that was about, but she backed away as Zuzana continued to plant noisy assurances all over his face.

54

Recognition

Karou expected Ten to be waiting outside the door and follow her, but the she-wolf must have assumed she would stay in with her friends tonight; she was nowhere to be seen.

With a thrill at the unexpected freedom, Karou wove her way quietly toward the kasbah's back gate, through the narrow lanes of the ruined village, hearing the scurry of rats at her passing. Several times she had to go airborne and drift over obstacles and collapsed walls, but was careful to keep below the roofline and out of sight of the sentry tower. She had a moment to herself and she was not going to risk it.

Once or twice she got the feeling that she was followed and looked back, but saw no wolfish slink in the shadows. She did catch a glimpse of white and for an instant feared it was Thiago himself, but it was only some of his clothing, laundered and draped on a roof to dry. She breathed. The White Wolf was the last person she wanted to see right now.

Well, maybe not the very last. That position was reserved for Akiva, but there she was safe. Akiva was far away in the Hintermost, apparently, and what the hell was he up to? Had he really saved Ziri? The evidence was flimsy.

One dead hummingbird-moth.

Deep memories stirred: the feel of the living shawl that Akiva had gifted her that night at the Warlord's ball, the fanning of those soft, furred wings, and then the tickle as the creatures began to eat the glittering sugar that dusted her chest, neck, and shoulders. She still felt shame for the sugar, all these years later—that it had been meant for Thiago, and she had let herself be dusted with it, not quite admitting to herself that she was ready to surrender to him, to let him . . . taste her. She shuddered to imagine that fanged mouth on her flesh.

Instead it had been hummingbird-moths that tasted her, and later . . . an angel.

How strange and cruel life was. If there had come a whisper in her ear that long-ago morning that by nightfall she would be in the arms of the enemy—and *want to be there*—she would have laughed at it. But when it came to pass it had felt as natural and right as the steps in a dance that she had always known.

She wondered now: What if Akiva had never come to Loramendi, with his beautiful, startling talk—*love is an element*—his soft touch and sweet magic, his heat and humor and his firelight eyes, if she had never have known any suitor but the Wolf?

Had she been such a pliant thing that she would have let herself be taken by him, tasted and claimed? She wished she could believe that she would have awakened to her foolishness even without Akiva's coming, but her shame would not subside. She *might* have cringed at Thiago's touch and shaken herself awake, but . . . she knew that she would most likely have let the tide carry her along until it was too late.

Well. Her people would still be alive if she had. What was her own happiness compared to that?

She reached the river and slipped down to the bouldered place on its bank where she could sit hidden from view from the kasbah. She kicked off her shoes, put her feet on the cold-splashed stones, and watched the reflection of the stars pull into long, dancing streaks on the moving surface of the water. The scope of that glittering sky had a way of making her feel so small—minuscule, insignificant—and she realized she was relishing that feeling as a way of relieving herself of the pressure to *do something*.

After all, what can I *do?*

Really: What? The chimaera were loyal to Thiago, and Thiago would never compromise.

What, Karou wondered, *would Brimstone do?*

Her longing for him in this moment was so profound that it made her slip into hope—that malingering, wretched hope that he was not truly gone. She let herself imagine, just for a moment: *If Brimstone were here, what would be different?*

One thing, at least. *I would be loved.*

"Karou."

It was only a whisper, but she jumped at the sound of her name. *Who—?* She saw no one, she had heard no approach. Only . . .

A draft of heat.

A drift of sparks.

Oh god. No.

And then like a dropped veil, his glamour vanished and he was before her.

Akiva.

Light coursed through Karou and darkness chased it—burning through her, chilling her, shimmer and shadow, ice and fire, blood and starlight, rushing, roaring, filling her. Shock and disbelief. And rancor.

And rage.

And she was on her feet. Her fists were clenched, her fists were stones, so tightly clenched, her whole body was taut with rage at the sight of the angel, every sinew stretched and her skin drawn tight so she felt the blood in her temples, pounding, and the fury in her fists, pulsing, and in her closed palms: the *scald*. Her hamsas burned and she was opening her hands and lifting them and Akiva did not defend himself.

When the magic of the marks hit him, he lowered his head and endured it.

Magic poured off Karou, and Akiva shook under the onslaught but didn't move—not away, not toward—and Karou knew that she could kill him. She'd wished she'd done it before and here he was to give her another chance. Why else would he be here—why else?—and what else could she do but kill him?—there *was* nothing else—after what he had done—after what he had done—after what he had done—but . . . how could she kill *Akiva*?

How could she not?

Hadn't he done enough without forcing yet another impossible choice on her? Why was he here?

He dropped to his knees, and the air between them rippled with Karou's crippling magic and with memory. The day of her death, this is what she had seen, *this*: Akiva on his knees, sick with the weight of this same magic coursing off Thiago's soldiers, and he had struggled to hold his head up and look at her—*just like this*—with horror and despair and *love*—and she had wanted more than she had ever wanted anything to go to him and hold him, whisper to him that she loved him and was going to save him, but she couldn't, not then, and she couldn't now, not because of shackles or pinions or the executioner's ax but because he was the enemy. He had proven it beyond any horror she would ever have believed, beyond any betrayal she could ever have dreamed, and he could never be forgiven, not ever.

But... then... her hands fell to her sides.

Why? She hadn't meant to drop them. Her hamsas were hot against her own thighs and her breath was ragged and coming in gasps and she couldn't make herself raise her hands back up. Akiva was shaking and racked with magic, and the pair of them were again in the eye of a storm of misery—their *world* was a storm of misery and they were caught in its center, in the deceptive stillness that had allowed them to forget, once upon a time, that all around them was a stinging whirl of hatred that *would* catch them—it was everywhere and everything and they'd been fools to think they could leave their small safe place and not be caught in that vortex like every other living creature in Eretz.

But they had learned, hadn't they?

Karou's gasps were in danger of becoming sobs, and her legs

were trembling. She wanted to drop to her knees, too, but she couldn't. It would be as good as extending a hand to him. She stood over him. Her palms were still hot with magic, but she kept them at her sides.

"I thought you were dead." Akiva's voice was choked. "And... I wanted... to die, too."

"Why didn't you?" Karou's face was hot and wet and she was ashamed of her tears and ashamed that she still hadn't been able to kill him. What was wrong with her, that even now she couldn't avenge her people?

Akiva lifted himself up off his hands, pushed back upright. He looked wrung out, pale and shaken and sick, the whites of his eyes red as they had been long ago. "It would have been too easy," he said. "I don't deserve peace."

"And I don't, either? Don't I deserve to finally be free of you?"

At first he said nothing, and Karou's words echoed in the silence. They were so ugly—edged in mockery to cover her anguish; she hated the sound of herself. When he did answer, his anguish was undisguised. "You do deserve it. I didn't come here to torment you—"

"Then why *did* you come?" she cried.

Even before Akiva rose to his feet, Karou felt as if she were fighting against something, but when he did stand, unsteadily, and she had to take a step away and tip back her head to look up at him, she knew what it was. The shape of him—the breadth and contours of his chest, the sharp line of his widow's peak that her fingers had traced so many times, and his eyes—above all his eyes, his eyes. Confronted with his realness, his nearness, Karou understood that what she was fighting was familiarity—familiarity of a magnitude that was a profound kind of recognition.

This was Akiva, and the recognition had been there even when he was a stranger, that day at Bullfinch when she had first laid eyes on him. It was why she had done such an astonishing thing as save the enemy's life. It had been there in the dance in Loramendi, even when he wore a mask, and it had been there again in the lane in Marrakesh, when he was, for all intents and purposes, a stranger again.

Except that he wasn't.

Akiva had never been a stranger, and that was the problem. A kind of call echoed between them, even now, and from the hollow of Karou's heart where there should have been only enmity and bitterness, came a slow pull of... longing. Rage rushed in and swamped it. *Foul heart!* She wanted to rip it out.

How could she still not hate him?

* * *

And when their eyes met, this was what Akiva saw: not the longing but a sudden flare of violence and loathing. He failed to recognize it as *self*-loathing, and he was lost. He looked sharply away, realizing only now—*fool*—that he had still had hope. Of what? Not that Karou would be glad to see him—he wasn't that big a fool—but maybe for a flash, a hint that something remained in her besides hate.

But that hope vanished and left him empty, and when he found his voice to answer her question, he *sounded* empty. Scraped and dry.

"I came to find the new resurrectionist. I didn't know that it was . . . you."

"Surprised?" she asked. The loathing was as thick in her voice as in her look, and could he blame her for it?

Surprised? "Yes," he said, though that wasn't the word for what he was. He was gutted. "You could say that."

She cocked her head in that birdlike way she had, and Akiva's heart was raw. She saw, and understood. She said, "You wonder why I never told you."

He shook his head, dismissing it, but there it was. She had never told him. In the requiem grove for that month that was the only real happiness of Akiva's life, in all their talk of peace and hope, all their love and discovery and their plans, so grand—to invent *a new way of living*—Madrigal had never spoken of resurrection. It was the White Wolf who had spilled the chimaera's great secret, gloating in the prison of Loramendi between lashes of the whip.

Akiva had kept nothing from her. He had wanted her to know him, truly and fully, from the terrible tally his inked knuckles boasted to the misery of his earliest memories, and love him for who he was, and all these years he'd believed she had. So what did it mean that she had kept such a secret? She may even have come straight from the work of resurrection into his arms and never breathed a word of it.

"I'll tell you why," said Karou. Her words were precise, a knife sliding between his ribs. "I never trusted you."

He nodded; he couldn't look at her. What had been emptiness filled with nausea, as powerful as if revenants were arrayed around him with their hamsas upheld.

"So are you going to kill me?" she asked. "That's why you came, isn't it? To kill another resurrectionist?"

Akiva's head snapped up. "What? No. Karou. *No.* Never." How could she even ask that? "There's no reason for you to believe it," he said, "but I'm done killing chimaera."

"You told me that once before."

"It was true then," he said. "And it's true now." After Bullfinch he *had* stopped killing chimaera.

And after her death, he had started again.

He couldn't stop himself from turning his hands, trying to hide the evidence tattooed on them. He wanted to tell her that everything he had done he had done because he was broken, because watching her die had destroyed him, but there was no way to say it that didn't sound like he was trying to pin the blame outside himself. There was no way to talk about what he had done, nothing to plead, and no mitigation. Even thinking about it, he came up again and again against the sheer magnitude of his guilt, and there were no words. Confession and apology were worse than inadequate—they were an affront; explanation was impossible. But he had to say something.

I lost my soul. "I lost our dream. Vengeance eclipsed everything. I barely remember the weeks and months after..." *After I watched you die, and part of me died, too.* "I can't account for what I've done, let alone atone for it. I would bring them all back if I could. I would die a death for every single chimaera. I would do anything. I *will* do anything, and everything, and I know...I know it will never be enough—"

"No, it won't. Not ever, because they're *gone*—"

"I know. I'm not looking for forgiveness. But there are still lives to be saved, and choices. Karou, the future will have chimaera in it or not, depending on what we do now."

"We?" Karou was incredulous. "What *we*?"

"*I*," he hastened to clarify. He knew that no "we" would ever again stretch to encompass the two of them. "And in the seraph ranks there may be others who are tired, and who want life, not death."

"They *have* life. Unlike my people."

Akiva had been thinking of Brimstone's last words—"It is *life* that expands to fill worlds"—but of course Karou couldn't know that. He wanted to tell her what Brimstone had said. He thought she would want to know, but coming from him, wouldn't it seem like a taunt? "It's not a life worth living," he said. "Not one worth handing on to children."

"*Children*," said Karou, and she was so bleak—and so beautiful. Akiva couldn't help himself—he looked at her and looked at her, and he ached, looking, knowing he would never again touch her or see her smile. "When both sides start butchering children," she said, "I think it's safe to say life has *lost*."

What did she mean? She saw his confusion. "Oh. You don't know yet?" Grim. "You will."

It hit him. Thiago. "What has he done?"

"Nothing *you* haven't."

"I've never killed a child."

"You've killed *thousands* of children, Beast's Bane," she hissed. He flinched to hear her speak the name, and he couldn't argue.

He hadn't done it with his own swords, but he'd opened the way for the killers. There were things he had seen that he would never unsee. Images swelled in him like screams—strobe memories, flashing, ugly, ugly, unforgivable. Akiva closed his eyes. This was what he was to her: a killer of children, a monster. She was working side by side with the White Wolf, and it was *Akiva* who was the monster. How had the world gotten so twisted around?

If Thiago had not found them out and come to the requiem grove that night, what might they have gone on to do?

Maybe nothing. Maybe they would have died some other way and accomplished nothing.

It didn't matter. The dream had been pure. Even in his despair, Akiva knew it, *felt* it, but he knew Karou couldn't. He took a step back from her, ventured to look at her again. She had her arms wrapped around herself, and her face was desolation. She was broken, as he had been all these years. And... *he* had broken her.

"I'll go," he said. "I didn't come to cause you pain, and please believe I didn't come to kill. I came because... I thought you were dead. Karou, I thought..."

His hand went to the thurible. What would it mean to her, he wondered, this vessel and its message: *Karou*. If it wasn't her soul, whose was it? His first thought on finding it had been that the name was a label, but it was clear to him now that it was an inscription.

"I found this in the Kirin caves," he said, and held it out. "It must have been left there for you to find." She looked startled by the sight of a thurible in his hands. He held it out; she hesitated, unwilling to come any nearer to him. "This is why I wanted to die," he said, and he turned the small square of paper so that she could read it. "Because I thought it was *you*."

* * *

Karou snatched the vessel from him and stared at the writing. She wasn't breathing.

Karou.

How many times, back in Prague, had she gotten notes just like this? Then, they would have been pierced through by Kishmish's claws and somewhat the worse for wear, but the paper was the same, and the writing...she would know it anywhere.

It was Brimstone's.

She stared at it until a gust of sparks pulled her out of her shock, and she knew that Akiva had gone. She didn't have to look around. She felt his absence, the way she always had—as cold rushing in to fill the void he left behind. Her heart was hammering, she held the vessel to her chest and imagined she could feel the soul within vibrating against her heartbeat. That was pure fancy; there could be no hint through the silver of what—*who*—was inside. But it *had* to be....

It had to be.

Her hands shook. All it would take was twisting the vessel open. An impression of the soul would filter out and she would know at once.

She held it ready. Hesitated. What if it wasn't?

Her thoughts were scattershot; they came and cascaded away, but one came and came again. *Akiva had brought her the thurible.* Thiago—her ally—lied to keep her isolated and alone.

Akiva—her enemy—brought her the thurible that might . . . that might . . . that might contain . . . *Brimstone.*

Did it?

A twist of the wrist and Karou opened the vessel. Half a second. The soul skimmed against her senses.

And she knew.

55

The Emperor's Prowess

A bare foot, highly arched. A slender ankle festooned in golden bangles.

Nevo didn't mean to see, but the music of the bangles drew his attention at the moment the girl stepped through the door and he glimpsed this secret sight before he could jerk his chin down and pin his gaze to the ground.

The concubine of the night, leaving the harem to be escorted across the skybridge to the emperor's inner sanctum. She was veiled and cloaked as the women always were, in a hooded robe that concealed even her wings, and she would scarcely have registered as a person at all but for that glimpse of foot. It was the most Nevo had ever seen of one of Joram's concubines, and he was caught off guard by its effect on him.

Instantly he wanted to help her.

Help her what? Escape? That was rich. It was his duty to ensure that she didn't. He was part of the Silversword escort standing ready to deliver her across the bridge. They were six, a virtual parade. It was ludicrous: six guards to walk a girl across a bridge.

A *girl*—not a woman? Nevo couldn't have said why he thought so—it was hardly the foot—but he guessed that she was young. And then, she hesitated.

When the harem doors clanged shut behind her, she stood frozen in place.

Nevo sensed frantic energy beneath all that gauzy cloth. He could see her veil stirred by too-quick breathing, and her cloak by courses of shivers, not from cold, but terror. It had to be her first time making this walk.

The thought pierced him.

Several times a week he drew parade duty, as they called it, and he had learned that you could infer a lot from the manner of a woman's bearing, even beneath so much concealment. Slow, steady steps, short quick frantic steps; head held high or darting left and right, peering through the screen of her veil at the world outside her prison. He had seen—or guessed at—weariness and resignation, pride, dejection, but he had never seen a girl freeze before, and he tensed, thinking she was going to bolt.

The skybridge was a slender span of glass, the city far below, and sometimes the women chose to leap rather than be delivered across it. Under those cloaks their wings were pinioned, and to fall was to die—or try to die. A guard would leap after her. If he caught her, she was punished; if he didn't, *he* was.

It had happened before, though not in his own time here. Nevo was only twenty; he had had his silver sword only two years, and been promoted to the emperor's personal detail just two months ago. He didn't know what to do in a situation like this.

Not a one of his fellow guards moved or spoke. They waited, and so he waited, too, unaccountably nervous. And when the girl began, finally, to propel herself so-slowly forward, trembling, Nevo came to understand something. He had thought the six-guard parade a ridiculous display: Lest anyone fail to take note of the emperor's prowess, or to count the women who were his and the bastards he sired, here were six guards standing each over eight feet tall in their extravagant helmet plumes to draw all eyes to the spectacle.

But maybe there was more to it than that. Because in this moment, if Nevo alone were this girl's escort, he couldn't swear that he would do his duty. As powerful as his loyalty to the emperor was, there were stronger impulses, like the urge to protect the helpless.

Fool, Nevo, he chastened himself with an inward snarl. Some said Joram's magi could read thoughts, and he hoped it wasn't true, because in the space of seconds he had allowed such ridiculous visions to flit through his head—saving this girl, taking her somewhere safe. Godstars, there was even a lean-to dwelling in the picture, a garden behind it, and a great overarching sky with no spires as far as the eye could see, no Tower of Conquest, no Astrae, no Empire. Just a small, safe place, and himself hero to an unknown, faceless girl.

All because of a glimpse of foot?

Pathetic. Maybe his bunkmates were right, that Nevo needed some "tending to" in the soldiers' comfort house. He told himself he would go, resolved on it as he marched, his boot heels too slow on the glass walk. The escort was grouped in two triads with the girl between, so that Nevo walked right behind her, adjusting his steps to match her mincing pace. She looked so small—they always did, framed by the giants of the guard. He could hear her uneven breathing—the high, fluting gasps of near-hysteria—and feel the waves of heat rolling off her cloaked wings.

Her perfume was so delicate it might almost have been her natural scent.

He wondered what color her hair was, and her eyes.

Stop it. You'll never know.

The march was short over that span of glass, Astrac opening beneath them and closing again when they came to the other end. The girl was delivered. A steward met her at Alef Gate and she went in and was gone without a glance at her escort.

Absurdly, that stung. As if she should have taken note of him, somehow understood that he felt sorry for her?

Nevo knew that in his Imperial Guard uniform he was as anonymous to her as she should have been to him, and the thought made him restless and angry. He had lost himself to a uniform—this shining silver costume of a uniform with its bouffant plumage and its overlong bell sleeves that would interfere with a clean draw, if ever he were called on to draw his sword, which he never was, except in the training arena, and even that was more dancing lesson than fighting. The Silverswords were not what he had thought when he was selected from the ranks of the common army to join them. He'd been chosen for his height, not even for his swordsmanship, which he had once been proud to know was exceptional. But the recruiter hadn't seen him fight. He had been interested only in his look, the upshot of which was that in all his finery Nevo was indistinguishable from any other Silversword in Astrae. Maybe his own mother could pick him out, but certainly the emperor's terrified concubine wouldn't recognize him if she saw him again, two times or two hundred.

And why should he care if she did?

He didn't care.

Alef Gate closed, and the concubine's perfume was too frail to linger on the air. She was gone to her duty, and Nevo would go to his and think no more about her.

As it happened, his post was here at Alef Gate. With another of his triad, he relieved the standing guard and took their places. The other guards of the parade went on to their own posts, most of them farther inside the great glass tower than Nevo had ever been. The emperor's private quarters had been described to him as a kind of castle-within-a-castle, occupying the deep inner core of the Tower of Conquest. Alef Gate was the outermost entrance; inside it, corridors branched labyrinthine, so that there was no direct conduit to successive gates—Beit, Gimel, Dalet, and on through the alphabet. Nevo had been only as far as Beit, but the other guards said that it tested the memory to find one's way within. It was all clouded glass, so much glass, thick and rich with a sheen like honey, and strong. In training they were invited to test it with their swords, and strong as Nevo was, he'd been unable to breach the walls even with his booted foot, even with the hilt of his sword. The corridors curved, layer upon layer of that glossy unbreakable glass, and were riddled with false doors and dead ends, all of it designed to confuse and trap invaders or assassins.

Good luck to them, thought Nevo. Ten guarded gates stood between himself and the emperor; no one was getting through there. Tonight he himself was glad to be as far from the center as possible. Guards on Samekh Gate sometimes heard... weeping.

Weeping.

The women at the comfort house might not *weep*, but Nevo knew he would not be going there, and as he stood at his post through the long, dull night, it felt as if his true work and challenge—other than standing still for long stretches of time—was in keeping himself from wondering what was happening within. It was ridiculous, how that merest of glimpses had made this girl real in a way that all the women and girls of the past two months had not been. Well, they *had* been, certainly, but he had managed to overlook it. Would that he could now.

He indulged in a different folly to distract himself. It was equally futile but less likely to drive him mad, and it was: wishing that he had never been plucked from the army to join the Silverswords.

It was not a rational wish. The guards' pension was better—it went to his family—and the chances of survival *much* better than in the army, but unlike most Silverswords, Nevo had been a soldier first and knew the difference, and the difference was profound.

Out beyond Astrae, across this land and the next, soldiers had kept the beasts at bay for centuries, fighting and dying and finally winning. There was honor in that, even glory, though

Nevo would have given up the glory for simple honor—to feel right in his days and nights, to *do* something. . . .

Of course, it was more complicated now. The Chimaera War was over and a new one was brewing, but it was hard to feel the simple righteousness there had always been when fighting beasts.

The Stelians were seraphim. Beyond that, he knew next to nothing about them; no one did. The Far Isles were, quite literally, on the far side of the globe, trading suns and moons with the Empire in turn, never sharing day or night or anything else; if they had wronged the Empire in some way, it had not been felt by ordinary folk, who bore no animosity toward their distant, mysterious cousins. Nevo's gauge was his own family, and he could well imagine the talk there would be when it got out that Joram had declared war.

"On *who?*" his father would demand, looking dumbstruck. "On a people whose king he doesn't even know the name of?"

"If there *is* a king." His mother. "I've heard they have a *queen.*"

"Oh, have you now. And that the air elementals are her spies?"

"Indeed. And she can kill with a look, and cooks up storms in a great pot to send out over the seas." She would be smirking. His mother had a laughing smirk and a love of nonsense, and his father had a booming laugh, but a dark furrow of worry, too.

"What a fight to pick," Nevo imagined him fretting. "It's like pelting stones into a cave and waiting to see what comes barreling out."

And Nevo *was* waiting to see. Envoys had been dispatched with Joram's declaration two weeks ago and hadn't returned or been heard of. What did it mean? Perhaps they'd gotten lost searching for the Far Isles and hadn't delivered the scroll at all. Saved from war by poor navigation?

Wishful thinking.

He stifled a yawn. It was finally morning, or nearly. His relief would be here soon—

Alef Gate crashed open.

Nevo leapt airborne. Chaos poured out. Noise and wings and sparks and rushing and shouting and . . . what was the protocol? He protected the gate from *without*. What did he do when chaos burst from *within*? No one had ever said, and who was this? Stewards and servants, and a handful of Silverswords, too.

"What's happened?" Nevo barked, but no one heard him over the roaring coming from within.

The bellowing, the fury.

Joram.

The girl, thought Nevo. And while stewards and servants stumbled over each other trying to escape the path of the emperor's rage, he pushed inside. Beit Gate was abandoned; where was Resheph? Had he been one of those to flee? *Flee?* Unbelievable.

Nevo rushed through the door and was deeper in the inner sanctum than he had ever been. He didn't know the way, but Joram's rage was like a river he traced upstream. When he took a wrong turn, he doubled back and found the right way. Minutes were lost to the glass labyrinth. The emperor's voice came and went now. The howling gave way to words, though Nevo couldn't make them out.

Gimel Gate, Dalat, Hei, Vav, all unguarded; the Silverswords had either rushed out or in, leaving their posts. Nevo's first thought was to be appalled by the lack of discipline, but then he realized that he, too, had left his post, and he began to be afraid. It was the only time he wavered; he could still go back—maybe in the madness his breach would be overlooked.

Later, it would be some consolation to know that it wouldn't have mattered. By now, nothing he said or did could matter. All was done and decided long before he burst at a flying run into the emperor's bedchamber.

Plashing fountains, orchids, the chatter and squawk of caged birds. The ceiling seemed leagues overhead—all glittering glass spangled by constellations of lights that gave the illusion of the night sky. In the middle of it all, the bed was raised on a dais, like some monument to virility. It was empty.

Joram stood in the center of the room with his hands on his hips. He was powerful, thickened by age but toughened, too, and marked with old battle scars. His jaw was square, his face red with rage and hard with scorn. He wore a robe; it showed a triangle of chest, and seemed somehow vulgar.

A handful of other guards were here, standing around looking—Nevo thought—stupid and large. Eliav was one of them. The Captain of the Silverswords had himself been on Samekh Gate, and would have been the first on the scene—save Namais and Misorias, of course, Joram's personal bodyguards, who slept by turns in the antechamber. They stood just paces from their master, their faces seeming chiseled from wood. Byon, the head steward, was leaning heavily on his cane, his palsy much more pronounced than usual.

"You didn't place it there?" Joram demanded of the old seraph.

"No, my lord. I would have woken you at once, of course. For something like this—"

"A basket of fruit?" Joram was incredulous, and then—"A *basket of fruit!*"—his fury returned and flashed through the chamber as heat and light.

Nevo took a step back. He scanned for the girl. He hadn't been thinking clearly, or thinking *at all*; it hadn't even occurred to him until this moment that he would see her unveiled, and certainly not that she, like Joram's chest, might be... exposed. As soon as he caught sight of her—peripherally, a blur of flesh on the far side of the dais—he realized this was the case, and his instinct was not to look, not to turn toward her, but only to back out to the door and be away from here.

"Explain to me how it came to be here." Joram's fury turned to ice. "Through so many guarded doors to arrive at the foot of my bed."

It was her stillness that made Nevo turn his head.

She *was* young; he had been right. And she was exposed. Naked. There was a girlish fullness to her face, but her breasts were full, too, nothing girlish there. Her hair was red and wild, and her eyes were brown. She was slumped against the wall, making no effort to cover herself, staring at him—at *him*—without expression.

Without motion.

Almost as soon as Nevo settled his eyes on her, she tipped slowly sideways. He watched it happen, remembering how slowly she had walked across the skybridge. *This was like that,* his mind tried telling him, just like that. But then: the rubbery jounce and splay of limbs as she subsided to the floor, the tinkle of her bangles settling, and stillness. The fire of her wings dimmed. Died. On the wall behind her was a streak of blood which, traced upward by the eye, led to a red stain on the glass.

Her head had done that.

She had been thrown.

Nevo was hot and cold and sick. He thought of the Shadows That Live—his instinct was to blame beasts, and he knew the fabled assassins were at large again, somehow still alive—but this wasn't what they did. The Shadows slit throats.

And, of course, he knew who had done it. His eyes roved wild over the lavish room as snatches of conversation penetrated his dismay. He knew *who*, but not *why*.

"Every guard who was on duty," he heard Joram say.

Eliav, in horror: "My lord! *Every—?*"

"Yes, Captain. *Every. Guard.* Did you think, after a lapse like this, that you might live?"

"My lord, there was no lapse. Your doors never opened, I swear it. It was some sorcery—"

"Namais?" Joram said. "Misorias?"

"Sir?"

Joram said, "See it done before the city wakes," and the guards replied, "Of course."

The emperor kicked out at something—a basket—and it tipped and sent pink orbs spinning, and one struck the bed dais and burst with a sound such as the girl's skull may have made on the wall. Nevo looked at her again. He couldn't help himself. The sight of her there, dead, and no one else seeming even to notice, made the whole scene feel like a vivid hallucination. It wasn't, of course. It was all happening, and he understood with a kind of seeping clarity that he was going to hang.

But not *why*.

Only that it had something to do with a basket of fruit.

56

A Surprise

Shaken awake, Zuzana sat up and didn't know where she was. It was dark; the air was thick and the smells were pungent—earth and sharp animal scents with an undertone of decay. A touch, gentle on her shoulder, and Karou's voice. "Wake up," she was saying softly. Zuzana became aware of her aching muscles and remembered everything.

Oh, right. Monster castle.

She blinked her friend into focus in the dim candlelight. "Hell time is it?" she muttered. Her mouth was so dry it felt like the desert itself had curled up and spent the night in there. Karou put a bottle of water into her hands.

"It's early," she said. "Not yet dawn."

"Early's stupid," groaned Zuzana. At her side, Mik still slept. She took a swig of the water and swished it around. Better. She blinked in the dim and focused on Karou. She felt a small jolt, and her sluggishness slid away. "You're crying," she said.

Karou's eyes were wet; there was an unblinking brightness to them, and a hard set to her jaw. Zuzana tried to interpret the look but failed. She couldn't tell if her friend was happy or sad, only that she was *intent*. "I'm fine," Karou said. "But I need your help again."

"Yeah, okay." Zuzana hoped it wouldn't entail cleaning hideous wounds. "What with?"

"A resurrection. I have to finish before Thiago or Ten come up." Karou smiled, but again it was impossible to interpret, neither happy nor sad, but steely. "I want it to be a surprise."

57

A Basket of Fruit

"A basket of fruit," repeated Akiva, incredulous.

When Joram had declared war on the Stelians, he must have prepared for many scenarios, but Akiva doubted it had ever entered the emperor's mind that his chosen foe might... *turn him down.*

He was back in Cape Armasin with his regiment, where the news had traveled on the tongues of scouts and soldiers and in small scroll missives tied to the legs of squalls; it came in scraps and whispers, lies and truth and guesses mixed with official dispatches that were just as full of lies as the gossip was, and it was a few days before Akiva, Hazael, and Liraz had enough pieces to make a puzzle.

It had not been Joram's envoys, it seemed, who delivered the Stelian response. Indeed, the envoys had not returned at all, on top of which communication with advance troops staging in Caliphis had been severed, and a reconnaissance mission had likewise fallen off the map. Every seraph sent in the direction of the Far Isles had vanished. That news alone chilled Akiva, and also stirred his fascination. What was happening over the edge of the world?

And then . . . a basket of fruit.

Such was their reply. Truly, it was nothing more sinister than that. It wasn't a basket of envoys' heads or entrails; the fruit wasn't even poisoned. It was just fruit, of some tropical variety unknown in the Empire. The emperor's tasters had declared it "sweet."

There was a note. Of its message, reports differed, but the report Akiva believed came from a nephew to an imperial steward, and it was this, in archaic Seraphic, in a feminine hand, and stamped with a wax seal depicting a scarab beetle: *Thank you, but we must respectfully decline your overture, being more enjoyably occupied at present.*

The nerve of it, the staggering gall. It took Akiva's breath away.

"I still don't understand," Liraz said, after the initial shock wore off. "How does this explain the Breakblades?"

"Breakblades" was what Misbegotten called Silverswords, after their elegant weapons that would never withstand a blow in real combat—not that they ever saw any. The only indisputable fact of the entire mystery was this: Two days past, Astrae had awakened to the sight of fourteen Silverswords swinging from the Westway gibbet.

"Well," said Hazael, "that would be the *manner of delivery* of the basket of fruit. You see, when our father woke in the morning, it was simply sitting at the foot of his bed, and no one could tell him how it had gotten there. Through ten guarded gates, into the heart of the inner sanctum where he believed himself safe from all comers, even the Shadows That Live."

"Even the Shadows That Live could not have done this," said Akiva, and he tried to fathom what magic could account for it. Invisibility alone was no help against closed doors. Had the Stelian emissary passed through walls? Beguiled each guard in turn? Simply wished the gift there? That was a thought. Just what were the Stelians capable of? Sometimes, when he was deep inside himself working a manipulation, Akiva imagined skeins of connection tracing across the great dark surfaces of oceans and coming at length to islands—islands green in honeyed light, morning air ashimmer with evaporating mist and the wings of iridescent birds, and he wondered: Did his blood make him Stelian? Joram's blood didn't make him his; why should his mother's make him hers?

"Fourteen Breakblades swinging on the Westway." Hazael let out a low whistle. "Imagine the sight, all that silver blinding in the sun."

"Can the gibbet hold fourteen Breakblades, giants that they are?" Liraz wondered.

"Maybe it will collapse under their weight, and good riddance," said Akiva—meaning the gibbet, not the guards. He had no love of Breakblades, but he couldn't wish them dead. He shook his head. "Can the emperor believe he's safer now?"

"If he does he's a fool," said Hazael. "The message is clear. Please enjoy this lovely fruit while contemplating all the ways we might kill you in your sleep."

Grim as it all was—as bleak the picture of the gibbet bowed

by the weight of fourteen guards—the most upsetting news came as an afterthought, and from a Misbegotten. Indeed only a Misbegotten would have taken note of it, or cared.

Melliel was the older half sister who had spoken up on behalf of the Misbegotten at the end of the war. She was thick, scarred, and inked; she fought with an ax and kept her gray hair hacked short as a man's. There was nothing feminine about Melliel except her voice, which even in barked greeting had a ring of music to it. She had sometimes sung at campfires on campaign, and her song-stories had been transporting as few things ever were in a battle camp. She was posted in the capital, or had been until the day before. Now she was with a detachment of Misbegotten going west, into the mists and mysteries of the vanished troops. As if the Empire hadn't lost enough soldiers in the final battles of the war. All of its armies had bled, but none more than the Misbegotten.

"Of course he would send Misbegotten," Liraz had hissed, hearing their mission. "Who cares if bastards come back?"

Melliel, though, said she was glad to go—glad to be free of the spider's web that was Astrae. It was she who told them what else had happened at the Tower of Conquest while the Breakblades swung.

"A shrouded body was...released...through Tav Gate that same morning." Tav was the last of the Tower's gates. It was the gutter door, belowground and egress-only; it was where waste was flushed out to sea.

Akiva steeled himself. "Who?"

Melliel's jaw worked. "There's no way to know for certain, but...apparently no one thought to dismiss the harem escort.

They waited two hours at Alef before a steward noticed and sent them away."

Akiva felt the news in his gut first and his fists an instant later—a hot surge that made them clench so tight his forearms burned. From Liraz came a choked noise; Hazael's breathing grew hoarse and he turned abruptly to pace away trailing sparks. Turned and paced back. His fair face was red. Liraz was shaking, her fists clenched as tight as Akiva's.

The harem escort was the procession of Silverswords that marched the concubines to and from the emperor's bed. "Parade duty," they called it. Akiva's mother had made that walk years ago, who knew how many times—on one return with himself beginning in her belly. Liraz's and Hazael's mothers, too, and Melliel's, and untold other girls and women. And the morning of the hangings, it would seem, the concubine who should have emerged from Alef had been sent out Tav instead, along with the night's refuse.

"Terrible what happened to her," Akiva heard in his head—the cruel, goading voice of his father the first time he had ever deigned to speak to him. Had his mother's body been sent out Tav Gate, too?

A wave of weariness took him. How could life be so unrelentingly ugly? The war was over, but both sides were still slaughtering civilians; the emperor casually killed concubines in his bedchamber and sent his bastards into the unknown to die drumming up more war. There was nothing good in the world, nothing at all. And now that even his memories of happiness were corrupted, Akiva found himself in freefall.

Had she meant it? Had she truly never trusted him? He

wanted to deny it; he *remembered.* He remembered those days—those nights—more clearly than any others in his life, and how she had curled into him in sleep, and how, when she woke to the sight of him, her brown eyes had come alive with light. Even on the scaffold, and again in Marrakesh, after the wishbone was snapped but before she understood...

Before she knew what he had done.

Maybe he had seen only what he wanted to see. It didn't matter now, anyway. There was no more light in her eyes, not for him and, worse: not at all.

In the morning, when Melliel departed with her troops, Akiva stood on the rampart with Liraz and Hazael and saw them off. A part of him wished he were going, too, mists and mysteries and vanished troops and all, to see the Far Isles, and maybe meet the one who had written such a mad message to the emperor.

But his place was here, on this side of the world. His challenge was here, and his penance: to do what he had told Karou he would, which was anything and everything.

What was anything? What was everything?

He knew, but it seemed to loom before him as huge and insurmountable as the mountains of the south.

Rebellion.

With Madrigal, in the temple, everything had seemed possible. Was it? Would he find any sympathy in the ranks? There was a restiveness there, he knew, and a quiet desperation. He thought of Noam at the aqueduct, asking wildly when it would all end. There would be more like him, but there were those, too, who would claim women and children in their tally and laugh as the ink dried. That would always be true; there would always be both kinds of soldiers. How was he to find the good, recruit them, trust them to secrecy while he went about the slow and scraping work of building a rebellion?

Melliel's troops were just a shimmer on the horizon now. The rocky swell of the cape headland blocked the view of the sea from here, but its clean scent was in the air, and the sky was great and endless. Finally, their Misbegotten brethren vanished into it.

"What now?" asked Liraz, turning to him.

He didn't know what she meant. Liraz. He still didn't know what to make of his sister. She had gone along with the bird summoning warily, and freeing the Kirin, but she had seemed more narrow-eyed and watchful than ever since his return from the rebel camp. With the news that the chimaera had taken to returning the civilian attacks, he feared that she would argue for giving up their location to their superiors.

There was a restless energy in her, her wings kicking off sparks as she paced. "How does one begin?" she asked. Stopped, fixed him with a stare, and held up her hands. Her black hands. "You said one has only to begin. So how do we?"

Begin? *Mercy breeds mercy*, Akiva had told her. He hardly knew what to say. "Do you mean . . . ?"

"Harmony with the beasts?" she supplied. "I don't know. I know that I'm through taking orders from men like Jael and Joram. I know that every night a girl must cross the skybridge knowing that no one will help her. Those are *our mothers*." Her voice was raw. "We're swords, they tell us, and swords have no mother or father, but I did have one once, and I can't even remember her name. I don't want to be this anymore." Again, she lifted her hands. "I've done things—" Her voice cracked.

Hazael drew her against him. "We all have, Lir."

She shook her head. Her eyes were wide and bright. No tears, not Liraz. "Not like me. You couldn't. You're good. Both of you, you're better than me. You were helping them, weren't you? While I was... while I..." She trailed off.

Akiva took her hands in his, covered up the black marks so she didn't have to look at them. He remembered what Madrigal had told him, years ago, with her hand on his heart and his on hers. "War is all we've been taught, Lir," he told his sister now. "But we don't have to be that anymore. We'll still be us, just—"

"A better us?"

He nodded.

"How?" Her restlessness overcame her. She shook him off to pace again. "I need to do something. Now."

Hazael spoke. "We start to gather others. That's our first step. I know who to start with." Yes, Akiva realized. He would.

"It's too slow," Liraz said fiercely.

And Akiva agreed. The idea of *steps*—of a careful progression of plans and recruitment and scheming and subterfuge—it was far too slow.

"Liraz is right. How many more would die while we whisper secrets?"

"What, then?" asked Hazael.

In the deep distance, the sky was cleaved by a line of stormhunters on the move. The massive birds were drawn by some inner compass to knots of gathering wind, to deluge and turmoil and churned seas, hail and shipwreck and knives of lightning;

no one knew why, but right now, Akiva felt the same pull in himself—toward the center of his own brewing storm.

"It was always going to be the first step," he said. "It's just coming eighteen years late." He'd known what he had to do then, and he knew it now. As long as Joram remained in power, their world would know war and nothing but war. Hazael and Liraz were furrow-browed, waiting.

Akiva said, "I'm going to kill our father."

58

Honey and Venom

The body lay on the floor. It was a near-perfect likeness to the one Karou mourned, and when she came out of her trance and saw it there, she gave a little sob and had to fight the urge to drop to her knees and bury her face in the crook of its neck. But *it* was just that: an *it*, still a shell, no soul yet animating it to return her embrace. She got a hold of herself, pulled the vises off her arms and hands quickly—too quickly. The sun was up, and Ten was sure to come sniffing around any minute. Karou hadn't wanted to lose time unscrewing the clamps, and in one or two places they snagged her flesh coming off.

"Ack! Halt!" cried Zuzana. "Stop abusing yourself!"

Karou ignored her fluttering hands and said, "Hurry. Light the incense."

"I think someone's coming," said Mik from the doorway.

Karou nodded. "Boards," she said, and he closed the door and secured it. They hadn't replaced the crossbar—it would have made too much noise to hammer those great iron nails back into the wall. Instead, Mik had come up with the idea of gouging a pair of grooves into the dirt floor, into which he now settled planks, propping them at an angle to the door, wedged under handle and hinges. Karou hoped it would hold.

Light pad of footsteps, soft scrape of claws on the stairs.

The incense was lit. Zuzana handed it to her, and Karou's hand shook setting it on the brow of the body. Smoke made a fluting trail upward before dispersing on a puff of Karou's breath. The scent of sulfur; this had given Brimstone his name. Karou wondered what it had been before he became the resurrectionist, when he was a thrall in the pain pits of the magi.

The door shuddered lightly as Ten tried pushing it open and met with unexpected resistance. An instant of startled silence, and then a fist thudded on the wood. "Karou?"

She looked up sharply. It wasn't Ten. It was Thiago. *Damn.*

"Yes?" she called.

"I've just come up to see if you need anything. How is the door blocked?"

How indeed, thought Karou, who had never had the opportunity to ask after her crossbar. He thought he had taken care of her irritating need for privacy? Well, there is more than one way to skin a cat. Or a wolf. She said only, "Just a second."

A further pause, Karou fumbling with the thurible—she winced when the chain rattled, afraid he would somehow guess what she was doing—and then his fist came down on the door again. "Karou?"

"*Juuust* a minute," she sang, her voice covering the scrape of the thurible twisting open.

She dropped to her knees beside the body. Watched, waited.

The soul effused from the vessel, overwhelming her with its presence. It was fireflies in a garden. It was eyes shining from shadows. It was flicker and fork, honey and venom, slit pupils and smooth, sun-warmed enamel.

It was Issa.

Karou was conscious of the beats of her own heart, one, two, three; distinct, almost painful pulses. Four, five, and the serpent-woman opened her new eyes and blinked.

Karou held in a sob; time hung still, the sob expanded within her. Thiago hit the door harder. "Let me in," he said, his voice cloaked in calm that didn't manage to hide its spiking anger. Karou didn't answer. She held Issa's gaze.

What has she been through? How did she die? What does she know? What will she say?

Down the length of the new body, flesh that had been inert came slowly alive. The subtle contraction of muscles, twitch of fingers, the beat of a heart. Issa's chest rose with the intake of her first breath. Her lips parted, and her first exhalation—her very first—carried the words *Sweet girl.*

Karou's sob escaped and her face found the place it wanted, against Issa's neck where human flesh transitioned to cobra hood—the odd mix of warm and cool that Karou had known since she was a child and Issa had held her on one hip, rocked her to sleep, played with her, taught her to speak and sing, loved her and been half a mother to her. Yasri had been the other half; between them the two chimaera women had raised her. Twiga had never taken much of a role, and Brimstone...

Brimstone. The instant Karou had touched Issa's soul back

at the river she had known her, and had felt the queerest split decision of emotions: elation and defeat, love and disappointment, joy and savage despair. Neither side had overtipped the other. Even now the emotions were a balanced scale. Issa was not Brimstone, but... Issa was *Issa*, and Karou held her and felt her arms, shaky and uncertain and new, climb up and wrap around her in return.

"You found me," Issa whispered, and from her queer balance of happy and sad, the words tipped Karou into confusion. Because she hadn't found her.

Akiva had.

But there was no time to think about that now. Karou sat up and back, in the process giving the serpent-woman a clear view of her surroundings. When she saw Mik and Zuzana, her eyes went wide. She smiled, and, oh, her face was so lovely—it was not the face that Karou had known and loved, but it was similar in its quiet Madonna beauty, its flawless skin and sweetness—and her delight was so instant and pure. She knew Zuzana the same way Zuzana knew her: from Karou's sketchbooks; Mik had not been in the picture yet when the portals burned. Zuze gave a dopey smile and half wave, and Issa let out a rusty little laugh.

Softly, Karou said, "Issa, I have a lot to tell you, as I hope you have a lot to tell me, but that's Thiago—" She gestured to the door just as it juddered from a low kick.

Issa's eyes clouded at the mention of the Wolf. "He lives," she said.

"Yeah. And he's going to be very surprised to see you." *Hello, understatement.* It was imperative that Thiago not find out how

Issa came to be here; Karou said as much, and helped Issa to a semisitting position. Then she motioned to Mik to take hold of one of the wood planks while she took the other.

"*Karou,*" said Thiago, and his false calm had all rubbed off. "Open this door. Please."

Karou nodded to Mik, and they wordlessly pulled away the boards and stood back so that Thiago's next kick blasted it open, startling him—and Ten behind him—with its gunshot report.

"Good morning?" said Karou, making it a query as she looked with puzzled innocence at the blasted-open door. "Sorry. I was finishing a resurrection. I didn't want to be interrupted halfway." She looked to Ten. "You know how I am about that."

Thiago's brow furrowed. "A resurrection? Who?" He cast a glance into the room and saw only Zuzana and Mik. The open door concealed Issa, but Karou shoved it back, and when Thiago saw who was there, his eyes widened, then narrowed. Ten's, too, before she turned a look of fierce suspicion on Karou.

Before either could speak, Karou said, in a tone of mild reproach, "You never told me Issa's soul was in there." She gestured to the pile of thuribles. "Do you know how much faster the resurrections would have been going if I'd had her helping me all along instead of Ten?"

She had the satisfaction of seeing the White Wolf speechless. He opened his mouth to reply and nothing came out. "It isn't," he said finally. "It couldn't be."

"It is," said Karou. "As you see."

There was, of course, no possible way that Issa's soul could have been in that stash of thuribles, and they both knew it.

Those were all soldiers who had been under Thiago's command and died at the battle of Cape Armasin; Issa would never, could never have been among them. Yet here she was, and Karou watched Thiago's expression flash from astonishment to confusion to frustration as he tried to come up with a way to account for it.

He settled on disbelief. "Whose soul is it really, and why have you wasted resources on such a body?"

It was Issa herself who answered him. "Such a body?" she asked, looking down at herself. "Since when have Naja been a waste of resources?" It was a fair question; Issa herself was not a warrior, but plenty of her kind were, like Nisk and Lisseth.

Thiago's reply was curt. "Since we developed the pressing need *to fly*, and Naja have no wings."

"And where are *your* wings?" Issa shot back. She turned to look Ten up and down. "And yours?"

More fair questions. Thiago didn't answer her. "Who are you?" he demanded.

"I assure you, Thiago, it is as Karou says." Unsteadily she took possession of her body, raising herself to rear up slowly on her serpent coil, which was banded muscle as thick around as a woman's hips. Already, the tip of her tail twitched in the way Karou remembered. The marvel of creation struck her as it hadn't in many weeks; she had gotten so worn down that she'd lost her amazement—for resurrection, for magic, for *herself*. She had remade Issa. She had done this.

Issa told Thiago, "I am Issa of the Naja, and for eighty-four years I served at Brimstone's side. In that time how many bodies did he craft for you? The dauntless Wolf. No less than fifteen, surely. And you never once said thank you." Her beautiful smile made it sound not like a scold, but almost a fond remembrance.

"Thank him? For what? He did his job, and I did mine."

"Indeed, and you asked no thanks, either. Or adulation."

There was no sarcasm in Issa's voice. Her tone was as sweet as her smile, but anyone who knew Thiago at all would understand that she mocked him. Adulation was wine to the White Wolf; more: It was water and air. Whenever he would return to Loramendi from a successful campaign—the very hour of return, the *moment*—his gonfalon would unfurl from the palace facade. Trumpets would blast and he would stride out to the cheering of the city. Runners would have come before him to make the people ready. They didn't resent it; for all that the cheers were arranged, they were real, and Thiago had reveled in them.

There was a tightness around his mouth now. "All right then, Issa of the Naja, tell me. How did your soul come to be here?"

Issa didn't hem and haw, or shoot any furtive glances Karou's way. She said, with perfect honesty, "My lord general, I do not know. I don't even know where 'here' is." Only then did she turn to Karou, eyebrows raised in question.

"We're in the human world," Karou told her, and Issa's eyebrows climbed a little higher.

"Well, that's strange news. I'm sure you have much to tell me."

And you me, thought Karou. *I hope*. Now, if she could just get rid of the Wolf. *And* his spy.

"Where did she come from?" Thiago asked in a tone that cut straight to the lie. "Where did she come from *really*?"

He stared at Karou, and she didn't flinch. "I told you," she said, and pointed to the mountain of thuribles.

"That's not possible."

"And yet, here she is."

He just stared at her, as if he could drill the truth from her with his eyes. Karou stared boldly back. *You tell your lies*, she thought. *I'll tell mine.* "And the best part," she said, "is that I won't need Ten's help anymore. I have Issa now. And I have my friends." She gestured to Zuzana and Mik, who were watching everything from the deep well of the window.

"Well then, this is a happy day," Thiago replied, his tone conveying anything but happiness.

Karou had known, of course, that he would be displeased—that she had blocked the door, performed a resurrection of her own choosing, introduced a mystery in the person of Issa, and was clearly lying to his face—but still, the look of malice he turned on her struck her as out of all proportion.

Malice. Glittering, poisonous malevolence.

Okay, *now* Karou flinched. She hadn't seen that look in his eyes since... since she was Madrigal, and remember how *that* had turned out. "It *is* a happy day," she said, feeling herself backpedaling. Not that she had forgotten that look, but seeing it again, she remembered the heat of the black rock under her cheek, the parting of the air as the blade fell. Issa reached for her hand, and she gripped it tight, so grateful for her presence. "I really will work much faster now," she said. "Isn't that what matters?"

That, and the fact that it was Akiva who brought the thurible, that he was here, *right under your nose.*

"As you say," Thiago said, and Karou was sure she did not imagine, as he swept her room with a glance, that his head lifted in just the way it had when he had caught her scent across the court. The flare of his nostrils was subtle but unmistakable, and his eyes were narrowed with suspicion.

He would get nothing but incense here, she told herself. Nothing but the sting of brimstone.

At least, so she very much hoped.

"I'm sure I don't have to remind you what's at stake," he told her, and she shook her head no, but as he turned to go, she wondered what he meant. The fate of their people? The success of the rebellion? She had defied him; she couldn't help thinking he meant something more personal than that.

What was at stake? She felt balanced on a precipice and buffeted by gales. What *wasn't* at stake?

And then, in her doorway, the Wolf shared a look with Ten that was so fraught with scheming—with *thwarted* schemes—that Karou had a flash of insight that chilled her and sent her mind racing back over the past days and weeks.

The constant watching, the questions, all the hints and omens. "You could be Kirin again," Ten had told her. "I would resurrect you. You'd just need to show me how."

The suggestion had been repellant: Put her soul in Ten's hands? Even if the pit didn't figure into the plan—and it did—it had felt so wrong. And now Karou understood why.

Ten was meant to replace her. Thiago didn't want to *help* Karou. He wanted to *not need her.*

Karou felt as though she were opening her eyes and seeing the White Wolf clearly for the first time since he'd found her wandering in the ruins of Loramendi.

He still wants to kill me.

Heat was building in her chest and radiating out to her limbs, creeping up her neck as a flush. She wanted to scream. She wanted to get right in his face and scream as loud as she could, but even more than that, she wanted to *laugh.* Did he really think Ten could do this work? It had taken her years to learn it at Brimstone's side, and even with his guidance, it was as much gift as practice. She would never forget her pride in the first "Well done" she'd earned, or the surprise and respect in Brimstone's voice when he had seen, against all his expectation, that she had a sympathy for magic.

Ten could no more conjure a body than Virko could play a concerto on Mik's violin.

Karou understood Thiago's game now; it had failed, and he still needed her. So his game would have to change.

To *what?*

59

Sweet Girl

"Stop looking at her boobs."

"What?" Mik turned to Zuzana, pink spots blooming on his fair cheeks. "I'm not!"

"Well, *I* am," Zuzana declared, regarding Issa. "I can't help myself. They're *perfect*. Nice job, Karou, but couldn't she maybe wear a T-shirt?"

"Seriously?" said Karou. "How many nude models have you drawn?"

"None," said Mik.

"Well, okay. Maybe *you* haven't, but I'm sure you've seen your share of boobs."

"Not really." His eyes drifted again toward Issa. "And, you know, never on a snake goddess."

"She's not a goddess," Karou said fondly—though she did *look* like one. She was still marveling: *Issa is alive. Issa is here.* "She's a Naja, and they don't wear clothes."

"Right," said Zuzana. "They just wear *snakes*."

"Yep."

The first thing Issa had wanted to do, after greeting the chimaera host—which had taken a good part of the morning—was go through the kasbah and summon snakes to her. Karou had followed behind, a little disturbed to realize that the serpents had been there all the time, including one highly venomous Egyptian cobra. Now, back up in her room, they were wreathed around Issa's waist and neck, and one was twining through her hair. While Karou watched, a coil of its body slipped down over her brow to rest on the bridge of her nose. Laughing, Issa lifted it gently back up.

"They tell you anything interesting?" Karou asked her, switching from Czech to Chimaera. She was remembering Avigeth, and how the coral snake had told Issa how the hunter Bain hid his wishes in his beard. If not for that, Karou may never have made it to Eretz.

Issa's laugh evaporated. Her face grew serious. "Yes," she said. "They say it stinks of death since you came here."

Karou felt chastened, like the snakes were tattling on her. "Yes, well," she said. "We've done what we had to do." Right away the "we" felt dirty, and she thought of Thiago telling her, "We are in this together."

They weren't, though. It was clear now that they were in this very, very separately.

She must have sounded defensive. Issa gave her a curious look. "Sweet girl, I have no doubt of that." She paused. Even the snakes paused and ceased their twining. Karou knew they were attuned to Issa's mind and emotions, that their stillness echoed hers, and that the time had come to talk. There had been too much going on earlier, too many chimaera crowding around. There was something about the mystery of Issa's appearance—she was the only known survivor of Loramendi—that buoyed their spirits.

Zuzana and Mik had a buoying effect, too. At breakfast, Karou had watched with amazement as her friend, who did not even share a language with the chimaera, performed a mocking pantomime of Virko's violin playing, complete with shrill sound effects and her own Munch's *Scream* reaction, that drew roars of laughter from the stern-faced revenants, Virko included. Zuzana had managed to form more of a bond with these soldiers in one meal than she herself had in over a month.

Her shame had kept her from trying. She saw that now; she'd believed she deserved their contempt. Did she still believe it? Not all their contempt, anyway—not the part based on Thiago's lies.

Ziri had been in the hall at breakfast, too, and though they hadn't spoken, there had been a powerful connection in their shared look. A secret, and more? Karou had hoped Ziri would be a friend, and it seemed that now he *was*, and she realized she had Akiva to thank for that, too. The angel had saved Ziri's life, and he had brought her Issa's soul.

Why?

Issa was before her now, her snakes still but for the flicker of tongues, her own Madonna face quiet but watchful. Waiting. Waiting for Karou's question?

All morning she'd fought asking it, afraid of what Issa would tell her. Now, though, she had to know. She took a deep breath. "Is he really gone?"

Issa's lips trembled, and she knew. Karou felt a sharpness behind her eyes.

"He was still alive when he sent us away," said Issa. "But he did not expect to remain so."

"Sent you away?" Karou repeated. Of course, Akiva had found the thurible in the Kirin caves. *Why had he been there?* Home of her first childhood, it was also where they had planned to meet, once upon a time. Where they had planned to build their rebellion. Then the "us" struck her. "Yasri and Twiga, too?"

"He allowed Twiga to remain with him, but Yasri and I were to survive. For *you*, when you came. As he knew you would."

"He did?" Karou was tentative. She fought back her tears with deep breaths. "He believed me?" She had told Brimstone that she wasn't some butterfly to shoo out a window, and she'd meant it.

"Of course. He knew you, child." A twist of a smile, so bittersweet. "Better than you knew yourself."

Karou let out a little laugh, and an edge of sob escaped on it. "Well, that's certainly true," she said.

Issa's eyes were wet-bright, but with an effort of will she kept the tears from spilling. Karou reached for her hands and clasped them tightly, and they held on to each other while they told their stories.

Zuzana and Mik had gone back to sleep, lulled by the afternoon heat, and the sounds of the kasbah drifted through the closed shutters—sparring in the court, the ring of blades. Voices.

"After the portals burned," Issa said, "we knew it wouldn't be long. Joram pressed the attack as he never had before. Our armies shrank by the day, and more and more folk arrived at the gates, coming to Loramendi for...safety." Issa swallowed. Her voice dropped to a whisper. "The city was so full." She looked down at her hands and Karou's, still clasped together. "The seraphim took great losses, too. Joram sent them to die, so many, so many, knowing that we would run out of soldiers first, and we did. Such a simple calculus in the end. Loramendi came under siege. That's when Brimstone..." The tremor overcame her voice and Issa snatched a hand out of Karou's to press against her mouth. Karou still held her other hand and wished she could do more. Nothing made you feel so useless as another person's grief.

Issa was struggling; when she lifted her eyes again, she looked stricken. It was such a haunted look that Karou felt a stab of fear. "Issa—"

But Issa rushed over her. "We wanted to stay with him to the end." She squeezed Karou's hands. "Of course, I wanted to see you again, and help you, but to leave him, after..." She couldn't finish. Issa smashed her lips together, pressed them white. Her whole face was rigid with the effort not to weep. She took a deep breath. Another. "But he still needed us. So Yasri and I...died, too."

Too?

What was she skipping? A nameless horror gripped Karou. What had happened in Loramendi? Images pinwheeled; she shook her head. She saw Issa and Yasri bleeding quietly from painless wounds until their lashes fluttered shut. Or had they sipped requiem tea and slipped into sleep? And at the end of it, she imagined Brimstone and Twiga silent, hunched, and stoic as they gleaned the souls of the two women who had been their companions for decades.

"Couldn't he have gotten you out alive?" she asked plaintively.

Issa looked at her, and Karou knew she'd said the wrong thing. As if the decision might have been lightly made!

"No, child." She was so sad. "Even if we could have made it out, what would we have done, waiting in hiding, but grieve and worry, grow hungry and thirsty, be discovered, be killed? Stasis is kind; we didn't even have to be brave. We were messages in bottles." She smiled. "*Messengers* in bottles."

And what was the message? As Brimstone faced his death after a life begun in slavery, endured in pain and sacrifice, prolonged and protracted by war, and soon to end in brutality, what had he wished to tell her? Feeling that she was failing some test, Karou couldn't bring herself to ask. Yet, anyway.

He had sent their thuribles out with messenger birds, Issa told her—bat-winged crows, or squalls, as Kishmish had been—to be hidden in places that she might find them. Yasri's soul, she learned, was in the ruins of the temple of Ellai.

"Did he think I might go there?" Karou asked. "Could he imagine that place would mean anything to me now?"

Issa was taken aback. "Yes, child. Once you broke the wishbone and remembered—"

"Once I remembered dooming my people?"

"Sweet girl, what are you saying? *You* didn't doom us. A thousand years of hatred doomed us."

"To war, maybe. Not annihilation."

"The end was coming. Maybe in one year or one hundred, but it was always coming. How long can a war go on?"

"Is that a riddle? *How long can a war go on?*"

"No, Karou. The riddle is: How might a war *end*? Annihilation is one way. Joram's way. *He* did this, not you. You dreamed a different way. Akiva, too. You, the pair of you, you had the capacity not to hate. The audacity to love. Do you know what a gift that is?"

"A gift?" Karou choked. "A gift like a knife in the back!" On the bed, Zuzana stirred, and Karou lowered her voice. "It was false. It was crazy. It wasn't love. It was stupid—"

"It was brave," countered Issa. "It was rare. It *was* love, and it was beautiful."

"*Beautiful.* Are we even talking about the same story? I died, and he betrayed everything we dreamed of?"

"He was devastated, Karou," said Issa. "What do you think *you* would have done?"

Karou stared at Issa. Was she defending Akiva?

"What would you have done if the seraphim had taken *you*, tortured you, and made you watch as they cut off *his* head? And think: What might you have done, the pair of you together, if Thiago hadn't stopped you? What might the world be now?"

"I . . . I don't know," said Karou. "Maybe Thiago would be dead, and Brimstone would be alive." For an instant—if only for an instant—it seemed as though it were all Thiago's fault and not hers at all. She had believed back then that they had Fate on their side, but the Wolf had bullied it into submission, and here was the result.

The serpent-woman asked softly, "Tell me, what *are* you doing, child?"

Karou couldn't answer. *Killing angels. Killing children.* She pressed her lips together. *Avenging you*, she thought next, and the hypocrisy hit her like shattering. If that was all she was doing, how was she any better than *him*?

No. It wasn't the same. She released a ragged breath, and words hissed out: "Fighting for the survival of the chimaera races."

But *was* she? The rebellion was in Thiago's hands, not hers; with all his secrecy, how could she know *what* they were fighting for?

What was it Akiva had said to her by the river? That the future would have chimaera in it or not, depending on what they did now. Well, he'd said a lot of things. Karou had been so shaken by his presence, by her fury—by her longing—that it hadn't really sunk in. He'd talked of life, and choices. Of the future, as if there might be one.

And what had she said? Anything she could think of to hurt him.

She knew she had to tell Issa everything, not least of all how her thurible had come to Karou, but it was so hard to speak Akiva's name, and impossible to meet her eyes while doing so. She told from Ziri's return to Akiva's appearance at the river, before backtracking to Marrakesh and even Prague. Of course, Issa hadn't known about any of that, and Karou was so ashamed, admitting that she had...fallen for him again. She left out the kiss. Issa made no judgments and spoke only to coax Karou's words from her, but Karou felt scrutinized. She tried to keep her voice even, her face straight, to prove that Akiva was nothing to her now but one more seraph enemy. When she was done, Issa was silent a moment, and thoughtful.

"What?" Karou asked. She sounded defensive.

"So," said Issa, and she laid her words down with even precision, like cards on a table. "Akiva followed Ziri here." She paused. "Do you fear that he'll reveal this position to the seraphim?"

The question slammed Karou into a muffled, white-light bubble of shock. *Oh*, she thought. *That*.

She'd been worrying about keeping Akiva's visit secret from the chimaera—not about keeping the chimaera rebels secret from Akiva. What did *that* mean? She'd told him she never trusted him, and that was a lie he had believed all too easily, but now? How could she still trust him now?

If she didn't, though, wouldn't she have rushed back to the kasbah and urged Thiago to make immediate preparations to leave? It hadn't even occurred to her to do that.

Because it wasn't Akiva that she feared.

"No matter what happens," he had told her in Marrakesh, just before they broke the wishbone, "I need you to remember that I love you." She had promised—breathlessly, unable then to fathom a reality in which she would wish not to remember it. She kept the promise against her will; she *wanted* to forget, but the knowledge held fast: Akiva loved her. He wouldn't hurt her. This she knew.

In a wisp of a voice and loath to admit it—it felt as though *she* were the one defending him now—Karou told Issa, "He won't."

Issa nodded, solemn and sad, looking into Karou and knowing her so well that Karou felt like a diary lying open, all her secrets and failings there to read, and her traitor's heart pulsing blood onto the page. "All right, then," Issa said, trusting Karou's trust, and that was that.

"Now." Issa turned to the table and tooth trays. With forced lightness, she said, "Perhaps we should get to work, lest the Wolf decide we're not worth the trouble of our sassing mouths."

There was more to say, Karou knew. There was the message; there was a gap in Issa's story, and whatever it was that she'd left out haunted her. Karou had never seen Issa look like that. *She'll tell me when she's ready*, she thought, trying to believe that it was for Issa's sake that she didn't come right out and ask, when she knew very well that it was just her own fear.

60

The New Game

Karou had told Thiago the truth: The work really did go much faster with Issa's help, and Zuzana's. Two pairs of clever hands and she could delegate every task but the actual conjuring. After Ziri turned up to tithe—insistent, even imploring, to repay her for her magic—Karou felt as if she were scarcely doing anything at all. Her room was too full. It was stuffy, Ziri's wings took up space, and Issa's tail seemed to be everywhere she wanted to place her feet, but she felt . . . happy. *Actual* happy, not *Holy Grail* happy. And the task that she was happiest to delegate? Even more than the tithe, it was the math.

"I'm good at math," Mik volunteered, overhearing her complaints about wing-to-weight ratios. "Can I help?"

When it turned out that he *could*, Karou dropped to her knees to genuflect. "Gods of math and physics," she intoned, "I accept your gift of this clever, fair-haired boy."

"*Man*," corrected Mik, insulted. "Look: sideburns. Chest hair. Sort of."

"Man," amended Karou, rising and bending again in mock prayer. "Thank you, gods, for this man—" She interrupted herself to ask Zuzana, in her normal voice, "Wait. Does that make you a *woman*?"

She only meant that it was strange to go from thinking of Zuzana—and herself, too—as a *girl* to a *woman*. It just sounded weirdly old. But Zuzana's response, employing full eyebrow power in the service of lechery, was, "Why, yes, since you ask. This man did make me a woman. It hurt like holy hell at first, but it's gotten better." She grinned like an anime character. "So. Much. Better."

Poor Mik blushed like sunburn, and Karou clamped her hands over her ears. "La la la!" she sang, and when Ziri asked her what they were saying, she blushed, too, and did not explain—which only made *him* blush in turn, when he grasped the probable subject matter.

By the end of that first day, they had built five new soldiers for the rebellion, double Karou's average when working with Ten, and that was with a late start and having to teach Zuzana and Mik the basics. They had followed Thiago's wish list and specifications to appease him, even when Zuzana's drawn-at-random thurible—the one she'd been pestering Karou about since her first afternoon—turned out to contain Haxaya. The fox soldier had been Madrigal's friend once, and her soul was the touch of sunset and laughter, with a bite like the sting of nettles; Haxaya was someone you wanted on your side . . . which started Karou thinking about sides.

Who could she trust? The soldiers of the chimaera army were and had always been fiercely loyal to their general. But she had Issa, of course, and there was Ziri, who took a risk even coming here to tithe. Maybe the rest of Balieros's renegade patrol. They remained in stasis, so she couldn't know for certain. She thought Amzallag was unhappy with Thiago's tactics, and possibly Bast. She liked Virko. He had a jovial go-along nature, and judging from his vomiting he was no fan of these terror missions, but she couldn't see him defying the Wolf.

What was she even thinking? She couldn't see *herself* defying the Wolf, let alone asking others to. She'd told Ziri her suspicions about the Wolf's desire to kill her, and, uncomfortingly, he'd shown no surprise. "He needs to be in complete control," he said. "And you proved a long time ago that you're not under his spell."

Yes, she had proven that, all right. The question that echoed in her brain now was: *What can I do?*

She couldn't go along with him. His course was barbaric, and that was bad enough, but it was also ruin. Look what he'd brought down on the southern folk. She kept catching herself thinking that if the soldiers understood the cause and effect—if she could just make them *see*—then they could not support his strategy. But, of course, they did understand. That was the worst part. They had followed his orders anyway, all except one patrol.

And she couldn't stand up to him, either. Thiago might as well have been their god, and what was she? A known angel-lover in human skin? Even if anyone *was* to listen to her, she was no leader. It had been a long time since she was even a soldier, and she was afraid. Of responsibility, of the Empire, of the odds against their survival, and most of all, of Thiago himself. Right now, she was afraid of seeing that malice in his eyes again.

"Maybe another day," she had said to Zuzana, closing Haxaya's thurible and setting it aside. "Right now, let's just try to make the Wolf happy."

And he *was* happy with their work.

"Well done," he said, when they presented him with the five new soldiers. His mask was back in place. He was all mild benevolence at dinner, even pouring wine—wine? That was a rare commodity, and Karou hadn't brought it—he raised a glass to the five new revenants. "To survival," he said, and she wondered: *Whose?*

Turning over these soldiers to him—these *weapons*—she did not forget for a second what he would use them for, and it sickened her, but open defiance would not serve. She saw the way the others watched him: with an avid mixture of awe and fear, hoping for his notice, and beaming when they received it. And she saw how he worked the crowd, winning his soldiers again and again, making them feel like his chosen hands, his strength at the end of the world.

She watched him pour the wine, and when she saw the orb shape of the bottle, she lost her taste for it. It wasn't chimaera grasswine, so called for its pale greenish color, but a seraph vintage, rich and red; one of the soldiers must have brought it back from some town they'd sacked.

She sat back in her chair, stirring her couscous with her fork.

"No wine for you?" Thiago asked, taking the bench at her side.

"No, thank you."

"Some believe it's bad luck to refuse a toast," he said. "That its blessing will pass you over."

What, his toast to survival? "So if I don't drink your wine, I won't survive?"

He shrugged. "I'm not superstitious. But it is good wine." He drank. "Our pleasures are so few in these times, and we agreed earlier, today is a good day. Five soldiers join the fight, Issa is come to us...somehow." They both glanced at Issa, who sat farther down the table with Nisk and Lisseth, who were Naja—though Naja as reinterpreted by Karou. "And, of course, you have your friends." He tipped his head in the direction of Zuzana and Mik.

The humans were sitting cross-legged on the floor in a circle of soldiers, pointing at things and learning more Chimaera words: *salt*, *rat*, *eat*, which unfortunate combination led to Zuzana rejecting the meat on her plate.

"I think it's chicken," Mik said, taking a bite.

"I'm just saying there were a lot more rats around here earlier."

"Circumstantial evidence." Mik took another bite and said, in passable Chimaera and to guffaws of laughter, "Salty delicious rat."

"It's *chicken*," insisted one of the Shadows That Live. Karou wasn't sure which it was, but she was flapping her arms like wings, and even producing chicken bones to prove it. *Now I've seen everything. The Shadows That Live, doing chicken impressions.*

Her friends' presence changed the tone of the kasbah so much, and so much for the better, and she had loved having their help today as much as she'd loved their company. But watching them from Thiago's side and knowing what she now knew, she began to get a bad feeling.

"Yes," she said, striving for a light tone. "I have my friends. But they're just visiting. They'll be leaving soon."

"Oh? What a shame. They've been so useful. Surely they can be persuaded to stay."

"I don't think so. They have commitments back home."

"But what could be more important than helping you?" Karou felt her field of vision narrowing like a lens, zeroing in on her friends. Here, then, was to be his new game. Thiago's voice was velvet. "I would hate for you to lose them."

Lose them? There was a rushing in Karou's ears. Thiago's threats were as clean and pristine as he was, but she had no doubt that what lay beneath them was blood. Her friends were a vulnerability. She cared about them. Clever fingers and math notwithstanding, Thiago would keep them here for one reason: as a means of controlling *her*. She dropped the pretense. "I'll have Ten back instead," she said softly. "Just let them leave."

"Oh, I don't think so. Ten has many fine qualities, but I think we can agree they serve her better in *compelling* the resurrectionist than in being one herself."

"I don't need to be compelled. I've done everything you've asked."

"Where did Issa come from?"

The question caught her off guard. Her hesitation was fractional, but it was there, and provoked a wan smile from him. "I already told you," she said.

"Indeed."

Karou felt turned to ice. She sat there watching as Zuzana fashioned the chicken bones into a rattly marionette. It had joints of twine and a chipped bowl for a head, but she somehow made that damn thing seem *alive*, sidling up to soldiers begging for scraps. The soldiers clapped and beat the drums Karou had brought, and Zuzana danced her marionette until its head fell off, after which they urged Mik to play for them.

"Try the wine," Thiago said, getting up to go. "It's very rich. You know what they say about angel wine? The bloodier the better."

She didn't drink it. Later, with Issa in the court, Karou watched him, but he only sat against a wall, alone, with his head tipped back and his eyes closed, listening to the music.

Other eyes were open, though. In heavy shadow, in the gallery, Ten paced. She was watching Karou, and didn't try to disguise it, and didn't shift her gaze even when she pivoted to change direction in her pacing. Back and forth, back and forth, untiring. She might have been the Wolf's hostility made flesh—animal flesh, along with predator instinct and sharp teeth, hungry for the kill order she had been cheated out of.

Karou's skin prickled all over and she scanned the assembled soldiers, all held rapt by Mik's playing. Some eyes were closed and others were open and she didn't know what she was even looking for. "I don't think I did you a favor by resurrecting you," she said softly to Issa. What was it Issa had said before, that stasis is kind? "You were safer in the thurible."

Issa's reply was equally soft. "My safety is not important."

"What? It is to me."

"*You* are important, Karou. And the message is important."

The message. Karou was mute. A space hung between them—a silence that was deeper than the music, waiting for her to fill it with a question. What had Brimstone wanted her to know? It was time to ask. She would never again hear his voice, but there were his words at least, his message. "Is it good or bad?" she asked Issa. The wrong question, she knew. She just couldn't help herself.

"It's both, sweet girl," said Issa. "Like everything."

61

A Lot of Dead Akivas

"How did the Stelians get into the inner sanctum?" Hazael mused. "If Akiva could figure *that* out—"

Liraz cut him off. "Even if he could, we're not assassins."

"Not for lack of trying."

In the wake of the basket of fruit, it was reported that Joram kept to the Tower of Conquest, and had even suspended his audience with citizens. There was no way to get to him. At least, none that they had figured out.

"You know what I mean. We're not *sneaks*, and we're not the Shadows That Live. Our father will see our faces before he dies."

"I know. You prefer your victims to know who's killing them." Hazael recited this as if he'd heard it a hundred times.

Akiva spoke. "This time especially. And there must be witnesses."

They looked over at him, surprised. He had been doing a

kata, seeking *sirithar*, trying to find a place of calm wherein an answer might come to him. He had failed on both counts: no calm, and no answer.

"The people have to know that it was us," he said, sheathing his swords. "Or they'll just blame the Stelians or the Shadows That Live, and Japheth will have no choice but to take up his father's wars."

Japheth was the crown prince. He was the crown prince because his next-oldest brother had murdered his oldest brother, then been murdered himself in the temple that same night while praying to the godstars to shrive his sin. He was remembered as the Unshrived; the brother he had slain was the Avenged, and Japheth was just Japheth. He was no paragon; he was a soft skulkling, afraid to leave the Tower of Conquest even under full escort. He was a coward, but the right kind of coward—who would shrink from war even if he didn't have to fight it himself. At least, that was Akiva's hope.

"So the Misbegotten become the enemy," said Hazael, melancholy.

"The citizens despise us anyway," said Liraz. "They'll be glad it's us."

"They will," said Akiva. "They'll say that Joram should have known, and that it was his own fault for putting so many bastards in the world. It will shock them, and it will end with us."

"And by *us*, you mean…"

"All of us." Akiva's words were heavy. "All of our lives will be forfeit."

"So we three decide the fate of three hundred?" asked Hazael.

"Yes," said Akiva. He looked out to sea. Three hundred. *Only three hundred.* So many already lost. Akiva had decided *their* fates, hadn't he? He had set this in motion. Oh, the war had been going on for years, but once the portals were burned it was over in months. With Brimstone hamstrung by his lost supply, Joram had hit the chimaera with every breathing body under his command, and all had sustained massive casualties: the Dominion, the Second Legion, even the scouts and the Empire's navy, but the Misbegotten were hardest hit, being expendable, endlessly renewable. Being the smallest force to begin with, their loss ratio was staggering, with only one in four having made it through alive. "We'll warn the others," he said. "They'll leave their regiments and join us. Can you think of anyone with less to lose?"

"Slaves," said Hazael.

"We *are* slaves," said Akiva. "But not for very much longer."

Over the following days they began, cautiously, to feed warnings out to their bastard brethren; word of mouth only, as troops passed through Cape Armasin. Some all-night flights were needed, under glamour, to reach distant postings. The Misbegotten were scattered to the four corners of the Empire, a few with this regiment, a few with that. Akiva thought of Melliel and her team, but had no way of reaching them. He wondered what they had found over the curve of the horizon, if they were alive, if any of the troops they'd gone to find were alive, and whether they would make it back. None had yet, not of all of Joram's envoys, scouts, and advance troops. *No one* who had flown toward the Far Isles had returned.

One might think this would cool the emperor's ardor for this conquest, but rumors coming out of the capital suggested very much otherwise. Hazael squeezed every scrap of news out of anyone who passed through—and there were more and more travelers these days as nobles under army escort came across the water to survey their new holdings—and the scraps added up to a strange mosaic indeed.

"Is he planning an invasion?" Akiva wondered. "It makes no sense."

"A thousand pure white surcoats," Hazael had reported. This was the sort of gossip they had from lords and their servants. "He's having a thousand pure white surcoats made, with matching standards." Hazael paused. "For the Dominion."

"The Dominion?" Less and less sense. For one thing, the Dominion color was red. White signified surrender, and Joram did not surrender. But the color was a mere detail compared to the salient issue of: What were they *for*? New surcoats and standards . . . to make an impression on the enemy? What sort of impression did white make? And what would embolden Joram to send more forces into that void, let alone the Dominion? Surely he wouldn't risk vanishing his elite army into the mysteries. The Misbegotten maybe, but the Dominion?

"Jael himself is pushing for it," said Hazael. "There's a rumor that it's his idea."

Jael? The Captain of the Dominion was many monstrous things, but he was no fool. And then there was the matter of the harpers. Joram had called up the harpers from the monastery of Brightseeming to cease their devotions to the godstars and come to Astrae, where they were to be appareled in white to match the Dominion.

"There's something going on," said Akiva. "Something that hasn't made its way into rumor. But *what?*"

"I think you're going to find out." It was Liraz, coming into the barracks with a scroll in her hand. She handed it over. It bore the Imperial seal. Akiva froze, knowing what it must be, and looked up at his brother and sister.

"Go on," urged Hazael, tense.

So Akiva broke the seal and unrolled the scroll, and read the summons aloud. "To appear before His Eminence, Joram the Unconquered, First Citizen of the Empire of Seraphim, Protector of Eretz, Father of Legions, Prince of Light and Scourge of Darkness, Chosen of the Godstars, Lord of Ashes, Lord of Char, Lord of a Country of Ghosts—"

Hazael grabbed the scroll to see if the last three were really written there, which they were *not*, and it was he who continued reading. "In gratitude for heroic service to the realm, is summoned Blood Soldier of the Misbegotten, Akiva, Seventh Bearer of that Name..." Hazael stopped reading and looked up at Akiva. "You're the *seventh?* That's a lot of dead Akivas, my brother. Do you know what that means?" He was very grave.

"Tell me. What does it mean?" Akiva prepared himself for mocking doom. Six bastards had carried the name before him? It *was* a lot; too many. Some must have died in infancy, or at the training camp. Hazael was probably going to tell him the name was cursed.

But no. His brother said, "It means that the cremation urn is full, no room for your ashes. You have no choice." He smiled his hapless, open smile. "You *have* to live."

62

Chain

Heroic service to the realm.

For "heroic service to the realm," Akiva was summoned to Astrae. If this had happened months ago, in the wake of Loramendi, it might have made sense. But medals had long since been pinned, spoils divvied. Akiva had been overlooked with the rest of the Misbegotten, so why was he summoned now?

Liraz was uneasy. "What if Joram knows something?" she asked. They were in flight, nothing but the Halcyon Sea in all directions. She liked flying over the sea—the vastness, the clean and ashless air, the quiet. But she did not care for their destination.

"What could he know?" said Akiva. "But even if he does, there may never be another chance like this."

There may never come another chance to stand face-to-face with their father and end his brutal life. Liraz had never even seen Joram up close. Now she would, and he would bleed. "I know," she said, and left it at that. Any protest she might make would sound like fear—of Joram. Of failure.

Liraz *was* afraid. It was a stinging fear, like flying into a sandstorm; it shamed her, and she would never admit to it. Fearless Liraz. If only they knew what a lie it was. She wanted to say, *It's too dangerous.* She wanted to convince her brothers that in Astrae—in the Tower of Conquest, no less—there would be too many factors beyond their control. *Better we vanish now,* she thought, *and undercut Joram from outside the Empire than fly into his trap. His* web.

Though she didn't voice her fears and was certain she didn't show them, Hazael drew a little closer to her side and said, "Joram probably just wants to use our illustrious brother to his own ends. To fight the rebels? Who better than Beast's Bane? Especially with all focus on this mad Stelian conquest."

Liraz said, "Or it's to do with the mad Stelian conquest. Akiva *is* Joram's only link to the Far Isles."

Akiva was flying off to the side, lost in thought, but he heard. "I'm no link. I know no more of Stelians than anyone."

"But you have their eyes," she said. "That might earn you a parley, at least."

Akiva looked disgusted. "Could he think I'd play emissary for him? Can he imagine that I'm his creature?"

"Let's hope so," said Liraz, her voice sharp. "Because the alternative is that he suspects you."

Akiva was silent a long moment, before finally saying, "You don't have to be part of this. Either of you—"

"Damn you, Akiva," she snapped. "I *am* part of it."

"Me, too," said Hazael.

"I don't want to put you in danger," said Akiva. "I can kill him alone. Even if he does suspect something, he could have no idea what I'm capable of. If I can get to him, I can kill him."

"You can kill him. You just might not get out," Liraz finished for him, and his silence was his acknowledgment. "What, die and be done? How very easy for you." With Liraz, most strong emotion manifested as anger, but in this case the emotion really was anger. With what they had set in motion, she wouldn't even have her regiment to return to and the illusion of a life. She would be outcast, traitor to the Empire, and she knew she didn't have it in her to build a movement behind her. Akiva could; he was Beast's Bane. And Hazael. Everyone loved Hazael. But who was she? No one even liked her but these two, and she sometimes thought that was only habit.

"I don't want to die, Lir," Akiva said softly.

She couldn't tell if he meant it. "Good," she said. "Because you aren't going to. We're going with you, and any dying is going to be done at the other end of our swords."

Hazael backed her up, and on Akiva's face, gratitude vied with the emptiness that Liraz had started thinking of as his "death wish" look. She remembered a time when Akiva had laughed and smiled, when in spite of the violence of their lives he had been a full person, with a full range of emotion. He had never had Hazael's sunshine demeanor—who did?—but he had been *alive*. Once upon a time.

Fury stirred in Liraz for the girl who had done this to her proud, beautiful brother. How many times now had he gone away to find that . . . creature . . . and come back broken? Broken and broken again. *Creature*. It sounded ugly, but Liraz didn't know how to think of the girl: Madrigal, Karou, chimaera, human, and now resurrectionist. What was she? It wasn't disgust she felt for Karou, not anymore; it was indignation. Incredulity. A man like Akiva crosses worlds to find you, infiltrates the enemy capital just to dance with you, bends heaven and hell to avenge your death, saves your comrade and kin from torture and death, and you send him off looking gut-punched, diminished, carved hollow?

Liraz didn't know exactly what Karou had said to Akiva this last time, but she knew that it had not been kind, and as the three of them flew on in silence, she found herself imagining what she would say to *her* in the unlikely event that they ever found themselves face-to-face again. It was a surprisingly satisfying way to pass the time in flight.

"There." Akiva saw it first, and pointed. The Sword.

In its golden age, Astrae had been known as the City of a Hundred Spires. One for each of the godstars, the spires had been slender towers of impossible height, like the stems of flowers growing toward the heavens. They had been crystal, sometimes mirroring the storm clouds of the emerald coast, other times scattering prisms of dancing light over the rooftops below.

That city had been destroyed in the Warlord's uprising a thousand years ago. This was the new Astrae, built by Joram on the ruins of the old, and though he had tried to restore the dead city of his ancestors, that had been raised by the lost arts of magi, this by slaves. The spires weren't even half as tall as their precursors, and they weren't fluid upthrusts of crystal as the old had been, but were glass, seamed and riveted, held together by steel and iron. Of them all, the Tower of Conquest stood tallest, its silhouette shaped like a sword—*the* Sword—making an apt symbol of the Empire, especially when its edge reflected the fire of the setting sun, as it did now.

Blood and endings, Liraz thought, seeing that great blade rising red from the distant cliffs. An apt symbol indeed.

She disliked Astrae; she always had. There was an atmosphere of strain and subtle fear, a culture of whispers and spies. How right Melliel had been, calling it a "spider's web"—even down to the dangling dead displayed to all comers.

The Westway gibbet was the first thing they saw on reaching the city. Beside the fourteen guards there hung another, older corpse that she took for the unfortunate sentry from Thisalene, and yet another pair who'd been hung by their ankles, wings dragging open and catching every breeze to send them eddying in circles like broken dolls. Their crime—or ill luck—Liraz couldn't guess. She had an impulse to scorch a black handprint into the wood of the support post and burn the gibbet out of existence. Night was falling; blue fire would lick the darkening sky, full of dreams and visions. *Not yet*, she told herself.

Soon.

The three came down to the Westway and presented themselves for entry to the city. Liraz found herself gritting her teeth in expectation of the greeting Silverswords reserved for Misbegotten, which was, at best, to see how long they could keep them waiting, and at worst, open taunting. Breakblades had no use for soldiers in general: Cloistered as they were in the scented calm of the capital, they only wondered what had taken others so long to win the war. As for Misbegotten, bastards were beneath their notice.

In Liraz's case, *literally* beneath. She stood as high as their breastplates; they enjoyed pretending not to see her. Like all Breakblades, these two were near seven feet tall, not including helmet plumes. Maybe a couple of inches were boot heel, but even barefoot they would have been giants. They were giants that Liraz knew she could fell with a stroke, which made it all the more maddening to endure their disrespect.

"Slaves enter by the Eastway," said the one on the left, bored, without even looking at them.

Slaves.

Their armor marked them clearly as Misbegotten. They wore vests of dark gray mail over black gambesons, with shoulder guards and breeches of black leather reinforced with plate. The leather was worn, the mail was dull, there were dents and repairs in the plate. For the purpose of their audience with the emperor, they wore short capes, which were in better shape than the rest of their uniform since they were rarely worn. Capes were a bad idea—nothing but a claw-hold for the enemy.

Well, that and a place for their badge: an oval escutcheon containing links in a chain. *Chain.* Supposedly it signified strength in solidarity, but everyone knew it really meant bondage. Liraz thought of the chimaera rebels feeding the slavers their chains, and she understood the impulse. She saw herself tearing off her cape and stuffing it down the Breakblade's great gorge, but it was fantasy. She did nothing, said nothing.

Hazael, however, laughed. He was the only person Liraz knew whose fake laugh sounded real—disarmingly so. The Breakblade darted a glance at him, brow creasing. Dumb brute, couldn't tell if he was being mocked. *Always assume so,* she wanted to tell him. Hazael elbowed her. "Because of the badge, he meant," he said, as if she'd missed the joke.

She didn't laugh; she couldn't even imagine being able to laugh the way her brother did—the tumbling, easy sound of it, the loose-muscled abandon. When she did laugh, the sound was sharp and dry even to her own ears—a hard crust of laughter compared to Hazael's warmth and give. *If I were bread*, she thought, *I would be a stale soldier's ration, just enough to live on.*

Akiva didn't laugh, either. Devoid of antagonism or any kind of reaction, he held the Imperial summons up inches from the guard's face and waited while he read it. Disgruntled, the guard waved them through.

My *brothers*, Liraz thought, entering Astrae between them. How different they were from each other, Hazael with his fair hair and laughter, Akiva saturnine and silent. Sunshine and shadow. *And what am I?* She didn't know. Stone? Steel? Black hands and muscles too tense for laughter?

I am a link in a chain, she thought. Their badge had it right—not in bondage but in strength. She strode between her brothers, three abreast down the center of the broad city boulevard. *This is my chain*. Their armor was dull in the moonlight, in the lamplight, in the firelight of their feathers, and folk drew back from their passage with looks of wariness. *Oh, Astrae*, she thought, *we have kept you too safe if it is* us *that you fear.* They were neither loved nor respected by the people, Liraz knew, and soon they would be infamous and outcast, but she didn't care. As long as she had her brothers.

63

Luck Friction

"They're unreal, aren't they?"

Ziri flushed. He hadn't heard Karou come up beside him, and she'd caught him watching her friends kiss. Had he been staring? What had she seen in his face? He tried to look nonchalant.

She said, "I think they breathe at least half their air out of each other's mouths."

It did seem like that, but Ziri didn't want to let on that he had noticed. He'd never known anyone to act like Zuzana and Mik. They were out in the chicken yard right now—of all places unconducive to romance, not that they seemed to mind. He could see them through the open door, washed white by sunlight. Zuzana was balancing on the edge of the rusty live-stock trough so she was taller than Mik, leaned over him with both arms wrapped entirely around his head, her hands splayed, fingers tangled in his hair. *His* hands, though. His hands were cupped around the curve of her pale legs, tracing lightly from the backs of her knees up her thighs and down again. It was that more than the kissing that had made Ziri forget himself and stare. The startling intimacy of the touch.

He had witnessed affection in chimaera, and he had witnessed passion, but the one had generally been reserved for mothers and children, and the other for dark-corner encounters during the drunken revels of the Warlord's ball. He had lived all his life in a city at war, spent most of his time with soldiers, and had never known his parents; he'd never seen affection and passion so perfectly paired, and... it *hurt*, somehow. It wrenched an ache from his chest to watch them. He could scarcely imagine having someone who was *his*, to touch like that.

"It must be a human thing," he said, trying to make light of it.

"No." Karou's voice was wistful. "More of a *luck* thing." He thought he saw a flash of pain on her face, too, but she smiled and it was gone. "Funny to think it's only been a few months since she was afraid to even *talk* to him."

"*Neek-neek*, afraid? I don't believe it." There was a ferocity in the tiny Zuzana that had started Virko calling her *neek-neek*, after a growlsome breed of shrew-scorpion known for facing down predators ten times its size.

"I know," said Karou. "She's not exactly timid." They were in the mess hall; the breakfast hour had gone. Ziri had just finished sentry duty and scraped the dregs of breakfast onto a plate for himself: cold eggs, cold couscous, apricots. Had Karou already eaten? Her arms were hugged around her waist. "It was the only time I've ever seen her like that," she said, smiling in the soft way of good memories. Her face had become so much more alive since her friends arrived. "She didn't even know his name for the longest time. We called him 'violin boy.' She'd get so nervous every time she thought she might see him."

Ziri tried unsuccessfully—not for the first time—to picture Karou's human life, but he had no context for it, having seen nothing of this world beyond the kasbah and the desert and mountains surrounding it.

"So what happened?" he asked, setting his plate on the table. The hall was empty; Thiago had called an assembly in the court, and he had planned to eat quickly and go straight there. Finding himself alone with Karou, though, he lingered. He didn't want to gulp down food in front of her, for one thing, and for another, he just wanted to stand here, near her. "How did they... finally?" He meant to say "fall in love," but it embarrassed him too much to speak of love—especially now that she knew how he'd felt about her as a boy. She had to have read it on his face and in his blush when he'd told her how he'd been watching her at the Warlord's ball all those years ago. He wished he could take back that confession. He didn't want her thinking of him as the boy who used to follow her around. He wanted her to see him as he was now: a man grown.

She understood his meaning, though, even if he didn't use the word *love*. "Well, since she was too afraid to talk to him, she drew him a treasure map. She hid it in his violin case when he was performing—they worked at the same theater, but they'd never spoken—and she left early that night so she wouldn't see him get it. In case he got all pained-looking or something, you know, and she just couldn't take it. She'd already decided that if he didn't follow the map to the treasure, she would just never go to work again and that would be the end of that."

"What was the treasure?"

"*She* was." Karou laughed. "That's Zuze being shy. She won't talk to him, but she'll make herself the object of a treasure hunt. Right in the middle of the map was a drawing of her face."

Ziri laughed, too. "So obviously he went. He followed it."

"Mm-hmm. He went to the place and she wasn't there, but there was another map, which led to another, and finally to her. And they fell in love and they've been like this ever since."

At "like this" she gestured out the open door, to where Zuzana was now gingerly treading along the edge of the trough, holding Mik's hand.

Ziri had never heard anything like that story of a trail of treasure maps. Except possibly the story of the angel who had come disguised into the cage city of the enemy to dance with his lady.

He liked Zuzana's story better. "A luck thing," he said.

"Yeah," said Karou. She looked at him, and away again. "I think they both have to be lucky. It's like, luck friction. One's flint and one's steel, striking together to make fire." She hugged her arms tighter around herself. "It's better when they tell the story themselves. They're funnier than I am."

"I'll ask them," he said. He was conscious that Thiago's assembly would be starting, and that he needed to be there. "The way they're learning Chimaera, it won't be long before they *can* tell it."

She didn't say anything. The softness of good memories was gone. She looked over her shoulder, furtive, and then up at him, piercing. "Ziri," she said in a hush, "I have to get them out of here."

"What? Why?"

"Thiago's threatened them. As long as they're here, I have to do exactly what he says. And I really want to stop doing what he says." She said the last part quietly, burningly, and Ziri had the impression of something shifting in her, a girding up, a gathering of breath and strength.

"Do Zuzana and Mik know?"

"No, and they won't want to go. They like it here. They like being part of something magical."

So did Ziri. He'd relished those hours spent in Karou's room with her and Issa and Mik and Zuzana, even if he had been tithing. They had been lively and filled with laughter and warmth, with resurrection instead of killing. "I'll help you. We'll get them to safety."

"Thank you." She touched his hand and said again, "Thank you."

Then Zuzana called something to her in their human language and came spinning through the door.

"Are you coming?" Ziri asked Karou. "Thiago's assembly will have begun."

"Not invited," she said. "I'm not supposed to worry myself over such matters. Will you tell me what he says? What he's planning?"

"I will," Ziri promised.

"And I have something to tell you, too." Again, that girding and gathering, and a keen new resolve. Gone was the trembling girl Thiago had found in the ruins.

"What is it?" Ziri asked, but the small human whirlwind reached them then.

"Later," Karou said as Zuzana grabbed her hand and pulled her away with a distracted *hello* over her shoulder to Ziri.

He left his breakfast uneaten and went out the door. What did she want to tell him? He could still feel her touch on his hand.

Once, when he was a boy and she was Madrigal, she had kissed him. She had taken his face in her hands and kissed him lightly on the forehead, and it was ridiculous how many times he had thought of it since. But his moments of happiness were a sad, small lot, and the kiss hadn't had much competition for best memory. Now it did.

Now he had the memory of Karou's shoulder warm against his own as they slept side by side, and the memory of waking beside her. What would it be like to wake beside her every morning? To lie down with her every night? And . . . to fill, with her, the hours between. All the hours of night.

"A luck thing," she had said.

Supposedly he was lucky. Lucky Ziri. Because he had his natural flesh? It was a claim none of his comrades could make, so he didn't argue if they wanted to call him lucky, but he'd never felt it, growing up without a people, no life but war, and even less now that the war was over—whatever that meant, as the killing raged on.

Then he thought of the screams of the dying, the smoke of the corpses, and he was ashamed to question his own luck. He was alive; that was not nothing, and it couldn't be like this forever.

Everyone was already in the court when he got there—except Ten, who came slinking in a moment after Ziri and sidled up to the Wolf to whisper in his ear. Thiago paused to listen, and then his glance slid, cool, to lock on Ziri. It made Ziri's flesh crawl, and then the Wolf spoke.

"As you all know, we lost a team in our strikes the other night, our first casualties, but their safety did his duty and returned with all their souls. Ziri." Thiago nodded to him. There were cheers in the assembly, and someone reached out a heavy hand to jostle Ziri's shoulder. But Ziri didn't for a moment believe this speech was headed anywhere good, and he braced himself, and was unsurprised by the rest.

"But you need a new team now. If Razor will have you?" Thiago turned to Razor.

No, thought Ziri, his jaw clenching. *Anyone else.*

"Your wish, my general," came Razor's hiss of a voice. "But I can't promise he'll play hide-in-safety on my team, or keep that pretty skin of his."

"Hide-in-safety" was a slur used in stupid bravado by soldiers who couldn't see the value of preserving the souls of the fallen. Ziri tensed at the implication that he would ever choose to hide, but then he thought of what they would certainly be doing, and there was no conviction in his outrage. He *would* rather hide. Better yet, he would rather prevent the slaughter from happening at all.

But of course, that wasn't going to be an option. Ziri had been a soldier now more years than he hadn't. He'd never loved the life, but he was good at it, and never, at least, while the Warlord was alive, had he abhorred it. He did now.

"There's a string of towns on the Tane River, east of Balezir," said Thiago. He smiled with the sick exaltation that Ziri knew heralded *grievous harm*, and said, "I want the angels to wake in Balezir tomorrow and wonder why the Tane runs red."

64

A Nicer Number

Karou was bent over a necklace when Ten came to her doorway, but in truth, her thoughts were far away, in Loramendi. She could still barely get her mind around what Issa had told her. Both good and bad indeed. But *good* and *bad* were words for a child's primer, and did not come close to representing the magnitude of tragedy on the one hand, and on the other… hope.

Head-clearing, shoulder-lifting, this-changes-everything *hope*. At least, it *could* change everything.

Or Thiago could crush it and carry on his campaign of terror until chimaera truly were beyond all reach of hope. It was up to Karou to persuade them. *No big deal*, she thought, staring at the teeth in her hand and staving off the wild laugh that wanted to burst from her. *They love me here. I think I'll call a meeting.*

In the doorway, Ten cleared her throat.

Karou gave her a flat, sideward glance. "What do *you* want?"

"Hostile," said Ten, entering uninvited. "I just came with a message." She was so casual. Karou assumed the message was from Thiago, but she should have known something was amiss from the amusement in Ten's voice. "He was sorry he couldn't say good-bye to you himself."

"Good-bye?" That was rich. "Where's *he* going?" The days of Thiago leading missions were long over. He was as much a fixture of the kasbah as Karou was. More, because theoretically she could fly away any time she wanted to.

"To the Tane," said the she-wolf.

The Tane was a river in the east of Azenov, the landmass that made up the heart of the Empire's lands. Karou looked up sharply, but it was Issa who asked, with undisguised contempt, "Whose message is this, she-wolf?"

"It's from your *friend*," said Ten; she said it like it was an illicit word, a piquant naughtiness to speak behind one's hand. "Why, whom did you think I meant?"

Karou went to the window, and there he was in the court with his new team. With Razor. Even as she watched, they gathered the air beneath them and took flight. This time, Ziri *did* look to her window, and across the distance she saw his face was rigid with anger, and his eyes, as he lifted his hand in farewell, were full of regret.

Her heart was pounding. It was because he'd helped her yesterday, or maybe because of this morning. Whatever the particulars, she hadn't been careful enough.

"Where's Ziri going?" asked Zuzana, leaning past her to watch the team's departure.

"On a mission," Karou heard herself say.

"With *Razor?*" Zuzana made a choking sound of disgust, which, being comical, missed the mark by a thousand miles. She had no idea. "What's in that gross sack of his, anyway?"

I guess Ziri is going to find out, Karou thought, feeling sick. Razor was her fault. She had put that slick, wrong-feeling soul into that powerful body and awakened him. And now Ziri was at his mercy—to say nothing of all the seraphim who had fallen and would fall victim to him.

She had heard... that he *ate* them.

She didn't want to believe it, but you had only to stand downwind of him to catch the abattoir reek of his mouth—rotting flesh in shreds caught between razor teeth. As for his sack of stains, she didn't want to know. *Ever.* She just wanted it to end, but there he went, to make mayhem on the Tane.

"Seven's one too many for a team, isn't it," remarked Ten. "Six is a nicer number."

A nicer number? Karou understood, and whirled on her. "What? Say what you mean. That only six will return?"

"Anything could happen," replied Ten with a shrug. "We always know that when we go into battle."

Karou's chest was rising and falling with her quickened breath. "You always know that, do you?" she spat back. "When was the last time you went into battle? You or your master?" Her hand flashed out; she snatched a knife off the table. It was the little one, barely bigger than a nail file; she used it for a hundred things, like slicing the incense cakes and prying teeth loose from jawbones, and pricking her fingertips for the small bursts of pain she sometimes needed at the end of a conjuring.

"Come here, Ten," she said, gripping it. "How about a little resurrection? No need to march all the way to the pit. I'll just throw your body out the window."

Ten laughed. At the little knife, and at her. It sounded like barking. "Really, Karou. Is that how you want to play?" She flung a hand in the direction of Zuzana and Mik. "And which of them dies first? The Wolf will probably let you choose."

"Well, you'll already be dead, so I guess you'll miss it."

Issa grabbed Karou's arm and took the knife. "Sweet girl, stop this!"

Shaking with fury, Karou snarled, "Get out!" Still laughing, Ten did.

Karou turned to Mik and Zuzana, who were flat against the wall, holding hands, and wearing identical *Um, what?* expressions. She brushed past them, back to the window, and looked into the deep, empty sky. Ziri was gone, and down in the court, earthbound and easy to pick out from the milling troops of the small but ever-growing army, was Thiago. Looking up at her.

Karou slammed the shutters.

"What?" asked Zuzana, starting to flutter and hop. "*What what what?*"

Karou exhaled a long, shaky breath. Ziri was a soldier, and a Kirin, she told herself. He could take care of himself. At least, that was the surface of her thoughts. Underneath, in the sucking currents of her wild, fist-beating powerlessness, she knew... she knew that she would probably never see him again. "Tonight," she said. "I'm getting you out of here."

Zuzana started to argue.

Karou cut her off. "This is not a good place for you," she said in a rasping whisper, as emphatic as she could make it. "Have you wondered how I died?"

"How you—? Uh. Battle? I assumed."

"Wrong. I fell in love with Akiva, and Thiago had me beheaded." Plain and brutal. Zuzana gasped. "So now you know," said Karou. "Will you please let me get you to safety?"

"But what about you?"

"I have to take care of this. It has to be me. Zuze. Please."

In as small a voice as Karou had ever heard her use, Zuzana said, "Okay."

Mik asked, "Um... how?"

It was a good question. Karou was watched, that much was clear, and not just by Ten. She didn't have Ziri to rely on now, and she couldn't risk resurrecting Balieros's patrol—it would be too transparent. There was no one else she could be sure of, but she did have one idea that didn't involve any other chimaera.

She took another deep, uneven breath and considered Zuzana and Mik. They were emphatically not soldiers, and it wasn't merely that they were human, but that they were supremely... first world, utterly unaccustomed to hardship of any kind. The hike here had almost done them in, and Zuzana had only been sort of joking when she said that losing at cakewalk was the worst day of her life. Could they handle the tithe? They would just have to.

"Could you walk back out of here, if you had to? At night, when it's not so hot?"

They nodded, huge-eyed.

Karou scraped her lip between her teeth and worried it. "Do you think..." she asked haltingly, hoping it wasn't the worst idea she had ever had, "that you might like to learn... to, um, turn invisible?"

She would have given much in that moment for a camera, to preserve forever the expression on her best friend's face.

The answer, needless to say, was *yes.*

* * *

They worked at it all day.

"This is a little less awesome than it could be," was as close as Zuzana came to complaining about the tithe, but her glee, when she came visible again after her first success at glamour, was bright and beautiful, as she was bright and beautiful, and Karou couldn't help it—she grabbed her into the kind of overlong, too-tight hug that could really only mean: *This is it, I've loved knowing you.* When she finally drew back, Zuzana's eyes were wet, her mouth skewed into an angry don't-cry grimace, and she didn't say a word.

Karou still had to pull off some resurrections so that she might present soldiers to Thiago, lest he guess that her attention had been elsewhere that day. She managed it with Issa's help—three new soldiers—and she managed to get through dinner, too, eating mechanically, and now more than ever, she scanned the host and wondered: Who among them had the courage to stand up to the Wolf?

For such a reason as she was now ready to give them, she told herself, there must be some.

Zuzana and Mik gave away nothing, sitting as usual on the floor among soldiers, learning words in an otherworldly language they would never again have the opportunity to speak. *Friend, fly, I love you.* Virko thought this last one was hilarious, but Karou felt pulped by it. Mik played Mozart that night, and Karou saw Bast moved to tears, and later, much later, in her room, she handed vises to her friends, and put one on herself, and led them out unseen into the desert night. They took only what fit in their pockets—money, dead phones, passports, the compass—and canteens slung over their shoulders. Everything else they left.

Karou walked a little way with them, then flew back to the kasbah to watch and make sure that their absence went unnoticed.

It did.

Tucked into her tooth tray she found a folded paper: a drawing of Zuzana and Mik, and written out phonetically, the Chimaera for "I love you." She broke down then, and Issa held her, and she held Issa, and they both wept, but by the time the sun rose and the kasbah came to life, they were calm again. Pale and subdued. Ready.

It was time.

Once upon a time,
chimaera descended by the thousands
into a cathedral beneath the earth.

And never left.

65

Beast Requiem

It was a choice. When the end came, every chimaera in Loramendi had it to make. Well, not the soldiers. They would die defending the city. And not the children. Parents chose for them, and the seraph invaders would later remember very few children in the city when the siege finally broke the iron bars of the Cage. Maybe none, in fact. So much had already burned and collapsed. It was hard to make an accounting in all the rubble.

So the angels never guessed what lay buried beneath their feet.

Go down to the cathedral beneath the city. Carry your babies and lead your children by the hand. Go down into the airless dark and never come out.

Or stay above and face the angels.

It was a choice of deaths, and it was easy. The one below would be gentler. And perhaps... possibly... less permanent.

Brimstone didn't promise. How could he? It was only a dream.

"You were always the dreamer between the two of us," the Warlord said to him, when Brimstone came to propose it. They were two old men—"old monsters," as the enemy would have it—who had risen from the most abject slavery to tear down their masters and carve out for their people a thousand years of freedom. A thousand years and no more. It was over, and they were very tired.

"I've had better dreams," said Brimstone. "That the cathedral was for blessings and weddings, instead of resurrection. I never dreamed it a tomb."

The cathedral was the massive natural cavern that lay beneath the city. Few had ever seen its carved stalactites but the revenants who woke on its great stone tables. Whatever blessings and weddings Brimstone had dreamed for it when first he found it and built a city on it, it had only ever seen the one purpose: revenant smoke and hamsas.

And now this.

"Not a tomb," said the Warlord, putting a hand on his friend's hunched shoulder. "Isn't that the point? Not a tomb at all, but a thurible."

In a thurible, properly sealed, souls could be preserved indefinitely. And if the cathedral were sealed, its vent shafts blocked and its long corkscrew stair collapsed and concealed, Brimstone had proposed that it might serve, in essence, as a massive vessel for the preservation of thousands of souls.

"It may only ever be a tomb," he warned.

"But whose idea is this?" asked the Warlord. "Am *I* to

convince *you*, who brought it to me? You could look out the window today, see the sky raining fire, and say that it has all been for nothing, everything we've ever done, because now we've lost. But folk were born and lived and knew friendship and music in this city, ugly as it is, and all across this land that we fought for. Some grew old, and others were less lucky. Many bore children and raised them, and had the pleasure of making them, too, and we gave them that for as long we could. Who has ever done more, my friend?"

"And now our time is done."

The Warlord's smile was all rue. "Yes."

The tomb—the vessel—could not be for them, because the angels would leave no stone unturned until they found the Warlord and the resurrectionist. The emperor must have his finale. This might be Brimstone's dream, but its fulfillment would depend on another.

"Do you believe that she'll come?" the Warlord asked.

Brimstone's heart was heavy. He couldn't know if Karou would ever find her way back to Eretz; he hadn't prepared her for anything like this. He'd given her a human life and tried to believe that she might escape the fate of the rest of her people, the endless war, the broken world. And now he would hang it all around her neck? Heavy, heavy, keys to a shattered kingdom. The weight of all these souls would be as good as shackles to her, but he knew that she wouldn't shirk them. "She will," he said. "She'll come."

"Well then, we do it. You named her aptly, old fool. Hope, indeed."

So they put it to the people to choose, and the choice was

easy. Everyone knew what was coming; their lives had shrunk down to huddling and hunger—and fire, always fire—as they waited for the end. Now the end was here, and... like a dream this hope came to them; it came in whispers to their dark dwellings, their ruins and refugee squats. They knew, all of them, the devastation of waking from hopeful dreams to darkness and the stench of siege. Hope was mirage, and none trusted easily to it. But this was real. It was not a promise, only a hope: that they might live again, that their souls and their children's souls might bide in peace, in stasis until such a day...

And this was the other hope, heavier still, that Brimstone hung around Karou's neck, and the greater task by far: that there may come such a day at all, and a world for them to wake to. Brimstone and the Warlord had never been able to achieve it with all their armies, but Madrigal and the angel she loved had shared a beautiful dream, and, though that dream had died on the executioner's block, Brimstone knew better than anyone that death is not the end it sometimes seems.

By the thousands the folk of the united tribes filed down the long spiral stair. It would be crushed behind them; there would be no way out. They beheld the cathedral and it was glorious. They pressed in tight and sang a hymn. It was possible that it would never be more than their tomb, and yet, this was the easy choice.

The hard choice and true heroism was in those who chose to stay above, because they couldn't all go. If every chimaera vanished from Loramendi, the seraphim would guess what they had done and go digging. So some citizens—*many*—had to stay and give the angels satisfaction. They had to *be* the angels' satisfaction, the hard-won corpses to feed to their fires. The old stayed, as did most who had already lost their children, and an undue number of the ravaged refugees who had endured so much and had but this one thing left to give.

They sacrificed themselves that some might yet know life in a better time.

This was what Karou went armed with this morning, as well as her literal arms: her crescent-moon blades slung at her hips and her small knife pushed down the side of her boot. With Issa at her side, she headed to the court where the Wolf and his soldiers were already awake and gathered in the clean, crisp air, several teams armed and ready to fly. Amzallag's team was one, and Karou felt her heart reaching toward the soldier. She wished she could tell him her news alone, and some of the others, too, who would be most powerfully affected by it.

Amzallag had children. Or he had had them, before Loramendi fell.

"We'll hit them north of the capital," Thiago was saying. "The towns are poorly fortified, and sparsely guarded. The angels haven't seen battle there for hundreds of years. My father had let his edge grow dull. He took a defensive stance. Now we have nothing left to defend."

It was a bold statement, and was met with a shifting of weight by some soldiers. It sounded almost as though he were blaming the Warlord for the fall of their people.

"We do, though," Karou spoke up, stepping out from the same archway she had hidden beneath to watch Ziri and Ixander spar. Thiago turned his benevolent-mask to her; how thin it was, how utterly unconvincing. "We have something to defend."

"Karou," he said, and he was already skimming the scene for Ten, traitor-sitter. Peripherally, Karou saw her on the move.

"There are still lives to be saved," Karou said, "and choices." They were Akiva's words, she realized once they were out. She flushed, though nobody could know that she was parroting Beast's Bane. Well, he was right. More right than he could have known.

"Choices?" Thiago's look was cool, flat. Ten's hand closed on Karou's arm.

"You remember the choice we talked about yesterday," said the she-wolf in a low growl.

"What choice is that, Ten?" Karou asked full-voice. "Do you mean the choice between Zuzana and Mik, and who you would kill first? I choose neither, and they're out of your reach. Get your hand off me." She yanked her arm free, and turned back to the host. She saw some confusion, and shuttling of glances back and forth between herself and Thiago. "The choice I mean is to protect our own innocents from the seraphim, instead of slaughtering theirs."

"There are no innocent seraphim," said the Wolf.

"That's what they say when they kill our children." She couldn't help sliding a glance in Amzallag's direction. "Some even believe it. We know better. All children are innocent. All children are sacred."

"Not theirs." A low growl edged Thiago's voice.

"And all the folk on both sides just trying to live?" Karou took a step toward him. Another. She couldn't feel her feet; maybe she wasn't even walking, but drifting. In her state of anxiety and pumped-up courage her heartbeat roared in her ears. Her courage was a guise. She wondered if courage always was, or if there were those who truly felt no fear. "Thiago, I've been trying to work something out, but I've been afraid to ask you." She swept the host with a look. All these faces, these eyes of her own creation, all these souls she had touched, some beautiful, some not. "I wonder if everyone here understands but me, or if any of you lose sleep wondering." She turned back to Thiago. "What is your objective?"

"My objective? Karou, it is not required of you to understand strategy." She could see he was still trying to work out what audacity brought her to question him, and how he might reassert his control without open threats.

"I didn't ask your strategy, only your objective," she said. "It's a simple question. It should have a simple answer. What are we fighting for? What are we killing for? What do you see when you look into the future?"

How hard and unblinking his eyes, how immobile his face was. His wrath was ice. He had no answer. No good answer, anyway. *We're fighting to kill*, he might have said. *We're killing for vengeance. There is no future.* Karou felt the collective waiting of the chimaera and wondered how many of them would be satisfied with that. How many had lost all ability to hope for more, and how many might find a last scrap of it once they knew what Brimstone had done.

"The future," Thiago said after an overlong pause. "I once overheard you planning the future. You were in the arms of your angel lover, and you spoke of killing *me*."

Ah, yes, Karou thought. It was a skillful evasion on his part. To these soldiers, that image—a chimaera entwined with a seraph—was enough to eclipse her question. "I never agreed to it," she said, which was true, but she sensed that the curiosity she had kindled was waning; she would lose whatever small ground she might have gained. "Answer my question," she said. "Where are you taking us? What do you see in the future? Do we live? Do we have lands? Do we have *peace*?"

"Lands? Peace? You should ask the seraph emperor, Karou, not me."

"What, *the beasts must die*? We've always known his objective, but the Warlord never mimicked it like you are. These terror killings only bring worse down on the people you've forsaken." To the soldiers, "Are you even trying to save chimaera, or is it just about revenge now? Kill as many angels as you can before you die? Is it that simple?" She wished she could tell them what Balieros's patrol had done, and what they had witnessed in the Hintermost, but she couldn't bring herself to reveal that secret. What would Thiago do if he knew?

"You think there's another way, Karou?" He shook his head. "Has all their gentle treatment led you to believe they want to make friends? There's only one way to save chimaera, and that is by killing the angels."

"Killing them all," she said.

"Yes, Karou, killing them all." Scathing. "I know this must be hard for you to hear, with your lover among them."

He would keep coming back to that, and funny thing: The more times he mentioned it, the less shame Karou felt. What had she done, really, but fall in love and dream of peace? Brimstone had already forgiven her. He had more than forgiven her;

he had believed in her dream. And now... he had entrusted it to her—not to Thiago, but to her—to find a way that their people might live again.

And she had thought the pile of thuribles in her room was a burden? Ah, what a little perspective could do. But the sense that had overcome her when Issa told her about the cathedral wasn't the pinned-in-place trapped feeling that she suffered doing Thiago's bidding. No. It was as if she'd been on her knees and Brimstone had grasped her hand and raised her to her feet. It was redemption.

She looked at Issa, who gave a little nod, and she took a deep breath. To the rebels she said, "Most of you or maybe even all of you cheered at my execution. Maybe you blame me for all of this. I don't expect you to listen to me, but I hope you'll hear Brimstone."

That caused a stir. "Brimstone?" some said, skeptical. They looked to Issa, as they should.

Thiago looked to her, too. "What is this?" he asked. "Does Brimstone's ghost speak through you, Naja?"

"If you like, *Wolf*," returned Issa. To the soldiers: "You all know me. For years I was Brimstone's companion, and now I am his messenger. He sent me out from Loramendi in a thurible to serve this purpose, and to do so meant that I could not die beside him as I would have chosen. So listen well, for the sake of his sacrifice and mine. It is grotesque to imagine that killing and mutilation and terror could ever deliver to us a life worth living. They will bring what they always have: more killing, more mutilation, more terror. If you believe vengeance is all that is left to you, hear me." How lovely she was, raised tall on her serpent's coil, and how powerful with her cobra hood flared wide, her scales gleaming like polished enamel in the dawn light. She was beaming, beatific, and radiant with emotion.

She said, "You have more to live for than you know."

66

Kill the Monster. Change the World.

"The emperor will receive you now."

Akiva had been staring over the skybridge at the gray glass domes of the seraglio where he had been born. It was so closed and silent, so unknowable from the outside, but he had dim memories of noise and shafting light, children and babies, playing and singing—and he looked around at the voice. It was the head steward, Byon, leaning on his cane and dwarfed beneath the high, heavy arch of Alef Gate and the pair of Silverswords who flanked it. He was white-haired and grandfatherly at a glance, but only at a glance. It was Byon who maintained the lists of the emperor's bastards, canceling the dead so their names might be given to the newborns. Seeing him, Akiva couldn't help wondering if he would outlive the old seraph, or if that crabbed hand would draw the strike through his own name. He had stricken six Akivas already; what was one more?

For a moment he felt himself to be nothing more than a

placeholder for a name—one is a succession of flesh placeholders for a name that belonged, like everything else, to the emperor. Expendable. Endlessly renewable. But then he focused on what he had come here to do, and he met Byon's rat-black eyes with the cultivated blankness that had been his default expression for years.

He was no placeholder. There would be no eighth Misbegotten bearer of the name Akiva; fathering bastards was only one of many things that Joram would not be doing after tonight. Along with starting wars. Along with breathing.

"Remove your weapons," Byon instructed.

This was expected. No arms save the guards' own were permitted in the emperor's presence. Akiva hadn't even worn his usual pair of swords crossed at his back—the cape that was part of his formal uniform interfered with them. He had buckled a short sword at his hip only to make a show of laying it down on request, which he did.

Hazael and Liraz likewise disarmed and laid down their weapons.

Their visible ones, anyway.

Akiva's own glamoured blade hung from the opposite hip from the one he had laid down. It couldn't be seen, but anyone studying him closely might notice a quirk in the play of shadow along his leg where it hung invisible, and of course it could be felt—cold steel—by any who brushed too near or thought to search him or embrace him, which Akiva thought a small enough risk—the embrace, anyway. As for the search, this was the first test of the emperor's suspicion.

Had he brought the Prince of Bastards here to *use* him, or to *expose* him? Akiva waited out the steward's scrutiny. There was no search. Byon gave him the merest nod, and when he turned and vanished into the Tower of Conquest, Akiva fell into step behind him, and Hazael and Liraz behind him in turn.

The emperor's inner sanctum. Hazael had made inquiries; they knew roughly what to expect—the interlocking passages of thick, honey-hued glass, gate after guarded gate. Akiva committed each turn to memory; this way would be the only way out. They would glamour themselves; that was the plan. In the tumult that would follow the assassination, in the rush and stomp of guards they would vanish and retreat. And escape.

He hoped.

Another passage, another turn, another gate, another passage. Deeper into the emperor's inner sanctum. Akiva's anticipation grew taut.

How weary he was of this brute response to all problems: Kill your enemy. *Kill, kill.* But right now the brute response was the *only* response. For the good of Eretz, for an end to war.

Joram must die.

Akiva reached for *sirithar*—the state of calm in which the godstars work through the swordsman—but didn't come anywhere close to it. He managed to hold his heartbeat steady, but his mind raced—through scenarios, magical manipulations, even *words.* What would he *say* when he faced his father and unsheathed his blade? He didn't know. Nothing at all. It didn't matter. It was the deed that mattered, not words.

Do the thing. Kill the monster. Change the world.

67

The Only Hope Is Hope

Amzallag bulled forward and fell to his knees before Issa. "Who?" he asked, almost whispering. "Who went into the cathedral?" A few other soldiers leaned forward with intense, restrained yearning.

"Thousands." Issa's voice was tender. "There was no time to make a record. I'm sorry."

Karou stepped forward. "All the children went," she said, looking to Issa for confirmation. "And all the mothers. The chances are very good for your families."

Amzallag looked stunned. On his tiger features "stunned" came across as a wide-eyed version of his constant ferocity—ferocity that was more Karou's doing than his. His soul was as plain as tilled earth and as steady as a carthorse, but with this body she had given him he could hardly help but look ferocious. His jaws with their kitchen-knife fangs were agape and his deep orange eyes were unblinking. Although he was kneeling—his stag forelegs buckled before him and tiger haunches bunched in a crouch—he still towered above Issa, and his arms, when he reached for her hands, were huge and gray. *Before he sees his family again*, Karou thought, *I can give him a gentler form.*

But that was getting ahead of herself. Way ahead.

While Amzallag's big hands took Issa's, Karou watched Thiago. When Amzallag said "Thank you," in a voice like the saddest pull of a violin, Thiago's fangs showed in a fleeting snarl.

"I am only a messenger," said Issa.

At that, Thiago's eyes slid from her to Karou. "Tell us again," he said, "how exactly that was accomplished."

"How what was accomplished?" Issa asked. Amzallag released her hands and rose, turning himself with smooth tiger movements to stand at her side—and Karou's side—across the court from the Wolf. The move was deliberate, and sent a clear message of allegiance. Karou's feeling of triumph was compromised, however, by the inquisition she felt coming.

"How you arrived among us," Thiago said. "One morning, here you were. It is very strange."

"Strange it may be, but I can't satisfy you. The last thing I remember before waking is, of course, dying."

"And where was it Brimstone planned to send your soul, in the grip of his squall? You must know that at least."

Karou interrupted. "Is this all you have to say? We've just told you that thousands of our people can still be saved, and you talk of squalls? Thiago, our children can live again. This is enormous news. Can't you be glad?"

"My gladness, my lady, is tempered with realism, as yours should be. Live where? Live how? This changes nothing."

"It changes everything!" she cried. "Everything you're doing is hopeless. Can't you see? It is futureless. This brutality, the civilian attacks? Your father would be sick. Everything you do to the seraphim, Joram will return a hundredfold, a thousandfold." She was appealing to the host now. "Did Thisalene give you satisfaction? *The angels must die?*" She pinpointed Tangris and Bashees, and fought against the fear that would have snatched her voice right back into her throat. To call out the Shadows That Live? Was she mad? *Remember the chicken impression,* she told herself with a surge of hysteria.

"In Thisalene," she said, "you slew a hundred angels." The sphinxes met her look in their inscrutable way. "And hundreds of chimaera died for it." One sphinx blinked. Karou continued, taking in the others. Oh, her heart, it was beating furious-fast. "And the rest of you. You let them die. You gave them hope—the Warlord's smiles, the messages. *We are arisen?* And then? All those folk of the south, they couldn't believe that you would start this fight, call the enemy down on them in such impossible numbers, only to abandon them. Do you know..." Karou swallowed. Her own cruelty felt icy, spiky, to put it to them like this. "Do you know that they died watching the sky for you?"

She saw Bast take a stagger-step back. Some others were breathing as though their throats had gone tight. Virko was staring at the ground.

"Don't listen to this," snarled Ten. "She can't know what happened there."

"I do know what happened," said Karou. She hesitated. Was it betrayal to tell of Balieros's defiance? *He* would tell them, if he were here; she felt sure of it. The future of the rebellion hung in the balance, and she had this weight to slam heavy on the scale. How could she not use it? "Because one team did what none of the rest of you would. Do you really believe Balieros and Ixander, Viya, Azay, and Minas succumbed to some town guard? They died fighting Dominion in the south. They died defending chimaera. While you were doing what?"

The sun was climbing, the heat growing heavy. The court was bright and still. Thiago answered her. "While we were doing what the angels were doing, and yet it's us you scathe, not them. Would you have us lie down and bare our throats to them?"

"No." Karou swallowed. This was difficult ground she was treading: how to argue for a different course without coming across as some starry-eyed peacenik—naive at best, an enemy sympathizer at worse, which they already believed she was. It all came down to this: She could offer them no real alternative to fighting. When she had dreamed together with Akiva of the world remade, she had believed that he would bring his people forward as she would somehow bring hers—as if the future were some country they could meet in, a land with different rules, where the past might be overcome—or overlooked?—like a seraph knuckle tally erased from the skin.

Now, on the outside of the bubble of that foolish love, Karou saw how grim their dream would have become had they been left to pursue it, how dirty, how bruised. Those tally marks would never have faded. They would have remained always—between herself and Akiva, chimaera and seraphim—and the hamsas would, too. They couldn't even touch properly. To have believed that they might join two such sets of hands together, the dream seemed madder than ever. And yet... *the only hope is hope.* Brimstone's words, back then and again now, as gifted her by Issa.

"Daughter of my heart," was the message Brimstone had sent just for Karou. She wanted to cry again right here in the court, thinking of it. "Twice-daughter, my joy. Your dream is my dream, and your name is true. You are all of our hope."

Her dream. A dream dirty and bruised is better than no dream at all. But she had had Akiva then, and the hope that he might bring the seraphim to their new way of living. What did she have now? Nothing to promise, and no plan. Nothing but her name.

"No," she said again. "I would not have us bare our throats. Nor would I have you thrust our people to their knees in your rush to slaughter theirs. Nor would I have you leave our future buried under the ash, so that you might bury theirs."

Thiago's eyes narrowed as he tried but couldn't at once find words to answer that.

Karou went on. "Brimstone once told me that to stay true in the face of evil is a feat of strength. If we let them turn us into monsters..." She looked at Amzallag, the gray hue of his flesh, at Nisk and Lisseth, who stood just behind Thiago, still recognizable as Naja but with none of Issa's beauty and grace. At all the others, overlarge, overfanged, winged and clawed, and unnatural. She had done this, the literal work of turning these chimaera into the monsters the angels believed them to be.

"Someone has to stop killing," she implored Thiago. "Someone has to stop *first.*"

"Let it be them, then," he said, so cold, his lips trembling with the effort not to fall into a full wolf snarl. His fury was palpable.

"We can only decide for ourselves. At least we can stop the assaults long enough to think of another way, instead of making it worse, always worse."

"We are destroyed, Karou. It can't get any worse."

"It can. It *has*. The Hintermost? The Tane? What is Razor doing right now, and how will it be answered? It can get worse until there is no one left. Or maybe . . . maybe it can get better." Again Akiva's words came into her head, and again Karou spoke them, this time without blushing. "Eretz will have chimaera in it or not, depending on what we do now."

And that was when the Shadows That Live spread their silent wings and lifted with the grace of dreams and nightmares to float over the heads of their comrades and land lightly at Karou's side. They didn't speak; they rarely did. Their stance was clear: elegant heads held high, eyes defiant. Karou was breathless with a sudden swell of emotion. Of power. Amzallag, Tangris, Bashees, Issa. Who else? She looked to the rest. Most seemed stunned. In more than a few pairs of eyes, though, Karou saw malice to match the Wolf's, and knew that there were those among them whose hate would never again be touched by hope. In others, she saw fear.

In too many others. Bast would come, though; Karou willed her to take a step. She was on the verge. Emylion? Hvitha? Virko?

And Thiago? He stood staring at Karou, and she remembered the way he had looked down at her in the requiem grove in another life. She saw that savagery in him again, the flaring nostrils and wild eyes, but then... she saw him pull it back. She witnessed the moment that he mastered his fury, and, with calculation and cunning, and *effort*, put his mask back in place. It was worse than hate or fear, this lie of mildness. This huge, huge lie. "My lady Karou," he said. "You make a powerful argument."

Wait, Karou thought. *No*.

"I will take it under consideration," he said. "Of course. We'll consider all possibilities, including—as we now may, with glad hearts—how to glean the souls from the cathedral."

Her new surge of power shrank to nothing. By giving her this small victory, the Wolf took away her chance for a greater one. Now none of the other soldiers need gather their courage to come to her side, and their relief was profound. She could see it in their posture, in their faces. They didn't want to choose. They didn't want to choose *her*. How much easier it was to let themselves be led by their general. Bast wouldn't even look at her. *Cowards*, she thought, starting to shake as all of her pumped-up courage collapsed into frustration. Could they really believe that the White Wolf would consider ending—or even pausing—in his crusade? *Victory and vengeance*. He would have to tear his gonfalon down, make a new one. She thought with yearning of the Warlord's symbol: antlers sprouting leaves. New growth. How perfect, and how out of reach.

And now, so quickly, the rest of these soldiers were out of her reach, too. Thiago was accustomed to wielding power, and she was so very not. Effortlessly he took back what little she had gained and turned the army's energy to his plans.

His plans for gleaning the buried souls from the cathedral.

Amzallag himself was the first to volunteer. He went forward, avid, and others followed him. Karou stood rooted in place, all but forgotten. Issa took her hand and squeezed it, communicating her shared dismay, while the Shadows That Live melted away before she could even thank them, and soon the direct heat of the sun drove most of them from the court.

The day passed away in this atmosphere of new energy. Karou and Issa watched and listened, and Thiago did entirely appear to be doing what he had said he would: considering all possibilities, such as how they might conduct an excavation in enemy-patrolled territory, and even what they might do in the south to help more chimaera reach the Hintermost. It was exactly what Karou wanted, and she could barely breathe, because she knew it was just another move in the Wolf's game. A feint. But what did it conceal? What was his true game?

Night fell, and she found out.

68

Sirithar

Akiva followed Byon through one last set of doors. Fragrance and humidity greeted them; a billow of steam obscured Akiva's vision at the moment he crossed the threshold, and he heard his father's voice before he saw him.

"Ah, Lord Bastard. You honor us with your presence." It was a powerful voice, honed on bygone battlefields crying death to the beasts. Whatever he was now, Joram had been a warrior once.

And he looked it. Akiva bowed; he was rising as the steam cleared, and saw that they were in a bath, and that Joram was naked. The emperor stood on the steaming tiles, hale and solid, his flesh rouged by heat, surrounded by the small army of servants apparently required to purify his royal person. A girl tipped a pitcher of water over his head and he closed his eyes. Another was on her knees, washing him with a lather as thick as whipped cream.

Akiva had envisioned this meeting many different ways, and in none of them had his father been naked. *He suspects nothing*, he thought. *If he did, he would meet me clothed and armed*. "My lord emperor," he said, "the honor is all mine."

"*Our* honor, *your* honor," drawled Joram. "Whatever shall we do with such an excess of honor?"

"We could always hang it from the Westway," said another voice, and Akiva didn't have to see that cut-in-half face to know whose it was. Sunk back on a tiled bath bench in a pose of informality that he alone would dare in the emperor's presence, was Jael. Well, that was a convenience, as, of course, Jael could not be allowed to live any more than Joram could. He, blessedly, was fully clad. "If only there was room on the gibbet," he said like a lament, and low laughter rumbled through the others assembled here. Akiva gave their faces a quick scan. None lounged like Jael, but all seemed enough at their ease that he took these bath-time councils to be a common occurrence.

Joram's mouth carved a smile from his cruel face. "Room can always be made on the gibbet," he said.

Was it a threat? Akiva didn't think so. Joram wasn't even looking at him; he closed his eyes and tipped back his head for another sluice from his attendant's pitcher, after which he shook his head hard, spraying water. Namais and Misorias, standing near as ever, both blinked at the spray but elsewise moved not a muscle. Joram's personal guards—brothers—were said to be deadly fighters. They were Akiva's first concern. Silverswords were present, as well, two pairs each along facing walls: eight Breakblades with condensation fogging their silver armor, their plumes gone limp in the steam. He wasn't worried about them.

In fact, as his father stepped out of the shallow pool of lather, away from the white-garbed girls and toward a servant holding a robe, Akiva found his worry draining away. He may not have envisioned a bath in his planning, but in all ways, here was his optimal scenario: a light guard presence in a contained environment, a limited number of witnesses whose word would be taken on faith, and, most important: the absence of suspicion.

Nothing in the eyes of these seraphim hinted at wariness.

There was Crown Prince Japheth, glassy-eyed with boredom. He was a blandly attractive seraph of around Akiva's age, with some indefinable flaccidness about the set of his features that spoke of weakness. Akiva knew that Japheth was no paragon. He would be better than his father; that was what mattered. Beside him was white-haired Ur-Magus Hellas, head of the emperor's circle of useless magi, said to have the emperor's ear. His look of heavy, half-lidded condescension was all Akiva needed to see to know that his own magic remained his secret. A few other faces were unfamiliar, uniform in their haughtiness.

"Let me look at you," commanded Joram.

"My lord," replied Akiva, and stood where he was as his father centered himself before him and inspected him with a squint. He had put his robe on, but hadn't closed it; Akiva wished he would. It seemed a strange intimacy to kill a naked man. Joram was so near that Akiva could have reached out and tapped him on the breastbone. Or pierced him through the heart. He had the unwelcome thought that his father's steam-pink breast would give like softened butter. He was aware of his own heartbeat pulsing in the tension of his hand. His hand, his arm, his body wanted to draw his sword and be done here, but his mind buzzed with questions.

What is this about?

And something else. *Terrible what happened to her.* If Akiva didn't find out now, he never would.

He held his father's stare. Or perhaps his father's stare held him. Joram's eyes were so like Liraz's and Hazael's: blue, down-tilting at the outer-corners, generously lashed in gold. Unlike theirs, though, their father's were devoid of any trace of soul. His stare was infamous; it was said one saw one's own death in it, or at least the utter worthlessness of one's life. It brought seraphim to their knees; the unworthy were said to open their own throats for terror and shame.

And Akiva did see death in the emperor's eyes, but not his own.

He felt a thickness in his throat. He knew what it was: It was emotion, but... for what? Not for Joram, not remorse for what he was going to do. Was it for the faceless, all-but-forgotten woman who'd given him her tiger's eyes and stood aside as the guards took him? Or... for the face he had seen in silver that day, small and terrified and mirrored over and over in the shin plates of Silverswords. For himself. For all that he had lost and all that he had never had and never would have.

"Yes, you'll do," said Joram at last. "It's lucky, after all, that I let you live. If I'd had you killed, who would I send to them?"

Send to them.

"*They* may choose to kill you; what do I know of Stelians? You should say your good-byes, just in case."

From across the room, Jael spoke. "It's bad luck for soldiers to say good-bye, brother. Have you forgotten? It tempts fate."

Joram rolled his eyes, turning away from Akiva. "Then don't say it. What do I care?" He walked out of easy reach; Namais and Misorias were right there. Akiva had let an opportunity go by. There would be another. He would make another. "Be ready to go in the morning." Joram spared Hazael and Liraz a backward glance; if he noted their resemblance to himself, he gave no sign. "*Alone.*"

"Go where, my lord?" asked Akiva. He had already made his plans for the morning, of course—to vanish without a trace—but the loose thread of a mystery was here just waiting for him to pull it. His mother.

"To the Far Isles, of course. The Stelians believe that I have something of theirs, and they want her back. Jael, you'll remember. I never bother with their names. What was she called?"

"I do remember," said Jael. "She was called Festival."

Festival.

"Festival. A name like that and you'd expect her to be *fun.*" Joram shook his head. "Can they imagine I'd have kept her all this time?"

Festival.

The name, it was like a key in a lock. Images. Perfume. Touch. Her face. For an instant Akiva remembered his mother's face. Her voice. It was a long time ago—decades—they were fragments only, but the effect was immediate: it was focus and clarity, like light honed to a beam.

The effect was *sirithar.*

Akiva had thought he knew *sirithar.* It was a part of his

training; he had done dawn katas for years, seeking the calm center of himself; it was elusive, but he had believed he knew what it was. This was different. This was true and instant and indelible. No wonder he hadn't understood; no doubt none of his trainers had ever achieved it, either.

It was magic.

Not the magic he had discovered for himself, cobbled together out of guesswork and pain. He may as well have lived his life scraping and scratching in the dirt, only now lifting his head to see the sky and its infinite horizons, its unguessable fathoms. Whatever the source of power or the tithe, it wasn't pain. In fact, the pain in his shoulder was gone. *What is this?* Light and lift and weightlessness, a depth of calm that made the world around him seem to slow and crystallize so that he saw everything—Japheth's jaw straining to stifle a yawn, a flicker of a glance shared between Hellas and Jael, the sphygmic jump of Joram's jugular. The heat and stir of breath and wings, every movement painted strokes of intention on the air. He knew the servant girl was going to rise from her crouch before she did: her light moved ahead of her, she seemed to follow it. Joram's hands were going to lift; Akiva anticipated it and then they did. The emperor at last closed his robe, tied its sash. He was still speaking, each word as clear and real as a river stone. Akiva understood that what he heard in this state would be committed perfectly to memory.

That he would never forget his father's last words.

And that he knew what his last words would be.

"You'll go to them," Joram was saying with the disengaged certitude of absolute autocracy. Akiva realized he need never have feared he was suspected. Joram was so swollen with his own legend it would not occur to him that he might be disobeyed. "Show them who you are. If they'll hear you, give them my promise. If they surrender now and yield up their magi, I will not do to them as I have done to the beasts. The Stelians fare well enough snatching envoys out of the air, but what will they do against five thousand Dominion? Have they even an army? They think they can turn *me* aside so easily?"

You do not begin to understand how far they are beyond you. A part of Akiva wanted to turn in a circle and marvel at the rivers of light swimming through the layers and layers of glass of the Sword, to hold up his own hands and stare at them as if they had been remade, as if he himself were an entirely new creature built of those same rays of light.

Light veiling fire.

A voice, out of the distant past. "You are not his." It was her voice, a resonant vibrato, accented and full of power. It was that day. "You are not mine. You are your *own*." She hadn't wept. *Festival.* She hadn't tried to hold on to him or grapple with the guards, and she hadn't said good-bye. Good-byes tempt fate, as Jael had said.

Had she thought she might see him again?

"Did you kill her?"

He heard himself ask the question and was aware of many things at once: the sudden stillness of the counsel; the clench of Namais's and Misorias's fists on their hilts; a flare of interest from Japheth, who lost his urge to yawn. Behind him, he didn't even have to see Hazael and Liraz to know that their muscles relaxed into readiness; he knew Liraz was already smiling her unnerving battle smile. "Did you kill my mother?"

And he saw his father's eyes, unsurprised and full of contempt. "You have no mother. As you have no father. You are a link in a chain. You are a hand to swing a sword. A hull to dress in armor. Have you forgotten all of your training, soldier? You are a weapon. You are a *thing*."

Those were the words. Akiva had heard them echo backward through the shimmer of *sirithar*. He already knew they were Joram's last.

And so he dropped the glamour from his sword and drew it from his sheath. He was moving within the tide of time; it would be done before the witnesses could even register their shock. Namais and Misorias began to move, but they existed in another state of being. Akiva was fire veiled in light. They couldn't hope to stop him. He crossed the space to the emperor in the time it took a blink of surprise to crease his cold eyes.

How could he not see the change in me? Akiva wondered, and he slid his blade through the silk of his father's robe and into his heart.

69

Scratching

It was Bast who came scratching at Karou's window. The shutters were secured by their long brass latches, and across the room Mik's planks were sunk in their floor gouges, jammed up under handles and hinges. Door and window were both shut tight, and Issa and Karou were within, uneasy. Karou paced. Issa twitched her tail. They were waiting for something to happen.

And something did.

The scratching at the shutters. A hoarse whisper. "Karou. Karou, open the window."

Karou shrank back. "Who's there?"

"It's Bast. I'm on sentry duty, I shouldn't be here."

"Why are you?" Karou's anger flared. If Bast had come across the court this morning, others might have, too. And...what if they had? Karou didn't even know what she would have done. She was so out of her depth she wanted to curl up and cry. *Oh, Brimstone, did you really think I could do this?* Well, he couldn't have known that the Wolf would live through the war to thwart her at every turn, could he?

"It's... it's the Wolf," came Bast's reply, and Karou felt as though the air were sucked out of the room. Here it was, the clatter of the other shoe dropping. What had he done? "He's taken Amzallag and the sphinxes. I saw them from the tower."

Taken? Karou and Issa exchanged a sharp look. Karou yanked the window open. Bast clung to the ledge, wings half-open and lightly fanning to keep her balanced on her too-narrow perch.

"Taken them where?" Karou demanded.

Bast looked stricken. "To the pit," she whispered.

Afterward Karou would wonder if Bast had been Thiago's pawn or his conspirator, but in that moment she didn't suspect her. Her horror seemed real, and maybe it was. Maybe she was thinking how it could have been her making that walk, with how close she had come to taking Karou's side. And maybe—probably—she was thinking that it was a mistake that would never again tempt her.

One does not side against the Wolf.

With shaking hands Karou buckled her knife belt back on and felt better with the weight of her crescent moons at her hips. The open window was before her. Issa was at her side, but couldn't come through it with her. Karou turned to her.

"I'll follow, sweet girl." Issa moved the door, scales rippling. "Go. I'll be right behind you."

And Karou did go, out into the night. She was already away and over the rampart when Issa pulled up the planks and set them aside. She opened the door.

And came face-to-face with Ten.

70

Long Live the Emperor

The emperor dropped to his knees. His eyes died; the hate flickered out of them as life poured red from his chest. No one caught him, and he keeled over with a splash into the shallow channel of the bath. Water and lather bloomed pink.

A servant girl screamed.

Namais and Misorias were in motion. Akiva blocked their strikes; nothing had ever been easier.

He sensed the guards coming off their walls, their shock blunting the air. At least one got tangled in his own bell sleeve fumbling for his hilt, and cursed. As one, Hazael and Liraz unsheathed their swords.

The Silverswords might have believed they had the advantage from numbers alone—eight to two—but at the first crossing of blades their confidence evaporated. This was no exercise of parries and thrusts such as they were used to, no nice *ching* and chime of silver. Hazael and Liraz wielded their longswords two-handed, such power in their strikes as had rent the armor and hide of countless revenants. Decades of battle, hands black with their terrible tally, and their onslaught caught the guards like a force of nature.

They weren't two fighting off eight. They were two cutting through eight. Slight as Liraz was, her first blow dislocated the shoulder of the guard who blocked it. His *uff* of pain was followed by a clatter as his sword flew from his hand; she didn't finish him as he staggered back but spun toward another guard with a low lightning kick that took him out at the knee. His *uff* bit at the heels of his comrade's, and he was down, too.

Hazael's first strike shaved through his opponent's blade, leaving the guard holding a pretty silver stub.

All of this transpired in the gasp between breaths—the Misbegotten schooling the swaggering Silverswords in the vital difference between a *guard* and a *soldier*—and the guards' eyes flared wide in understanding. The posture of the remaining five changed from menacing confidence to a defensive hunch. Readjusting their grips, they formed a loose circle around the Misbegotten, and their volley of glances, one to another, was easy to interpret:

Go on, attack them.

You attack them.

They needn't have worried. Liraz and Hazael didn't wait. Waiting gave the enemy time to think. They themselves didn't need to think any more than their swords did. They attacked. They were *nithilam*. The clangor was deafening, and the nickname "breakblades" proved well-founded as the guards' flashing, brittle weapons shattered at the slash of steel. Across the room, one of the unknown counselors ducked just in time as a flying shard of silver sword embedded itself in the wall where seconds earlier his head had been.

The Breakblades were all disarmed, lightly injured, and when one made a halfhearted try for a sword, Liraz had only to grin and shake her head, and he halted like a guilty child.

"Just stand there," she told them. "Demonstrate for us your great skill at *standing there*, and you'll be fine."

The others stood taking up space—so much space, such big bodies, and such poor training. Their lives had never been in danger before, and if Liraz and Hazael had wanted to kill them they'd have found it pitifully easy. But they didn't want to kill them. They'd scarcely drawn blood. Joram had been one target, and he lay dead and unattended in shallow water that had deepened now from pink to red. Jael was the other.

But Jael was gone.

"Akiva," said Liraz. "Jael."

Akiva already knew. The three Misbegotten held the center of the room. It was quiet. All told maybe two minutes had passed since Akiva's blade had entered his father's heart. He had disarmed Namais and Misorias—they had put up a better fight, but not good enough—and had rendered them unconscious with the hilt of his sword to forestall any heroics that might force him to kill them. One had landed facedown, and in the moment it had taken Akiva to turn him over with his foot and prevent him from drowning in the shallow red water, Jael had vanished.

Where? If he had escaped through some secret door, he had failed to take his nephew along. Akiva took a long, level look at the crown prince. Japheth had pulled one of the serving girls against him as a living shield. She was frozen, crushed to his chest, her long braid caught in his fist where a better man would have held a sword.

And here is the new emperor, Akiva thought.

Wherever Jael had gone, he must now raise the cry. Akiva braced for the response that must come. He was surprised that it hadn't already; he'd expected the guards at Samekh Gate to hear the ring of blades and come rushing in; it was then that he and Hazael and Liraz were to have glamoured themselves invisible and taken to their wings to find their way out under cover of chaos.

There was, however, no chaos.

Maybe, he thought, sound didn't travel well through all these interlocking glass walls. In the eerie calm, Akiva's newfound state of *sirithar* left him, like something that had come and gone of its own volition, and his senses were robbed of their newfound scope. In this dimness and diminishment, he surveyed the room. The gallery of flatterers sat pinned in place, aghast; mouths gulped fishlike at the humid air. His eyes skimmed over them. Hellas had lost his smugness.

And there was Japheth, clutching the serving girl. Akiva supposed this display shouldn't surprise him, but to hear someone is craven is one thing. To see it made so plain is another. But what was he to do? Their purpose here today must be made clear. It was the assassination of a warmonger, not mutiny against the Empire entire, and not a grasp for power for themselves.

So, holding the crown prince's gaze, Akiva spoke the words

of accession. "The emperor is dead. Long live the emperor." In the atmosphere of steam-heat and shock, his voice was heavy, solemn. He crossed his arm over his chest, pressing the hilt of his sword to his heart, and gave Japheth a small nod. Behind him, Hazael and Liraz did the same.

Japheth's terror gave way to confusion. He glanced aside, looking to the council for explanation as if this possibility had never occurred to him. The bath girl took advantage of his confusion and writhed free, darting for the door like a creature freed from a trap. Akiva let her go. The door slammed open as she blew through it and he thought surely now the guards must come flooding into the room.

And still they did not.

Bereft of his living shield, Japheth dropped to his knees and began to crawl slowly backward, trembling. Akiva turned away, disgusted. "We're done here," he said to his brother and sister. Whatever was going on outside this bath, it wouldn't do to wait any longer. It would have been easier to go with chaos for cover—ten gates standing open as their guards rushed to respond—but they would make do, and fight if they had to. He was ready to be gone, to put Astrae and his own treachery behind him.

He made it as far as the door.

It was not Silverswords, with their heavy-booted incompetence and pretty, useless blades, who forced him back. It was Dominion. Not guards but soldiers: ready and calm and *many*. A score, more. *Two* score, crowding the room but bringing no chaos with them, no tide of easy escape. Only grim faces and swords already slick with blood.

Whose blood?

And . . . they brought with them something else, something utterly unexpected, and at the first touch of that wave of debilitating and so-familiar nausea, Akiva understood. As the soldiers winched a tightening circle around him and his brother and sister, around the shamefaced disarmed Breakblades and the corpse of the emperor, they carried grisly . . . trophies . . . before them, and he knew that this had all been orchestrated. He had played a part written for him by Jael, and he had played it perfectly.

The Dominion were holding out *hands*. Dried, severed hands, marked with the devil's eyes. Revenant hands, as powerful as they had ever been when upheld by their true owners: the chimaera rebels they had killed and burned in the Hintermost.

Akiva felt the assault of the magic as if it entered his bloodstream and curdled him from the inside. He tried to hold out against it, but it was no good. He began to shake and couldn't stop.

"Thank the godstars," he heard the counselors murmuring. "We are saved." Fools. Did they not yet wonder what Dominion were doing inside the Tower of Conquest?

Their captain was with them. "Nephew," he said. For a second Akiva thought Jael was addressing him, but he was looking at Japheth. "Allow me to be the first to offer my congratulations," he said. He was flushed—from the heat, from fear?—his scar a long gnarl of white. He moved to Japheth, who remained on his knees, and told him, "This is no meet pose for the ruler of the Empire of Seraphim. Get up."

He held out his hand.

Akiva understood what was going to happen, but the pulsing sickness of the hamsas met the dullness that had descended in the aftermath of *sirithar*, and he could do nothing to stop it.

Japheth reached for his uncle's hand and Jael took it, but did not raise his nephew to his feet. He pivoted behind him. Japheth gave a gasp of pain as Jael crushed the prince's soft hand in his swordsman's grip and prevented him from rising. A glint of metal, a jerk of the arm, and it was done inside a second: Jael drew his dagger across his nephew's throat and a fine red line appeared there.

Japheth's eyes were wide and rolling. His mouth gaped and no sound came out but a gurgling. The red line grew less fine. A drip became a rivulet. A rivulet a rush.

"The emperor is dead," Jael said before it was strictly true. He smiled and wiped his blade on Japheth's sleeve before dropping him with a shove that sent his body to join Joram's in the red water. "Long live the emperor."

Akiva felt himself as stunned and fish-mouthed as the counselors.

As for Jael, he couldn't have looked more pleased. He turned to Akiva and executed a mocking bow. "Thank you," he said. "I was so hoping you would do that."

From there, Akiva's best-case scenario went very badly wrong.

71

The Pit

By the time Karou reached the pit, it was already done.

Amzallag, Tangris, Bashees. They lay dead in the starlight and Thiago stood by their bodies, calm and shining in all his white, waiting. Waiting for *her*. Others stood by in a loose semicircle, and Karou should have taken one look at the scene, spun right around in the air, and fled back to the questionable safety of her room. But she couldn't, not with those bodies lying there, Amzallag and the sphinxes, their slashed throats still pumping blood into the scree and their souls anchored by failing tethers. Because they had taken her side.

This was to be the price? She would never have another ally. If she let this stand, she might as well abandon the chimaera cause right here and now.

She was dazed with disgust and fury as she dropped down, landing heavily before the Wolf. The blood spatter across his chest and sleeve read as black in the night. Behind him:

mounds of earth from the excavation of the pit; a line of shovels standing upright like fence pickets; Karou could hear a low drone, as of a distant engine, but realized it was flies. Down in the dark. She was a moment surveying the terrible scene before she found her voice. Choking, she said, "And here stands the great hero of the chimaera, murderer of his own soldiers."

"They weren't my own soldiers, apparently," he replied. "Their mistake." And he turned to Amzallag's body. It lay at the very verge of the pit. Thiago braced himself and, with one clawed wolf's foot, dug in and gave a powerful shove so that the body rolled. It had to weigh five hundred pounds, but once the shoulders overbalanced the edge, their bulk dragged at the rest. It was slow, so slow...and then sudden. Amzallag's body tipped into the pit and disappeared into that foul darkness.

Lisseth did the same to the sphinxes' bodies, which were much lighter, and there was almost no sound, as if the landings were soft—Karou knew, and didn't want to picture, what it was that cushioned them—but stench rose, and flies, flies by the hundreds. They rose in a buzz of black and seemed to carry the putrescence with them. She backed away, fighting her gag reflex. She could almost feel the air in her mouth, thick and choking, fume and liquid. She staggered back, looked aghast at Thiago.

"They aren't all monsters like you," she said. "Like the rest of you." She scanned the captains assembled around them—Nisk, Lisseth, Virko, Rark, Sarsagon—and they met her eyes, blank and unashamed except for Virko, who looked down when she lit on him.

"Monsters, yes, we are monsters," said Thiago. "I will give

the angels their 'beasts.' I will give them nightmares to haunt their dreams long after I am gone."

"Is that it, then?" she snapped. "That's your objective, to leave a legacy of nightmares when you die? Why not? Why wouldn't it be all about *you*? The great White Wolf, killer of angels, savior to no one."

"Savior." He laughed. "Is that what you want to be? What a lofty goal for a traitor."

"I was never a traitor. If anyone is, it's you. All of that today about excavating the cathedral? Was it all lies?"

"Karou, what do you think? What would we do with those thousands of souls? Our resurrectionist can barely build an army."

Such contempt in his voice. Karou's was its equal. "Yes, well, I'm done building your army, so I'll need something to keep me busy." She was practically spitting now, her head filled with the white noise of rage. She would get Amzallag's soul, and the sphinxes', too. Amzallag had not lived to have the hope of his family only to die now.

"Done, are you?" Thiago smiled. *Killer, torturer, savage.* He was in his element. "Do you really think this is a game you can win?" He shook his head. "Karou, Karou. Oh, your name does amuse me. That fool Brimstone. He named you *hope* because you rutted with an angel? He should have named you *lust*. He should have named you *whore*."

There was no sting in the word. Nothing Thiago said could wound her. Looking at him now, she could scarcely understand how she had let herself be led for so long, doing his bidding, building monsters to ensure his nightmare legacy. She thought of Akiva, the night he had come to her at the river, the crushing pain and shame in his face, and love, still love—sorrow and love and *hope*—and she remembered the night of the Warlord's ball, how Akiva had always been the right to Thiago's wrong, the heat to the Wolf's chill, the safety to this monster's menace.

She fixed Thiago with a narrow stare and said quietly, coolly, "It still eats at you, doesn't it? That I chose him over you? You want to know something?" *Love is an element.* "It was *no contest.*" She hissed the last words, and a spasm of fury wracked Thiago's cold, composed face. That beautiful vessel that Brimstone had made; it hid such a black, deadly thing within.

"Leave us." He spoke through clenched teeth, and the others were shaking out their wings to obey before Karou had even a moment to regret her words. With the sound of wings and the great, dust-stirring gusts of their backbeats, the fanning fumes of rot, the sting of dirt on her bare arms, her face, she felt the phantom twitch of her own once-wings, so deep was her impulse to flee. Like the night of the Warlord's ball, when she danced with Thiago and every second her wings had ached to carry her away from him.

Away, away. *Get away from him.* She gathered herself to leap, but before she could leave the ground, Thiago moved. Fast. His hand flashed out, clamped around her arm—her bruises screamed—and he held. Tight.

"It *does* eat at me, Karou. Is that what you want to hear? That you *humiliated* me? I punished you for it, but the punishment was...unsatisfying. It was impersonal. Your protector Brimstone made certain I was never alone with you. Did you know that? Well, he's not here now, is he?"

Caught in his grip, Karou looked after the departing soldiers. Only Virko looked back. He didn't stop, though, and all too soon the darkness gathered him and he was gone with the others, wingbeats fading, dust settling, and Karou was left alone with Thiago.

His hand on her arm was a vise; Karou knew how Brimstone had made the Wolf's bodies. She knew the strength in him, and she didn't hope to break his grip. "Let me go."

"Wasn't I kind? Wasn't I gentle? I thought that was what you wanted. I thought it would be the best way with you. Coaxing and kindness. But I see I was wrong. And do you want to know? I'm glad. There are other means of persuasion."

His free hand, suddenly, was at her waist, thrust under the edge of her shirt to clutch at her bare skin. Her own free hand flew to the crescent-moon blade sheathed at her hip, but Thiago batted it away and seized the weapon himself, flinging it into the pit. It was only seconds before the other followed it, and Karou was shoving uselessly at his chest in her struggle to get free of him.

It all happened so fast, and she was off her feet, hitting the scree so hard her vision went dark and her breath was driven from her lungs. She was gasping and Thiago was over her, heavy and far too strong, and the useless thought looping in her mind was, *He can't, he can't hurt me, he needs me*, and all the while he was laughing.

Laughing. His breath on her face; she turned away from it, struggled, every muscle straining against him, every gasped breath a lungful of stench from the pit.

She was strong, too. Her body was Brimstone's work as much as his was, and it wasn't empty strength, either—she had trained all her life. She got an arm free and twisted, wedged her shoulder between them, pulled up a knee and threw him off, rolled clear as he came lunging right back at her and she was up and reaching for the sky, for escape, when he tackled her from behind and she went down hard again. Her face in the scree this time and pain flaring through her and she was pinned, his weight so heavy on her shoulders she could get no purchase to throw him off, and then his voice was in her ear—"*Whore,*" he breathed—and his breath was hot, his lips were on her earlobe, and then the sharp points of his fangs.

He bit her. *Tore* her.

She screamed, but he slammed her head into the scree again and the scream choked off.

She couldn't see him. He was holding her facedown in the dirt and rocks when she felt his clawed fingers dig under the waistband of her jeans and tug. For a second, her mind went blank.

No.

No.

The screaming wasn't her voice. It was her mind, and it was the same foolish, outraged loop again: *He can't, he can't.*

But he *could.* He *was.*

The jeans stayed put, though, even when he yanked so hard it dragged her a foot across the ground, her cheek feeling every rock, and so he rolled her over again to get at the button and he was on her and he was smiling and her blood was on his lips, on his fangs, it dripped into *her* mouth and she tasted it. The stars were above him and it was when he let go of her arm to grab both sides of her jeans and try to lever them off that her fingers closed on a rock and she smashed his smile from his face.

He gave a grunt of pain, but his face stayed right there. His blood joined hers on his fangs and his smile came back. His laugh, too. It was obscene. His mouth was a grimace of red and he was still on her.

"*No!*" she cried, and the word felt like it pulled from her soul.

"Don't act so pure, Karou," he said. "We're all just vessels, after all." And when he yanked at her jeans this time they peeled down and caught on her boots, bunching around her calves. She felt rocks beneath her bare skin, gouging. The screaming in her head was deafening and useless, useless, as his knee came down between hers and wedged them apart. His snarl was pure animal and Karou fought. She fought. She didn't fall still. Every muscle was in motion, working against him. His clawed fingertips lacerated her arms holding her, and the rocks tore at her back, at her legs, but the pain was so far away. She knew that she must not lie still, she must never lie still. He shifted his grip on her arms so he was holding both her wrists with one hand—to free his other hand, to free his other hand—but she tore out of his grip and reached for his eyes. He pulled back just in time and she missed and dug grooves in his cheeks instead.

He backhanded her.

She was blinking and the stars were swimming. She was shaking her head to clear it when she remembered her knife.

In her boot.

Her boot seemed such a very long way from her hands. He held her wrists so tightly she could barely feel her fingers, and when he paused and drew himself up again to fumble at his own clothes—*not so white now,* she heard herself think from very far away—he had to let one of hers go. She let it fall aside this time, limp. She closed her eyes. Outside the circle of their ragged breathing, the desert silence was like a void, eating sound, swallowing it. She wondered: If she screamed, would they even hear her at the kasbah? If they did, would anyone even come?

Issa. Issa should have been here by now.

What had they done to Issa?

Karou didn't scream.

Thiago forgot her free hand as he lowered himself onto her, and she turned her head aside and squeezed her eyes shut. She didn't look at him. His breath came in wolfish pants now, and she shifted her hips and turned, twisted to deny him, and she didn't look as she groped under the bunched denim of her jeans for the top of her boot. For her knife. That small hilt, it was cool in her hot hand. In the pain and breathlessness, the squeezed-shut blindness, the fug of rot and the buzz of flies, the scraping, shifting scree and the press and wrench of flesh, that hilt was everything.

She eased it free. Thiago was trying to push her hips flat. "Come, love," he said in his purr of a voice. "Let me in." Nothing had ever been as perverse as that soft voice, and Karou knew that if she looked at him she would find him smiling. So she didn't look.

She sank her blade to the hilt in the soft hollow of his throat. It was a small knife, but it was big enough.

Heat poured over Karou and it was blood. Thiago's hands abruptly forgot her hips. And when she did open her eyes, he wasn't smiling anymore.

72

A Sad Waste of Pain

"Kill everyone," Jael commanded his soldiers with morbid good cheer.

Akiva still stood in the center of the bath, his brother and sister with him, and they still held their swords, though with the sick pulse of the devil's marks, he knew they were in no condition to defend themselves against so many soldiers.

"Not *everyone*," corrected Ur-Magus Hellas, who had moved to Jael's side, and who, unlike the rest of the council members, was manifestly unshocked by all that had transpired. A conspirator.

"Of course," said Jael, all lisping courtesy. "I misspoke." To his soldiers: "Kill everyone but the Misbegotten."

Hellas's look of smug complacency vanished. "What?"

"Certainly. Traitors must have a public execution, must they not?" said Jael, deliberately not taking Hellas's meaning. He turned to the bastards, still with that repulsive cheer. "As my brother said earlier, room can always be made on the gibbet."

"My lord," said Hellas, affronted and only just beginning to be afraid. "I mean *myself*."

"Ah, well. I am sorry, old friend, but you have conspired in my brother's death. How could I trust you not to betray *me*?"

"*I?*" Hellas went red. "*I* have conspired? With *you*—"

A cluck of the tongue, and Jael said, "You see? Already you are singing songs about me. Everyone knows it was Beast's Bane who killed Joram and poor Japheth, too, his own blood. How could I let you leave this room, to go and spread lies about me?"

The magus's red face drained white. "I wouldn't. I'm yours. My lord, you need a witness. You said—"

"The bath girl will serve as a witness. She will serve *better*, because she will *believe* what she says. She saw the bastard slay the emperor. The rest, well, she'll be distraught. She'll believe she saw it all."

"My lord. You... you need a magus—"

"As if you are capable of *magic*," Jael scoffed. "I've no need of frauds or poisoners. Poison is for cowards. Enemies should *bleed*. Take heart, my friend. You die in noble company." He gave the slightest of gestures—little more than a twitch of his hand—and the soldiers moved forward.

Hellas cast wildly about for some protector. "Help!" he cried, though he had certainly played a part in ensuring that no help would be forthcoming.

The other council members cried out, too. Akiva felt more pity for them, though there was little enough space in his own mounting misery to waste pity on this coterie of cruel, handpicked fools.

It was a bloodbath. The Silverswords, big useless brutes and already disarmed, struggled and died. One Dominion soldier dispatched both Namais and Misorias—still unconscious—with light sword strokes to their throats. He might have been scything weeds, so dispassionate was the gesture. The bodyguards' eyes flew open and both experienced the moments of their death with a brief thrash and skid in the dregs of the red bath. The remaining servant girls were not even spared; Akiva saw that coming and tried to shield the one nearest him, but there were too many Dominion, and too many hamsa trophies arrayed against him. The soldiers shoved him back to Hazael and Liraz before silencing the girl's screams with no evidence of remorse.

They were their captain's men through and through, Akiva thought as the scene played out before his eyes. He had witnessed—and partaken in—more than his share of carnage, but this massacre staggered him in its callousness. And its cunning. Watching it, and knowing that he would be blamed for it—that the infamy would be *his* while Jael took up the mantle of emperor—Akiva burned hot and cold, furious and powerless.

He cast wildly about for some trace of the clarity and power that had earlier possessed him, but he sensed nothing beyond his mounting desperation. He looked to his brother and sister; they stood back to back. He could see their strain.

There were four council members besides Hellas; they died more or less as they had watched their emperors die: shocked, outraged, and helpless. Hellas squealed. He tried to get airborne, as if there were any escape in the vaulted glass ceiling, and the soldier's sword caught him in the gut instead of the heart. The pitch of the squeals sharpened, and the magus grabbed at the blade where it entered him; he clutched it as he sank back to the floor, staring down at it with disbelief, and when the soldier jerked the blade free, fingers scattered. Hellas lifted his maimed hands up before his face—blood, so much blood; it fountained from stumped fingers—and that was what he was looking at, in abject horror and still squealing, when the soldier corrected his aim and delivered a clean thrust to the heart.

The squealing stopped.

"I don't believe he even *tried* to do any magic," Jael observed. "And all that pain to tithe, too. What a waste. A sad waste of pain."

Then he turned a piercing look Akiva's way and pointed to *him*. Akiva tensed to defend himself—or try. His grip on his sword was weak and worsening as sickness pulsed at him from all sides. But the soldiers were well attuned to their captain's gestures; they did not attack.

"Now here," Jael said, "stands a magus."

Akiva *was* still standing, though he thought not for long. The sensation of so many hamsas trained on him, it dragged him back years to the scaffold in the agora of Loramendi, Madrigal, and how she had looked at him, and how she had laid her head down on the block; how it had fallen and echoed and he had screamed and been able to do nothing. Where had that state of true *sirithar* been then? He shook his head. He was no magus; a magus could have saved her. A magus could save himself and his brother and sister from these soldiers with their clawed, gnarled trophies, their stolen strength.

Jael mistook his reaction for modesty. "Come now," he said. "You think I don't know, but I do. Oh, this display of glamour, the swords? That was very good, but *the birds? That* was marvelous." He whistled wetly and shook his head: a heartfelt compliment.

Akiva took care to give away nothing. Jael might suspect, but he couldn't *know* the birds had been his work.

"And all to save a chimaera. I'll admit, that puzzled me. Beast's Bane, help a beast?" Jael was looking at him, drawing out a pause. Akiva didn't like the look or the pause. Always, their encounters had played like a high-stakes game: exaggerated courtesy veiling mutual distrust and deep dislike. They had gone far beyond the need for courtesy now, but the captain kept up the charade, and in it there was a ghost of *glee*. He was toying with a smile.

What does he know? Akiva wondered, feeling certain now there was something, and he would have given much in that moment to put a sharp end to Jael's glee.

"She tasted of fairy tales," Jael said. The words struck a chord of familiarity—and a note of dread, too—but Akiva couldn't place them. Not until Jael added, almost singing, "She tasted of *hope*. Oh. What does *that* taste like? Pollen and stars, the Fallen said. He did go on about it, foul thing. I almost felt sorry for the girl, to have felt the touch of such a tongue."

A roaring in Akiva's ears. *Razgut.* Somehow, Jael had found Razgut. What had the creature told him?

"I wonder," asked Jael, "did you ever find her?"

"I don't know who you mean," Akiva replied.

Jael's smile unfurled fully now, and it was a nasty specimen, malicious and excited. "No?" he said. "I'm glad to hear it, since there was no mention of any girl in your report." This was true. Akiva had said nothing of Karou, or the hunchback Izîl who had hurled himself from a tower rather than give up Karou, or of Razgut, either—who at the time Akiva assumed had died with the hunchback. "A girl who worked for Brimstone," Jael continued. "Who was *raised* by Brimstone. Such an interesting story. Far-fetched, though. What interest could Brimstone possibly have taken in a human girl? For that matter, what interest could *you* have taken in a human girl? The usual kind?"

Akiva said nothing. Jael was too happy; it was clear that Razgut had told him everything. The question, then, was how much did Razgut *know*? Did he know where Karou was now? That she was carrying on Brimstone's work?

What did Jael *want*?

The captain—no, Akiva reminded himself, Jael was the emperor now—said with a shrug, "Of course, the Fallen also claimed the girl had *blue hair*, which really strains credulity, so I thought, how can I trust all the other things he's telling me about the human world? All the other fascinating things you left out of your report. I had to get creative. By the end, I believed he was telling the truth, strange as it all sounds, and what I can't make out is how the three of you failed to report on their *advancements*. Their *devices*, nephew. How is it that you failed to mention their wondrous, unimaginable weapons?"

Akiva's sick feeling was deepening, and it wasn't just from the hamsas. It was all coming together. Razgut and weapons. Pure white surcoats. Harpers. Pageantry. *To make an impression*, he had thought when he'd heard the rumors, but it hadn't made any sense. No one could imagine that the Stelians would be impressed by white surcoats and harps.

Humans, on the other hand…

"You're not invading the Stelians at all," Akiva said. "You're invading the human world."

73

The Scream

Thiago seemed to not quite understand why all of a sudden he couldn't breathe, or what the small pinch at his throat had to do with it. His hand flew to the blade, pulled it out, and as his blood poured out all the faster—onto Karou, all onto Karou—he looked at the knife with...*condescension.* Karou had the idea that his last living thought was, *This knife is too small to kill me.*

It wasn't.

His eyes lost focus. His neck lost strength. His head came down heavy on her face; for a moment he floundered, then twitched, then stopped. He was dead weight. He was *dead.* Thiago. Dead and heavy. His blood kept flowing and Karou was pinned under him, her knees still splayed, her ankles caught in her pushed-down jeans, and her own panicked gasping breath was so loud in her ears she imagined the stars could hear it.

She pushed him off, partway anyway, dragged herself the

rest of the way out from under him, kicking at his legs to get free, and then she rose, unsteady, and pulled at her jeans. She fell and rose again. Her arms were shaking so violently it was a few tries before the jeans were up, and then she couldn't manage the button. She couldn't stop shaking, but she couldn't leave it undone, it was unthinkable, and it was this that brought the tears—her frustration that she couldn't make her fingers perform this simple action, and she *had* to do it, she couldn't leave it. She was sobbing by the time it was finally done.

And then she looked at him.

His eyes were open. His mouth was open. His fangs were red with her blood and she was red with his blood. Her vest that had been gray was sodden and black in the starlight, and the White Wolf, he was... exposed, he was obscene, his intention laid bare and as dead as the rest of him.

She had killed the White Wolf.

He had tried to—

Who would care?

He was the White Wolf, hero of the chimaera races, architect of impossible victories, the strength of their people. She was the angel-lover, the traitor. The whore. Those who would have stood with her were gone—murdered right here or sent away to die. Ziri wouldn't be coming back. And Issa, what had they done to her?

Am I alone again?

She couldn't bear to be alone again.

She still couldn't stop her shaking. It was convulsive. She was having a hard time drawing breath. She felt light-headed. *Breathe*, she told herself. *Think.*

But no thoughts came, and scarcely more breath.

What were her options? Flee or stay. Leave them, let them die—*all of them*, all the chimaera in Eretz, and let the souls lay buried—or stay and . . . what? Be forced to resurrect Thiago?

Just the thought of it—of the skim of his soul against her senses, of life returning to those pale eyes and strength to those clawed hands—dropped Karou to her knees to retch. Both options were unbearable. She couldn't abandon her people—a thousand years Brimstone had borne this burden, and she broke after a couple of *months*? "Your dream is my dream. You are all of our hope."

But she couldn't face the Wolf again, either, and if she stayed, they would make her bring him back.

Or kill her.

Oh god, oh god.

She retched again. It racked her, spasm after spasm, until she was a shell, as raw on the inside as the outside—*a vessel*, she heard his voice in her head, *we're all just vessels*, and she retched again and it was just bile. Her throat stung, and when the rasp of her own choking finally died away, she heard a sound, and it was near.

And it was *wings*.

She panicked.

They were coming back.

* * *

"Invade the human world?" Jael looked affronted. "You malign me, nephew. Is it an invasion if we are welcomed?"

"Welcomed?"

"Yes. Razgut assured me they will worship us as gods. That they already *do.* Isn't it wonderful? I've always wanted to be a god."

"You're no god," Akiva said through clenched teeth. He thought of the human cities he had seen—images of lands at peace that had struck him as so alien when he had first arrived. Prague with its beautiful bridge, people congregating, strolling, kissing on the cheeks. Marrakesh, its wild square filled with dancers and snake charmers, the teeming lanes where he had walked beside Karou before...before they had broken the wishbone, and with it the fragile happiness he had known could not last. "They'll take one look at your face and brand you a monster."

Jael reached up and ran a finger down his scar. "What, this?" He shrugged, unconcerned. "That's what masks are for. Do you imagine they'll really care if their god wears a mask? They'll give me what I want readily enough, I have no doubt."

And what was that? Akiva didn't know much about human battle, but he knew some. He remembered the strange cafe Karou had taken him to in Prague, decorated with gas masks from a bygone war. He understood that they could poison the air and make all things die gasping, and that they could pump each other full of metal in the time it took an archer to draw back a bowstring, and he knew that Razgut had not lied to Jael. Humans *did* worship angels. Not all of them did, but many, and their worship could be as deadly as their weapons. Bring the two things together—bring them into Eretz—and it would make the war of the last thousand years look like a shoving match.

"You don't know what you're doing," he said. "It will mean the end of Eretz."

"The end of the Stelians, anyway," said Jael. "For the Empire, it will be a new beginning."

"This *is* about the Stelians, then? *Why?*" Akiva couldn't understand what stoked this hatred of Stelians. "Send *me* to them, as Joram wanted to. I'll be your envoy, your spy. I'll carry your message to them, but leave human weapons in the human world."

Akiva hated abasing himself to Jael, and Jael just scoffed. "My message? What message could I have for those fire-eyed savages? *I'm coming to kill you?* Dear nephew, that was a fool's mission, and Joram was the fool. Did you believe all that about serving as envoy? I just needed him to bring you here. For reasons that I think have been made clear." He gestured around the blood-spattered, corpse-strewn bath.

Yes, his reasons were clear, all too clear now. While Akiva had been planning to deliver Eretz from Joram, Jael had been waiting in the wings, and not just waiting. Orchestrating. Maneuvering his bastard scapegoat right into place.

"And if I hadn't killed him?" Akiva asked, disgusted that he hadn't felt the jerk of puppet strings all along.

"That was never a risk," said Jael, and Akiva understood that even if he hadn't killed Joram—if, by chance, he had come here as a loyal soldier to receive his emperor's gratitude and orders—he would have been framed for the murder anyway. "The moment you walked though that door, you were an assassin and a traitor to the realm. It helps that you *are*, of course. It's good to have a true witness. The servant girl owes you her life. Hellas, alas, owes you his death. But don't feel too badly. He was a viper." Jael, calling someone a viper. Even he saw the hypocrisy in it, and laughed. Akiva didn't know if he had ever seen anyone enjoy himself quite so much.

Hazael was the first to succumb to the sickness of the devil's eyes. He dropped to his knees and vomited onto the blood-spattered tile. Liraz edged closer to him, looking soon to follow suit.

"You think we have no other allies?" Akiva asked. "That no one else will rise against you?"

"If *you* can't succeed, nephew, who could?"

It was a fair question. A devastating question. Was this it, then? Had he failed his world—and Karou—so spectacularly?

"I'm a little sorry I can't have you in my service," said Jael. "I could use a magus, but it would be so hard to trust you. I can't shake the feeling that you don't quite *like* me." An apologetic shrug, and his gaze slid past Akiva to lock on . . . Liraz.

Through his weakness and his nausea, Akiva felt a surge of fury and dread and helplessness, but there was the edge of something more, something hard and glittering that he hoped, he hoped might be the edge of *sirithar*, coming within reach once more.

"*You*, though," Jael said to Liraz. "So lovely. It appears that I'll have need of new bath attendants when I move into these quarters." He looked at a dead girl on the floor and smiled that splay of a smile that tugged his scar white and pulled puckers along the remains of his nose and lips.

Liraz gave a hard laugh; Akiva heard his sister's weakness in it, and her struggle to bear up under it. "You can't trust him, but you think you can trust *me*?"

"Of course not. But I never trust women. I learned that lesson the hard way." He reached up to touch his scar, and when he did, his eyes gave the slightest flicker in Akiva's direction. That was all, but it was enough.

Akiva knew who had cut Jael.

Hazael rose from his knees. It had to take extraordinary effort, yet somehow he managed a version of his lazy smile when he said, "You know, I've always wanted to be a bath attendant. You should take me instead. I'm nicer than my sister."

Jael returned the lazy smile. "You're not my type."

"Well, you're not *anybody's* type," said Hazael. "No, wait. I take it back. My *sword* says she'd like to know you better."

"I'm afraid I must deny her the pleasure. I've been kissed by swords before, you see."

"I may have noticed."

"Festival," said Akiva abruptly, and all eyes turned to him. It was Jael's that he held. "It was my mother who cut you." He didn't want to talk about his mother with Jael; he didn't want to open the door to his uncle's memories—what lay on the other side of it could only be horrific—but he had to buy time. And . . . he had hoped her name might be the key to unlocking *sirithar.* It was not.

"So you *have* guessed," said Jael. "Do you know, that might have been my favorite part of the day. When you assumed it was Joram who killed her? He may as well have, though. He did give her to me."

Give her . . . ? Akiva couldn't think about it. "She can't be the reason you hate the Stelians. One woman?"

"Ah, but not just any woman. Women are everywhere, beautiful women are *nearly* everywhere, but Festival, she was wild as a storm. Storms are dangerous things." He looked at Liraz again. "Thrilling. Stormhunters know. That there's no ride in the world like a storm in fury." He motioned to a soldier. "Take her."

Akiva thrust himself in front of the soldier; he felt slow, sluggish. Hazael was moving, too. Liraz managed to swing her sword, but the sound it made, careening off a Dominion blade, was weak, and it flew from her grip to fall with a muffled thud onto the pile of bodies that had been Joram, Japheth, Namais, and Misorias. Disarmed or not, she was not cowed. "Kill me with my brothers, or you'll wish you had," she spat.

"Now I'm insulted," said Jael. "You would *die* with them, sooner than scrub my back?"

"A thousand times."

"My dear." He pressed a hand to his heart. "Don't you see? Knowing that is what makes it sweet."

The soldiers closed in.

Two score Dominion with the severed hands of dead revenants upheld, and Hazael still dealt a death before his own came to him.

His slice took a soldier in the face. His blade lodged in bone, and as the soldier fell, the weight pulled Hazael forward, so the thrust that was coming to him sank deep. Up under one raised arm it slipped, where there was no protection from mail or plate or even leather. It went through him and out between his wings. He stumbled, looked at Akiva, then down at the sword. He let go of his own, gave up trying to free it from the skull it was wedged in, and even as Hellas had, he reached for the blade he was spitted on. But his hands weren't working. He batted at the hilt; he crumpled, and Akiva saw it all through the flare of clarity he had been desperate for.

Sirithar, come too late. Like a blood daub, after the killing is done.

Hazael fell. Liraz threw herself to her knees to catch him.

Akiva experienced in splendid light the howl that shaped his sister's mouth. He heard her banshee grief and saw it, too. Sound had form, it was light, everything was light, and everything was grief, and Liraz was trying to hold Hazael's head as his eyes glazed, but a pair of Dominion grabbed her, dragged her, and Hazael's head fell. Akiva knew his brother was dead even before his head hit tile, and the thrum he felt inside his skull was like the thousands of summoned wings that had drubbed the skies of the Hintermost.

There were no birds this time. Or if there were, it was the sky that brought them, the sky itself, which at that moment... moved. Outside, over the city and over the sea, as if it had been grasped in a great fist and dragged, the sky lurched. It slid. It gathered, contracting upon one locus and dragging everything to its center: the Tower of Conquest. The sky was a continuous skein, so the disturbance was felt over the whole orb of Eretz.

Campfires as distant as the southern continent flared with the sudden drag of winds. In the jagged ice palaces atop the Hintermost, stormhunters stirred and lifted their great heads. On the mountains' far side, Sveva and Sarazal and the Caprine emerged from their long passage through the tunnels to blink up at a night sky that seemed set in motion. And on the far side of the world—day where in the Empire it was night—a woman standing at the railing of a terrace looking out over a pale green sea felt the tug of wind at her hair and looked up.

She was young, strong. She wore a diadem on her black hair, a stone scarab set in its burnished gold; her wings were flame and her eyes were, too, and they cut narrow as, overhead, clouds were dragged so fast they blurred. On it went and on, the clouds blurred to streaks, wheeling birds and shadows caught in an inexorable wind. Her eyes stirred to sparks as across her city, her island—her *isles*—her people stopped what they were doing to watch the sky.

And when it ceased and a profound stillness fell, she knew what was coming, and reached for the railing.

The lurch had been like the gasp that precedes the scream, and then came...

The scream.

Silent, expulsive. The clouds surged back the way they'd come, racing over the pale green sea.

And on the world's far side, back at the source of this great unnatural gasp and scream, the unbreakable glass of the Hall of Conquest...shattered. The Sword, symbol of the Empire of Seraphim, exploded outward with massive force.

The moons were watching. Their reflections were carried by a million flying shards, so it could be said that everywhere a splinter stuck and stabbed, so, too, stabbed Nitid and Ellai. When the sun rose, dagger fragments of glass would be found embedded in trees many miles away, and in corpses, too, though those were fewer than might have been, had it been day. Pierced birds and angels lay broken on rooftops and a

Silversword had crashed through a dome of the seraglio, creating a breach through which dozens of concubines escaped in the confusion, many carrying Joram's babies in their bellies, others cradled in their arms.

The Sword met the dawn as a steel skeleton, layer after layer of glass gone, all of those labyrinthine corridors peeled away, all those birdcages and painted screens, and that dais of a bed, gone as if they had never been.

The day—dazzling, cloudless—grew into a patchwork of hush and horror, rush and rumor and bodies washing up on beaches as far away as Thisalene.

What had happened?

It was said the emperor was dead at the hand of Beast's Bane, and the crown prince, too. It surprised no one that Beast's Bane and his bastard cohorts were gone, or that the ragged Silverswords who had survived the night found, on storming the Misbegotten barracks, that it was empty, not hide nor hair of a bastard soldier anywhere in Astrae.

Across the Empire this would prove true. The Misbegotten had gone with the clouds, it was said.

They hadn't, though. The clouds had fled to the far side of the world, where the young queen of the Stelians had set aside her scarab diadem, bound back her black hair, and set out with her magi to trace the source of the extraordinary disturbance.

As for the Misbegotten, they had gone to gather at the Kirin caves and await their brother Akiva, seventh of the name, to pledge selves and swords to his cause.

74

The Cure for Ennui

"I feel like a fly when it's trapped in the window and almost dead." Zuzana's voice sounded as limp as her hair felt.

"That's it exactly," agreed Mik. "Fan faster."

It was Zuzana's turn wielding the fan, an artifact of crackly palm fronds they had found on the roof of the hotel. Mik, wearing only shorts, was in the chair, tilted back with his feet on the bed and his head back to expose his throat to the breeze. "You are a goddess of air circulation," he said.

"And *you* are a specimen of glistening maleness."

Mik's laugh was dulled by heat coma. "I was surrounded by monster soldier torsos for a week. I know that I am a glistening specimen of *scrawn*."

"You're not scrawny." Up and down went the fan as Zuzana formulated a compliment. It was true that being surrounded by bronze-hard pectorals and biceps bigger than her head cast Mik's physique in a new light, but really, who needed biceps bigger than her head? Well, unless their job was *killing angels*, in which case that might come in handy. She told Mik, "You have perfect violin-playing muscles."

"And you, with your mighty puppeteer arms. We put the chimaera to shame."

She stopped fanning and fell backward onto the bed. It was a bad bed in a cheap hotel, and the flop jarred her teeth. "Ow," she said without conviction.

"Hey. Your turn isn't even half up."

"I know. I just succumbed to ennui."

"Just now."

"Just exactly now. You saw it happen."

Mik let his chair rock forward, and used the momentum to pitch onto the bed beside her. "Ow," she said again.

"I know a cure for ennui," Mik told her, half rolling toward her before giving up and flopping onto his back. "But it's too hot."

"It is *way* too hot," agreed Zuzana, who had no doubt what his cure entailed. "How are there even *people* in this country? Who can make babies in heat like this?"

"So let's go," he said. "The coast. Home. Australia. I don't know. Why are we still here, Zuze?"

"Here" was Ouarzazate, the biggest city in southern Morocco. It looked like a film set for *The Mummy* or something, which it probably was, seeing as how it was a movie studio town at the edge of the Sahara desert. It was a little bland, a lot hot, and though their hotel ostensibly had air-conditioning, it had ceased to function some time in the night, which they had not noticed, since the nights actually *were* cool enough for curing ennui and populating countries.

Why *were* they still here, a full day after their invisible escape from monster castle, feet freshly blistered from the hike and resulting tithe bruises at the height of their purple glory?

"I don't want to go," Zuzana admitted in a small voice. "Back to tourists and angel cults and puppets and real life?" She was whining and she knew it. "I want to make monsters and do magic and help Karou."

"That's real life, too," he said. "And more to the point, real death. It's too dangerous."

"I know," she said, and she did, but it just felt all wrong leaving Karou there. If Thiago had killed her once, how could she know he wouldn't again? "Damn it, why doesn't she have a *phone*?" she grumbled. Karou was rich; she couldn't splurge on a satellite phone or something? Whatever. If Zuzana could just know her friend was okay, *she* would be okay, too.

Which is not to say that she would stop whining.

She'd agreed to leave the kasbah, and here she was. Fine. She hadn't said she would leave the country. She just couldn't get over the feeling that if they went any farther away, the whole magical spell of the past week would evaporate and leave her with nothing but a crazy story to tell her grandkids about how, for a week, in a giant sandcastle at the edge of the Sahara desert, she had been a resurrectionist's apprentice and built great winged soldiers for an otherworldly war.

And they'd make loopy crazy gestures behind her back because hell, it did sound completely insane.

And then? She'd have no choice but to blink invisible—because *oh my god, she could do that now*—and swat their ruffian hides with rolled-up newspaper as they ran screaming from her cabbagey old-lady kitchen.

"I'm going to be the scariest grandma in the world," she muttered, grouchy and kind of looking forward to it.

"What?"

"Nothing." She flipped over and buried her face in her pillow. She screamed into it, got a mouthful of musty hotel pillow, and instantly wanted to bathe her tongue in running water. Of course the pillowcase had been washed since the last occupant, she told herself. *Of course.* That was why it tasted like stale stranger head.

Mik's hand was on her back, making slow circles. She turned her face to him.

"I'm finger-painting with your sweat," he informed her. "That was a heart."

"A sweat heart. How romantic."

"Oh, you want romantic? Okay. What does this spell?"

She felt his fingertip slide over her skin, and spoke each letter as it formed. "Z-U-Z-A-N-A. Zuzana. W-I-L-L. Will. Y-O-U." She paused. "You." She lay very still, listening with her skin for the next letter. "M." Her voice dropped. She watched Mik's face. He was smiling to himself, mischievous, his eyes on his work. Strawberry stubble covered his jaw. A beam of sunshine slipped through a broken slat in the shutter and glanced across his eyelashes; they looked dusted with light.

"A." Zuzana said. *Oh god. Zuzana will you* M-A—

Her heart pounded. Could he feel it through her back?

When they'd talked about marriage back in Prague she'd been dismissive. Well. She'd been embarrassed to have been caught thinking about it; that wasn't who she was, some flit girl who dreamed of wedding gowns, and she was just way too young.

R, she felt. "R," she whispered.

Mik's hand fell still. "Wrong," he said. "That was a K."

"K? That's not how you spell—" She cut herself off.

"How you spell what?" Mik's voice was teasing. "I was writing *Zuzana will you make me a sandwich?* What did you think?"

She jerked her shirt down over her back. "Nothing," she said, rolling off the bed.

Mik caught her around the waist and dragged her back. "You didn't think—? *Oh*. How embarrassing for you."

Her face was hot. He'd done it again. Jesus. Apparently she *was* a flit girl who dreamed of wedding gowns. "Let me go," she said.

But he didn't. He held her. "I can't ask you that yet," he whispered in her ear. "I still have two tasks left."

"Very funny."

"I'm not joking." He sounded serious, and when she looked up at him, at his sweet, earnest face, he *looked* serious. "Were *you*?" he asked.

Well, yes, she *had* been joking about the three tasks. Seriously. She wasn't a fairy-tale princess. Only, she kind of felt like one right now, and it wasn't the worst feeling she'd ever had. "No," she said; she stopped trying to get away. "I wasn't joking, and here's your second task. Get the air-conditioning back on, so you can cure my ennui."

75

It Was Near and It Was Wings

Karou was in her room. It was night. Again. A day had passed since the pit. Somehow.

The door was closed, but Mik's planks were gone. They had taken them, and the shutter bolts, too, and her safety, which, it was now clear, had never been more than an illusion.

She pictured the moon's racing swerve around the world, and the world's hurtling course around the sun, and the glitter of the stars in their arcs—but...no. That was illusion, too, just as the rising and setting of the sun was a trick. It was the *world* that moved, not the stars, not the sun. The *sky* moved, panning across that vastness as it rolled through space, hurtling end over end, and that hurtling was what kept her pinned here. One of billions.

It doesn't matter what happens to me, she told herself. *I am one of billions. I am stardust gathered fleetingly into form. I will be ungathered. The stardust will go on to be other things someday and I will be free. As Brimstone is free.*

Stardust. This was science, she had heard it and read it—all matter came from the explosions of stars—but it sounded like the humans' own version of Eretz myths. A little drier, maybe: no rapist sun, no weeping moon. No *stabbing* moon. That was the Kirin story: The sun had tried to take Ellai by force and she had stabbed him as Karou had stabbed Thiago. Nitid had wept, and her tears became chimaera. Children of regret.

Karou wondered: Had *Ellai* wept? Had she bathed in the sea and tried to feel clean again? That could have been part of the story: Her tears gave the seas their salt, and everything in the world was born of violence, betrayal, and grief.

Karou had bathed in the river. Her tears wouldn't make it to the sea; they would water date palms in some oasis; they would become fruit and be eaten, and perhaps be wept again through other eyes.

That's not how it works.

Yes, it is. Nothing is ever lost. Not even tears.

What about hope*?*

She was as clean as it was possible to be without hot water and soap. She had submerged herself in the rushing water until her arms and legs were numb, her bruised, torn skin scrubbed free of blood—her own blood and . . . not only her own blood. Not even mostly.

And not only Thiago's, either.

She heard a sound and it was near and it was wings.

She jolted her mind from the memory like it was a face she could slap.

Think of something else.

Her pain. That would serve. Which pain, though? There

were so many, and she had become too much a connoisseur of pain to let them blend into one haze. Each scrape, each contusion was its own entity, like stars in a constellation. A constellation called what? *The Victim?*

She looked like a victim. Raw. Brutalized. The right side of her face had been dragged over the scree. Her lip was split, her cheek purple, scraped and scabbing. Open blisters on her palms wept from the handle of the shovel. The shovel. *Don't think.* Her earlobe. That was the pain she decided to focus on; she could do something about that. It was torn and swollen where the Wolf had bitten her; she might have mended it the way she had mended Ziri's hands and cut smile, but she didn't think she would be able to maintain the focus she would need, and anyway, she couldn't bear the thought of the vises. Her whole body was ache and sting and scream.

"You make beautiful bruises," Thiago had told her once. *You don't*, she thought, looking at the ugly mottling that covered her arms, the splayed finger marks that told what he had done to her.

Tried to do, she reminded herself.

Had Ellai stabbed the sun in time, she wondered, or had the sun had his way? The story was unclear. Karou decided to believe that Ellai had protected herself, as she had. She held a curved upholstery needle over a candle flame to sterilize it. A hand mirror was propped on the table in front of her, and when she looked at it she zeroed in on her ear, avoiding any focus on her face. She didn't want to see her face.

All those years of martial arts training, she thought as the needle began to glow. You'd think fighting could look like it does in movies: plenty of space to deliver elegant choreography, land clean kicks, and glare cool glares. *Ha.* There had been no space, only grappling and panic, and Thiago's strength had counted for a hell of a lot more than her repertoire of fancy kicks.

Of course, she *had* killed him. She might look like a victim, but she wasn't. She had stopped him.

If only that could have been the end of it.

A sound and it was near and it was wings.

It echoed in her head, the wingbeats, and the thud, the thumping sound dirt made when it was flung from the shovel. And the flies. How did flies find the dead so fast?

She felt like she was still at the edge of the pit, that fetid darkness threatening to drag her down. She jammed the needle through her earlobe, hard. It served to thrust the memory away again, but she knew the memory was like the flies—she might shoo it away, but nothing could keep it from coming back—and the piercing *hurt.* Her small sharp gasp was enough to wake Issa.

Issa. There was the night's one blessing. She still had Issa.

"Sweet girl, what are you doing?" The serpent-woman uncoiled from her place in front of the door and gave a little hiss of exasperation when she saw the needle stuck through Karou's earlobe like a fishhook. "Let me do that."

Karou let her take the needle. What if she didn't have Issa? If, after everything else, they had taken Issa from her, too? "I couldn't sleep," she whispered.

"No?" Issa's voice was soft, and so were her hands. She eased the needle through Karou's flesh and pulled the first stitch taut. "My poor child, it's little wonder. I wish I had some dream tea to give you."

"Or requiem tea," said Karou.

Issa's voice was *not* soft when she said, "Don't say such things! You are alive. As long as you are alive, and *he* is..." She tapered off. *He who?* Whatever she was going to say, she rethought it. "As long as you are alive, there is still hope." She took a breath, steadied her hand, and asked, "Ready?" before she put needle again to flesh.

Karou winced. She waited until the needle was through. "I'm sorry," she said. "Was it...? Is that how you and Yasri...?"

"Yes," said Issa. "It was peaceful, child, don't be sad." She sighed. "I wish she were here, though. She would know what to give you. She had a dozen tricks for helping Brimstone sleep."

"We'll get her," Karou said, wondering when, wondering how, and wondering what the place looked like today. Thiago had put the temple to the torch and the requiem grove, too. It had been eighteen years; had the trees grown back? The grove had been ancient. She remembered arriving in the moonlight to the sight of the treetops, the glint of the temple roof showing through, and how her heart would race knowing Akiva was waiting for her below. Akiva, waiting to gather her out of the air. Akiva lying beside her, tracing her eyelids with his fingertip, his touch as soft as hummingbird-moths, as soft as the drift of requiem blossoms falling in the darkness.

She closed her eyes and clasped her arms, one hand over each forearm, and felt the tenderness of her bruises. Thiago, her ally; Akiva, her enemy. How twisted it was. What makes an enemy?

No. She couldn't forget. She dug her fingers into her bruises to shake herself out of her memories. Ink lines inscribed on killing hands make an enemy. Ash palisades where cities once stood make an enemy.

Issa tied off another stitch and cut the thread. Karou thanked her and wondered *What now?*

The sun would rise; she couldn't stay in her room forever. She would have to face the chimaera. She couldn't wait for her bruises to fade. Would they even notice? They took her bruises for granted. How much did they know of what had happened at the pit?

Not all of it, that was certain, and—dear gods and stardust—they had better never find out.

A sound and it was near and it was—

"Karou."

A choked whisper. Karou blinked.

"Who's there?" Issa's voice was sharp, and Karou knew she hadn't imagined the whisper. It came from the window, and this time it was not Bast.

"Please."

The voice was disembodied, the word pulled long, and it was too low a whisper to ring with the richness of his voice, but Karou knew who it was. Her body flashed hot and cold. *Why? Why would he come back here?* She stood up fast and her chair smashed backward.

Issa stared at her. "Who is it, child?"

But Karou didn't have time to answer. The bolts were gone

from the shutters. The window came open. Issa startled, the heavy muscle of her serpent's coil rippling in the candlelight, and Karou shrank from the intrusion—and from the heat—as Akiva simultaneously appeared, in the soft glimmer of a vanishing glamour, and crashed to the floor.

76

Dead Weight

He wasn't alone. Karou felt the presence of others even before the glamours fell away and revealed them. The two from the Charles Bridge. She knew them at once, though they looked so different now. The sister—Liraz—whose beautiful face had been so sharp and dangerous; it was transfigured by misery. She was gasping, and her eyes were red pits of grief—though nowhere near as red as Akiva's, which looked as they had that long-ago day when Madrigal had worn a hijacked body to free him from his cell in Loramendi. The whites had gone bloodred from burst capillaries. What had done that? He looked waxen, ravaged by exhaustion.

But neither of them was so altered as their brother. Who was . . . dead.

They cradled his body between them, and neither seemed up to the task. As they lowered him to the floor, he slipped and landed heavily. A moan came from Liraz, who dropped to her knees and picked up his head with such gentleness.

Hazael, Karou remembered. *His name was Hazael.* His eyes were open and staring, his skin livid, neck and limbs already rigid. His wings had burnt out; his flame feathers were nothing but bare quills now, the barbs all turned to ash and fallen away. He had been dead for some time.

Karou's body was still flashing from hot to cold and back; she stood frozen in place, trying to make sense of the scene. It was Issa who moved slowly forward and bent over Hazael to touch his face. Karou only watched, a queer detachment settling over her—that old unreality returned, as if her life were a shadow play cast on a wall—and she expected the fierce sister to snarl and shove Issa away, but she didn't. Liraz reached for Issa's hand and gripped it. The serpents in Issa's hair and around her neck grew still and taut, ready to strike if it came to that.

"Please." Liraz's voice was strangled. Her eyes shifted from Issa to Karou and they were wild. "*Save him.*"

Karou heard the words, but in her slowed-down state they seemed to drift in the air. Her gaze swung to Akiva. The way he was looking at her... it was like touch. She took an involuntary step back. His face was a silent plea; he was nearly as gray as the corpse of his brother, which they had laid down on the space of floor where Karou conjured bodies. The resurrection floor. They were all looking to her. Even Issa had turned to her.

Save him?

They had come to her *for help*? After burning Brimstone's portals—*and Brimstone*—after destroying her people, they had brought her their slain brother to resurrect?

How far had they carried him? They were racked with tremors from the effort. Akiva slumped against the wall. His arms hung at his sides. He looked more dead than alive, more dead even than when she had first seen him, bleeding on the battlefield at Bullfinch.

"What happened to you?"

It might have been *her* asking *him* that question, but it wasn't. It was Akiva, and he was looking at her cheek, her lip, and her newly stitched earlobe. Self-consciously, she untucked her hair from behind her ear and concealed it. "Who did that to you?" he asked. Weak as his voice was, it burned with anger. "It was *him*, wasn't it? It was the Wolf."

He was not wrong, and all Karou could think of, seeing the fury on his face, was the living shawl he had made her once, the so-soft touch of moth wings on her shoulders. Once upon a time, Thiago had torn her dress, and, down from the false stars of the festival lanterns, Akiva had summoned a living shawl to cover her.

She had made a choice that night, and it had not been the wrong choice.

But that was then. So much had happened since.

Too much.

She ignored his question, hating the physical evidence of her vulnerability, wishing her arms were covered, and wishing she had mended herself. What was a little more pain, after all? She must not show weakness, not now. She stepped forward, turning her attention to Hazael. Akiva had brought her his dead brother? Well, he had also brought her Issa. And he had given her Ziri back, she mustn't forget that, whatever may have happened since. She lowered herself to her knees beside the body—slowly; everything hurt—and wondered that they had brought his body so far.

Bodies are only dead weight—*we're all just vessels, after all*—but knowing that was one thing; leaving a body behind was another. Karou understood that well enough. It is bodies that make us real. What is a soul without eyes to look through, or hands to hold? Her own hands trembled and she clasped them to keep them still.

The wound was under Hazael's left arm. His heart. It would have been a quick death.

"Please," Liraz said again. "Save him. I'll give you anything. Name your price."

Price? Karou looked at her sharply, but there was no trace of the cruelty or severity she remembered, only anguish. "There is no price," she said. She glanced at Akiva. *Or if there is*, she could have added, *you've already paid it.*

"You'll do it?" Liraz's words trembled with hope.

Would she? Karou knew she was their only hope—she whom they would have slain in Prague just for bearing the hamsas on her hands—and there was irony there, but she took no pleasure in it. She couldn't bear the sight of Liraz's hands—they were so *black*—but they were so tender on her brother's neck, her fingers so soft on his dead cheek, and Karou knew she should not feel sympathy for this killer of her people, but she did. Who among them, after all, had clean hands? Not her. *Oh, Ellai, my hands will never be clean again.* She clenched them suddenly and her blisters burned from her work with the shovel. It felt to her as if to do this one thing, save this life . . . it might be a salve. Not just for these seraphim but for herself, after the horror of the pit and the shovel and what she had had to do, and... and the lie she was now forced to live. She wanted to do this. A tick on her knuckle for a life saved instead of taken.

"I can't preserve this body," she said. "It's too late. And I can't make him look the same, either." Maybe Brimstone would have known how to conjure those fiery wings, but they were far beyond her. "He won't be a seraph anymore."

"It doesn't matter," Akiva said. She met his eyes, his red, red eyes, and she wanted to do this for him. "As long as he is himself," he said. "That's all that matters."

Yes, she told herself, and wanted to believe it as firmly as he did. *Soul is what matters. Flesh is vessel.* "Okay." She took a deep breath and looked down at Hazael. "Give me the thurible."

Her words were met with a silence that was like sinking.

Sinking.

Oh no. No. Karou stared at Hazael's dead face, his open blue eyes, his laugh lines, and her upwelling sorrow overwhelmed her with its force. *No.* She bit her lip, willing it to stillness. She was rigid. She had to be. Her grief... if she let it out, it would be a magician's scarf, one grief tied to another to another, it would never end. She didn't want to look up again, to see the stricken faces frozen in that terrible silence.

"We didn't... we didn't have one." Liraz. Whispering. "We brought him *here*. To *you*."

Akiva was hoarse. "It's only been a day. Karou. Please." As if it were a matter of persuading her.

They didn't understand. How could they? She had never told Akiva how it worked, how tenuous the soul's connection grew after death, or how easily it could be cast adrift if it was not contained. She had never told him, and now there was nothing in the air or aura of this dead angel—soldier, killer, beloved brother—no impression of light or laughter to go along with those blue eyes and laugh lines, no stir of any kind to brush against her senses and tell her who he was because . . . he *wasn't.*

She looked up. She forced herself to meet Akiva's red eyes and Liraz's so they would see and understand her sorrow.

And know that Hazael's soul was lost.

77

To Live

It was her sorrow that undid Akiva. One look and he knew. Hazael was gone.

"No!" Liraz's cry was choked, airless, nearly soundless, and she was in motion.

Akiva didn't have the strength to restrain her. She couldn't have much strength left, either. Even after the sickness of the hamsas, she had borne most of Hazael's weight on the long journey here—and for what, all for nothing—and sometimes *his* weight, too, catching him by an arm and screaming at him to wake up when he would start to slide into the darkness. The darkness, the darkness. Even now it was lapping at him.

What had he done in Astrae?

He didn't know. He had known only the thrum in his skull and the gathering, the pressure, the pressure, and he had grabbed Liraz and held her to him, fallen on Hazael and held him, too, and the blast when it came—from *where*?—had carried them clear. Far away, far, and not one dagger of all the glass of the shattered Sword—not one splinter—had touched them.

They had brought Hazael to a field and he was already dead. But what is death? Akiva had thought of Karou. Of course he had. *Hope*, he had told himself, on his knees in the grass, weak and dazed and numb. *Her name means hope.*

But not in their language, and not for them.

Liraz lunged at Karou and Akiva reached after her but he was too slow. She hit Karou and slammed her backward. There was a chair lying on its side. They went down. Karou cried out in pain.

Liraz found air. "You're lying!" she screamed.

Screamed.

Akiva was moving, but it was like wading through darkness; the serpent-woman was faster—the serpent-woman was Issa, he knew her from Karou's drawings. She must have been the one in the thurible. *Thurible thurible thurible.* Why hadn't he had a thurible? But maybe the blast had torn away Hazael's soul; maybe it was already gone when they laid him in the field, and there had never been a chance of saving him. They would never know. Hazael was gone, that was all that mattered.

And Liraz was screaming.

Whatever Karou might have decided to do with them, it was out of her hands now. "Just save him!" Liraz screamed at her and the sound was terrible, it was raw and so loud, and Akiva imagined eyes snapping open all over the kasbah.

Issa was strong where Liraz was weak and broken. The serpent-woman threw her off Karou, thrust her back to Akiva; she could have killed her, her serpents could have sunk fangs into his sister's flesh, but they didn't. Issa shoved her to Akiva and he caught her. Liraz struggled, but sobs broke her and she collapsed in his arms. "No no no," she was saying over and over. "He can't be gone, he can't, not him." He held her and sank with her back down beside their brother's body, and he cradled her while she sobbed. Each sob was like a tempest racking her rigid form, seizing her, shaking her. Akiva had never even seen her cry before, and this was beyond crying. He held her, weeping, too, and looked over the top of her head to where Issa was helping Karou to the edge of the bed.

He saw the gingerness of her movements, the pain on her face, the *cuts* on her face, and the sorrow in her swan-black eyes when she looked at him, and silent tears slipping down her cheeks, but he couldn't process any of it. Darkness was tilting and weaving around him, Liraz's sobs were sending shudders straight to his heart, and Hazael was dead.

The cremation urn is full, he heard in his brother's lazy, jovial voice. *You* have *to live*.

And here he was again: alive while others died. Oh, black fatigue. He just wanted to close his eyes.

And then, at the door, a knock. Karou snapped to face it. A guttural female voice demanded, "Karou? What's happening in there?"

When Karou snapped back toward him there was still the sorrow in her eyes, but dismay was distorting it, and distress. She wiped away her tears with the back of her hand and struggled to her feet. Her face contorted with pain from the effort—what had he done to her, that...animal?—and she seemed to want to say something, but there was no time because the door was opening. Liraz lifted her head, her sobs trailing away as she came back to herself and realized what she had done.

She was alert, her face white around her wet, red eyes. She reached for Hazael's rigid hand and gripped it. The grief left her face, resignation settling her features into an unnatural calm.

Akiva understood that she was ready to die.

He knew he had no right to be horrified—he'd been fighting the same feeling for so long—but he was horrified anyway, and he felt himself caught in a spiral of helplessness. At the tugging edge of blackness, trapped once more in the enemy stronghold, a profound new urgency arose. He was *not* ready.

He wanted to live. He wanted to finish what he had finally started, all these years too late. He wanted to remake the world. With Karou, with Karou.

But he didn't think that was going to happen.

The first figure through the door was Thiago's she-wolf lieutenant. Slinking bestial creature, she went into a hunch and growled at her first sight of the angels. But Akiva didn't even look at her, because behind her, paused on the threshold, cheeks scored by scabbed gouges that confirmed his worst suspicions, was the White Wolf.

78

The Angel and the Wolf

"Visitors, Karou? I didn't know you were having a party."

Oh, that voice, the calm and disdain, the hint of amusement. Karou couldn't make herself look at him. *Life in those pale eyes, strength in those clawed hands.* It was wrong, so wrong. And *she* had done it. Her bile rose; she could have fallen to her knees to retch all over again.

"I didn't, either."

It was the only way, she told herself, but her trembling intensified as she struggled to stifle it. She fixed on a point behind him, but the shifting forms of Lisseth and Nisk filled the corridor, and she didn't want to look at them, either. She would never forget or forgive the coldness of their faces when she had come limping back from the pit, blood-drenched and shaking, in shock, trailing behind Thiago.

As for Thiago himself…

He entered the room. She could hear the dig of his claws in

the dirt floor and she could smell the musk scent of him, but she still couldn't look at him. He was a blurred white presence in her peripheral vision, crossing the room to face the angels from her side. From her side, as if they were together in this.

And . . . they *were.*

She had made a choice. To deserve Brimstone's belief in her and the name he had given her. To work for the salvation—and resurrection—of her people, by any means necessary, by *any* means. And Thiago was necessary. The chimaera followed *him.* This was the only way, but that didn't make it any easier to stand beside him and feel the weight of Akiva's stare, and when she turned to him—she had to look somewhere—to see the loathing and confusion on his face, and the incredulity. As if he couldn't believe she would suffer the nearness of this monster.

I am a monster, too, she wanted to tell him. *I am a chimaera, and I will do what I have to do for my people.*

Such false courage. Her expression was defiance, but it was pinned in place. The fire of Akiva's eyes had always been like a fuse that set the air alight between them. Now was no different. She burned, but it was with shame to be facing him from the Wolf's side. The angel and the Wolf, together in a room. It seemed to her now that she had always been headed toward this moment, and here it was: The angel and the Wolf faced each other, and Akiva was red-eyed, gray-faced, broken and sick and grief-stricken, and *she* . . . she stood beside the Wolf, as if the pair of them were lord and lady of this bloody rebellion.

It's not what you think, she could have told Akiva.

It's worse.

But she said nothing. He would get no explanations or apologies from her. She forced herself to turn. To Thiago. She hadn't set eyes on him since they returned from the pit. She made herself look at him now. If she couldn't do that much, what chance was there for all that lay ahead?

She looked.

The Wolf was the Wolf, imperious and breath-catching, a work of Brimstone's highest art. He wasn't his usual impeccable self, which was no surprise considering the past day and a half. His sleeves were pushed up, bunched and wrinkled over his tanned and muscled forearms, and Ten's attention to her master's hair appeared to have slipped. It had been gathered back by hasty hands and tied in a white knot. Some strands had escaped, and when he pushed them back it was with a flicker of impatience. As for that hated, handsome face, it bore scratches from Karou's nails, but the wound where her blade had slid up under his chin, that was sealed and mended as if it had never been. It had been an easy fix, nothing like Ziri's hands or even his smile; only a few layers of tissue to draw back together along a tiny slit. Karou could scarcely have killed him more cleanly if she'd *planned* to bring him back to life, and she'd had pain in plenty for the tithe.

It was his eyes, oh god, it was his eyes that were hardest to look at. *Life in those pale eyes.*

We're all just vessels, after all.

Behind her own eyes came the sting of tears and she looked down. She didn't know what to do with herself. She hugged her bruised arms to her body and cast wildly about for something to say. Angels in her room, one of them dead and one of them Akiva; here was a pretty predicament.

It had been only a space of seconds since the Wolf entered. His stillness and silence did not yet ring strange, but soon they would.

If Liraz hadn't screamed, Karou would have helped the angels get away. She would have burned incense to cover their scent. She owed Akiva that much and more. No one would have needed to know they had ever been here. But it was too late for that. Now Thiago would have to do something about them, and—Karou had seen it in his eyes in that brief glance—he was at an even greater loss than she was.

His course of action should have been clear; he had dealt with Akiva before: tortured him, punished him not only for being a seraph but for being Madrigal's choice, and everyone close to him knew how he hungered to finish what he had started. The White Wolf should have been laughing now; he should have been drunk on his bloody delight.

But he wasn't.

Because, of course—of course, *of course*—he wasn't really the White Wolf.

79

Done

"So, is this what it looks like?" Thiago asked.

"What does it look like?" Akiva asked, hating to speak to the Wolf at all. They hadn't been face-to-face since the dungeon in Loramendi, and now that they were, talking was not what Akiva wanted to do.

"It *looks like* a dead angel." Indicating Hazael, Thiago turned from Akiva to Karou and back again with a contemptuous half laugh. "Did you come to pay a call on our resurrectionist? I'm sorry, but we don't service your kind. Perhaps you are aware, we are at war."

"The war is over," snarled Liraz, with a passion Akiva knew she didn't feel for their victory. "*You lost.*"

"Did we? I like to think that remains to be seen."

Slowly, Akiva reached a restraining arm around his sister's shoulder. If she launched at the Wolf the way she had at Karou, the serpent-woman would not be shoving her back to him alive. Maybe death was what Liraz wanted, or thought she wanted in her mourning, and maybe death was going to happen, here, tonight, no matter what they did, but Akiva would not court it further than he already had by coming here, and that had been pure desperation.

He looked to Karou, trying to guess what she was thinking. She would have helped Hazael; he had seen the truth of her sorrow. What now? Would she help them? *Could* she? Those bruises on her arms...She still held her arms cradled against herself, and though Akiva was fairly sure she was trying to conceal her bruises—why did she look so ashamed?—the effect was that he kept finding his eyes drawn to them. And...he had seen her tithe bruises when he came before; the memory had haunted him. These were different.

These bruises weren't made by brass clamps, but by *hands*.

All at once, they were all he could see. A wave of fury overcame him and it was *he* who needed to be restrained. He was on his feet and it was only the insistent tug of darkness, the infuriating weakness, that made it so easy for Karou—*Karou*—when he lunged or staggered forward, to step between him and Thiago and shove him back. Her brow was drawn hard and her eyes were fierce; her look asked *Are you mad?*

And he *was*. He was also pathetic. He stumbled over Hazael and it was Liraz this time who caught *him*. They were both so weak, so debilitated and demoralized, that they just sank together to the dirt floor beside their brother's body. This without the chimaera even having to flash a hamsa in their direction. They were just so done, so painfully, obviously, pitifully done.

"Just do it," hissed Liraz, and Akiva couldn't even bring himself to argue. "*Kill us.*"

Karou regarded them with that hardness she'd shown when she shoved him—it was anger, Akiva thought, that he had again forced her to decide his fate. She had changed so much in just a few months. The sharpness, the bleakness. He remembered how she had been back in Prague and Marrakesh, in the little time they'd spent together before the wishbone: the softness and mobility of her expressions; the shy, incongruous smiles; and the rapid-flare flushes that had spread up her fair neck. Even her anger had been a flashing, vital thing, and he hated this new carved-mask hardness, and he hated his part in bringing it about. But at that moment, if he was given the choice, he would still have said he wanted to live.

It was only in the next moment that this conviction was shaken.

Karou turned to Thiago—to *Thiago*, of all living creatures in two wide worlds—and shared a look with him that was brief and secret, unguarded and full of pain—but it was *shared* pain and it was... *tender.* It was so profane, that tenderness, and so unbearable, that Akiva forgot everything else. All his dwindling vitality gathered in a last-gasp burst of strength and he flew at Thiago.

And Thiago caught him by the throat with one clawed hand. He held him at arm's length; he made it seem easy. Their eyes met, and as Akiva felt his throat crush closed in the Wolf's vise grip, he saw a trace of that perverse tenderness lingering in his enemy's gaze. With that, he just let go. His eyes rolled back. His head fell.

He let the darkness have him, and there was a part of him that hoped it would decide to keep him.

* * *

When Akiva collapsed, the Wolf's relief was as profound as his abhorrence for the words he had forced himself to speak, and for the sound of them issuing from this throat that was Thiago's throat, as this voice was Thiago's voice. And these hands that were a dead match for Karou's bruises? They were Thiago's, too.

But the nightmare? That was all Ziri's.

He wanted to ease the angel down to the floor, but he made himself thrust him roughly back to the other seraph, the beautiful female who looked as lost as she did savage. She caught Akiva, staggering under the dead weight of him—but no, not dead weight. Akiva wasn't dead. The Wolf wouldn't let Beast's Bane die so painlessly. As for Ziri . . . he wouldn't let him die at all, if he could help it.

If.

That the first test of this deception should be to decide the fate of the seraph who had saved his life, it was . . . unfair. He wasn't ready to be tested. The skin still fit too ill, or he wore it poorly. It wasn't the physical fit. As a vessel it was strong, graceful; it had a suppleness and tensile power that felt *enhanced*, and he knew it was a thing of beauty to behold, but he couldn't overcome his revulsion for it. When he had taken possession of it...Oh, Nitid, the taste of Karou's blood had still been in its mouth.

That was gone now, but his revulsion lingered, and the worst part: So did hers. And how could it not? Ziri had seen the state of Thiago at the pit; he knew what he had done to her—or *tried* to do, he hoped only *tried* to do, but he hadn't asked, how could he ask her that? She had been drenched with blood when he found her, and shaking with a violence that was like shivering in killing cold, and even now she could barely bring herself to look at him.

How many days past had he been gripped by the hope that she could see him for who he was—not a child anymore but a man grown, a man and...maybe a flint of luck to strike, his flint to her steel and his luck to hers. A man she might love. And now he was *this*?

If there was a will at work in the cosmos, the stars were ringing with laughter now. He could almost laugh himself. Had ever a hope been so annihilated?

But if it was unfair, at least it was his own doing. He had seen what needed to be done, and he had done it.

For her. For the chimaera, and for Eretz, yes, but it was her he had thought of when he dragged his blade across his own throat. He hadn't even known whom to pray to, the goddess of life or of assassins. What a foul gift he had given Karou: his sacrifice. His body to bury. The enormity of this deception to carry forward.

And...the chance to change the course of the rebellion and claim the future. That was enormous, too, but right now the deception felt like everything.

What was already done—the dying—was the easy part. Now he had to *be* Thiago. If this was going to work, he had to be convincing, starting right here with these seraphim. Which was why he was so immeasurably relieved when Akiva lost consciousness and he could put a quick end to the encounter, at least forestall the inevitable and try to think what to do.

"Take them to the granary," he told Ten, with what he hoped was the Wolf's gentle and authoritative contempt. And after she obeyed, with Issa assisting the female seraph with Akiva's body, and Nisk and Lisseth carrying the dead one between them, he closed the door behind them and fell back against it, squeezed his eyes shut and raised his hands to his face. But oh, how he hated the touch of them. He let them fall. He hated the touch of his own hands. *His* hands? He held them apart from his body—*his* body?—and in the tension of his misery they were rigid as rigor mortis, like the hands of the angel whose death he had made himself mock.

There was no escape from the vileness, because the vileness was *him*.

"I am Thiago," he heard himself say in low, choked horror. "I am the White Wolf."

And then, first at one hated hand, then both, Ziri felt a light touch and opened his eyes. Karou was right before him, pale and weeping, bruised and shaking, black-eyed and blue-haired and beautiful and very near, and she was looking at him—*into* him, to *him*—and holding both his hands in both of hers.

"*I* know who you are," she said in a fierce sweet whisper. "*I* know. And I'm with you. Ziri, Ziri. I see you."

And then she laid her head on his chest and let him hold her in his murderer's arms. She smelled of the river and trembled like a breeze on a butterfly's wing, and Ziri cradled her as if she were their world's last hope.

And maybe she was.

80

The Deception

A sound and it was near and it was wings.

Karou had been sure it must be Thiago's cohorts returning, and she had neither fled nor hidden. She had frozen like a prey thing, on her knees in the dirt and rocks and blood and vomit and flies and horror, waiting to be found.

And when she saw who it was, when he dropped down before her, his Kirin hooves scattering stones, there had been no room in her shock to be glad—Ziri was alive and he was *here*—because the undone way he stared at her only sharpened her shock. He looked to the Wolf and back at her. His jaw was loose with disbelief; he actually took a halting step backward, and Karou saw the grotesque tableau as he was seeing it. The indignity of the Wolf's pose, clothes twisted and wrenched asunder in an unmistakable display, and the little knife lying where he'd dropped it, looking like a letter opener, or a toy.

And her. Shaking. Bloody. Guilty.

She had killed the White Wolf. If she had been thinking at all, she wouldn't have believed that it could get any worse than that.

But, oh, it had.

Now, in her room, she laid her head on his chest and felt his heart beating against her cheek—fast and faster; she knew it was Ziri's heart now, not Thiago's, and she knew, too, that its rushing was for *her*—and she tried to quell her revulsion for his sake.

She had hoped that her little Kirin shadow might prove an ally, but she had never imagined . . . this.

After that first instant of slack astonishment he had lunged to her side and he had been so careful with her, so present and good and unfaltering—none of his shyness now; he was all focus and strength. He had held her shoulders, carefully but firmly, and made her look at him.

"You're all right," he had told her when he was sure that the blood that painted her wasn't her own. "Karou. Look at me. You're all right. He can't hurt you anymore."

"He can, he will," she had said, near hysteria. "He can't be dead, it can't stand. They'll make me bring him back. He's the White Wolf. *He's the White Wolf.*"

That was it, all there was to say. Ziri knew it, too; they didn't have to talk what-ifs. It was Ziri who saw what to do and who did it. Karou grasped his intent when he drew his crescent-moon blade; she gasped, tried to stop him. He said he was sorry. "But not for myself. That part's all right. I'm just sorry to leave you alone, for the time between."

Between. Between bodies.

"No! No!" *No no no no no no no.* "We'll think of something else. Ziri, *you can't do this*—"

But he did, and with a practiced hand, and his blade was very sharp.

She held him while he died, and his round brown eyes were wide and unafraid, and they were sweet, in the instant before they dulled, they were sweet and hopeful as they'd been when he was a boy following her around Loramendi. That was who she thought of as she held him dead in her arms—the boy he had been—and again now, as he held her in his new arms. She thought of the boy so that she wouldn't betray him by shuddering. It was so unfair, after the magnitude of his sacrifice, and so cruel, but it was all she could do not to wrench herself away, because though he was Ziri, his arms were the Wolf's, and his embrace was anathema.

When she couldn't stand it another moment, she used a pretense to draw back. She reached into her pocket, stepping away, and drew out the thing that she had put there days earlier and half forgotten.

"I have this," she said. "It's... I don't know." It seemed stupid now. Ridiculous, even—what was he supposed to do with it? It was the tip of his horn, a couple of inches long, that had snapped off in the court when he'd fallen unconscious. She wasn't sure what had made her take it, and now, as he reached for it, she wished she hadn't. Because there was a shyness in his voice when he said, "You kept this," that made it clear he was reading too much into it.

"For you," she said. "I thought you might want it. That was before..." Before she had buried the rest of him in a shallow grave? Again, her stomach felt like a clenching fist. It had been the best she could do, and at least it wasn't the pit. Not the pit for the last true Kirin flesh, dear Ellai, be it only so much stardust gathered fleetingly into form. It had been hard enough to shovel dry dirt onto his face. She'd kept thinking she should change her mind. After all, it was up to her. She had two bodies freshly dead. She could mend either one. She could have put Ziri's soul back where it belonged; he'd done what he'd done and it was so brave, but then it was in her hands. His soul was in her hands.

Ziri's soul felt like the high roaming wind of the Adelphas Mountains and the beat of stormhunters' wings, like the beautiful, mournful, eternal song of the wind flutes that had filled their caves with music he could not possibly remember. It felt like *home*.

And she had put it in such a vessel. Because he was right, after all. This was the only way to take control of the chimaera's fate. Through such a deception.

If they could pull it off.

It wouldn't be easy even under ordinary circumstances, but so soon, while they were both still reeling and hadn't even been able to talk or plan, to come to such a test. The angels must be dealt with.

Karou turned away and went to her table. She righted the chair that she had toppled when Akiva fell through her window, and eased herself into it. The backs of her legs were so torn up from thrashing under Thiago's weight, and her whole body pretty much felt like it had been clamped in vises. But that would all pass in a day or two; the rest was here to stay.

The problems, the terrible responsibility, and the lie that at all costs must go no further than this room.

Issa and Ten returned, minus Nisk and Lisseth.

"I want them gone," said Issa in a dangerous tone, and Karou knew that she meant Nisk and Lisseth, not the angels. "They're savages, leaving you out there with him like that. The others, too."

Karou tended to agree, but still. "They were following orders." She pointed out that they had followed worse orders than that.

"I don't care," said Issa. She was even more disgusted with the pair because they were Naja, and she wanted to believe better of her own kind. "There has to be some basic understanding of right and wrong, even when it comes to orders."

"If we made that a rule, we'd have no one left. Well." She glanced at the Wolf. At Ziri. "Very few." Balieros's team must be resurrected soon, along with Amzallag and the sphinxes, whose souls she had gleaned from the pit. She needed soldiers she could trust. "Anyway, we can't start disappearing everyone we don't like. That would be suspicious. And," she added somewhat after the fact, "wrong."

In fact, they had disappeared no one, and she didn't plan to start. Razor didn't count. He had died attacking a seraph stronghold called Glyss-on-the-Tane—the same engagement in which Ziri had been lost, to the sorrow of all. No one need ever know what had really happened when Razor had tried, and failed, to carry out Thiago's order, or that one of the two of them *had* returned—though only to the comfort of a shallow grave and the starring role in this enormous subterfuge.

"Let *me* have the two Naja," said Ten, clicking her teeth

together. "This wolf mouth has a hunger. I'll say they *asked* me to eat them."

"Don't be terrible," Issa protested mildly.

"No?" Ten peered around at Karou. "But wasn't that the whole inducement?"

Karou couldn't help but smile, which hurt her raw cheek. Ten was no more Ten than Thiago was Thiago; she was Haxaya, and it was easier with her. As much as Karou had grown to hate the she-wolf, there just wasn't the same level of physical aversion as with the Wolf. It was good to have Haxaya's dark humor in the mix—even if one couldn't quite tell when she was joking. When Karou had awakened her old friend in Ten's body—Ten having fatally underestimated Issa and her usually docile bands of living jewelry—she had put it to her straight: the terrible situation, and what she must do or else be returned forthwith to her thurible.

Haxaya's answer, with a smile that seemed made for Ten's wolf jaws, had been, "I've always wanted to be terrible."

"Can you be slightly less terrible?" she asked her now. "No eating the Naja, or any other comrades, even despised ones." As an afterthought, she added, "Please."

"Fine. But if they *do* ask me—"

"They're not going to ask you to eat them. *Ten.*"

"I suppose not," she conceded with what sounded like true disappointment, and maybe it was.

And here they were, Karou's allies: Thiago, Ten, and Issa. And they were looking to her. *Oh god*, thought Karou, feeling tipsy with panic. *What now?*

"The angels," she said, willing her pulse to even itself out.

“They escape,” said Issa. “Simple. He’s done it before.”

Karou nodded. Of course, that was it. Get them gone, see the last of Akiva, finally and forever. That was what she wanted.

So what was that ache in her chest?

We dreamed together of the world remade, she kept thinking. It had been the most beautiful dream, and could only have arisen as it did: born of mercy and nurtured in love. And she couldn’t think of the future, and peace, without remembering Akiva’s hand to her heart and hers to his. “*We* are the beginning,” she had said then, in the temple, and everything had seemed possible with his heart beating under her hand.

And now, his heart was beating right over there, in the dark, in the granary. So near, and yet so very far away. There was no way she could imagine, no collision of impossible events, that would bring his heartbeat under her hand ever again, or join the two of them back together in the dream that was theirs—not hers and Ziri’s, not even hers and Brimstone’s, but hers and Akiva’s.

No way she could imagine.

81

Veins of Chance

One world on its own is a strange enough seethe of coiling, unknowable veins of intention and chance, but two? Where two worlds mingle breath through rips in the sky, the strange becomes stranger, and many things may come to pass that few imaginations could encompass.

82

Top Three Reasons for Living

Zuzana and Mik were at Aït Benhaddou when it began. *It.* The thing that would never be eclipsed, that would own the third-person singular, neuter pronoun "it" forever.

Where were you the day it *began?*

Aït Benhaddou was the most famous kasbah in Morocco, much bigger than monster castle, though lacking the zest of monsters. It had been restored by World Heritage funds and movie money—Russell Crowe had "gladiated" here—and it was sanitized and set-dressed for tourists. Shops in the lanes, rugs draped over walls, and at the main gate, camels batting their astonishing eyelashes as they posed for photographs—for a price, of course. Everything for a price, and don't forget to bargain.

Mik was bargaining. Zuzana was sketching in the shade while he, pretending to peruse a selection of kettles, purchased an antique silver ring that he suspected was not actually silver, and probably not antique, but indisputably a ring, which was the main thing. *Not* an engagement ring. He'd gotten the air-conditioning back on all right, but he wasn't about to count that as one of his tasks, and never mind, ahem, curing Zuzana's ennui. *That* was most certainly not a task. It was one of his top three reasons for living—the other two being the violin and holding Zuzana's hand—and it was an activity he performed—*participated in*—with a feeling of deep gratitude to the universe.

To win her hand, though, he required a challenge. Two more challenges.

He felt a curious commitment to this whole task idea. *Who got to do things like this?* Monsters and angels and portals and invisibility—even if the last one was a little hard to enjoy on account of all the *ouch*. For that matter, how many people ever got to buy maybe-antique maybe-silver rings for their beautiful girlfriends in ancient mud cities in North Africa and eat dried dates out of a paper bag and see *camel eyelashes*, for god's sake, and... *hey, where are all the people going?*

There was a sudden tide of rushing in the narrow lane, and hollering in Arabic or Berber or some language that was not Czech or English or German or French, and Mik watched in perplexity. The locals were hollering and rushing and then doors were swallowing them up and the lanes were empty of all but tourists: tourists blinking at each other as the dust quite literally settled, and, behind the doors, the hubbub intensified.

Mik pocketed the ring and returned to Zuzana, who was still sitting in the shade, but no longer sketching. She looked up at him, unsettled. "What's going on?"

"I don't know." He looked around. A few families still lived within the walls here; he caught a glimpse of a bright TV screen as a door swung open and shut. It was such an anachronism: a TV in this place... and then... and then the hollering turned to screaming. Such a pitch of screaming. It seemed to mingle joy and terror.

Mik grabbed Zuzana's hand—a top-three reason for living—and pulled her across the way to where the TV was, to see what in the hell—or in the heavens—was going on.

83

Good-Bye

When Akiva awoke, Liraz was sleeping by his side and they were in darkness, though, of course, it is never true darkness where seraphim are. Their wings, even burning dull in exhausted sleep, cast a sly luminescence that reached to the high timbered ceiling over their heads, the sloping mud walls at their sides. It was a large space, and windowless; he couldn't tell if it was night or day. How long had he slept?

He felt...well, *invigorated* was a hard word under the circumstances, it sounded full of life, and he was not that, but he was a good deal better. He pushed himself up to sit.

The first thing he saw was his brother. Hazael lay on Liraz's other side; her body was curved toward his, and for a wild instant, hope leapt in Akiva that it was three of them again, that Karou had resurrected his brother, after all, and Hazael would sit up and start telling ridiculous stories about all he had seen and done while he was a disembodied soul. But that hope quickly went the way of most hopes: Acid bitterness devoured it, and Akiva felt like a fool. Of course, Hazael was dead, still and forever. There were beginning to be flies, and that couldn't stand.

He woke Liraz. It was time to honor their brother.

The ceremony wasn't much as ceremonies go, but then they never were: a soldier's funeral, the corpse its own pyre. The official words were impersonal, so they changed them to fit Hazael.

"He was always hungry," said Liraz, "and he fell asleep sometimes on the watch. He saved himself a thousand times from discipline with his smile."

"He could make anyone talk to him," said Akiva. "No secret was safe from him."

"Except yours," murmured Liraz, and it stung, the truth of it.

"He should have had a true life," he said. "He would have filled it up. He would have tried everything." He would have married, he thought. He could have had children. Akiva could almost see him—the Hazael that might have been, had the world been better.

"No one has ever laughed more truly," said Liraz. "He made laughing seem easy."

And laughing should be easy, Akiva thought, but it wasn't. Look at the pair of them, black hands and splintered souls. He reached for his sister's hand, and she took it and gripped it as tightly as a sword hilt, as if her life depended on it. It hurt, but it was a pain he could easily bear.

Liraz was altered. Layers were stripped away—all her harshness and the tough veneer that even he had scarcely seen through since they were children. Hugging her knees, with her shoulders hunched and her firelit face soft with sadness, she looked vulnerable. Young. She looked almost like a different person.

"He died defending me," she said. "If I had gone with Jael, he would still be alive."

"No. He would have hanged," Akiva told her. "You would still have been taken, and he would have died in misery for failing you. He would have chosen this."

"But if he had lived just a little longer, he could have gotten away with us." She had been staring into the flames that consumed their brother, but she blinked away from them to fix on Akiva. "Akiva. What did you do?" She did not ask, "And why didn't you do it *in time?*" but the ghost question hung there anyway.

"I don't know," he said, to the asked question and the unasked, and he stared into the cremation fire as it burned fast and infernal, leaving only ash for an urn they didn't have.

What did he have in him, to have done such a thing, and why hadn't it shown itself when he needed it most—not just in time to save Hazael's life, but years ago, to save Madrigal's? Had the years of devotion to *sirithar* honed his sympathy for magic? Or was it triggered by that sudden surge of memories of his mother?

Liraz asked, "Do you think Jael is alive?"

Akiva didn't know what to say to that, either. He didn't want to think about Jael, but it couldn't very well be avoided. "He may be," he allowed. "And if he is…"

"I hope he is."

Akiva looked at his sister. The tough veneer had not returned. She still seemed vulnerable and young. She had spoken simply, quietly, and Akiva understood. A part of him hoped it, too. Jael deserved no such easy death as the explosion would have dealt him. But if he *was* alive, there were things to be done.

He rose and looked around. Mud walls, wooden door, no guards with outstretched hamsas to keep them weak; this dark place couldn't hold them. Where was the Wolf, and why had he allowed his prisoners to rest and regain their strength?

And where was Karou? With Thiago? The idea brought gut pain, like a stab. Akiva couldn't shake the memory of the look that had passed between them. That one look made him question everything he'd thought he knew about Karou. "I think it's time to be going." He held his hand out to his sister.

Once, Liraz would have rolled her eyes and risen without help. Now, she let him pull her to her feet. But once she had risen, she stood rooted beside the remains of Hazael's pyre, staring at it. "I feel like we're leaving him here."

"I know," said Akiva. To have flown so far bearing his weight, and to leave now with nothing? It seemed, in that moment, unthinkable. He looked around again, saw a jug inside the door.

"Water," Liraz told him. "The Naja woman left it." Akiva went and got it, offered it to Liraz, and then drank deeply himself. It was sweet and good and much needed, and when it was gone, he carefully filled the jug with Hazael's ashes. Maybe it was foolish or morbid to keep such physical residue, but it helped, somehow.

"Okay," he said.

"To the caves? The others must be thinking we died in the blast."

The Kirin caves, where once upon a time he and Madrigal were to have met to begin their revolution. It was his Misbegotten brothers and sisters who awaited him there now, and with them a future that did not yet feel real. His sense of purpose was intact: to finish what he had started, end the killing, create—somehow—a new way of living. But without Karou by his side, the dream lay ahead of him with all the magic of a dusty path to a flat horizon.

"Yes," he said. "But there's something we have to do first."

Liraz let out a long breath. "Please tell me it doesn't involve saying good-bye."

Good-bye. The word hurt. *Good-bye* was the last thing Akiva ever wanted to tell Karou. He thought of their first night together, how at the Warlord's ball and later at the temple they had whispered "hello" to each other, again and again like a shared secret. It had been on his lips the first time he kissed her. That was what he would say to her if he could have what he wanted. *Hello.* "No," he told Liraz, and reminded her it was bad luck to say good-bye.

To which she replied, deadpan, "Bad luck? By all means, let's not start having any of that."

* * *

It was neither "hello" nor "good-bye" that Akiva interrupted his escape to say, stealing glamoured again into Karou's room to take her and Issa by surprise.

The Wolf, bless the godstars, was not there, but when Karou shot to her feet she threw a quick, uncertain look to the door and it was another gut-stab to Akiva—a reminder that Thiago was near, and had full access to that door.

"What are you doing here?" Karou asked, startled. Her peacock-blue hair was braided over one shoulder, and sleeves now hid the bruises on her arms. The swelling of her cheek had come down some, and her anger seemed to have gone, too. A flush spread up her neck, sudden color overtaking her pallor. "You were supposed to go."

Supposed to go. This wasn't the surprise it might have been. Their imprisonment had been a sham. When Akiva had laid his hand to the door to burn it, it had sighed open. It wasn't even locked. He'd let out a small breath of a laugh and peered through the crack to see an ugly little courtyard piled with rubble, and no guards.

"We are going. But there's something I have to tell you." Akiva paused, seeing Karou tense. What did she think he was going to say? Was she afraid that he'd come to speak of love? He shook his head, wanting to assure her that those days were over, that she had no more such torment to fear from him. Tonight he brought a new torment. Again he was the bearer of an impossible choice. He said, "I am going to seal the portals."

Whatever she was braced for, it wasn't that. Her voice was a gasp. "*What?*"

"I'm sorry. I wanted to warn you," he said, "so you could decide which side you'll be on."

Which side: Eretz or the human world? *Which life will you give up?*

"Which *side?*" She came out from behind her table. "You can't. Not this portal. I need it. *We* need it." What began as astonishment was becoming outrage, edged with panic. Issa moved to her side in a ripple. "Haven't you burned enough? Why would you even try—?"

"To save both worlds," said Liraz, "from corrupting each other."

"What are you talking about?"

"Weapons," said Akiva simply. He paused. He couldn't begin to imagine compressing all that had happened in the Tower of Conquest into a neat explanation to offer her. "Jael. He may be dead, but if he's not, he'll be coming here for weapons. With the Dominion."

The whites of Karou's eyes were rings around her black irises, and she put out a hand to steady herself on her table. "How could he even know about human weapons?" A flash of fury. "Did *you* tell him?"

Another stab, that she could believe that Akiva would arm Jael, but it was no satisfaction to him to tell her the truth. He wished he could lie and spare her. "Razgut," he said.

She stayed frozen a moment in her stare, then shut her eyes. All the rose-flush that had colored her cheeks drained away, and she made a small, anguished moan. At her side, Issa whispered, "It is not your fault, sweet girl."

"It is," she said, opening her eyes. "Whatever else isn't, this *is*."

"And mine," said Akiva. "I found a portal for the Empire." The portals—and hence the human world—had been lost to seraphim for a millenium; Akiva had changed that. He had found one portal, the one in Central Asia, above Uzbekistan. Razgut had shown Karou the other. "They could come by either portal. Jael planned it as a pageant, to play on all that humans believe angels to be."

Karou was clutching Issa's hand and taking long, shallow breaths. "Because things weren't bad enough already," she said, and began to laugh a broken laugh that Akiva could feel in his heart.

He wanted to fold her in his arms and tell her it would be all right, but he couldn't promise that, and, of course, he couldn't touch her. "The portals must be closed," he said. "If you need time to decide—"

"To decide what? Which world I'll be in?" She stared at him. "How can you ask that?"

And Akiva knew that Karou would choose Eretz. Of course, he had known it already. If he hadn't, he thought that no magnitude of threat—worlds at stake and lives—could have induced him to close the doors between them and trap himself forever in a world where she was not. "You have a life here," he said. "There may never be a way back."

"Back?" She cocked her head in that bird way that was pure Madrigal. She was bruised and shadowed, standing before him, breathing fast and summoning courage like a glamour. With her hair pulled back, the line of her neck was exaggerated, like an artist's rendering of elegance. The planes of her face were also exaggerated—too thin—but they still vied with softness, and that interplay seemed the very essence of beauty. Her dark eyes drank the candlelight and shone like a creature's, and there was no question in that moment that, whatever body it was sleeved in, her soul belonged to the great wild world of Eretz, terrible and beautiful, so much still unmapped and untamed, home to beasts and angels, stormhunters and sea serpents, its story still to be written.

She said, in a voice that was hiss and purr and the rasp of the blade to the sharpening stone, "*I am chimaera.* My life is there."

Akiva felt something course through him, or many things: a tremor of love and a chill of awe, a wave of power and a surge of hope. *Hope.* Truly, hope was as unkillable as the great shield beetles that lay inert for years beneath the desert sands, waiting for prey to happen near. What possible grounds had he for hope?

As long as you're alive, he had told Liraz, only half believing it himself, *there is always a chance.*

Well, he was alive, and so was Karou, and they would be in the same world. It was possibly the thinnest grounds for hope that he had ever heard of—*we are alive and in the same world*—but he clung to it as he told her his plan to fly to the Samarkand portal and burn it first, before doubling back for this one. He wanted to ask her where the rebels would go now, but he couldn't. It wasn't for him to know. They were enemies still, and once he left here, Karou would vanish from his life again, for long or forever, he couldn't know.

"How much time do you need?" he asked through the tightness in his throat. "To retreat?"

Again she glanced toward the door, and Akiva felt the burn of fury and envy, knowing that she would go to the Wolf as soon as he was gone, and that they would plan their next move together, and that wherever the chimaera rebels went, Karou would still be with Thiago, and not—and never—with him. All his restraint broke. He took a heavy step toward her. "Karou, how . . . ? After what he's done to you?" He started to reach toward her, but she shrank back, gave a single sharp shake of her head.

"Don't."

His hand fell.

"You don't get to judge," she said in a violent half whisper. Her eyes were wet and wide and desperately unhappy, and he saw her hand lift by old instinct to her throat, where once upon a time she had worn a wishbone on a cord. She had been wearing it their first night together; they had broken it when the sun threatened dawn and they knew they must part, and in the days that followed it had become their ritual. Always in parting. And if the wish had blossomed over the days and weeks to become their grand dream of a world remade, it had begun much more humbly. That first night, the wish had been simple: that they might see each other again.

But Karou's hand found nothing at her throat and fell away again, and she faced Akiva squarely and spoke coolly, and what she said was, "Good-bye."

It felt like a final tether snapping. *As long as you're alive, there is always a chance.* A chance of what? Akiva wondered, throwing a glamour over himself and his sister together, and pushing himself out into the night. That things will get better? How had the rest of the conversation gone, back at that grim battle camp?

Or worse. That was it. *Usually worse.*

84

Apocalypse

Karou felt Akiva's departure as she always had: as cold. His warmth was like a gift given and snatched away, and she stood there with her back to the window, feeling chilled, bereft, and undone. And *angry*. It was a childish, cartoonish anger—facing Akiva, she had wanted to beat her fists at his chest and then fall against him and feel his arms close around her.

As if *he* might be the place of safety that she was always seeking and never finding.

Karou breathed. She imagined she could feel him growing farther away and farther, and the distance hurt more with every phantom wingbeat. She took gulps of breath to fight back sobs. Issa's arm was around her. *Be your own place of safety*, she told herself, straightening. No crossbar in the world could protect her from what lay ahead, and neither could a tiny knife tucked in her boot—though there her tiny knife would most certainly remain—and neither could a man, not even Akiva. She had to be her own strength, complete unto herself.

Be who Brimstone believes you are, she told herself, willing the strength to suddenly well up from some unknown depth. *Be who all those buried souls need you to be, and all the living, too.*

"Sweet girl," said Issa. "It's all right, you know."

"All right?" Karou stared at her. Which part? The threat of human weapons to Eretz, or the threat of seraphim *here*. The havoc the angels could cause to human society just by existing, let alone by soliciting guns for a war beyond human ken… What had she done now? How could she have turned Razgut loose on Eretz with his poisoned soul and such deadly knowledge as he possessed? How many more such mistakes did she have it in her to make, huge enough to destroy worlds? What, exactly, she wanted to demand of Issa, was "all right"?

Issa said, "To love him," and Karou felt a jolt go through her at the unexpectedness of it.

"I don't—" she tried to protest, out of habit of shame.

"Please, child, do you think I don't know you at all? I'm not going to say there is some easy future for you, or even any future at all. I only want you not to punish yourself. You've always felt the truth in him, then and now. Your heart is not wrong. Your heart is your strength. You don't have to be ashamed."

Karou stared at her, blinking away the tears. Issa's words—her permission?—hurt more than they helped. There was *no way*.… Surely Issa could see that. Why was she torturing her by talking as though there was? There wasn't. There was not.

Karou steeled herself. *Be that cat*, she remembered from a drawing in her lost sketchbook. The cat that stands out of reach on a high wall, needing no one. Not even Akiva. "It doesn't matter," she said. "He's gone, and we have to go, too. We have to get everyone ready." She looked around her room. Teeth, tools, thuribles, it would all have to go with them. As for the table, the bed, and the door, she felt a wave of regret. Rough as they were, they were so much more than she'd had on the run with the rebels before they came here. She swallowed, felt all the hollow horror of being shoved out a door into darkness.

"Issa." She started to tremble as the full dread of this new predicament took hold of her. "Where will we go?"

* * *

Coiling, unknowable veins of intention and chance. Later, Karou would wonder where they might have gone, and how everything else would have fallen out differently, unknowably.

If the Dominion had not already arrived.

* * *

The chimaera host was gathered in the court and ready to fly when they heard a sound in the distance, a mundane sound with no place in this wasteland silence. It was the honking of a horn. The incessant, insistent honking of a horn, and the crunch of tires grinding over the trackless hill, careless with urgency and far too fast. More than a few of the soldiers broke formation to rise into the air and see over the wall. Karou was first.

Her breath and heartbeat caught in her throat. Headlights

on the slope. A van. Someone was hanging out the passenger window waving both arms, shouting, drowned out by the honking.

That someone was Zuzana.

The van skidded, fishtailed, stopped. Zuzana was out and running through the kicked-up dust, and Karou knew what she was screaming before the words came clear.

And she knew that the blame for two worlds' fates was on her shoulders now.

"Angels! Angels! Angels!"

Zuzana was sprinting. Karou dropped out of the air, catching her friend by the shoulders.

"Angels," Zuzana said, breathless and wide-eyed and white. "Holy hell, Karou. In the sky. Hundreds. *Hundreds.* The world. Is freaking. *Out.*"

Mik came running around the van to Zuzana's side, and lurched to a halt. Karou heard rushing on the hill like a landslide and knew the chimaera were gathered behind her.

And then...she felt heat. Zuzana, looking past her, gasped.

Heat.

Karou spun around, and there was Akiva. For a long moment, he was all she saw. Even the Wolf was only a white blur, moving to take his place at her side. Akiva had come back, and his beautiful face was tense with remorse.

"Too late," she said softly, knowing that this world that had nurtured her in hiding, that had given her art and friends and a chance at normal life, would never be the same again, no matter what happened next.

The chimaera host, bristling in the presence of the enemy,

was watching Thiago for a sign that did not come. The pair of seraphim stood not a wingspan away, and their mythic, angelic perfection was everything the "beasts" were not. Karou saw them with her human eyes, this army she had rendered more monstrous than ever nature had, and she knew what the world would see in them if they flew to fight the Dominion: demons, nightmares, evil. The sight of the seraphim would be heralded as a miracle. But chimaera?

The apocalypse.

"No. It isn't too late," Akiva said. "This is the beginning." He put his hand on his heart. Only Karou could know what he meant, and, oh, she did know—*we are the beginning*—and felt heat flare in her own heart, as if he had laid his hand there. "Come with us," he said. He turned to Thiago, standing at her side. His voice scraped and his eyes burned hot, and Karou knew how hard it was for him to make himself address the Wolf, but he did.

He said, "We can fight them together. I have an army, too."

EPILOGUE

The Kirin caves. Two uneasy armies seethe and roil. Only the sprawl of the caverns keeps the peace, by keeping them apart.

The Misbegotten claim to feel the sickness of hamsas even through stone. The revenants, enraged by the cold calculations writ black on the knuckles of their enemies, will not desist from pressing their palms against the walls that divide them. It is not a good beginning. Each army burns to hack off the others' hands and hurl them over the drop into the ice chasms below.

Akiva tells his brothers and sisters that the magic of the marks doesn't penetrate stone, but they don't want to admit it. Every hour he wishes Hazael were here. "He would have them all playing dice together by now," he tells Liraz.

"The music helps, at least," she says.

She doesn't mean the music of the caverns. The wind flutes haunt them all, waking beast and angel both from nightmares more alike than they could ever imagine. The Misbegotten dream of a country of ghosts, the chimaera of a tomb filled with the souls of their loved ones. Only Karou is soothed by the wind music. It is the lullaby of her earliest life, and she has been surprised by deep and dreamless sleep these two nights they have spent here.

Not tonight, though. It is the eve of battle, and they are gathered, several hundred altogether, in this largest of the caverns. Mik's violin fills the space with a sonata from the other world, and they are all quiet, listening.

Common enemy, their commanders have told them. *Common cause.*

For now, anyway. It is implied or believed that soon this will change—revert—and they will be released to once more freely pursue their hate as they always have, chimaera against seraphim, seraphim against chimaera. The hope—Karou's, the Wolf's, Akiva's, and even Liraz's—is that their hate will turn to something else before that day comes.

It feels like a test for the future of all Eretz.

Zuzana's head is on Karou's shoulder, and Issa is on her other side. The Wolf isn't far; Ziri has grown easier in his new body, and, lying back on his elbows beside the fire, he is elegant and exquisite, the former occupant's cruelty absent from his face unless he remembers to try to put it there, and his smiles no longer seem learned from a book. Karou feels him looking at her, but she doesn't look back. Her eyes are pulled elsewhere, across the cavern to where Akiva sits at another fire with his own soldiers around him.

He is looking back at her.

As ever when their eyes meet, it is like a lit fuse searing a path through the air between them. These past days, when this has happened, one or the other would turn quickly away, but this time they rest and let the fuse burn. They are filled with the sight of each other. Here in this cavern, this extraordinary gathering—this seethe of colliding hatreds, tamed temporarily by a shared hate—could be their long-ago dream seen through a warped mirror. This is not how it was meant to be. They are not side by side as they once imagined. They are not exultant, and they no longer feel themselves to be the instruments of some great intention. They are creatures grasping at life with stained hands. There is so much between them, all the living and all the dead, but for a moment everything falls away and the fuse burns brighter and nearer, so that Karou and Akiva almost feel as if they are touching.

Tomorrow they will start the apocalypse.

Tonight, they let themselves look at each other, for just a little while.

. . . to be continued

Acknowledgments

Whew.

It always comes as a relief to get to this page, because it means I have finished a book—a thing that gets easier in some ways over time, but not in all ways. Every story is its own challenge, and in the middle I find myself relying on the quote "It always seems impossible until it is done." Because it *does*. (I didn't know who said that until just this moment when I googled it, and now that I know it was Nelson Mandela, finishing a novel doesn't seem like such a big accomplishment after all. Thanks a lot, Nelson Mandela.)

Ha. But truly, it *is* an accomplishment, and I owe deep thanks to some wonderful people:

First and best, my husband, Jim Di Bartolo, who is not only my earliest and most crucial reader, but also my fort holder-downer and slack picker-upper when I am struggling to balance writing with life. My books would not be what they are without you, and neither would my life, which I would not trade for any other life, real or fictional, not for anything. Thank you for the happy!

Clementine, age two, who, when I left in the mornings to write, would call after me, "Say hi to Karou!" Look, my little Pie, I finished the ham! Very soon, I would like to write a book for you.

Always, my parents, for everything they've always done to help me be me. I am so lucky to have you.

My agent, Jane Putch, friend and partner. I truly would be lost without you. Thank you.

With my arms flung as wide as they will go, a huge thanks to the amazing teams at Little, Brown Books for Young Readers in the U.S. and Hodder & Stoughton in the U.K. for parallel amazing publishing experiences that make this all twice as much fun. At Little, Brown, thanks especially to Alvina Ling, editor extraordinaire; Lisa Moraleda, Bethany Strout; Victoria Stapleton; Melanie Chang; Andrew Smith; Megan Tingley; Stephanie O'Cain; Faye Bi; the design team; and everyone else who squeezed the publishing schedule to within an inch of its life to accommodate my pace and get the book out on time (ish). I'm sorry for any stress I have caused. Thanks also to Amy Habayeb and the rights team—getting the foreign editions in the mail is one of my favorite things!

At Hodder, massive thanks to Kate Howard and Eleni Lawrence and the rest of the team. Everything you do blows me away.

And thanks, lastly, to the readers of *Daughter of Smoke & Bone* for such marvelous enthusiasm and support. There is no motivation quite like the excitement of readers, and it has been a truly amazing year. From the depths of my heart, I hope you like this one, too.

XO

Turn the page for a sneak preview of

Dreams of GODS & MONSTERS

by LAINI TAYLOR

AVAILABLE SPRING 2014!

Editor's note: The following is unedited and may change in the final book.

1

Nightmare Ice Cream

Nerve thrum and screaming blood, wild and churning and chasing and devouring and terrible and terrible and terrible—

"Eliza. *Eliza!*"

A voice. Bright light, and Eliza fell awake. That's how it felt: like falling and landing hard. "It was a dream," she heard herself say. "It was just a dream. I'm okay."

How many times in her life had she spoken those words? More than she could count. This was the first time, though, that she'd spoken them to a man who had burst heroically into her room, clutching a claw hammer, to save her from being murdered.

"You...you were screaming," said her roommate, Gabriel, darting looks into the corners and finding no sign of murderers. He was sleep-disheveled and manically alert, holding the hammer high and ready. "I mean...really, *really* screaming."

"I know," said Eliza, though she knew it more by the rawness of her throat than actually remembering it. "I do that sometimes." She pushed herself upright in bed. Her heartbeat felt like cannon fire—doomful and deep and reverberating through her entire body—and though her mouth was dry and her breathing shallow, she tried to sound nonchalant. "Sorry to wake you."

Blinking, Gabriel lowered the hammer. "That's not what I meant, Eliza. I've never heard anyone sound like that in real life. That was a horror movie scream."

He sounded a little impressed. *Go away*, Eliza wanted to say. *Please.* Her hands were starting to tremble. Soon she wouldn't be able to control it, and she didn't want a witness. The adrenaline crash could be pretty bad after the dream. "I promise, I'm fine. Okay? I just..."

Damn.

Shaking. Pressure building, the sting behind her eyelids, and all of it out of her control.

Damn damn damn.

She doubled over and hid her face in her bedspread as the sobs welled up and took her over. As bad as the dream was—and it was *bad*—the aftermath was worse because she was conscious but still powerless. The terror—the terror, *the terror*—lingered, and there was something else. It came with the dream, every time, and didn't recede with it but stayed like something a tide had washed in. Something awful—a rank, leviathan corpse left to rot on the shore of her mind. It was...remorse. But god, that was too bloodless a word for it. This feeling the dream left her with, it was knives of panic and horror resting bright atop a red and meaty wound-fester of *guilt*.

Guilt over *what*? That was elusive, but she knew from lifelong experience that it would stay with her for days: this sense that she had done something unspeakable. This conviction that she didn't deserve to live.

It sucked.

When the sobs finally subsided and she lifted her head, Gabriel was sitting on the edge of her bed, looking compassionate and alarmed. There was this pert civility about Gabriel that suggested a better-than-fair chance of bow ties in his future. Maybe even a monocle. He was a neuroscientist, probably the smartest person Eliza knew, and one of the nicest. Both of them were research fellows at the Smithsonian's National Museum of Natural History—the NMNH—and had been friendly while not quite *friends* for the past year, until Gabriel's girlfriend moved to New York for her postdoc and he needed a roommate to cover the rent. Eliza had known it was a risk, cross-pollinating life hours with work hours, for this exact reason—*this*.

Screaming. Sobbing.

It wouldn't take much digging for an interested party to ascertain the…depths of abnormal…upon which she'd built this life. Like laying planks over quicksand, it sometimes seemed. But the dream hadn't troubled her for a while, so she'd given in to the temptation to pretend she was normal, with nothing but the normal concerns of any twenty-four-year-old doctoral student on a tiny budget. Dissertation pressure, evil lab-mates, grant proposals, rent.

Monsters.

"I'm sorry," she said to Gabriel. "I think I'm okay now."

"Good." After an uncomfortable pause, he asked brightly, "Cup of tea?"

Tea. Now there was a nice glimpse of normal. "Yes," Eliza said. "Please."

And when he ambled off to put on the kettle, she composed herself. Pulled on her robe, rinsed her face, blew her nose, regarded herself in the mirror. She was puffy, and her eyes were bloodshot. Lovely. She had pretty eyes, normally. She was accustomed to getting compliments on them from strangers. They were big and long-lashed and bright—at least when the whites weren't pink from sobbing—and several shades lighter brown than her skin, which made them seem to glow. Right now they looked a little crazy.

"You're crazy," she told her reflection—experimentally, as though testing the statement for a ring of truth.

No ring. Eliza didn't think she was crazy. Only periodically... *possessed.* Which, of course, was exactly what a crazy person *would* think. But she didn't mean possessed by a ghost. She was possessed by the dream, and that wasn't crazy at all.

Ha.

When Eliza joined Gabriel in the kitchen, the oven clock read 4 AM. Tea was on the table, along with a pint of ice cream, open, with a spoon sticking out. He gestured to it. "Nightmare ice cream. Family tradition."

"Really?"

"Yeah, actually."

Eliza wished that ice cream had been her family's response to the dream. She reached for the carton. "Thanks," she said. She ate a couple of bites in silence, took a sip of tea, all the while tensed for the questions to begin, as they surely must.

What do you dream about, Eliza?

How am I supposed to help you if you won't talk to me, Eliza?

What's wrong with you, Eliza?

She'd heard it all before.

"You were dreaming about Morgan Toth, weren't you?" Gabriel asked. "Morgan Toth and his pillowy lips?"

Okay, so she hadn't heard that before. In spite of herself, Eliza laughed. Morgan Toth was her nemesis, and his lips were a fine subject for a nightmare, but no, that wasn't even close. "I don't really want to talk about it," she said.

"Talk about what?" Gabriel asked, all innocence. "What is this 'it' you speak of?"

"Cute. But I mean it. Sorry."

"Okay."

Another bite of ice cream, another silence cut short by another non-question. "I had nightmares as a kid," Gabriel offered. "For about a year. Really intense. To hear my parents tell it, life as we knew it was pretty much suspended. I was afraid to fall asleep, and I had all these rituals, superstitions. I even tried making offerings. My favorite toys, food. Supposedly I was overheard offering up my older brother in my place. I don't remember that, but he swears."

"Offering him to who?" Eliza asked.

"*Them.* The ones in the dream."

Them.

A spark of recognition, hope. Idiotic hope. Eliza had a "them," too, and though rationally she knew that her own "them" were a creation of her mind and existed nowhere else, it wasn't always possible for her to believe this. Sometimes, especially in the aftermath, the feeling was too powerful—that she was a victim of something outside of herself, that it couldn't be a product of her own brain activity, but a real, external phenomenon—and then every scientific fact she knew about dreams went out the window.

She asked, "What were they?" before she quite considered what she was doing. If she wasn't going to talk about *her* dream, she shouldn't be prying into *his*. It was a rule of secret-keeping, in which she was well-versed: Ask not, lest ye be asked.

"Monsters," he said with a shrug, and just like that, Eliza lost interest—not at the mention of monsters, but his *of course* tone. Anyone who could say "monsters" in that offhand manner had definitely never met Eliza's.

"You know, being chased is one of the commonest dreams,"

Gabriel said, and went on to tell her about it, and Eliza kept sipping tea and taking the occasional bite of nightmare ice cream, and she nodded in the right places, but she wasn't really listening. She'd thoroughly researched dream analysis by the time she was ten—emphasis on: *monsters, being chased by*—and was as convinced now as she had been then that it didn't apply to her dream, or to her monsters.

They were something else entirely.

So when Gabriel summed up with "they're a manifestation of our waking fears" and "*everyone* has them," Eliza really wanted to say, *And I suppose* everyone *gets pacemakers when they're seven years old because "manifestations of their waking fears" keep stopping their hearts?* But she didn't, because it was the exact kind of memorable factoid that gets regurgitated at cocktail parties.

Did you know that Eliza Jones got a pacemaker when she was seven because her nightmares were so bad they stopped her heart?

Seriously? That's insane.

"So what happened to you?" she asked, cutting Gabriel off midsentence. "What happened to your monsters?"

"Oh, they carried off my brother and left me alone. I have to sacrifice a goat to them every Michaelmas, but it's a small price to pay for a good night's sleep."

Eliza laughed. *If only.* "Where do you get your goats?" she asked, playing along.

"Great little farm in Maryland. Certified sacrificial goats. Lambs, too, if you prefer."

"I don't think I have the stomach for it. And what the hell's Michaelmas?"

"I don't know. I pulled that out of the air."

And Eliza experienced a moment of gratitude because Gabriel hadn't pried, and the ice cream and tea and even her irritation with his scholarly jabber had helped to ease the aftermath. She was actually laughing, and that was something. And then her phone vibrated on the tabletop.

Who was calling her at four AM? She reached for the phone…

…and when she saw the number on the screen, she dropped it—or possibly *flung* it.

With a *crack* it hit a cabinet and bounced to the floor. For a second she had hope that she'd killed it. It lay there, silent. Dead. And then—*bzzzzzzzzzzzz*—not dead.

When had she ever been sorry to not have broken her phone?

It was the number. Just digits. No name. No name came up because Eliza had not programmed *that number* into her phone. She didn't even realize that she remembered it until she saw it, and it was like it had been there all along, every moment of her life since…since she'd escaped. It was all there—it was all right there. The gut punch was immediate and visceral and undiminished by the years.

"All right?" Gabriel asked her, leaning down to pick up the phone.

She almost said "Don't touch it!" but knew this was irrational and stopped herself in time. Instead, she just didn't reach for it when he held it out to her, so he had to set it down on the table, still buzzing.

She stared at it. How had they found her? How? She'd changed her name. She'd *disappeared.* Had they known where she was all along, been watching her all this time? The idea horrified her: that the years of freedom could have been an illusion…

The buzzing stopped. The call went to voice mail, and Eliza's heartbeat was cannon fire again: burst after burst shuddering through her. Who was it? Her sister? One of her uncles?

Her mother?

Whoever it was, Eliza had only a moment to wonder if they'd

leave a message—and if she'd dare to listen to it if they did—before the phone emitted another buzz. Not a voice mail. A text.

It said: *Turn on the TV.*

Turn on the…?

Eliza looked up from the phone, deeply unsettled. *Why?* What did they want her to see on the TV? She didn't even have a TV. Gabriel was watching her intently, and their eyes locked in the instant they heard the first scream. Eliza almost jumped out of her skin, rising from her chair. From somewhere outside came a long, unintelligible cry. Or was it inside? It was loud. It was in the building. Wait. That was someone else. What the hell was going on? People were crying out in…shock? Joy? Horror? And then Gabriel's phone started to buzz, too, and Eliza's unspooled a sudden string of messages—*bzzz bzzz bzzz bzzz bzzz*. From friends this time, including Taj in London, and Catherine, who was doing fieldwork in South Africa. Wording varied, but all were a version of the same disturbing command: *Turn on the TV.*

Are you watching this?

Wake up. TV. Now.

Until the last one. The one that made Eliza want to curl up in the fetal position and cease to exist.

Come home, it said. *We forgive you.*

2

The Arrival

They appeared on a Friday in broad daylight, in the sky above Uzbekistan, and were first sighted from the old Silk Road city of Samarkand, where a news crew scrambled to broadcast footage of... the visitors.

The *angels*.

Here were no mere three, as on the Charles Bridge months earlier. In flawless ranks of phalanxes, they were easily counted. Twenty blocks of fifty: a thousand. A *thousand angels*. They swept westward, near enough to earth that people standing on rooftops and roads could make out the rippling white silk of their standards and hear the trill and tremolo of harps.

Harps.

The footage went wide. Around the world, radio and television programs were preempted; news anchors rushed to their desks, out of breath and without scripts. Thrill, terror. Eyes round as coins, voices high and strange. Everywhere, phones began to ring and then cut off in a great global silence as cell towers overloaded and crashed. The sleeping slice of the planet was awakened. Internet connections faltered. People sought people. Streets filled. Voices joined and vied, climbed and crested. There were brawls. Riots.

Deaths.

There were births, too. Babies born during the Arrival were dubbed "cherubs" by a radio pundit, who was also responsible for the rumor that all had feather-shaped birthmarks somewhere on their tiny bodies. It wasn't true, but the infants would be closely watched for any hint of beatitude or magical powers.

On this day in history—the ninth of August—time cleaved abruptly into "before" and "after," and no one would ever forget where they were when "it" began.

* * *

Kazimir Andrasko, actor, ghost, vampire, and jerk, actually slept through the whole thing but would afterward claim to have blacked out while reading Nietzsche—at what he later determined was the precise moment of the Arrival—and suffered a vision of the end of the world. It was the beginning of a grandiose but half-assed ploy soon to fritter to a disappointing ending when he learned how much work was involved in starting a cult.

* * *

Zuzana Nováková and Mikolas Vavra were at Aït Benhaddou, the most famous kasbah in Morocco. Mik had just concluded bargaining for an antique silver ring—*maybe* antique, *maybe* silver, definitely a ring—when the sudden hubbub swept them up; he shoved it deep in his pocket, where it would remain, in secret, for quite some time.

In a village kitchen, they crowded in behind locals and watched news coverage in Arabic. Though they could understand neither the commentary nor the breathless exclamations all around them, they alone had context for what they were seeing. They knew what the angels were, or rather, what they weren't. That didn't make it any less of a shock to see the sky full of them.

So many!

It was Zuzana's idea to "liberate" the van idling in front of a tourist restaurant. The everyday weave of reality had by this time become so stretched that casual vehicular theft seemed par for the course. It was simple: She knew that Karou had no access to news of the world; she had to warn her. She'd have stolen a helicopter if she had to.

* * *

Esther Van de Vloet, retired diamond dealer, longtime associate of Brimstone, and occasional stand-in grandmother to his human ward, was walking her mastiffs near her home in Antwerp when the bells of Our Lady began to toll out of time. It was not the hour, and even if it had been, the tuneless clangor was overwrought, practically hysterical. Esther, who didn't have an overwrought, hysterical bone in her body, had been waiting for something to happen ever since a black handprint ignited on a doorway in Brussels and scorched it out of existence. Concluding that this was that something, she walked briskly home, her dogs huge as lionesses, stalking at her sides.

* * *

Eliza Jones watched the first few minutes on a live feed on her roommate's laptop, but when their server crashed, they hurriedly dressed, jumped in Gabriel's car, and drove to the museum. Early though it was, they weren't the first to arrive, and more colleagues kept streaming in behind them to cluster around a television screen in a basement laboratory.

They were stunned and stupid with incredulity, and with no small amount of rational affront that such an event should dare to unfold itself across the sky of the natural world. It was a hoax, of course. If angels *were* real—which was ridiculous—wouldn't they hew a little less closely to the pictures in Sunday school workbooks?

It was too perfect. It had to be staged.

"Give me a break with the harps," said a paleobiologist. "Overkill."

This outward certainty was undercut by a real tension, though, because none of them were stupid, and there were glaring holes in the hoax theory that just grew more glaring as news choppers dared to draw closer to the airborne host, and the broadcast footage became sharper and less equivocal.

No one wanted to admit it, but it looked...*real.*

Their wings, for one thing. Every feather was its own lick of fire. They were easily twelve feet in span, and the smooth rise and fall of them, the inexpressible grace and power of their flight—it was beyond any known technology.

"It could be the broadcast that's faked," suggested Gabriel. "It could all be CG. *War of the Worlds* for the twenty-first century."

There were some murmurs, though no one seemed to actually buy them.

Eliza stayed silent, watching. Her own dread was of a different breed than theirs, and was…far more advanced. It should be. It had been growing all her life.

She thought of her phone, left intentionally behind at the apartment, and wondered what new messages its screen held in store for her. And she thought of the extraordinary dark power from which she'd fled in the night, in the dream. Her gut clenched like a fist as she felt, beneath her feet, the shifting of the planks she'd laid across the quicksand of that other life. She'd thought she could escape it? It was there, it had always been there, and this life she'd built on top of it felt about as sturdy as a shantytown on the flank of a volcano.

A special thank you to the following readers for their wonderful contributions to the fan-generated series trailer for *Daughter of Smoke & Bone*:

Holly Faye Griffiths
Liesa Socquet
Yen Thu McGrath
Cici Whiteman
Danira Denise Corona Piñera
Katie Webber
Tris Kelsey
Kimberley Gill
Casey Devoron
Sammi Putelli
Angelina Nguyen
Iain Croall
Christine Tyler
Keely Shannon
Katie Toomey
Luz Dafne Corona Piñera
Eryka Krakowska

Watch the trailer at youtube.com/smokeandbonebook.